Battle of Loinnir

Mystifying Book 1

Dorian Moore

Cover art by: Megan Moore

ISBN: 979-8-9871601-0-7 (Paperback)
ISBN: 979-8-9871601-1-4 (Hardcover)
ISBN: 979-8-9871601-2-1 (eBook)

Dorian Dedication: I dedicate this book to Moore's pool. Only two weirdos would start off their friendship making up stories about an elf and a halfling while splashing in a pool all summer. Glad those weirdos were us. Also to my grandfather, you helped build the love of books and all things nerdy, wish you were here to read this.

Moore Dedication: To the best friend who was a constant, an anchor, even all those years that I wandered too far away to go cruising, well, ever. My platonic soulmate. You are absolutely the reason this book has finally come to fruition, because we both know I'm terrible at this kind of follow-through. And to my Mama, who allowed those weirdos to spend so much time in aforementioned pool and to be their weirdo selves so that this idea could bloom.

Prologue

"In the beginning, all races lived together and the world was filled with magic. The elves were wise and became the authority. The fae were peaceful and delicate; they spent their time trying to help nature thrive. The erebi had power, but were stronger when they could feed off the power of others. The elves did not allow this, and the erebi became jealous and began to plot a way to take control. The humans lived as witches and warlocks. They helped the elves, but they were consumed with the idea of gaining longer lives like the other beings around them.

As each race grew, the world began to suffer from the constant battles for power. Nature was being replenished with magics, only to be drained by the erebi. This weakened the fae and soon they were unable to heal the world and keep the natural magics strong; the world began to die. A war broke out among the beings as each tried to claim their right to land. It lasted for two hundred years. The humans suffered the most: while they had magic, their bodies were weak and most did not get the chance to grow old.

Our savior came in the form of a young woman: a powerful witch who was deeply in love. She watched as her husband was killed in battle, and her very being cried out in despair. She did not wish destruction, she only wanted to end the suffering. Her soul became pure, and drank in the white magic around her, filling her until her body seemed to burst.

The girl screamed out, feeling all the pain of those living, of those long past. As she screamed, the world ripped at the seams, breaking apart and creating the realms we now know today. She collapsed in exhaustion and left behind small rifts which the ancients could travel through. In fear of the young witch, and wanting peace, the races split, taking different realms for themselves; building doorways around the portals so they would always know where they lay. And so, a new world was brought forth.

The elves created a peaceful realm, though they never forgot their time of war, and always remained prepared for battle. They spread across their land and created kingdoms so all the elven people could thrive and grow. They named their new home Eloas.

The erebi created their own realm, but fought amongst themselves. Without the fae and elves their world could not replenish the magics, so the ancients broke into groups and warred with each other over power and land. Many tried to get through the portals where they could taste magic once again. Some simply wanted better lives without war; others sought more power. They named their realm Skia.

The fae took a smaller realm that they named Loinnir and made it beautiful. They let nature thrive and became strong once again without the constant drain on their energy.

But the witch had drained the human realm, Sula, of its magic, and when the other beings left, there was no more for them to feed off of. So the humans were no longer witches and warlocks, other than a few that were able to reach the ancients of their minds. The witch had done something powerful, something no one knew could be done. In taking in all that magic, she became immortal, and bore a mark on her wrist, so everyone knew what she was. The humans grew angry; even though she ended the war, she took away their magic, and she now had the power to live forever, something the rest of the humans were unable to do. They blackened her name, ran her out, and cursed her instead of praising her.

She went into hiding; some believe she rose above the world we know, her powers too great. Others believe she took her own life to end her suffering and loneliness. Perhaps she created a realm the rest did not know of, and she hides there still. But it is widely believed that there are still humans carrying her bloodline."

"What do you think, Mama?"

Ainadelothien loved this story, and made the queen recount it for her on a nightly basis. Tonight her baby brother joined, and was nestled in the bed beside her while her mother lay down to tell the tale of the ancients.

"I like to think, somehow, she was able to find a little peace for herself. Maybe she has been quietly hiding, watching her children grow and have children of their own. But now my darling," her mother rose and cradled her brother Toron within her arms, "it is far past bedtime for little princes and princesses." Ainadelothien received a kiss to her forehead and sleep started to make her eyes heavy.

"Night, Mama."

"Goodnight Aina, I love you." With that, the queen of Eloas shut the door and her feet padded down the hallway to place her son to bed.

Chapter One

Ana made her way slowly into the kitchen, following the clanging of kitchen utensils and the smell of breakfast. She vaguely remembered a time when she rose with the sun, bright and refreshed, but living in Sula did not give her the energy Eloas had. After years of living outside of her home realm, she now woke up groggy to the sound of her alarm clock just as a human might - clearly *not* the human standing in front of her, however.

Her roommate Melody was dancing around the kitchen, tight black curls bouncing in time to whatever music was playing in her headphones. She must have sensed the presence behind her, because a moment later she pulled the headphones from her ears and turned to face Ana, still watching from the doorway with amusement.

"Well good morning!" The young witch grinned from ear to ear, mischief dancing in her eyes. "Ya know, I've always had this picture in my head that elves are these kind, graceful, *pleasant* creatures at any time of the day. Seeing you roll out of bed every morning, though...I must have been *woefully* mistaken," Melody teased as the elf sidled up to the kitchen table. She winked at Ana and offered a cup of coffee as truce.

"I'm not *that* bad," Ana started to argue, even as she took the coffee mug like her life might depend on it. She nearly choked on the first chilling sip and Melody let loose an amused giggle. "*Mel!*" Ana sputtered before laughing and handing over the mug with an expectant arched brow. With a large grin, Melody took the mug from her hands and whispered a quick incantation over it, before handing it back. Ana took a tentative sip before drinking deeper and sitting the mug down with an appreciative moan. "Much better. You are getting pretty good at that one. Though, you *could* stop testing it out on my beverages."

Melody shrugged coyly. "And take the fun out of it?" She pulled out her phone to check the time. "Now hurry up, missy, we don't want to keep the customers waiting do we?"

Ana swatted at her with a dramatic eye roll. "You are more than capable of opening the store on the *one* day I'm actually late getting up. Not like you have any classes to run off to today."

Melody gasped. "You mean...you're trusting little old *me* to not burn the place down? I'm so honored." The witch placed a delicate hand on her chest in mock surprise before bounding forward and placing a kiss on her cheek. "Love you, see you in a few!" Just like that, Melody was racing down the stairs into Ana's magic shop, *Mystifying*.

Well aware the other woman would have everything under control, Ana took her time finishing her morning routine. They had come a long way since she found a teenage Melody behind the shop with nowhere to go. It was a bittersweet relationship for the both of them as they developed a sibling-like bond. It gave them both someone to lean on, but it didn't give back what they had each lost. Ana touched the preserved flower hanging around her neck and tried not to think of all it represented.

Then she felt the static of energy, a pulsing in the air that let her know the portal she was now protecting was opening below.

Her whole body reacted before her mind even fully comprehended what was happening. Mel was alone in the shop downstairs, and the portal stood in the back office. She was down the stairs in a few pounding heartbeats, adrenaline pumping through her as her eyes fell on an unharmed Melody before anything else. The witch's eyes widened as she caught the look on her face.

"Lock back up!" was all she said before grabbing the dagger she always kept under the counter and making her way into the office. Over the years she had her fair share of portal travelers, many of whom came with good intentions. She had once been a portal traveler herself. In fact, she had come through this very same portal. She also came across plenty of erebi attempting to cross over, to cause trouble or attempt to draw in human souls for whatever ancient they worked for.

Ana lost her breath when she caught sight of a woman lying on the ground with bloody parallel lines down her back. A fae who'd had her wings forcibly removed. Ana'd heard of such atrocity, but she had never seen it before. She thought she might be sick, but she managed to call out to Mel in a weak breath. The dagger in her hand suddenly felt like a block of lead, and she allowed her hand to drop to her side. She knelt beside the prone figure and searched for a pulse...and searched...and finally pulled her hand away.

"What was it-oh my goodness!" Melody stumbled back a step as Ana turned towards her. "Ana, what happened to her?"

"Stripped of her wings…but that shouldn't have killed her." She fought to keep her voice even, for Melody's sake, as her eyes searched for any other wounds that could be the cause of death. "I need you to call Aria." When Melody didn't move, Ana turned back to her and found her friend still staring at the body wide-eyed. "Mel," she soothed, "we need to get Aria here. Can you call her?"

Finally Melody nodded and turned away to find her phone. Ana let out a shaky sigh as she searched the room for a blanket. "I'm sorry," she murmured. The blanket settled heavily over the fae, and Ana couldn't help but consider it symbolic of the shroud of darkness and uncertainty that was now settling over her little shop.

Once Melody made the call, Ana came out of the backroom, closing the door softly behind her, as though that might block out what just happened. "Why don't you head out? Your Wicca group usually has a meeting in half an hour that you tend to miss. You should go and take comfort in your friends. I'm going to keep the store closed anyway, at least until I speak with Aria."

"I'm not going to leave you here alone, Ana."

Ana almost smiled at the prickle in Melody's voice. "If you stay I will just be worried about you. If you go, I know your friends will watch over you and you will get something out of meeting with them."

"Ana..." She heard the question in Mel's voice so she quickly held up a hand to stop her.

"Please, Mel. It would make me feel better, and we can't do anything until Aria gets here." Finally, Melody relented and gave a short nod. It only took her a few minutes to gather what she needed and pack it away in her messenger bag.

"Are you sure?" She tried once more before leaving but Ana nodded and practically shooed her from the store. Then in the silence she waited, and worried.

"Hey, Mel told me to get over here ASAP, what's wrong?" Ana looked up from where she'd been sitting with her head in her hands.

Even the worry in Aria's moss-green eyes did not retract from her beauty. A full-blooded fae, Aria was highly attuned to nature. She also had healing powers and the ability to speak with animals. She looked like she walked straight out of a forest with sharp pointed features, tan skin, and long silvery hair she kept braided down her back.

"We have a problem," Ana muttered, pushing herself to her feet. She led the fae to the back of the store, but stopped in the doorway. "Aria, just...I'm sorry for what I am going to show you, but something's wrong." Aria narrowed her eyes in confusion at the elf before stepping around her.

"She showed up an hour ago, already dead. Someone stripped her wings, but I am assuming something else killed her." Ana whispered, arms wrapping around herself as she hovered over the threshold of her office. Aria's entire frame visibly tensed as she leaned down to pull the blanket away.

"H...how did she end up here?" Aria turned to look at Ana. Even as tears pooled in her eyes, her voice hardened with determination, and Ana could feel the fae pulling herself together.

"I don't know. She was either trying to get through the portal while she was dying and didn't make the journey, or someone sent her through." Guilt and trepidation settled into the pit of her stomach. "Aria..."

"I'll go. It takes a special kind of monster to strip a fae of her wings." While Aria was born without wings, she'd grown up in Loinnir, and witnessed a few wing removals in her childhood. It was a wretched thing to do to a fae...not only was it extremely painful, but it often ripped away more than their wings. It could take part of who the fae was down to their very core. It lessened their magical abilities, and some fae even ended up losing their minds after a wing removal. They couldn't sleep or eat; some couldn't perform magic at all.

The Queen of Loinnir often used wing removal to punish those that crossed her. A vote had been made while Aria was still there on whether the queen could continue to do so, but the queen had won. Aria looked closely at the wound. "This wasn't the queen. Queen Gossamer always burned the wound, which actually helps it to heal quicker. This fae had her wings pulled by force," she traced a finger along the torn skin, "not by magic."

"Aria..." Ana knew they needed to find out what happened, but heaviness settled on her heart the second Aria said she would go. It had been years since the fae had come through the portal, looking for a new life. Ana also knew the queen of the realm did not allow the fae to pass through, which meant Aria could get in a lot of trouble by returning.

"You know that's exactly what you were working yourself up to ask. I *need* to go. She came here for a reason. She's fae, and we need to know who the hell is stripping fae of their wings, and why they would strip her wings *and then* kill her." She shook her head and draped the blanket back over the body. "We can't let that kind of sicko keep breathing, Ana. I'll go, I'll take her with me and give her a proper burial, and I will get some answers. I *won't* come back until I get answers."

Ana was silent for a moment. "I don't think you should go alone."

Aria grinned humorlessly. "I know, you've got to be our big bad protector all the time, watcher of the portal and all, but I can hold my own. You need to stay here with the store, Mel's got finals this week. I'll be *fine*, it was *my home* after all. I'll check in if I don't learn anything in a couple of days. Don't worry." The two women lifted the body up so that Aria could carry her through the portal, and Ana squeezed her friend's shoulder.

"Be careful."

"Tell Mel she better have aced that chem final by the time I get back. We didn't waste all of our time when we should've been running the store for nothing," the fae teased lightly. "See ya soon, Ana."

Ana gave a half smile, but darkness clouded her heart as she watched her friend step through the portal and disappear into another realm. With a deep breath, she went to open the store, more to distract herself than anything else.

℘ ℘ ℘

Erin let a frustrated sigh escape her lips as she searched her apartment for her camera. For something that she was so attached to, she sure lost track of it a lot. Flitting from room to room, she checked everywhere she could think of. "Aha!" she cheered as soon as she caught a glimpse of the camera strap sticking out from under a pile of dirty laundry. San Francisco was offering up a beautiful day, and her finger was itching to click some photographs, so Erin threw on her favorite brown leather jacket and was out the door. The breeze was coming off the sea and filling the air with a refreshing hint of salt. It was early spring so the city hadn't started to fill with tourists quite yet, but she knew it wouldn't be long.

She took a few shots as a trolley rode by on the street, and smiled back at a little girl waving at her from inside. Erin gave a happy wave in reply before setting on her way again. She was free as a bird with no real connections, but she never had the desire to leave California. Despite the fact that a feeling of belonging was not something that came to her easily, it had always felt like *home*. After spending her entire childhood being moved around through the foster system, there had been very little in her life she could depend on; rather than feel sorry for herself, Erin developed a fierce sense of independence and take-no-crap attitude.

Though her passion was nature photography, shots of people and buildings tended to sell more prints. Even with the business she got from tourists and local businesses, it had yet to bring in enough to pay the bills, so her primary income was waitressing and bartending, with photography reduced to a side job.

Erin took some more shots of the buildings, road signs, random people caught up in their own minds, and flowers breaking free from the concrete. As she wandered up and down the streets and took in the fresh air, she found herself wandering down roads she usually didn't walk. She saw a beautiful street where all the trees had already ' bloomed and the older buildings were covered in flowering vines. She took a moment to change her lens and ran her fingers through her short, cherry-red hair. She focused on close-ups of the buildings, the vines, and the signs - until one hanging wooden sign with looping black script that read *Mystifying* caught her attention.

Curious, Erin hung her camera over her head and stepped through the door. A soothing mix of smells greeted her, and an ethereal blond stepped away from a table set up in the corner to greet her.

"Welcome to *Mystifying*."

She was almost too beautiful and Erin was drawn in instantly. She nearly reached for her camera in an attempt to capture the glow the woman seemed to have. Instead, she smiled back and started walking around, taking in the natural honey-toned wood floors and the dark wood shelves covering the walls. A large dark wood table sat in the center with glass shelves displaying crystals, jewelry, and jars filled with ominous looking items.

She read some of the signs on the jars, looked at the covers of the books, and thought this had to be the strangest store she ever found herself in.

"Have you ever been in a magic shop before?" The woman smiled at her. After her childhood, Erin thought of herself as a quick judge of character; unlike some other retail workers, the smile actually met her soft blue eyes and she asked with true interest rather than going through a mental script.

"Uh...no I can't say that I have. It's not exactly what I would imagine."

"Are you practicing?"

At first Erin wasn't sure what she meant, and then realized she was asking if she practiced magic. Maybe this was a store she should have just taken a picture of and moved on.

"Ah, a non-believer. Well, I'm Ana, the owner of this little shop." She responded, apparently reading Erin's silence.

"Ana? Is that short for something?" Erin asked before thinking better of it.

"Why would you ask that?"

"Don't be offended, just Ana seems a little..." Erin looked over at the shop owner with a shrug, "a bit tame for you."

Ana threw her head back and laughed. "Actually it *is* short for something. You are just the first person to ever ask; the long version is

Ainadelothien." The shop owner watched her for a reaction, and for a moment Erin felt she was under some sort of test.

Erin's eyes did go wide as she took in the name. She liked how it rolled off Ana's tongue like a song, and thought it did fit *her*, if not the world they lived in. "Parents are big fans of Tolkien?"

"You could say that." The shop owner's smile seemed to hold a secret that Erin wasn't privy to.

"It's a pretty name; I see why you shortened it though. I'm Erin by the way. It's not short for anything," she joked dryly. Erin looked at the small table in the corner. She could just imagine a young Ana growing up with parents obsessed with "other worlds"; it was no wonder she owned a magic shop.

When Erin took a closer look at the table, she saw a bottle filled with liquid and herbs. There was a small bowl filled with herbs in the process of being crushed. When she got closer to the mixture her senses filled with the musky tones of lavender, chamomile, and lemon. "It's to help anxiety. You brew it as a tea." Ana seemed to glide around the room; every footstep was filled with the grace of a ballet dancer.

"That doesn't sound like magic, that sounds like a natural remedy."

"Well, what do you consider magic?"

Erin started to push away the question but then decided Ainadelothien was an interesting character, and she wanted to see where the conversation went. "I'm a fan of *Harry Potter*, so I guess some wand waving and special words. But *you* are the shop owner, why don't you tell me."

Ana nodded, a patient smile gracing her face. "Well, as you can see, no wands are sold here. A lot of magic simply stems from self-awareness and a deep connection to your surroundings. Some believe witches are simply people that have access to parts of the brain that other humans aren't able to reach." She paused, watching Erin for a moment. "What did you come in for today?"

"I just saw your sign, and thought I'd take a look around." Her fingers skimmed over heavy volumes, some of which seemed to be written in a language she didn't recognize. Curiosity had her leaning closer to some bottles to see if she could identify what they contained. Different colored liquids swirled inside many, while others held familiar herbs or dried flowers.

She wanted to pull her camera back out. She could get a few interesting shots, and there was just something special about exploring her surroundings through the lens. She could see Ana in shadow, the mystical books behind her, the herb mixture in focus. Before she even thought of asking, though, Erin talked herself out of it. Many shop owners didn't really appreciate someone coming in and snapping photos, especially if they didn't know what they would be used for.

"Or maybe you were just drawn to the energy. Some people have magic in them and don't realize it." There was that smile again, like she knew some big secret she wasn't sharing.

Erin scoffed at that. Maybe if Ana knew everything she had been through in her life, she would realize if there was something special about her, it would have come out from pure survival. "Well, it's my birthday next week. Is there something I should look at as a gift to myself? Maybe a candle that will bring me riches?"

"I think I have something you would like. It's a quartz, and it's meant to attune the wearer to their spiritual purpose. Plus, it makes a beautiful necklace." Ana went to some of the dangling jewelry, and pulled out a necklace with a rounded clear crystal. It had intricate metal work to hold in the stone, and Erin couldn't deny her instant attraction to the piece. She wasn't one to wear a lot of jewelry, but it *was* something she would have picked out for herself.

"It is beautiful, a good choice." A quick glance at the price also let her know it was within her cheap budget. "I'll take it."

Ana told Erin a few other properties of the quartz and how to care for the crystal as Erin paid and then placed it around her neck. "Happy early birthday. How old will you be, if you don't mind my asking?"

"Twenty-five."

Ana's brows rise slightly at that. "It is believed twenty-five is when those with abilities come to full power. Mystical beings reach their aging peak before aging slows for them and those with powers gain their full abilities. Maybe you were drawn here after all."

Something crashed in the back of the store, drawing Ana's attention away.

"Is everything okay?" Erin asked, glancing back toward the noise. There was a door to a back room, and she saw Ana staring at it with a wary gaze.

"I'm sure something just fell. Happy birthday, Erin. I hope to see you back soon."

Chapter Two

Briar's mother had been acting strangely for almost a month. The fae wished there was a way past her defenses so she could see what the future held, but as another seer, her mother had a natural defense against her intrusion. But it was more than that...it was as though a strong force was blocking her from seeing too deeply into any of the lives around her.

Something was coming, that much was clear. Nothing else would keep the future of everyone around her so fuzzy. Her mother clearly had some idea of what was happening, or she wouldn't have spent the month doing her best to avoid her. Briar might have thought she was just busy; her mother, Nia, was the strongest seer in Loinnir, which, much to her chagrin, also made her the advisor to Queen Gossamer. But that was too much of a coincidence.

Briar slowly made her way through the small village and wound deeper into the forest. The air was crisp and, just like others of her kind, she could feel life springing up at her feet as new flowers began to bloom. The ground started to change over from the full green grass to a thick blue moss as she neared the spring. Already, she could hear the music of moving water and melodic giggles of the young fae splashing one another from the banks.

Briar hoped the water would ease the tension building between her wings, but the stress of not knowing what was wrong, even as she felt so clearly there was *something* amiss, was too strong to shake. She stepped ankle deep into the water, the light film of her dress floating like a second surface, and panic abruptly pushed into her mind. She nearly fell right into the depths of the spring as the assault of a vision left her doubled over.

Flashes of images came to her in such a sudden burst the seer was certain her head would split in two. At first she couldn't make out the images separately, but after three deep breaths the jumble slowed enough to begin to make some sense. In her mind's eye parts of the forest suddenly began to die. Fae fell around her with veins black as the night sky, their wings deteriorating against the darkness that possessed them. An erebus with white skin and two long black horns stood before her mother, the queen, and the rest of the council. Another erebus stepped forward and killed the council members one by one, their blood soaking the ground below, until her mother stood as the last defense between the erebi and the queen.

Briar doubled over and lost the contents of her stomach as her mother's pain-to-come shot through her like an arrow to the heart. Erebi were coming and she had to warn everyone. Briar ran. She knew there was no time. She was on the other side of the forest and her vision was about to take place. Her mother was in the same dress she'd been wearing that morning and the sun was in the same spot it's in now. Her mother would be killed any minute and her realm was about to be taken over by erebi that would drain her land.

The war had finally come to them and her only choice was to try and escape to the realm of Sula. Maybe she could find people there who could prepare to fight back. She was already too late to save her mother, but maybe she could get the rest of her family, and they could make it to the portal to get help. Her bare feet raced toward her father's home. She didn't have long and the portal was in the opposite direction.

"Hello?" She ran in without knocking, but there was no sign of her father or her three half-sisters.

"Briar?" A timid voice came from above her head and Briar looked up to find her youngest sister Fern hiding in the rafters.

"Where is everyone else?"

"Queen Gossamer was having a concert so everyone else went to watch." Briar didn't need any further explanation. She knew Fern was afraid of the queen and did all she could to avoid her.

"We have to go." Briar held up her hands and Fern floated down with the grace of a flower opening to the morning sun. Briar hugged her tight.

"Have you seen something?"

"Yes, we have to get to the portal."

"What about everyone else?" Fern's small arms wrapped around Briar's neck and held tight. The moment Briar was out of the house, she spread out her wings and leapt into the air.

"There's no time. I'm sure they'll be fine, but we have to get to Sula for help."

"Is this because of the sickness taking the plants?" Briar looked down at her sister and asked what she meant. Fern was much more in-tuned with nature than she was. "The plants are starting to die. I can feel them crying for help. That's why I was in the rafters, I was afraid."

As soon as Briar broke free from the village and made it deeper into the forest, she understood what Fern meant. It was just like her vision, the plants were starting to turn black at the edges and curl into themselves. Then she spotted a line of erebi heading toward the village. The one with white skin led the way. Briar darted up past the foliage of the trees to avoid the erebi's black eyes, and covered Fern's mouth to make sure the younger fae stayed silent.

She started trying to plan an attack against the erebi to keep them from the village, to save her mother. Just as quickly as she came up with a plan, though, she saw her and Fern's demise. The realm's only chance was to make it to Sula and get help. Even as she knew she was leaving her mother to die, she flew toward the portal, clutching Fern against her as a reminder of what she was trying to save.

.℘ .℘ .℘

Erin left the store and shot a few pictures of the front of it before turning her lens to the buildings across the street. Energy was buzzing through her veins like she'd had too much coffee; she was practically rocking on the balls of her feet as she took in the world around her. The lighting was perfect at the moment, and it always gave her a small thrill when she knew she was creating something beautiful, making something she could leave behind. All that energy crashed against her ribs when a familiar face across the street caught her attention, and left her frozen in surprise. Her stomach dropped to the floor when she got a full-on look at the only constant in her childhood — his hair was grown out so it touched the collar of his shirt, and the blond hair was curled just enough to make it look like he'd simply run his fingers through it and let it dry, however it landed. Before she could get her mouth to work to call out his name, green eyes (as clear in her memory as one of her pictures) turned toward *Mystifying* as if drawn there. He seemed to have a similar reaction when he noticed her. It was like watching a cartoon as he jerked to a stop, and his mouth visibly dropped. She could feel his gaze drink her in as she did the same to him. He moved and bumped right into someone walking around him, and she might have laughed (if only she could remember how). Erin's heart hammered in her chest as she watched him quickly apologize and run across the street to her. She counted him lucky that it wasn't a busy street; in his hurry to get to her, he didn't even look before he ran across the road.

"Well, hello stranger." She wasn't sure how she managed to get the words out; she could feel her throat closing and quickly cleared it.

"Erin…" His green eyes searched her face and quickly lit up with a bright smile. "I can't believe it's you!" He pulled her into a hug, and she was surprised just how natural it felt to be pulled against his chest and surrounded by him. He still smelled like a forest, as though she were walking through the redwoods. "You have no idea…after you went into the last foster home and changed schools, I tried to get the information about where you were sent, but no one would tell me anything. You know how it is. Then I was placed in a home, and stayed with them until I aged out." He held her at arms length now, keeping his hands firmly on her wrists, as if he was afraid if he released her, she'd disappear.

Her initial joy at seeing him edged away as all the thoughts of growing up in a group home came bubbling to the surface. They weren't her favorite memories to say the least; about the only thing she liked to think about when it came to her childhood was the man standing in front of her. Even those memories turned bittersweet after they lost touch.

"I don't even know where to start, Gabe...almost ten years since I last saw you..."

"Are you free? Let's grab something to eat so we can catch up."

"Oh, I actually have to start heading to work." She saw the disappointment on his face and quickly amended. "I work at a local bar a few blocks away. It's an early shift, so we probably won't be busy. You can come and grab a bite and a drink. I'll have to work, but I should have plenty of down time." She shrugged, unsure if she really wanted him to see her there or not. The job was fine, she got tipped well, and even though some of the men could be rude, she was quite capable of holding her own. It just wasn't exactly the kind of place she wanted to take him to.

"Sounds good," Gabe answered happily, leaving her no way out of her offer. They started walking together and Erin searched for something to say. Finally, she laughed uncomfortably and got the ball rolling. "So how are *you* making money these days?"

He snorted at her phrasing, and instantly she felt more at ease. "I work at a local gym as a personal trainer. I do a few fitness classes and work with clients. It's fun, keeps me moving."

"Well, you fit right into California life."

Gabe shook his head with a grin that bordered on sheepish and scratched behind his ear. "Ah, I still prefer my food fried; I just can't get into tofu."

"I guess we might still get along after all." She bumped into his side good-naturedly before pointing out the bar where she worked.

Gabe sat at the stool she pointed towards, then she left him to get clocked in and collect her apron. She went ahead and placed an appetizer order for Gabe before she did a round to check on the three other customers, and waved a quick goodbye to Sean, who was already halfway out the door. She could feel Gabe watching her and tried to ignore how crazy her day was turning out to be. She hated working the bar during the day, but had drawn the short straw since she'd needed off to drive up to Napa Valley.

Gabe sat patiently while she got settled, and she couldn't stop herself from stealing glances his way. He was no longer the boy she'd grown up with, nor the gangly teenager who didn't quite fit into his body yet. His work at the gym certainly filled out his body. There was a lightness in his eyes that he'd always had, even during the darkest days. When he first arrived at the house he was around eight years old but had no memories. She remembered hearing the adults whispering about him, about the abuse he must have gone through to forget everything down to his own name and age. She'd been given up as an infant and spent her entire life in the system. Everyone whispered that something must be wrong with her because even when she was a baby, not one person attempted to adopt her. She stood there, staring at that lost boy with big green eyes and curly blond hair, heard everyone talking about him, and she couldn't take it. She walked right up to him and demanded he come play with her, and she didn't stop bugging him after that.

They'd been each other's best friends, and that was about the only thing either of them had any control over. Nothing had ever come between them until her last placement, when they'd lost touch.

The appetizer was ready, so she grabbed it from the window to the kitchen and then walked it over to him. His eyes widened in surprise. "I'm sorry miss, but I haven't ordered anything."

"Huh, my mistake." She met his grin with her own and then stole a mozzarella stick from his plate.

A loud crash had her jumping to attention. "I'm sorry!" Tony, one of the regulars, stood and reached to start cleaning up the glass he'd knocked over.

"No worries. Leave it, I'll get it." She grabbed the small trash can from under the counter and a towel to sweep the glass from the counter. On her second sweep, one of the thicker pieces of glass went through the cloth and sliced the palm of her hand. She drew back with a quick hiss of pain and Tony started to jump in to take over. She waved him away; the last thing she needed was a customer getting hurt. It only took one more swipe anyway to clean up all the shards, but suddenly there was a hand on her arm, and she turned to look up at Gabe. Without a word he took the towel and trash can from her and led her over to the small stool behind the bar.

"What are you doing?" She sat down, because he practically sat her there himself, and then her hurt palm was held between his own. "I'm fine, I heal quickly, I just need to wash it and get a Band-Aid."

"Still stubborn I see." He smiled at her and then did a quick scan of her workspace. It only took him a moment to find the bright red first aid kit.

"I can take care of it, Gabe." The feel of his hands on her was unnerving. She still couldn't believe he was there, forget about the fact he was touching her, and looking at her with the same wonder she felt.

"I'm well aware you are perfectly capable. I just want to do something for you." It only took him a minute to clean the gash and then wrap the bandage around it, but her heart was beating like crazy the entire time. "Hey Erin?"

"Yeah?"

"I really missed you."

She ignored the way her heart swelled in her chest. "I missed you too." She stood, "Now get out from behind my bar." She made a shooing motion towards him and got Tony a new beer. She did her best to not acknowledge Tony's grin as he raised his eyebrows at her. "Want me to drop another one? Thought he was going to propose there for a minute."

"Shut up, Tony." Once he was set, she turned back to Gabe and then stole one of his onion rings.

"Hey!" he protested half-heartedly.

"A girl's gotta eat, what can I say?" She chewed happily at his food, ignoring the slight throb from the cut on her hand. "Can I get you a drink? Or do you avoid alcohol so you don't wake up with more mysterious tattoos?" She reached out and rolled up his right sleeve to look at one of two tattoos he'd had when he showed up at the group home. She knew he had no idea how he got them or what they meant: one symbol was on the inside of his right wrist, and another was at the top of his spine. She traced the one on his wrist, and thought of all the times she'd done the same when they sat together watching movies or doing homework. The idea that someone would mark a child made her just as angry now as it did when they were younger. He might not remember what happened to him, but she thought he had to have been better off in the system.

"I guess I'll have a beer. I trust you to look out for me," he snarked. She jumped away from him, realizing she was still holding his wrist and tracing his skin. When her gaze shot to his she found him staring at her, a muscle in his jaw jumping.

"I'll make sure you get something really cool this time. Maybe I'll start looking up boy bands for you... I'm thinking tramp stamp all the way."

After Erin left, Ana looked toward the back door and waited to see if anyone would come out. She didn't hear another noise, so she grabbed her dagger and went to see what was waiting for her. Nothing seemed out of place, but the elf felt a strong dissonance around her that left her unsettled. "This is *my* shop. Just because I can't see you doesn't mean that I don't know you're here. Whatever you want, let's hear it. I don't have time or patience for games right now." After years of standing as protector over the portal between realms, Ana had seen her fair share of creatures come through. Mostly they meant no harm, but she had come across a few erebi and creatures looking for mischief. After finding the fae, however, she felt the world shifting, and knew more danger would be coming her way.

The hair on the back of her neck stood on end, and Ana spun, bringing her dagger up just in time to block an attack. She did a double take as she took in the erebus looming over her — the figure looked as though it was made of the deepest shadow she'd ever seen. The edges of it were like wisps, dancing along its body and fading into the air. The erebus's eyes sharply contrasted the rest of its body; bright orbs seemed to bore into her. They captivated her for a moment, threatening to hypnotize her, until she kicked out to force the erebus back.

With a jolt, she realized she recognized the erebus, and the memory of the last time she faced one had her stomach twisting into knots. It hissed at her and lunged forward again. She narrowly dodged a set of long, jagged claws swiping for her throat, and retaliated by thrusting her dagger into the erebus's chest. The elf grimaced when the beast shrieked in agony, ducking again as it flailed.

The blade shone black in the light once it was freed from the erebus's chest, and Ana shoved the body to the floor. "This is *so* not good." With a careful step over the lifeless body, the elf stole a glance into the store. "At least nobody came in," she sighed in relief. *That would've been a bit difficult to explain,* she thought to herself.

"Ana?" Melody called from the front door. Ana stepped into the store and waved the young witch in. "You okay?" Melody asked when she saw the look on Ana's face.

"Lock the door behind you, will you?"

Melody raised a confused eyebrow, but complied without argument. "What's wrong?"

"Come here," Ana called Melody over, "I had a visitor." She gestured towards the body, and gave a humorless laugh when Melody yelped in surprise. "Yeah…that's about how I responded when it *attacked me* out of nowhere." The elf grabbed a handful of tissues from her desk and wiped her dagger clean. Blue eyes examined the thick black blood now staining the tissue.

"What *is* it?"

Ana shrugged. "It's an infection erebus. They are fairly common because they can infect others and turn them into an erebus like them. It was hidden in shadow waiting to attack me when it first showed up. I was talking to a customer and heard something fall in here. I came back and the office looked empty...but I could *feel* it." She knelt down beside the body, and lifted its limp humanoid hand. Each finger ended in a thick, sharp point. "I've seen these erebi before, but it's been years. Hopefully Aria will come back with some answers soon."

Ana quickly let go and pushed Melody back when the erebus's body began to turn into a dark, billowing smoke. It hovered in the spot for a moment before getting sucked into the earth.

"Well at least he was nice enough to clean up after himself... Do you have any idea what just happened?" Melody gingerly swiped a foot over the spot.

"The dark energy of the erebus must have returned to his realm." Ana spoke quietly, her eyes frozen to the spot where the erebus was only moments ago.

.℮ .℮ .℮

"I'm hungry," Fern whispered, clutching Briar's hand.

"I know, can you get any of the animals to help?" It was dark and everything seemed to be in hiding. The infection erebi continued to patrol in groups, and they had to hide up in a tree to avoid being spotted. Fern had been quiet through their travels even though Briar knew how afraid she must be. She watched as Fern used her magic to try and reach out to any animals nearby, and a little bird seemed to appear from the darkness and landed next to them. Her sister reached out a finger and stroked its back briefly before it took off. It took two trips, but their new friend brought them a few clumps of berries. Fern gave the bird praise before it disappeared into the darkness again.

"Here." The young fae tried to hand some of the berries over, but Briar forced herself to turn it down.

"I was eating right before I found you. I'm okay."

"That was *hours* ago."

"You eat and then get some rest." She settled her sister back against her chest, letting her legs rest on either side of her on the wide branch.

"Do you see anything?"

"No, it's clouded." Fern grew quiet and thankfully didn't ask why. Anytime she closed her eyes and tried to see into the future and what path they should take, she just saw her mother standing before the queen while an erebus killed her. Whatever erebus decided to take over the realm was working quickly, taking out the queen and the counsel right at the beginning to get the rest of the fae to fall into line. Her father, Fern's mother, and their siblings had been in the crowd, but there was nothing they could do. "Tomorrow we'll fly the rest of the way to the portal and we'll find somewhere safe."

Fern sighed and drifted off to sleep but Briar stayed up longer, trying to get her vision to work...to see beyond her grief. It wasn't the first time she'd wished she held different powers. Fern could speak to animals and connect to nature, her father had the ability to shift, but she got her powers from her mother. She could see into the future, and fae with those powers tended not to live very long lives. Her mother spent a lifetime working for Queen Gossamer, seeing fae that betrayed the crown, snuck into other realms, or did anything that could endanger Loinnir. Now, her mother was gone, and their realm was under attack. She grew stiff watching another group of erebi pass under them. Their dark energy seemed to change the air around them, and she wondered if their presence was also making it hard for her to see the future.

She just had to get to the portal with Fern, and they could slip into Sula where they could stay hidden, for a time at least.

Chapter Three

Erin noticed her phone flashing a few days later and saw Gabe's name. They'd texted each other here and there over the last few days, but their schedules never seemed to line up for them to get together. Somehow it came up she was driving to Napa Valley for a photography shoot, and it happened to fall on a short day for him, so he was promptly invited along. Napa Valley was about a two hour drive, so it seemed like the perfect way for them to really catch up and get to know each other again after years apart.

"Hello?" She heard Gabe's deep voice greet her on the other end of the line and couldn't help but smile. If nothing else she knew he was still caring, still had a great sense of humor, and judging by his reaction at the bar the other night, he was still protective of her. She wondered what he thought of her and her changes. It hurt her when they lost contact, especially because she went through so much change the last two years she was stuck in the system. She was thrown into another foster home, and even though it was a good family, she was never able to be at ease after the problems she had in the previous home. Then she had to change schools, and moved further away from the area she always knew. Gabe had been her constant since she was eight; he had been a brother and a friend. But even that changed when they said their last goodbye.

"Erin?" His voice pulled her from her thoughts.

"I'm sorry, what was that?"

"I can shower at the gym, if you don't mind picking me up there? I can have my roommate drop me off for my class." Erin had insisted on driving because she already had her gear packed up for the trip. Gabe had an early class this morning, but then they were going to leave. She needed more pictures at dusk so she wasn't too worried about getting there early. Besides, if they made good time, they would still end up there by ten in the morning.

"That's fine, I'm getting ready and I'll have to finish a few things around here first anyway. I'll see you soon."

After they hung up, Erin looked at herself in the mirror and wondered what in the world got in her head to make her invite him. When she was taking pictures, she felt truly herself. She was able to connect with nature and forget about all of her problems. However, now she was extremely nervous about how the day would go. She wanted Gabe back in her life; she'd hated the years they spent apart, and that was putting a lot of pressure on her to make sure this went well. She finally decided on a pair of her comfortable jeans, but opted for a fitted white shirt and threw on her leather jacket. She was completely comfortable and would be able to move around easily, but she knew the outfit worked with her figure.

Why she was worried about her figure, she didn't want to let herself think about. Then she grabbed a scarf and put on brown leather boots before she went about moussing her hair. She loved to change her hair style and color, and figured she had probably tried about every option out there. At the moment, she had the sides of her head shaved short with a pile of hair on top that she styled.

Erin left a few minutes early, and picked up coffees and muffins for the ride before getting Gabe. It was clear he was fresh from the shower; tight curls held in lingering moisture, and his eyes were bright from his morning activity.

"Thanks for inviting me. Do I get to spend the rest of my day wine tasting?" His mischievous look left her chuckling.

"You can if you want to. I on the other hand will be getting paid to be there, so I should probably hold off."

Before she started driving, Gabe took her hand gently in his own and scrutinized the palm that he'd all too recently bandaged for her. She did her best to ignore how the small touch of his fingers sent her pulse racing. "You weren't joking about healing quickly were you?"

There was only a thin line on her skin to show she had cut it. His fingers traced the line with a soft touch and then he brought her hand up to his lips to place a soft kiss there. It was something he'd done a hundred times when they were children, but this time it sent her heart into her throat, and she had to clear it so she could get out her next words.

"Yeah, maybe living on my own, instead of in a house full of other kids, got my immune system really cranking. Right after graduating high school I was moving some of my stuff, and I had a pretty bad fall. I remember it only took a few days for all the scrapes and bruises to heal. It was never like that when I was younger; I still have the scars from Cujo. But nothing after falling down a flight of steps with a box full of stuff landing on me." She cringed at the memory of being attacked by a dog when she was nine.

She'd been placed in a foster home not long after meeting Gabe. It had been an okay place, but the boy that was also staying there decided to torment the dog. He'd gotten the poor thing all riled up and then shoved her at it. The dog had lashed out, and ripped up a good part of her leg and her hand before their foster father was able to get him off her. She'd been returned to the group house covered in stitches. She still had some decent looking scars and a healthy fear of dogs to remember the moment by.

"Huh." Gabe leaned back in his seat and released her hand so she could drive. She felt the loss of his warmth and tightened her grip on the steering wheel. "So you are a bartender, photographer, and newly invincible; what else should I know about you?"

"I'm also a waitress during the day."

Gabe sent her a surprised look. "*Three jobs?* Is that really necessary?"

"I *do* like to eat and have my own apartment."

"Get a roommate, like me." She raised her brow at him and was about to make a sarcastic comment, but he quickly amended. "I don't mean *me*. I mean…I have a roommate. I ended up bunking with Jason from school. Helps cut down the cost. None of your friends were willing to go in with you on a place?"

She shrugged uncomfortably. "I like my space." In reality, she had coworkers and people she joked around with…but she didn't really have *friends*. She found it hard to talk to others, and nearly impossible to build a genuine relationship. After a childhood spent being pulled from one place to the next, she found it wasn't smart to depend on other people. Gabe was the only person she'd ever really let herself lean on. When she'd lost him, it nearly killed her.

Gabe studied her for a moment and seemed to relent "It doesn't surprise me though, you were always a hard worker. While I was skipping class, you actually used your study hall to do homework and *study*." He cringed at that, making her laugh. "Did you go to college?"

"Not really. I took a business class and a few photography classes, but nothing really beyond that. I didn't want a bunch of loans so I only went when I could afford to. How about you?"

"I got a scholarship and took out a few loans. Went for personal training. Still paying off the bills though, so you were probably smarter, as usual," he lamented with a dramatic sigh. "I'm glad you still like taking photographs though; I feel like I spent more time looking at the lens of a camera than your actual face." Erin scowled at her passenger and stuck her tongue out at him when he laughed.

The rest of the ride passed in easy banter and petty fights over the radio. Erin felt more at ease than she had in years, so of course it was starting to freak her out. As a general rule, she didn't let people in. For the most part, she got plenty of human interaction through work and spent the rest of the time on her own. Gabe was different though. They'd shared time in and out of the group home, and even spent nearly four years together in a foster home.

When they were separated after being with the Gilbert family, she spent the next two years with the Wells family. She hid the fact that the Wells parents mostly ignored her and any of her needs, and that their son Chase, who was two years older than her, increasingly messed with her during her time with them.

Gabe was the one who eventually got her out of there; when she was fifteen, Chase finally took it too far. He decided if he had to put up with her in his house, then she was going to do what he wanted.

He tried to force himself on her, but she head butted him and was lucky enough to break his nose. His parents didn't do anything about the incident, just yelled at her for what she'd done, and let her know just how ungrateful they found her.

When she showed up at school with finger-shaped bruises, Gabe instantly pulled her aside. He'd already been questioning her about her life with the Wells family, suspecting that something had been off about her, but she'd been able to hide everything until then. When she told him what had happened, he marched her right to the principal's office to report it. Gabe told them that they were both returning to the group home, and that someone would have to go to the Wells to get her stuff, because he wasn't letting her set foot in that house again. She still couldn't believe how he'd outright refused to go back to the foster home he'd been placed at because he wanted to stay with her at the group home. The fact that she'd been hurt was probably the only reason they'd allowed it, but she'd always been grateful to him.

They spent the next year at the group home together. It was always harder for older kids to get placed, especially ones that had been moved around as much as they had, so she'd thought they would just age out together. When she was sixteen, though, she was told she'd be placed with another family. She'd been terrified, and had even asked Gabe to run away with her. Him turning her down was the last conversation they'd had before being pulled from one another.

When they arrived at the vineyard, Gabe offered to unload her Jeep while she spoke with the manager, then they wandered the grounds together. Once she started working, she fell into her normal rhythm. She might have even forgotten he was there if she couldn't feel his gaze on her. This was something they'd done many times before. As soon as she had her hands on a camera when they were younger, she couldn't be stopped. She took pictures everyday and more often than not, Gabe had followed her. He'd make up his own games, many of which involved photobombing her shots. She teased him with the memories as she worked. He just grinned fondly. "You know, I still have a box of old photos I took. When we were younger it would frustrate me to no end that I would get them printed, only to find you peeking from behind a tree or lying under a bush. I still pull them out sometimes when I need some cheering up."

"Well, now you have a fancy digital camera, so you can see right away how the pictures will look. I think that's cheating. It makes photobombing much harder."

"It must be so hard being you."

"It's easier when I have good company."

.ℰ .ℰ .ℰ

Briar's arms had long since grown tired, so Fern now flew alongside her. They were both silent, listening to the ongoing movement of erebi below. She had no idea how long they had been in the realm. At least some of them had to have been set up before, hiding near the portal and preparing their attack. The first wave would have already reached the village, and found the queen and her council attending the concert. Her vision was now both past and present. Her future — and the future of the realm — loomed like a black cloud ready to downpour.

Finally, Briar felt the pull of energy from the portal, and motioned for her sister to stop. Easing back leaves from the forest that had protected them from sight thus far, Briar got the full image of what was happening below.

Last she'd seen the ground foliage, only the edges were starting to die. The land she surveyed at that moment, however, seemed devoid of any magic, any energy. The roots of the trees were turning black, spreading out over the once rich earth below. Though she and Fern passed ahead of the massive army, two erebi stood guard at the doorway to their escape. One hardly looked like what she would expect from an erebus. He looked mostly human, with long black hair. When he turned his head, she caught sight of the red eyes and jagged scar on the right side of his face. The other erebus had yellow scales for skin, white eyes with black slits, and long talons jutting from his hands. He wore a long cloak, which covered the rest of him from view, but he gave off the feeling of *other*.

Briar turned back to Fern, and found her sister looking pale and ready to fall from the sky. "Fern?" She let the leaves fall back into place, forgetting the need to be quiet as she rushed to her sister's side.

"It's all dying. The plants are screaming in agony. They are begging for help. It feels like it's nearly ripping my insides apart." Fern's violet eyes stared into the distance, wide in silent horror.

"Shh..." Briar gathered Fern back into her arms and kissed the top of her head. "It will be okay. The portal is just below us. We can hide nearby and see if the two guards leave, or we can make a run for it. We just have to step through the portal and we'll be free." Fern nodded numbly, her brown curls bouncing in the breeze.

"Let me go!" A voice broke out below, female and pissed off.

"Come now, I've been ordered to send you back with a little message." Briar went back to watching through the leaves, her wings straining from the long journey and holding her place still above the trees. The black haired erebus was now out of sight, but two more were moving toward the portal with a struggling fae held between them.

"All this time she didn't know. She thought it was all lost. Drawing her out like this...you are signing your own death warrant-" One erebus silenced the wingless fae with a punch to the stomach and the two sisters looked at each other.

"We could try to grab her and get through the portal..." Fern suggested, her small features pinched with silent determination. It was either that or watch the erebus kill her. The portal was reaching out toward her with small tendrils of energy. It was just enough to give her the confidence she needed.

"Hold onto me, but if something happens, you get through that portal. Focus on the humans. There should be a protector on the other side. Understood?" She waited for Fern to agree, but the sight below left her frozen in shock.

One erebus, with a spike that seemed to grow from his wrist, stabbed the fae before Briar could react. Nausea washed over her and she felt dizzy, but Fern's small cry kept her from losing it. The erebus started to drag the fae to the portal and Briar dove, determined to push the fae from their arms and take her with them to Sula. She could *just taste* freedom...when a strong hand grabbed her ankle, and the erebus pushed the harmed fae into the portal. Her mind filled with mist; image after image flashed by...so quickly she couldn't make them out. So many different futures reached out to her that she swore her head would explode. She had to get Fern to the portal — even if she could no longer see. Something was *wrong*, and she needed to make sure her sister was safe.

"What's wrong with her?"

"She's one of them. Let's take her." The strong hand dragged her from the sky and she hit the ground hard. Her wings contracted painfully against her back, trying to avoid hitting the ground.

"Bri!" Fern's voice called to her from the mist, but she still couldn't see. Briar's heart pounded in her chest as she tried to slow the images flashing through her mind. Finally her vision cleared, and she turned on her side and proceeded to throw up on the dirt below. Her side hurt from hitting the ground so hard, but the twisting of her mind from the chaotic vision had her whole body fighting against itself. When her stomach was finally empty, she looked up and found the black haired erebus staring down at her with sharp eyes.

"Take them both, just in case."

"No!" She tried to struggle to her feet until the man hovering over her dragged her upright. Briar turned her head to find another erebus holding Fern, who was openly crying and trying to break free. "Please! Let her go!" She managed to shove an elbow into her captor's stomach and heard him groan, but didn't bother to turn. The second his grip loosened, she kicked back at him and pushed off his body to propel herself toward her sister and the erebus holding her. For just a moment, she had Fern in her grasp, but suddenly the hilt of a blade came down on top of her head. The last thing she smelled was honeysuckle before she sank into cool darkness.

.℘ .℘ .℘

Ana sat to balance the register while Melody locked the front door, switched the sign to 'CLOSED', and walked the floor to straighten up. The store was really just a front to have control over the portal. She had an endless amount of money thanks to the previous protectors, and probably the ones that came before them, but Ana always took the running of the store seriously. Luckily, those that had magic were naturally drawn to the place, and there were plenty of people who enjoyed coming to the store even if they did not possess magic. The routine of double-checking the deposit total, preparing the slip, and making a copy was practically muscle-memory, so she made a mental to-do list while she worked. She needed to make the run to the bank and grab some groceries, but didn't want to leave Melody alone in the store. She wanted to forget about the erebus that attacked, brush it off as one of the few random attacks that happen simply because they guarded a portal. She *wanted* to, but that, in addition to the fae that had been pushed through only to die on her floor, made it hard to write it off as incidental. Something in the pit of her stomach was setting off warning bells.

"Ana!" Melody's voice was sharp, making Ana think she may have called to her more than once. "You aren't going to make it to the bank in time if you keep sitting there staring. Go. I'll work on inventory, and I'm going to be hungry tonight, so it'd be really nice to have food when I go up." The last part was said with a grin, and it *did* help ease the knots in her gut.

"Okay. I'll have my phone on me, just call if you need anything." Ana gathered her stuff, panicked a little when she saw how late it was getting, and headed out. She paused until Melody locked the door, and gave a small reassuring wave before she left.

The bank was close, only a street down, which was very good, because she made it with only five minutes to spare. Annoyance was clear on the faces of the tellers, but she had everything ready, so it would be easy enough for them to get her out quickly.

Ana walked to the nearest market next. Knowing there was no longer a reason to rush, she wandered leisurely through the aisles and picked up a few extra things that she knew Melody loved. The witch was not her daughter, and she did her best to not "*parent*" too much; when she first came across Melody, the girl had been taking care of herself, living on the street, and still maintaining a solid course load at school. She knew she was responsible and more than capable...but it was hard when she wanted only the best for the girl, and wanted to protect her from the kind of trouble she had in the past. Idly she wondered if that caretaker drive stemmed from her failure to do the same for her brother.

Chocolate creme cookies and popcorn were added to the cart before Ana made her way to pay for the normal, healthier choices. A nagging sense of unease twisted in her stomach and left her tapping a foot as she waited on the cashier. "Probably just lingering stress," she told herself with a steadying breath.

She had only just stepped out of the shop when she heard her phone ringing. Looking less dignified than an elven princess should, she balanced bags and struggled to grab the phone. She would never get used to technology. It all still felt foreign to her, though she couldn't deny the convenience.

"Mel?" she questioned, readjusting the bags and starting the walk back to the store with the phone pinned between her ear and shoulder. At first she didn't hear anything on the other end, and the elf wondered if she'd been butt-dialed.

"Ana!" Melody's voice was thick with tears. At the panic in her young charge's voice, Ana's pace quickened. She only had to get over a block. She wasn't far. Whatever the problem was she would get there in time. She had to.

"Ana, I need help. Aria!" A thick sob she was clearly trying to choke back cut off her words. "It's Aria. Ana, I'm trying-" A small thud echoed through the phone, and Ana broke into a run. Melody must have dropped the phone, because she could still hear her, but the sound was muffled. She made it to *Mystifying*, and struggled with the bags of groceries still hooked on her arm. She dropped them and her phone at the door, so she could dig out her key. The second she was through, she felt the disturbing difference in energy.

"Ana…back here!" Melody's voice called from the office, but Ana had a sinking feeling she already knew what she would find. She ran, threw open the door, and froze in her tracks. She didn't see it all at once. It came to her in flashes: Melody on her knees, her body shaking; Aria's feet, bare and dirty with splotches of blood; the sound of Melody's sobs, Aria's head resting in her lap, forest green eyes staring blankly.

Slowly…oh so slowly…like she was moving through a fog, Ana crouched down beside them and checked for a pulse. She saw the blood, so much blood. Melody's hands were covered, probably from trying to stop the bleeding. Too much blood. No pulse. Melody pulled Aria closer, clearly knowing what she was going to say and trying to put it off for as long as she could. Her sobs turned to quiet whimpers of grief. Aria was gone, there was no saving her friend, the fae Ana had sent to her death.

Ana didn't speak, just put her hands on Melody's shoulders. She was numb, in shock. She should be used to death by now. It was very rare for elves to witness death, but not for her. How many had she seen? How many had she lost? But this one, Aria, her friend, so full of life and passion, living every day to the fullest, this one was *her fault*. Melody's grief was because of *her*.

Slowly Ana drew the witch away from the fae, pulled her against her shoulder and felt the moisture of her tears seep into her shirt. "She's gone sweetie, she's gone." The words came out soothing, coupled with the small circles she rubbed into the girl's back. Her voice was soothing for Melody's sake, but her mind raged.

Chapter Four

As dusk settled over the vineyard, Gabe set up Erin's camera stand for her, and stood back while she got different shots in the new lighting. The sun seemed to burn at the horizon, and deep hues of pink and gold painted the sky. When she was done he offered to load up her gear while she talked to the manager again, which earned him a grateful smile. Night fully coated the sky by the time she finished, so he offered to drive them home.

"Sounds good to me. Thanks for keeping me company today. I usually do all my shoots alone, so it was nice to have a pack mule... *company*! I meant company!" she teased.

"Well, in exchange, I was able to enjoy a lovely day at a vineyard instead of my apartment. I'll be happy to tag along whenever you require a pack mule. Or company." He grinned and tried to start her Jeep, but the engine wouldn't turn over. She groaned. "Try hitting the gas a little when you turn the key. Sometimes Tara needs a little push."

Gabe looked at her and started to laugh. "Tara?"

"Don't judge me, I was very fond of that cat!" she defended. There had been a feral cat that lived near the group home. She'd been watching a lot of Buffy at the time, so she named the thing Tara. Gabe caught her feeding the cat scraps on more than one occasion, and she'd even snuck the cat up to her room a few times when the weather was bad.

Gabe tried four more times to get Tara to start before he gave up and climbed out. She followed after him, praying he wasn't going to open the hood and tell her Tara was officially dead. It took her a while to scrape together enough money to buy the used Jeep. She'd made it two years just walking or taking public transportation, but when she started trying to get photography gigs she'd needed her own way around with her supplies. "Your cables have some corrosion. It's simple enough to replace, but we'll have to find a car shop."

"*Great*," Erin lamented. She pushed herself away from the vehicle to face him. "Sorry about this."

Gabe shrugged with a wry smile. "No big deal. We'll figure it out." They walked back inside to find out where the nearest store was. She was just grateful he knew a little something about cars, and that it seemed like an easy enough fix. Her gratitude faded a bit when they were told that at 7 o'clock in the evening, the places that would have what they needed would be closed. Of *course* they would!

"Well, what do you want to do? I can get us an Uber, or we can rent some rooms and get what we need in the morning." Both of those sounded like expensive options. She did know she was tired and hungry, though. The idea of taking a two hour ride home, and *then* having to take one again tomorrow to get her car, sounded like some level of Hell she didn't wish to explore.

"If you don't have plans for the morning, I'll just get us a room," Erin offered with a vague gesture towards the manager's desk. "In the morning we can get the cables and head home. It would probably be cheaper than having an Uber drive us all the way back. Plus it saves me a second ride back up here to get Tara and find someone else to fix her."

Gabe started to take out his wallet, but she held up a hand. "If you're okay sharing a room, I've got it. It's my fault we are here anyway and maybe the manager will give me a discount." She *hoped* the manager would give her a discount.

She watched with amusement as Gabe started to argue and then stopped himself. He was probably remembering how stubborn she could be and was debating if it was worth it. "Okay, but you'll let me get us some dinner."

"Deal," she replied.

Erin got them checked in, and the moment she had the key in hand, Gabe tucked her into the crook of his arm and led them to the dining area. They had a quick lunch there earlier, but the atmosphere changed with the darkening sky. The lights were set lower and each table had a candle burning. The moment they sat down, Gabe started them off with a bottle of wine. It didn't escape her notice that they were joined in the dining area with an array of couples both young and old. Gabe looked too good for this world with his tousled blond hair, forest green eyes, and a grin that promised trouble. Right now he was looking at her like she was the only woman in the world.

Once they ordered their food Gabe held up his glass of wine in a toast. "To an early birthday weekend. If I was going to get stranded anywhere, with anyone, I can't think of any better options than this one right here." He tilted his glass to her, but all she could do was stare.

"Erin, of course I remembered your birthday." Gabe frowned at her, reading her thoughts. "April 9th, this Tuesday... I didn't have my own to remember after all."

"I seem to remember we decided your birthday would be November 4th, the day you showed up at the orphanage." Erin set down her glass. Every year since they were separated she would go to the local bakery to get his favorite mini fruit tarts for his birthday. He'd always said something about it made him happy, like some good memory of his was tied to the treat. When they were growing up, it was always their birthday mission to find a new one to try.

"None of your memories ever came back?" she asked quietly. She knew how much it bothered him that he didn't know who he was or where he came from. He'd gone to therapy here and there as it was provided to him, but he was never able to remember anything before waking up at the edge of the road. His clothes were torn and dirty, but otherwise he'd seemed uninjured. He'd spent hours with the police until he was brought to the group home for emergency placement. When no one came for him and none of his memories returned, they'd started calling him Gabriel.

"No, I just had to settle for my memories of you," he replied. There was a tightness to the set of his mouth which gave away the fact that his lack of memories still bothered him.

"There were some good ones in there."

"I agree. You always brought light even in the worst of times." A little ball of warmth spread through her chest at his words. She knew how important he'd been to her survival when they were younger but it made her happy to think she might have done the same for him. He reached across the table and took her hand in his. "I should have run away with you when you asked. I've always regretted it."

"What? You have nothing to regret. I was just scared. We were kids. I mean, if we'd packed up our few belongings and snuck out that night, we would have been living on the streets. Instead, I aged out with a nice family and was able to find a job and an apartment. You went to college and have a job you enjoy. You can't regret that."

"I regret losing you."

She squeezed his hand. "You didn't lose me — we found each other again." She had her own regrets regarding their last moment together. She never should have asked him to run away with her; it hadn't been fair to place that on him. She still remembered sneaking up to his room in the middle of the night. A few hours earlier she'd been told she had a placement, but it required her to switch schools. They were taking her the next day so that they would have time over the weekend to get everything set up with the school. Gabe had been at work earlier, he'd found a fast food job to work so he had some of his own money. He'd already started saving up for when he aged out.

Erin wasn't supposed to go into the boy's room, but she and Gabe went into each other's spaces all the time; they just usually did it during the day when they wouldn't really get into trouble. Some of the other guys were asleep, however, most of them were still awake when she snuck in. Gabe had to deal with the usual crap they always gave him about her. She knew none of the guys so much as looked at her too long because of Gabe. Anytime a new person showed up at the house, he would immediately make it known that no one was to mess with her. She knew of two fights he'd gotten in to make sure of it, and she guessed there might have been a few others.

Gabe was unfazed by their taunting, and pulled her out into the hallway. There was a little sitting nook at the end, so he took her there where they would mostly be hidden from view. She'd barely sat down before she started crying. Erin wasn't one to cry; she could probably count on one hand how many times she'd cried in front of him, but she'd been terrified of what was going to happen. She asked him to run away with her. They would never have to worry about placements or anything else. They could start a new life together and not answer to anyone.

He told her it would all be okay while he rubbed circles on her back. They would still see each other all the time, if anything went wrong he would get her out of there, she just had to tell him. She'd expected him to go along with the plan, so she just sat there stunned while she came to the realization that he'd told her no. He hugged her and she was practically sitting on his lap so that they were hidden from view. She looked up at him, ready to make another argument for her case; when their gazes locked, though, there was something in his look that she couldn't quite place. He'd looked at her that way before, more and more so, recently. It made her mouth dry and her heart race.

"Are you going to be okay?" he asked her. Suddenly, they seemed so much closer. She wasn't sure which of them had leaned in, but now they were only a breath apart. Then his mouth was on hers. It was just a soft press of lips, but it sent her mind into a frenzy.

When Chase had attacked her, he hadn't kissed her. He'd just knocked her down and groped at her. Nothing about this felt the same. The press of Gabe's lips was clumsy, but warm and questioning. There was a hunger in it, but he'd been waiting for her to kiss him back.

She'd jerked away at the realization and then ran off. She couldn't even remember jumping away from him, or getting back to the girl's room.

In her memories, one moment he's kissing her, waiting for her to kiss him back, and the next she's sitting in her room, staring at the ceiling, trying to figure out what just happened. That was their last moment together. She always regretted not kissing him back. She should have stayed hidden in that alcove with him the rest of the night…taken in every last moment they had together. She'd loved him, he'd been her best friend, and there'd been attraction there. She'd been ignoring it for a few months leading up to that kiss, but her view of him had started to shift into more. Instead of exploring that, she'd run.

"So, why aren't you seeing anyone right now?" he asked. His lips tilted in amusement, which made Erin wonder if he knew what she was thinking about.

"Three jobs, remember?" She gave him a cheeky grin and finished taking the last bite of the seafood pasta she'd ordered.

"Ah, the old three job excuse. Oldest one in the book."

"Hmmm, you're right, I should be more creative. What about you? Why are you single?"

"Well, I blame my roommate. He leaves used socks all over the apartment like he's marking territory or something. For some reason, it seems to be a real turnoff." He flashed her a grin, which she couldn't help but return.

"I wonder if your roommate is aware you use him as an excuse that you can't get a girlfriend.

"I never said I couldn't!" He chucked a shrimp tail at her, completely unfazed that they were at a pretty upscale vineyard. "In all seriousness though, I just haven't found anyone that made me stop missing you." He sat back in his seat after dropping that bomb. She wasn't sure how to take that comment, so she turned her focus to her camera instead. She clicked a picture of him just as he went to sip his wine.

"I'll need you to sign a release for that photo. A hot man drinking wine will bring all the ladies here!" She grinned and shot another picture.

"Did you just call me hot?"

"Depends on if you agree to sign the release form."

Once they finished dinner they went up to the room together, and Erin instantly claimed the bed by the window. With an amused smirk, Gabe kicked off his shoes at the end of the second bed and grabbed the remote. "You got first dibs on the bed, I get to pick the TV show."

"That's fine with me. I'm probably just going to crash anyway. It was exhausting bossing you around all day," she teased. Gabe stuck his tongue out at her like a petulant child; Erin winked in response. Her smile remained for a long moment, until she glanced down at her clothes. Now that they were stuck there for the night, Erin wished she had worn something a little more comfortable. She settled into the bed after unwrapping her scarf and unclasping her necklace.

Gabe turned the lights off for her and turned down the volume of the TV, and still she couldn't drift off right away. Instead, she listened to the sound of his show and the small movements he made on the bed next to her. The wine made her limbs feel heavy, and her mind was exhausted, but her body just wouldn't give in. Eventually she gave up and rolled over to face him. He was sitting with his back propped up, but he looked away from the TV when he felt her watching him.

"I can turn it off if it's bothering you…" he started to apologize.

"No, it's not that. I just can't sleep."

"Come here." Gabe motioned for the spot next to him on the bed. She didn't move right away, though. As kids and teenagers they had spent plenty of time cuddling under a tree in the park or on a sofa watching TV; the thought of his arms around her now, though, made her feel light-headed.

After a moment's hesitation, she rose from her own bed and lay down next to him. His fingers instinctively went to her hair, and he pulled idly at the strands while she snuggled into his shoulder. "This is much easier now that your hair is so short," he whispered. His breath danced lightly along her cheek. The sound of his heart drumming away under her ear was soothing, and the feel of him playing with her hair started her drifting off. It had been years since she felt this safe and cared for. He shut off the TV and settled down around her, drawing her close. "Good night, Erin," he whispered to the top of her head, his lips brushing over her hair, then she was lost to dreams.

.♪ .♪ .♪

Briar awoke to her mother rubbing her back like she did when her visions made her sick, soothing circles that slowly settled her stomach and let her mind clear. Sometimes the visions came to her like dreams, almost pleasant and fleeting, but when someone was particularly conflicted or their future stood unclear, she would see all the ways it could go, until it became impossible to discern one image from the next. It always made her sick when that happened, and she would feel weak and tired afterwards.

Her mother understood; she often had the same problems. After years of practice she was able to control it better, but Queen Gossamer demanded a lot from her powers and it often left her feeling weak. "Mama?" she finally whispered, almost afraid to move her head. She could feel it pounding with a headache, and knew she would feel dizzy when she sat up.

"Shh," a voice soothed...but it wasn't her mother's. She also realized the hand rubbing her back was much smaller and the movements were random, rather than her mother's usual massage up her spine, around her wings, and then around the base of her skull.

"Fern?" It all came back to her and she jolted upright. "Are you alright?" Briar moved a little too quickly, and her head spun. She squeezed her eyes for a moment and took a few deep breaths through her teeth. Once the world seemed to still, she opened her eyes again. Her head wasn't pounding because of a vision; it was because someone hit her in the back of the head.

"I'm fine. You were out for a while, though." Her sister's voice was quiet and clearly afraid. It was her fault the younger fae was here in the first place, though she didn't know what would have happened if she had stayed in Loinnir.

"I'll be okay. Don't worry about me-" The sound of an iron door opening stopped her short. She moved quickly to cover her sister from view, though there was little she could do to protect her. The black-haired erebus entered, his red eyes glancing from her to Fern in one swift motion, taking in the whole of the room in one glance. His mouth was a thin line, the jagged scar crossing his face from the top of his lip up to his eyebrow. Whatever damaged him must have barely missed his eye.

"Finally awake I see. Get up, Blue. You're coming with me."

"Blue?" Briar's head was still a little foggy, but not so much that she didn't catch the name he called her. His eyes darted up to her turquoise hair and he simply raised one brow in response. "My name is Briar. And I'm not going anywhere other than home…" He stepped forward, and the strength in her voice fell short. His figure was large and intimidating. Darkness seemed to flow from him, so different from the energy she was used to feeling around others.

"You *are* coming with me. My leader has a job for you."

"And I suppose your leader believes the best way to get others to work for her is to kidnap them and rip them from their home?" Briar snarked, unable to resist being as contrary as possible.

He watched her in silence for a moment before his eyes darted to Fern. "Either you come with me, or I take the girl instead. Lyra won't be happy when she realizes the girl can't help her the same way you can."

Briar glanced behind her and found Fern cowering at the daunting figure of the erebus standing before them. "If I go with you...what happens to my sister?"

His voice was surprisingly soft when he answered. "I'll leave her here, lock the door behind me so no one else bothers her, and after your meeting with Lyra, you will be returned to her."

Seeing little choice, Briar turned and gathered her sister in her arms. "I'll be right back. I promise." She kissed the top of Fern's head before turning back to the man that now held her fate in his hands. She tipped her chin up, making herself look braver than she felt. "I've never broken a promise to her, don't make me a liar now."

The erebus led Briar down winding passages. All the walls were carved from solid stone, and she felt the heaviness of earth above, which led her to believe that they must be in a mountain, or at least far underground. The close walls and thick atmosphere left her feeling claustrophobic. She tried to ignore the pressure on her chest and focus on memorizing her surroundings, in case she had a chance to escape with her sister. "So your leader's name is Lyra?" Briar asked, as much out of curiosity as to break the unbearable silence.

Her captor turned to glare at her, the look so intense she recoiled a step. "Yes, we all have names, not that your kind cares. To you, we are all just evil that needs to be eradicated," he sneered.

"I'm sorry, are you trying to take the moral high ground right now?" She stopped. "I'd never met an erebus before they broke into my realm, killed people I've known all my life, and kidnapped me and my sister. You'd have a much stronger case if you were trying to make it while I wasn't being held captive."

"They killed your queen and her council. If anyone else died, it was because of choices *they* made against *my* kind. And you and your sister are perfectly safe; if you do as you're asked, I can take you both home once this is over."

"My *mother* was a member of the queen's council!" Briar barked, and the stab of agony threatened to unravel her tenuous hold on her self-control. Desperate to keep it together in front of Fern, she had kept quiet over their travels to the portal. Speaking the words aloud, though, made it all far too real. His eyes widened at her outburst, but his image blurred as tears filled her eyes. Instead of letting them fall, she bit the inside of her cheek hard until she tasted blood, and held her ground. This was not the place to show weakness. She was not prepared for any of this, but she had to be the shield for her sister. If she showed weakness, they could destroy the both of them.

"Does your sister know?" His voice was suddenly soft, and his eyes darted back to the hall they just came through. The abrupt change in the erebus's demeanor was unsettling. Briar shook her head.

"No, but she has a different mother. Her parents are safe as far as I can tell. Now, do *you* have a name or are you just meant to be my silent guard?"

"Doyle. And I'm sorry for your loss." He stared at her in silence another moment, which gave her a chance to stiffen her back and tuck her feelings aside. He seemed to abruptly do the same. "But it doesn't change all those that I have lost for simply being an erebus." He grabbed her arm and shoved her through a door. She found her captor, Lyra, waiting for her on the other side.

"Here is our little house guest." Briar took in the sight of the erebus that stopped her and her sister from escaping to freedom and getting help for their realm: she was covered in thick leather bindings that formed a makeshift armor across her dark, tattered clothing. Long hair the color of bronze was pulled back into a tight ponytail high on her head and hung just below the small of her back. She smiled, but it had a very sinister gleam with her yellow skin and green almost cat-like eyes.

"You and I share a problem. You see, the Queen of Skia, my half-sister as unfortunate as that is, allowed that erebi army to attack your realm. I don't think this is a very good move for Skia, because it puts us at war on two fronts. That never turns out well. So…" Lyra plopped down on a chair and crossed her long legs, brown leather boots bopping as if she were keeping beat to some tune in her head. "Here is what I propose: from what I hear, you are an observer fae. You do me a solid, and look into my sister's future to find a way to knock that crown off her little insipid head. You help me bring down the wicked witch, and I'll pull the erebi from your realm and send you and your little sis back to where you came from. Sounds like a pretty good deal now doesn't it?"

Briar gaped at her for a moment. "I can't just *see* on command. I've gone months without seeing anything before! If you can get me something that belongs to the queen, then it will help me concentrate and search for your answers."

"How nice. I love it when agreements are made so quickly. Here I thought I might have to do a bit more *convincing* in order to get your help."

"I am more than willing to help you," Briar replied. "I certainly have no love for the queen, as she sent an attack that killed people I care about. But I am going to have trouble concentrating when my sister grows sick from your realm. She does not have the power to see, she cannot help you. Her being here only takes away my concentration and energy."

"Well, how adorable is this?" Lyra stood and circled. Briar felt Doyle stiffen behind her. Lyra traced her fingers over her shoulder and then down her arm to grasp her hand. "Our guest feels as if she has the power to negotiate."

Briar hung her head for a moment and tried to think her way through this. Her top priority needed to be getting Fern back home. "I was simply hoping you could return her to our realm. I understand perfectly the situation I am in, and I will give you my full cooperation. I am not trying to negotiate; I am...asking a favor."

"But then my dear, what power would I have over you? If you no longer fear that I could snatch your sister and, let's say..." Lyra twisted a finger in the air as though she were thinking how Fern might be of some use, "torture her, and you could simply sit in your cell for the rest of your life with your arms crossed."

Briar straightened her spine and pulled her wings closer to her body to give herself all the strength she could muster. She stared Lyra down. "Why would I do that? I've been told that once you take out the queen I can return home, and you'll save my realm from the erebi. I certainly wouldn't go against my own best interest."

Doyle stepped forward and grabbed her upper arm. From the outside it would look like he was restraining her, but she felt the warning there. She also didn't miss the fact he shifted himself ever so slightly so he stood between her and Lyra. Apparently, he had no problem kidnapping her and her sister, but he feared what Lyra would do to her if she kept talking back. If this man was afraid of Lyra, then she probably should be too, but she had to hold her ground for Fern.

The bronze-haired erebus, however, grinned and stepped forward to pat Briar's shoulder. "Touché. Give me some time to think this over, dear. In the meantime, I will gather something of the queen's. I expect you to spend your time *seeing* what you can until I come back."

"Understood," Briar murmured. She turned away before she could be dismissed, and met Doyle's gaze.

He gave nothing away. His red eyes darkened until they were almost black as they each refused to turn away from each other's gaze. "I would like to return to my *room* now if that's okay with you? I can't focus on future events while a group of erebi stare me down."

An eyebrow quirked at that, and if she didn't know any better, she would have said his lips twitched up at the corners. With a blink the expression was gone, though, and he touched her elbow to lead her back down the cavernous path.

.℘ .℘ .℘

Gabe got up early the next morning to go in search of replacement cables. Erin decided to take another walk through the vineyard to get some early shots she missed out on the day before. The air was brisk and the sun was weak, so she zipped up her jacket and tucked in her scarf to help insulate. There had been a quiet awkwardness between them when they woke up, tangled up in each other. Gabe's fingers had still been curled in her hair, their legs were twisted together, and her arm was draped over him as she used him as a pillow.

They stayed like that for a moment, looking at one another before they both grinned and greeted each other with a shy "good morning". They moved slowly as they took turns showering, only to put back on the same clothes from the day before. They didn't talk about it, but there was a heaviness between them. This was more than reacquainting with an old friend. Maybe it started out that way, but there had been flirting and tenderness that went beyond friendship, at least for her.

Erin needed to get her mind off all of this, since it was more likely that Gabe just wanted to be friends again and she was getting ahead of herself. She wandered slowly between vines before reaching out to touch a bundle of grapes. It settled in the palm of her hand, and for a moment it was like she could smell and taste everything in the air that morning — from the lovely fragrance of the blooming flowers to the hint of sweetness left on her tongue by the pollen carried on the wind. She closed her eyes, and simply focused on the vines around her. She could feel them stretching out to grow further. She could taste the juice from the grapes on her tongue, even though it still rested on her hand.

The plant shifted, drawing Erin's gaze. What she saw made no sense — a small part of the vine had wrapped around her finger, and what had been clusters of tiny little bubbles had grown into full, ripe grapes in a matter of seconds. She shook her hand free with a small panicked yelp.

"Crazy," she muttered, staring at her hand and half expecting the vine to still be holding on to her.

"All fixed!" Gabe's voice rang out behind her. His presence startled her, and she couldn't hide her flinch as he came around to face her. "Are you okay?" He looked down at her hand, and Erin realized she was still holding it up. She dropped it and tried to ignore what just happened.

"Oh, yeah," she assured. "Did you still want to drive home?"

"Actually…" Gabe paused. It gave her a moment to shake off the feeling of being too aware of all the nature around her. She wondered what they put in their wine; it was freaking her out a little. "I don't mind driving us back, but do you mind if we walk for a few more minutes? It's a beautiful morning and I don't have any plans for the day." It *was* beautiful, and she was practically humming with energy. He held out his hand in question and it was impossible for her to not take hold. He was home to her. He was the sweetness of staying up late to share the candy one of them had hidden. He was the warmth of a hug after she'd had a bad day. He was the brightness of the sun when they were both too stubborn to return to the air-conditioned house, because they would rather be alone together. He was also the heartbreak of loss, but now she'd found him again, and she wasn't sure she could take more heartbreak. Not from him. But…she could deny him nothing.

They walked hand-in-hand further down the lane of vines, and his thumb made a soft brush back and forth against her skin. "Listen, I just want to make my intentions clear here, so things don't get confused." Erin tried not to stumble as he took a deep breath. "I was really excited when I ran into you the other day, and of course I wanted to catch up…find out who you are now."

She stilled and Gabe came to a stop with her. This was it. They shared one full day together, and now he'd decided it was best they go back to not knowing each other. She was sure they could be acquaintances, text some memes on occasion, but he had his own life to return to. She was not going to cry. She had no right to depend on him as she did when they were kids. Just because they crossed paths…

"Erin, I don't want to just get to know you as a friend. Not this time. We aren't kids anymore, and I feel like I've been missing a part of myself ever since we got separated. I don't want to feel that way again; I don't ever want to lose you. If you don't want more from this, that's okay, as long as I still have you in my life. But I'd drive myself crazy if I didn't at least let you know where I'm at."

72

"Wait." She was trying to make sense of his words. It was hard to make out his expression because her vision was a little blurry.

"Erin…" Gabe stepped closer to her. His hand came up to tuck against her cheek and he tilted her face to his. His thumb brushed over her bottom lip and a hazy warmth spread through her limbs. Then his other hand was at the small of her back, tucking her right up against him. He was no teenage boy any longer. There was a hunger in his gaze that she couldn't mistake. "Do you want me to stop?" He leaned closer, but still left space for her to back away if she wanted. He smelled like coconut from the hotel shampoo but she could still detect the undertone that was all him — forest in the sunlight.

She didn't move away. Instead, she tilted her head up more and rested her hands against his sides. Her fingers dug into his shirt and she used it to leverage herself to her tiptoes. Then his mouth was on hers. The brush of him against her was like lighting a match and throwing it towards a bundle of kindling. She was consumed by him in seconds. The feel of his muscles moving under her palms, the taste of the complimentary mint toothpaste from the hotel. His hands dug into her hips until they were flush together. They searched each other slowly, closing the gap of the last ten years and taking them beyond what they'd always been.

"Erin…" Her name was a whisper against her own lips. Gabe rested his forehead against hers and drew in a shaky breath. "Why didn't you kiss me back all those years ago?" he asked after they both caught their breath. He didn't move away.

"I don't really know." She brushed her lips against his once more, softly. "It was my first kiss and I wasn't expecting it. I didn't really know what it meant..."

"Well, do you know this time?" He teased, leaning to kiss her cheek, then her nose, then her other cheek. Her heart swelled in her chest at his tenderness.

"I kissed you back this time didn't I?"

Chapter Five

Sunlight danced through the branches around them, and Ana couldn't help but feel like it was mocking their agony. Soaking rain would have been more appropriate in this situation; both she and Melody had cried themselves into exhaustion, and simply had no more tears to shed. The weight of their friend's body seemed to be too much, but somehow the two of them managed to carry Aria to the cove of woods she'd loved so much in her life with the humans.

"You're sure this will work?" Melody questioned, her voice hollow.

Ana looked back to check on the witch before nodding. "Her magic will trigger it...the trees and flowers will surround her, draw her into the earth. No matter what realm they are in, if a fae is connected with nature, nature will claim them in death." She looked around, and gestured to a small clearing near some wildflowers. "Over here...Aria would have loved the flowers," she stated with a softer voice.

With Melody's help, they settled Aria's body down between the bright blooms. Then, she straightened and placed a hand on Melody's shoulder. "Come, Mel. We need to step back." Melody didn't respond right away, and Ana thought she might have to pull the witch back forcefully. Just as the foliage around Aria's body began to shift, however, Melody pushed herself upright and stumbled back into her. The elf kept a firm hold on her young friend, moving her back several steps as they watched vines and roots cover the body. Before long, their friend could no longer be seen beneath a blanket of green, flowers blooming in a stunning array of vibrant purples, rich blues, and happy tones of yellow.

Melody spun around and buried her face in Ana's shoulder. The young woman began sobbing, and Ana realized that both of them still had many tears to shed for their companion after all. The elf couldn't shake the heavy weight of guilt in the pit of her stomach; Aria wouldn't have gone back to Loinnir if she hadn't been asked to, after all. Aria's blood was on her hands, and she wasn't sure it would ever wash out. As she took in the sight of the new flowers which marked Aria's grave, Ana thought of how they'd become friends:

Ana was there when Aria first came through the portal. The fae was tired from her travels, but she was fascinated by the realm of Sula. She and Ana walked through the city and Aria asked about everything around them.

"Why did you leave such a beautiful world?" Ana asked after Aria finished telling her about all the colors, flowers, and smells in Loinnir.

"It was not all wonderful. It was my home, and it is beautiful…but a fae without wings does not have an easy life. All of our powers contribute, but the queen favors those with wings. Her closest friends and those of her council all are winged fae. Those without do not have many choices about their lives, and I just wanted to be free." Aria shrugged, but Ana could feel the fae's relief at finding herself in a new land.

They became fast friends. Aria wished to travel so she could see more of Sula. She became a collector of mystical items from around the world, and always stopped by to visit and show Ana what she acquired. Over the years she'd had a few girlfriends, but never settled down, too busy seeing the world to set down roots. She was there when Ana found Melody and took her in. She and Melody bonded quickly, and soon Aria stopped traveling so she could help Ana. Melody needed support and family and Ana suspected Aria had finally hit a time in her life when she was ready to be part of a family, too. Together, the three of them became a makeshift family of displaced magical beings. Now, they were missing a part of that family. Melody lost one of her support people; Ana lost one of her closest friends, and she was determined to find out why.

"Ana, there's something I forgot to tell you." Melody's voice brought Ana out of her thoughts. "When…when she was…um…" she shook her head briefly as if to clear the memory from her mind, "she said something about *her* coming back."

Ana stopped walking, confused. Realization hit her like a punch to the gut. There was only one person Ana could think of that Aria might have wanted to warn her about — the erebus that forced her out of her home...away from her brother...the one that killed her parents, destroyed their kingdom. If she was still alive, then what had been happening was not the work of rogue erebi. She was starting another war, using the same infection erebi she used to destroy Eloas.

"We have to go back. I need to look something up," Ana said, suddenly urgent. Melody gave her a concerned look, but followed her lead silently.

The drive back to the store was quiet, both women lost in their own thoughts. Ana's mind was racing over the implication that the same erebus that brought Eloas so much destruction and chaos, was now doing the same in another. The elf unlocked the store numbly, trusting Melody to take over the counter in the event that a customer walked in while Ana was researching. She headed for the office, to the shelves of books that were not for sale. She pulled any book on erebi that she could find, and dropped them on her desk.

"Do you need anything?" Melody asked, her voice hardly above a whisper, from the doorway. Ana looked up, her chest tightening at the way her young friend seemed to be curling in on herself in her grief. She didn't deserve to be suffering such pain. The college freshman should be stressing out about finals, bad dates, maybe even hangovers. Not losing her best friend at the hands of the same erebus that stole away Ana's innocence years ago.

"No, Mel," Ana murmured. "You can lock the store back up if you need to...I'll be back here for a while."

"I'll uh...I'll finish that inventory I never got around to," Melody murmured, her voice catching as her eyes filled with tears. "It'll keep me busy." Ana had to force back tears of her own while she passed the inventory list over to her friend. "Thanks." She watched Melody steel herself to go back into the store, shoulders straightening with fresh resolve. Ana took in a deep, shuddering breath before picking up the first book.

The sight of the she-erebus staring back at her from the pages of one of those books made every muscle in Ana's body tense. It had taken time, and almost a dozen books, but she'd found her. The depiction of the erebus was a basic sketch, but more than enough to take her back to the last time she'd seen her, the face vividly clear in her mind. Pure white skin, pitch black horns curving out of her forehead...eyes dark as voids. "Kali…"

"Aina, I'm scared!"

Aina dropped to her knees beside her little brother. Before they ran from their home, their mother put a spell on him so he would look human. Most likely her final task...there was no way anyone could have survived the onslaught she, Toron, and their Royal Guard Ethelron had narrowly avoided. Aina fixed her gaze on her younger brother, distracting herself from thoughts of their agonizing loss with the foreign look of Toron's humanoid ears. She would be able to enchant an item when they got to Sula so that he could cloak his appearance as he pleased, but Toron did not have control of his powers yet. "Shh, everything is going to be okay, Toron. You'll be safe soon," she soothed, scooping the elfling into her arms and rising gracefully once more.

With a glance over her shoulder, Aina registered that Ethelron was still fighting off a few erebi. "Run, Princess! You can make it!" Torn between listening to him and refusing to leave him too, she remained frozen in place for a moment. Ethelron finally looked up and held her gaze, eyes pleading with her to go, until an erebus managed to slice into his bicep with a dagger.

It took everything inside of her to turn from him, but she had to protect Toron. "You'll be safe soon," she whispered again.

"Optimistic for someone who just lost everything," a voice taunted behind her. Aina spun around and took a step back towards the portal. "You really think I am going to let you escape? I'm not a big fan of leaving my work half-done."

"I don't think you're going to have much choice." Despite the desire to avenge the murder of her parents and the impending destruction of her realm, Aina couldn't risk her brother's safety. Who knew how much longer the realm would be stable in the wake of Kali's devastation. She turned back around and leapt toward the portal.

"Not so fast." Kali's hand gripped her right shoulder, claws sinking deep into her skin. Aina gritted her teeth and instinctively released Toron.

"Toron, go! I'll be right behind you! Wait for me on the other side. Go!" The boy hesitated, tears filling his eyes, so she repeated the order vehemently. Once his blonde curls vanished from sight, she allowed her battle instincts to take over. Her free hand drew her dagger, and the elf turned towards the hand still anchored to her shoulder. In a single fluid movement, Aina sank her dagger into Kali's chest and dislodged the claws from her skin. *"You should have let us go."*

"T-this isn't over, Princess," Kali sneered weakly, scrabbling for a hold on Aina's wrist.

*"You really think you're going to be able to get out of here alive...*before *the realm collapses? Be thankful that I can't stay to rightfully avenge the King and Queen."* The venom and rage in her own words would have concerned Aina, if she'd had time to think about what she was doing. The ground shuddered violently beneath their feet, and she lost her grip on the ailing erebus. With only a flicker of a glance towards her Guard, Aina dove for the portal, and felt her heart shatter as she left her home behind for the last time.

She'd come into Sula through the very same portal in the corner of her office. At the time, the space had been a small bookstore owned by an elderly couple acting as protectors over the portal. Though they were human, the couple had been familiar with the supernatural, and took her in from the day that she stumbled into their office. Toron had not been waiting for her when she arrived, Ethelron never came through behind her, and weeks of searching left her feeling hollow and empty. In one horrible day, Ana had lost her entire family, her realm, and likely almost the entire population of her race.

Guilt tore at her with every breath; she'd failed her parents as she fled to the portal with her brother as they screamed behind her. She'd failed her brother, letting Kali slow her down…and she'd failed Ethelron, her friend, her loyal protector, who would only ever fail her if he were dead. In Sula, she started going by Ana, her given name too painful a reminder of her devastating defeat.

The shop owners had given her a job at the store and a place to stay, but it wasn't until the first fae crossed through the portal months later looking for help that Ana found a renewed sense of purpose. She worked alongside the humans for nearly fifteen years, expanding her knowledge and skills of the vast supernatural worlds, until the couple passed away and left her the shop. She'd spent those years thinking that the erebus responsible for destroying her realm was dead...only to find out this was not the case when a dear friend turned up dead by her hand.

$$\wp \ \wp \ \wp$$

Gabe drove them back to San Francisco, but they were in no hurry. Erin sat quietly beside him, watching the scenery pass them by.

Occasionally she sang along to something on the radio, but mostly she held his hand and gave him a warm smile when he looked her way.

"I guess this is my stop." Gabe pulled up to his apartment building and parked the Jeep. "So...there is a chance Jason is home, which means there may be a sock infestation. But, if you don't have plans...you are free to come in. I can make us some lunch," he offered. Erin winced in mock worry.

"Oh no, if you show me your apartment does that mean next time I have to show you mine? Is that part of dating? Because I'm going to need fair warning to clean."

Gabe chuckled and unlocked the front door. "Come on in, I'll try not to judge your mess when you invite me over. You do have *three jobs* after all, so I guess you have an excuse." He mocked her with a roll of his eyes as she entered the lobby, and tugged the door closed behind them.

The two stood quietly in the elevator, their sides touching as they rode to the third floor. As they entered, Erin had to do a double-take. The apartment was not what she would expect for two bachelors. The walls were a light gray brick with dark wood floors. They had a dark gray sectional that separated the open floor plan between the kitchen and living area. Very clean, very modern. She almost gulped as she thought of her mismatched furniture, bright colors, and scattered photos and artwork — not to mention the piles of stuff "decorating" the corners

"Did you guys do this? It's gorgeous." Erin crossed her arms over her chest and shook her head. "Now you are never coming to my place."

"Um, yeah, mostly. Didn't think I would be able to decorate?"

"No." Erin shook her head seriously while Gabe pouted.

"Well, here's another shocker: I can cook too!" Narrowed eyes searched his frame, a feigned look of seriousness on her face.

"Did you become a robot or something?" Erin followed him into his kitchen and sat on one of his barstools. "Is there something I can help you with?"

"No, I don't think you can be trusted." He handed her a bottle of water from the fridge, and she was two gulps in before she realized how thirsty she'd been. "If you want, you can play around with the TV, or explore for hidden socks." Flashing her a teasing wink, he started taking out food, so she decided to wander. The far wall was composed almost entirely of windows, so she went to take in his view of the city.

A few potted plants were scattered to grow under the natural light, but one was worse for wear. It didn't look like it was getting sun, so she picked it up to move it further over. When Erin sat it down, she touched the dying leaf, as though to encourage it. When her finger touched it, the leaf instantly brightened and came back to life. She watched as a flower in the center bloomed before her eyes, and she cried out.

"Are you okay?" Gabe called to her, and the clinking of kitchen work paused.

She couldn't answer, the breath caught in her throat. The flower's petals opened and seemed to smile up at her. She yanked her hand back, and accidentally knocked over the pot. It crashed to the floor, and the plant and dirt spilled across the wooden floor.

"Erin?" She heard him come around his counter, but still couldn't tear her eyes away from the plant as it quickly turned brown and died once more. His hand landed on her shoulder, but she pulled away, covering her mouth with trembling fingers.

"It's okay. I'll clean it up." He must have seen something in her face, because there was a small note of panic in his voice as he looked her over. "Erin, it's okay. Did you get hurt?"

"I have to go." The words barely made it past the lump in her throat. She'd almost forgotten about the incident at the vineyard, but now this? She couldn't pretend *that* hadn't happened.

"What? I thought you wanted to have lunch? It's just a plant, I'll clean it up-"

"I'll talk to you later. I'm..." Fearfully, she looked at the dead plant on the ground. "I'm sorry. I just...I have to go." She couldn't get away fast enough. She had no idea what was going on but it had to be real. She couldn't have just imagined *everything*.

She rushed into her Jeep and fumbled with her keys, but couldn't seem to get them into the ignition. It wasn't until she nearly dropped them altogether that Erin realized how badly her hands were shaking. With a growl of frustration, she dropped them onto the passenger seat and took a few deep breaths. When that didn't work, she rested her head on the steering wheel and squeezed her eyes shut. Maybe she was overreacting. Maybe all the excitement of finding Gabe again, and realizing they had a mutual attraction, was making her lose her mind.

Eventually, Erin calmed down enough to drive. She knew she wasn't ready for home, so she drove aimlessly for a while. Despite the fact that she needed to start working on the pictures she took, she felt an odd pull, and decided to follow it. She should have been surprised when she ended up on the road that led to the *Mystifying* store, but she wasn't. Instead, she pulled into an open spot and stared at the door. Her fingers clutched the necklace she had bought a few days before; maybe Ana had tricked her, given her something that would make her feel crazy instead of 'show her spiritual purpose'. Whatever it was, she was about to demand some answers.

Chapter Six

Ana looked up from her work when she heard the chimes for the front door. She'd been trying to get out a new shipment of books, desperate to keep her mind off of everything going on.

"Erin!" She recognized the woman from a few days before, before her whole world began crashing down around her ears. She forced a smile. "How do you like your necklace?"

"What did you do to me? I'm not crazy, *you* did something." The woman's cheeks were flushed with emotion as she let the door slam shut behind her. Melody shot to her feet behind the counter, and Ana could see her hand resting where the elf kept her dagger.

"I don't know what you mean." Ana kept her eyes on Erin, maintaining a calm expression, and came to stand beside Melody. She placed a hand on the witch's shoulder, and felt Melody relax her grip on the weapon.

Erin ripped the piece of jewelry from around her neck and threw it on the counter. "I demand to know what you did. You are messing with my life!" Her hazel eyes held a glint of panic, and Ana began to understand.

"Why don't you tell me what happened? Maybe then I can explain." Ana gritted her teeth, trying to be sympathetic. After burying one of her closest friends, the last thing she wanted to deal with was a crazy customer barging in. Melody had insisted on opening the store; *they were going to be there anyway,* she'd said. *It would help distract them.* Now Ana wished they had just left the doors locked. But, she remembered, there *had* been a reason she gave Erin the necklace in the first place. The woman had an aura around her. Ana could feel power brewing, and guessed some of that power was starting to make itself known.

Erin opened her mouth but froze, her words quickly dying on her lips. An expression took over her features, and Ana *knew.* The expression was one she had seen before, one Melody had worn too, when Ana first found her. "I'll believe you. I own a magic shop after all," Ana assured, her voice soft and soothing. Erin's anger finally seemed to melt away. She pulled out one of the stools beside the counter and sat heavily. No one spoke for a few minutes while Erin held her head and stared at the floor.

Ana pulled up a stool next to her, and motioned for Melody to give them a little space. The witch clearly wasn't sure about it, but she went to finish unpacking the boxes without argument. "Please tell me what happened." Ana gave her best impression of her ever-patient mother. Slowly and calmly, Erin told Ana about grapevines and flowers, clearly shaken by the experience. When Erin finished she looked up, and Ana got the feeling Erin was waiting for her to call the police. Instead, Ana laid a hand over hers and gave a reassuring squeeze.

"Did you maybe talk to your parents about this? Have you ever noticed anything odd like this happen around one of them?" Ana could see Erin was in a great amount of pain. She was clearly disturbed by what happened to her. That helped Ana put away her own pain, and focus on bringing comfort.

Erin pulled her hand away and stood from the stool. "Did *you* do this?" She seemed almost desperate for Ana to say she had, so she would have some kind of explanation. Sadly, Ana had to shake her head 'no'.

"You are reaching the age when one's powers become fully developed. You have always had this in you, but you didn't realize. Now, it is becoming too strong to just stay dormant."

Erin scoffed, a mask of annoyance hiding her grief. "I know you own this store and everything, but magic is *not* real."

"Then why do you think *I* did this to you somehow?" Ana nodded over her shoulder, knowing a way to clear it up fairly quickly. "Mel, would you mind?"

With a nod and an almost discernible eye roll, Melody closed her eyes and held her palms up. "Wha-" Erin made a strangled noise as Melody focused, and books rose from the boxes on the floor. Three of them floated into the air and started to circle her; she was clearly showing off a little. Then Mel's eyes opened, and she twisted her hands to the direction of the shelves. The books slid obediently into their spots.

.℘ .℘ .℘

Erin watched in awe, and felt like she was in some hidden camera show.

"Is...is this a trick?" She was having trouble making sense of what she was seeing. But then the girl's mocha brown eyes turned toward her, and Erin's mouth hung open when the necklace she had ripped off her neck suddenly started to float in the air. She watched the silver knit back together where she broke it. In shock, Erin held out her hand, and the newly fixed necklace folded gently into her offered palm.

"Melody is a witch," Ana explained. "A strong one too. She became aware of her powers at a fairly early age, considering her parents were non-magical. But from what you are saying about your show of powers, I believe at least one of your parents was fae. Did either of them ever show anything odd?"

"My parents are dead. Or they gave me up. I grew up in foster care." Her words were hollow. She was still staring down at the necklace in her palm and wondering when it was she lost her mind.

"I'm so sorry Erin."

"What are you trying to tell me? My parents were *fairies*? Fairies don't exist!"

"I understand this is a lot to take in. There are other realms out there, and portals that connect us. Fairies — better known as fae — elves, witches, erebi, or what humans might consider demons, *they exist.* Some are living amongst us, many simply stay in their own realm and never come into contact with humans."

"So you...are you a witch?" Erin asked, finally looking up at the shop owner.

Ana's smile was sad. "No. Witches are humans who, like I said before, can simply reach other parts of their brain. And I believe you are probably half human. If you were full-blown fae, your powers would have been more pronounced and shown up earlier. I, however, am not human."

"If you aren't human, what *are* you?" Erin tried to ignore the fact she was being told *she* was only *half* human, and focus on Ana.

"I am an elf. I am also orphaned, but I was born in another realm called Eloas. My brother and I came here to the human realm, which is called Sula, for safety about seventeen years ago." Ana moved around the store with ease as she spoke. Erin watched as she grabbed a few bottles and poured some things into a mug. Then she brought it over to her. "Drink this. It will help with the shock."

Erin sipped nervously at the brew, but it tasted sweet like honey and smelled wonderful. It did stop her heart from pounding, and when she got about halfway through, the buzzing in her ears finally stopped.

"How could I be a fairy without knowing? Shouldn't I have wings and be about five inches tall? And shouldn't your ears be pointed?"

Ana chuckled with amusement. "Many of the fae do have wings. Halflings are not gifted with flight however, only full-blooded. *Pixies* are small, and highly annoying; the fae are human size. As far as my ears..." Ana removed a small silver ring from her finger. Erin saw it had a small round blue stone, and the silver was shaped like a twig wrapped around her finger. Once the ring was off Ana brushed her hair to the side, and Erin watched in disbelief as Ana's sloped ears suddenly grew longer and pointed. "The ring is charmed."

Ana slipped the ring back on, and Erin noticed a tattoo peeking out from under her sleeve, though she didn't get a good look at it before Ana dropped her arm. By the time Erin looked back up to the blonde's ear, it appeared human once more. "It helps hide the elvish aspects of me. It also diminishes some of my abilities, but not enough for me to worry about most of the time."

Ana grabbed a candle and picked around for a crystal. She wrapped them gently in cheesecloth, and then wrote a brief sentence down on a slip of paper. "Now, unless your parents performed a memory charm, this will help connect you to your fae parentage. Before bed tonight, light the candle. Then sit the crystal in the flame. Say this sentence three times and then go to bed. For as long as the candle burns your dreams will connect you to whichever parent had powers. You will enter their world, and be able to see scenes from their life. Once the candle has burned out you will wake, but you will retain those memories. It will help you understand who and what you are, and why you were orphaned. Take all the time you need but then come back. I can help train you to control your powers." Ana held out the bag. Erin hesitated.

She glanced back at Melody, and the girl flashed her a reassuring smile. Erin took the bag and the strip of paper, and hurried out the door before she lost her nerve. When she got back to her Jeep, she noticed her cell phone was blinking with a text message. Gabe was checking to make sure she was okay. She almost texted back, but ended up putting her phone in the center console, leaving the message unanswered. What could she tell him anyway? She was some weird fairy half-breed who could bring plants back to life? It was probably better for him if she just stayed away, at least until she knew what was happening to her.

"Ana, are you sure this is the right thing?"

"What do you mean?" Ana watched Erin climb into her Jeep before she turned back to her friend.

"We just lost one of our own," Melody's voice rose with the sudden heat of anger, "and you are inviting a clearly unstable fae to practice under you?"

"The world around us is quickly becoming dangerous, Melody. I am supposed to be a protector over this portal; I would not be doing my duty if I stood by when someone clearly needs help. You know as well as I do, she won't be able to hide her aura once her powers are fully realized. Any erebi in this realm will be drawn to her. She is going to have to learn to control them." The elf paused. "And yes, we did just lose one of our own...maybe she will end up helping us. I've given her the option." Ana shrugged, but her mind was not as easy as she wanted it to be. The power coming off of Erin was palpable, and Ana believed she would be strong once she started reaching out for her powers. But she also sensed the woman was unstable and had trauma in her soul, which could make her magic dangerous if not properly guided.

"For right now, we have our own work to do. We need to start tracking any infection erebi we can that have made it to this realm. We cannot let them take hold. I am also going to have to come up with a plan for Kali. If she is coming back, she needs to be stopped before she has the chance to carry out whatever plan she has."

Melody let out a long-suffering sigh before she moved to set up in the center of the store with a map, candle and a stone to help her focus. Ana knew it could be hard work to perform tracking spells, especially on erebi, so she continued her work quietly, giving Melody the space she needed.

Some time later, Ana looked up at the door chime, and found herself fighting down both frustration and guilt. She'd forgotten to lock the door. While that typically wasn't a big problem, with Mel setting up for a spell, it could freak out some of the more skeptical customers. The last thing they needed was a non-believer screaming about how they were summoning demons or some other nonsense.

"Mel, hey! I'm sorry, I saw the closed sign...but I needed to check on you guys after…"

Ana stepped out of her office and smiled sadly at their visitors. Marisa, a dark-haired member of Melody's Wicca group, stood just inside the door with her father. "Mare, Asher, please come on in. Thank you for stopping by."

"I was just getting started on a tracking spell for these creepy infection erebi that have decided to try and make this place their new home." Melody gestured towards the book. "Keeping busy and taking out some nasties while I'm at it…"

Marisa smiled for a moment before becoming serious once more and turning to Ana. "I'm so sorry about Aria."

"Thank you," the elf replied solemnly. "You guys should probably know there has been a spike in dark energy. Something is going down, drawing erebi to the realm. I believe it is starting in Loinnir, but it's spreading. We all need to be careful, and keep watch."

Asher crossed his arms over his chest, watching Melody resume her work. "We've come across a couple ourselves just this week, which is unusual considering our last encounter was over a year ago. Do you have any idea what's behind it?" Asher was a very serious warlock. He came from a strict Korean family of magic users, and as far as Ana knew, the only time he'd broken from his family traditions was when he married Marisa's non-magical, non-Asian mother.

"Something Aria said makes me think that they are under the command of a much more dangerous erebus. She said that Kali, the one responsible for destroying my realm, is back, and it's looking like Loinnir is her next target. But I doubt the fae will be able to hold for long, and then she'll be coming here full force. I don't know how many erebi have made it here, so Melody and I are going to track down as many as we can and destroy them. The last thing that we need is those things hurting innocent people and creating an army."

"I'll stick around, help you-"

Asher put his hand up, shaking his head with a frown. "Absolutely *not*. It's one thing for you to help me deal with them as we come across them, but I am *not* okay with you going out and looking for trouble."

The young witch started to protest indignantly, but Ana shook her head as well. "Your father's right, Mare. Melody and I are prepared for this...I'd feel better if you both went to prepare your coven for the next wave. This isn't over."

Chapter Seven

Erin got back to her apartment and downloaded the photographs from the vineyard. She tried to focus, but each picture reminded her again of the vine reaching out and wrapping around her finger. She was editing the lighting on one picture, when she realized she'd spent the last ten minutes staring at the bag Ana had given her rather than doing the adjustments.

With an annoyed sigh, she got up and pulled out the white candle and small amethyst. She wasn't sure she wanted to do this. After going her entire life never knowing anything about her parents, never seeing them, and never knowing why they didn't raise her, she didn't know if she wanted to find out now. If she did this, she would be connected to one of her parents, see them both, hear their voices, and learn why they gave her up. That was a lot to ask an orphan to take in.

Her phone buzzed again and she saw Gabe's name pop up. *I don't want to bother you. I just want to know you are okay.*

If she closed her eyes, she could just see the concern in his eyes, and it made her type out a response. *I'm okay. Something came up.* If that wasn't the understatement of the year, she didn't know what was. She would have to figure out what to tell him, but now was not the time for that. Right now she had to decide if she was ready to find out the truth about herself and her parents.

Erin chewed on the inside of her lip as she took the bag into her bedroom and pushed the dirty clothes off her comforter. She pulled her blackout curtains closed over the large window at the head of her bed to block out the waning sunlight. It took her a few minutes to clear off the storage chest she had in place of nightstands, and then a few more minutes to find a lighter.

Finally, Erin lit the candle and let the flame grow strong before she carefully placed the stone. She watched as the fire curled around the amethyst, then remembered to say her chant. Sleep didn't come right away, her body tense and wired from the events of the day. Trying to calm herself, Erin took deep breaths of the fragrant candle and looked at some of the framed photographs she hung on the wall closest to her. They were some of her favorites, one of a seagull at Bodega Bay, who had politely coughed up a clamshell at her feet, another looking up the trunk of a Redwood, one of the fog rolling in behind the Golden Gate Bridge, and the final one was from the roof of her building during the first storm after she moved in.

The walls were still white, because she'd never gotten around to painting, her floors a latte-colored wood, which she'd covered with a chevron rug she found at a thrift shop. She watched the smoke rise into the air from the candle, and then she slipped away.

When her eyes opened, Erin was staring at the most beautiful colors she had ever seen. She was in a lightly wooded area, but she knew there was no place like it in the world she knew. This had to be the fairy realm, Loinnir. The ground was covered in blue moss other than two deep grooves where she was standing. It looked like the grooves were meant to be some type of road because they twisted through the clearing, around the corner, and out of sight. The trees were old and spindly with deep purple blossoms hanging from them like ripe fruit. Light was everywhere, she could even feel it vibrate off her skin. The air was sweet with a faint taste of honeysuckle.

Abruptly, she wasn't looking at the new world around her. Instead, she saw a woman crouched under one of the trees further away. Her face held such sadness; even from this far away, Erin could see her pain. "Are you okay?" She called out, moving closer to the woman. When the stranger stood, Erin saw she was no ordinary woman. She was a fairy...no, that word was far too childish. Ana called them fae. *Erin thought Ana had been breathtaking, simply in the aura around her, but when the fae stood, and her wings unfolded behind her, Erin gasped and forgot to breathe out again.*

A creamy white dress hung from her shoulders, both clinging to her and flowing out around her. Her hair, a rich chestnut color, barely reached the nape of her neck in the back and and sloped down to her shoulders in the front. When Erin got a good look at her face she knew it had to be her mother. It was almost like looking in a mirror. A straight nose, soft cheekbones, oval face, but her mother had sharp gray eyes as opposed to Erin's ever-changing hazel. Her wings unfurled from behind her and spread past the length of her arms. Almost translucent, every color on the spectrum seemed to swirl and dance within the light as it passed through. They looked delicate, but as Erin got closer she felt the gush of wind that one small flap in her direction caused.

"Can...can you see me?" Her voice was quiet as she waited on bated breath for her mother to look at her. But there was no answer. Her mother seemed to gather herself, squaring her shoulders before she started to walk down the path. There was nothing for Erin to do but follow silently and see where it led. She used her time to take in everything she could about the woman that she was so connected to, but had not seen since she was born. The woods grew thicker, but her mother seemed unfazed as she moved silently over the ground. Slowly, Erin realized that low hanging branches moved out of her mother's way like a gentle breeze was blowing them out of her path. Finally they reached a clearing. Her mother stretched out her wings and raised her chin before moving from the cover of the trees. When they walked forward, Erin saw a collection of other fae gathered around a stream. The water was crystal clear, and firefly-like bugs hovered above it giving off a blue light. The blue moss was replaced with an array of wildflowers and large green ferns.

Two fae seemed to be waiting for her mother. One had wild orange hair that cascaded down to her knees. She did not have wings, but peeking through her curls were two fox ears. She wore a long burgundy dress that offset the color of her fur. Her lips were a light pink and her large eyes the deep red of leaves in the fall. Beside her was a blonde fae. Her hair draped down her back in gentle waves, and she wore a small crown atop her head. Her crown looked like leaves entwined together, and glittered with stones. Her dress was a long collection of delicate lace with an open back to make room for her wings, which glittered silver in the sun. She had strong cheekbones and eyes of deep purple.

"Odette, we have gathered due to a strong accusation against you," the blonde spoke, voice dripping with authority. All the fae fell silent, and their eyes turned to Erin's mother.

"I understand, Queen Gossamer." Odette's gaze flitted to the one with fox ears. The woman's eyes were filled with tears. She left the queen's side and took Odette's hands. "Thank you for being here Sinopa," Odette whispered.

"Of course Odette…" The one called Sinopa pulled her into a tight hug and placed a soft kiss on the top of her head. Erin searched the crowd for some sign of what was about to happen. Instead, she was met with solemn faces all around. Only the queen watched the friends with a cold stare.

"Fraternization with humans and leaving Loinnir is a very serious accusation." The queen's eyes found Odette's. "Will you deny it?"

Odette moved from Sinopa. Her hands became fists at her side; Erin could see she was trying to keep them from shaking.

"N-" her voice cracked but she stood taller and tried again, "no. It is true that I have visited Sula." Sinopa gave a small shake of her head in warning but Odette continued on. "I have fallen in love with a human."

Gasps erupted around the crowd. Erin's heart started pounding. She had to be talking about her father. Somehow they had found each other in the human world and fallen in love. But from the reaction of the crowd, it was not something that would be taken lightly. Her mother was going to suffer for that love, Erin just wasn't sure how yet.

"I have made you one of my closest friends. I have kept you by my side. You have done more than bring harm to your home, you have brought harm to your queen." The queen's eyes looked down on the accused fae with disappointment. "You know the punishment then?" The queen's voice was soft.

"Of course." Odette nodded. She turned and brushed Sinopa's cheek. Sinopa was crying openly now. "Thank you for your friendship. I'll be okay, and I know you will do wonderful things. You don't have to be here."

"I'm not leaving you."

Erin's mother gave a short nod before she turned her back to the queen. Her wings spread out in beautiful glory behind her. Queen Gossamer stepped toward her, and Erin wanted to rush between them, to try to protect her mother. She knew it would do no good, however; this was something that already happened, and she wasn't really there, only observing. The queen spread a hand on Odette's back. "From this day forth you will be banned from the realm of the fae."

Then the queen's hand turned red. She held the base of Odette's right wing. Odette's skin started to burn and the queen's eyes turned red. With a great cry, the queen ripped the wing from Odette's back. Erin's mother screamed in pain and the air crackled with the magical energy the queen used. Odette fell to the ground in pain and Sinopa fell to her knees before her. She held Odette's arms and let her lean into her.

"Stand up and accept your fate." The queen's voice was ice cold.

Sinopa looked like she was going to argue, but Odette nodded her head. Tears were streaming down her face and she looked like she was struggling to breathe. With Sinopa's help she rose to her feet again. Sinopa was supporting her full weight as the queen burned the skin at the base of her second wing. Again, she gathered magical energy and ripped the wing away. Sinopa fell to her knees as Odette sagged against her. Odette sobbed into the ground, and Erin could see the deep scars on her back where her wings used to be. When Erin covered her mouth to keep from screaming, she realized she too had tears running down her face.

The queen handed the wings to a male fae beside her. "Burn them." Beside Odette, Sinopa turned into a fox and crawled from the dress she had been wearing. She curled up next to Odette and whined a heartbreaking cry. "Take Odette to the circle. She can return to Sula and the human she loves so much." With that, Queen Gossamer turned her back on the crowd and sauntered off.

.℮ .℮ .℮

Ana glanced over to Melody and nodded silently. The two crept forward towards the alley, where their latest targets were tormenting unwitting witches. Even if they had not been able to scry the location of these erebi, the yelps and screams would have been more than enough help. The elf carefully drew her dagger, and snuck a glance around the wall. Three erebi surrounded two young women, who looked barely twenty and absolutely petrified.

Ana heard Melody take a deep breath beside her before yelling out, "Can we make this more of a fair fight?" The creatures, startled, backed away, giving the young witches time to scramble towards them. "You're safe. Either of you any good with a dagger?" Both shook their heads in response to Melody's question. "Wonderful. Get out of here, go back to your coven and work on some protection spells." She didn't bother to look back to see if they followed through. Instead, she drew her own blade and stepped up beside Ana.

"Ok fellas, now that it's a little more even, let's dance shall we?" With a quick side glance to Melody, Ana grinned wickedly. The first erebus hissed and lunged for the elf, but Ana dodged it gracefully. With a spin, she ducked under an arching claw and buried her knife in the beast's chest. Melody had to leap out of the reach of another erebus's attack, and found herself at Ana's back. The two circled in unison, keeping watch on the two remaining erebi as they hissed and snarled, looking for an opportunity.

Melody feigned a step, and smirked when one of them took the bait. She knocked its blackened arm away with one hand, and stabbed it with the other. Ana watched Melody out of the corner of her eye as she fought down the remaining foe. Melody had grown much stronger as a fighter in the last year, but she'd always been better using offensive and defensive magic during fights while Aria had been the one to stand at her side for hand-to-hand combat. It was odd to see her in Aria's position now, knowing that she would never see Aria fighting at her side again. With a howl the erebus fell, the dark energy seeping into the ground.

"Well that wasn't so bad," Melody commented smugly, coming to stand beside her. Ana turned to her with a solemn face, unable to feel as smug with Aria's blood on her hands. "Come on, Ana..." She felt Melody's eyes search her face and her voice lowered, "let's get home and get some coffee...figure out our next move." Ana didn't mean to bring her friend down, but she wasn't quite able to hide her own feelings from the young woman she spent so much time with. She linked arms with her and patted her hand. "Those were some great moves you had back there." And this time she didn't have to force a smile.

.℮ .℮ .℮

Erin's vision went black once more. She was still crying over the pain her mother suffered, when she suddenly found herself in San Francisco. She knew the building before her well. Quickly she wiped away her tears with the back of her hand, and desperately searched the street she grew up on. She saw her mother across the road, and ran over to her. She had a bundle of blankets in her arms and a man standing beside her. This time Odette was wearing human clothing, but there were tears in her eyes once more.

"Odette...it is the only way to keep her safe." The man's voice was deep, laced with pain and concern. He had jet black hair and a peppered goatee. He wore glasses, and Erin could make out the start of crow's feet around his hazel eyes, giving him the appearance of someone that smiled a lot.

"It's not! You could be with her! She needs her father!" Odette looked down at the bundle in her arms and Erin saw a baby's face peeking out from within. Erin stood entranced by the sight before her: her mother, father, and a baby that was loved desperately by her parents.

"She needs both her parents, De." He held Odette's face with gentle hands. His eyes reflected only tenderness as he looked at his wife. "I'll not let you fight this battle alone. We will keep each other safe, and then we will come back for her. Together."

"Derek, the erebi are spreading out through the realms," she pointed out sadly. "Sinopa would not have risked traveling here if we weren't all in danger. The queen has been called to help fight them in Eloas, but Sinopa thinks it won't be long before they start trying to infest everywhere. Right now Erin is safe. She is only half fae, so it could be years before her magic starts to show. The erebi will only sense her once she starts to use it. You two would be safe, and at least she would have one parent, Derek. To leave her here..." She kissed baby Erin's forehead before looking back up to her husband with tear-filled eyes. "It is breaking my heart to walk away from her as it is. But at least if you stayed with her, I would know she is happy and loved."

Derek took the baby from his wife's arms and kissed both her plump cheeks. "It is impossible not to love her, and I desperately want to stay with her. But I cannot let you go on your own. If you are determined to help in the fight against the erebi, I will not leave your side."

"You know I have to. And even if I didn't, I can't be around her. They can trace me..." she shook her head grievously, "I can't risk them finding her. At least if I help in the fight, maybe this can all be over sooner."

"Then it is decided." Derek kissed his daughter once more and held her tightly. Then he handed her back to Odette and draped an arm around her while she stared at their daughter's face.

"You are so loved my little one. All we want is a long and happy life for you. We will come back for you as soon as it's safe. I love you, my baby girl." Odette leaned down and smelled her daughter's hair. Then kissed her face oh so softly, forehead, cheeks, little nose. Erin's heart clenched as she watched.

"Don't do it!" She called out, even though her words fell on deaf ears. "Stop! Stay with me! Stay! You don't come back." Erin fell to her knees but felt nothing. She wished with all her heart that they could just hear her. Then they could have a life together. But her parents walked slowly to the children's group home and climbed the steps. They seemed unsteady for a moment. but then they took each other's hands and rang the doorbell. Erin watched as the door opened, and they were led inside to leave their daughter behind. Erin squeezed her eyes shut, and held the image of the three of them together inside her mind.

Doyle followed behind Lyra, holding his head high and trying to appear as though he belonged there. Even Malux, the queen's pet, was not brought into the inner sanctum during council meetings. Some of the oldest erebi would meet with the queen. He had no love for the ancient ones; they were the main reason erebi like himself could not live a normal life.

They entered the large opening to the main cavern. Magical fire gave an eerie glow over the stone walls, casting shadows along Queen Flereous's face where she stood, in all her dark glory, at the center of the room. The ancient ones took different forms; some held such dark energy they simply became a wisp of darkness. Others were large beasts; some as much as twenty times his own size. The whole room was filled with their energy, and he wondered how many other beings gave up part of their magical energy in order to provide sustenance for the brutes around him to survive.

"Ah, dear sister. How grateful I am that you have deemed us worthy enough for you to join the council today." Eyes of every color swiveled in Lyra's direction as she sauntered into the throne room. They at least seemed to ignore him, a small mercy for which Doyle was grateful.

"Well, Flereous, apparently I have been missed amongst your halls. You've been working with Kali? I mean that is the only reason I can fathom for attacking Loinnir." Lyra circled the room, the fire flickering oddly against her yellow-tinged skin. Doyle noticed her fingers twitch toward her thigh, where he knew she kept one of her twin blades strapped between the layers of leather. There was no immediate sign of a threat, and yet her back was stiff and her fingers lingered close to the hilt of her dagger.

"Yes, Lyra, we have decided to help Kali in her new venture-"

"She and her brother have been trying to take hold of Eloas for *years* now, and they haven't managed!" Lyra snapped. "Now she wants to spread forces even thinner?" Doyle watched as a few erebi stood or stiffened at Lyra's tone. His own muscles began to prepare for a fight, even though he knew it would be pointless. If they decided to make a move against him and Lyra, they would both be dead in a matter of moments.

"The elves are much better fighters and strategists. You know they keep gathering forces from other elven kingdoms and pushing back." Flereous continued as though she were bored of the whole transaction happening before her. "Her brother will continue to hold there while we help her deal with the fae. They are weak, and not made to fight. They are *nature lovers* and have already rolled over into her hands. Then, she can use them and their resources to finish off the elves."

"Yes, then Kali and her brother Zepar hold all this power. Who do you think they will turn against then? Don't you think it might be their desire to hold *all* the realms, ours included?"

"They could try, and they would be quickly crushed." Flereous tilted her head, a clear sign of annoyance. Her veins began turning black as power coursed through her, contrasting against her pale skin. Her eyes seemed to reflect the fire around them, and they stared straight at Lyra.

"No need to show off, sister. I'm well aware of your power, but when they have two realms under their belt-" Lyra's words cut off as Flereous' secret weapons started down the cavern. The other erebi in the room instantly stilled, and Doyle watched as giants made of rock and molten flame joined their group.

Even compared to the ancient erebi, the rock twins were *huge*. Their heads brushed the top of the cavern as they entered, and the molten fire that held them together completely illuminated the room. "And you wonder why I don't come to your meetings more often," Lyra muttered, raising one thin brow before turning away. "It's your own grave you dig. The first thing they do is take out the royals." Lyra met Doyle's eyes, and he turned to follow.

Together they escaped the large room and started down a winding staircase. Their job there was done; she simply wanted to be seen, in the event the queen later noticed something missing. They would look to those that had *not* been in attendance before considering anyone present.

There was a small crawl space which would lead to a passage to the queen's room. As half sisters, Flereous and Lyra spent centuries at each other's throats. Flereous' mother was an old erebus with strong powers over flame; Lyra's own mother was a *common* erebus, and instead of special powers, Lyra was born with more intelligence, and a lithe body that was born to fight and move with ease.

Lyra had long-since ordered him to watch Queen Flereous and Malux in order to collect whatever information and weaknesses that he could. When he heard of the erebi being sent to Loinnir, Doyle was sent in order to capture an observer fae so Lyra could use her to help win against her sister. Over the years he had learned more than a few secrets of the queen, including many of her secret passages.

"Malux-" Lyra came out of the crawl space to come face to face with the queen's puppy. His face was drawn and pale, pinched in pain. Well, at least the half of his face that still looked human. Exposed to dragon blood, his human form had been tainted with that of a dragon; not only was he cursed with scaled skin, one shining draconic eye, and constant pain as his two forms fought with one another, but he also caught the eye of the queen and paid dearly for his rarity.

"Lyra," he drawled as his mismatched eyes swept over her in boredom. When they shifted past her and fell on Doyle, the erebus almost cringed away from the gaze. Quite a few of the queen's secrets had to do with the half-dragon. He'd spied on more than a few torture sessions, but always had to turn away and leave her to her fun.

"Did my sister grow tired of you? Or did she just choose a different play thing for the day?" Lyra crooned.

"Did you get yourself kicked out of the council meeting already?" Malux returned in a dry tone, his eyes finally leaving Doyle and turning back to the she-erebus.

"Yes, she called in the goons. Well, this chat has been nice, but I have more important people to talk to. I've wasted far too much time already with my sister's *pet*." Lyra and Doyle both moved past him in the narrow corridor. Doyle tensed, waiting for Malux to make a move to stop them, or question them on how they knew of the passage. He simply slipped through the door and left them.

Lyra moved into the passage that would lead to Flereous' bedroom and looked around. The king-sized bed took up much of the room, its high posters draped with red lace, contrasting the dark wood of the frame. Red satin dressed the bed, beckoning company. Lyra snorted. "Typical," she whispered as she started to move through.

"There," Doyle pointed to the painting inspired by Dante's Inferno. Lyra pressed on the wood grain that sprang open the hidden door.

Flereous was a collector of all things rare, and her most prized possessions she kept close. Choices were laid out before them, but the observer fae had said something *personal*. Lyra silently searched through while he watched the passage, straining to hear if anyone was approaching.

"This is it!" Lyra pulled back holding a gaudy gold ring with a heavy red stone. "It was from her mother. It's only an heirloom, no magic to it, so she shouldn't miss it anytime soon." Doyle closed the hidden latch as Lyra slipped the ring into a pocket on the inside of her top. She flashed a wink as she caught him watching her. He only rolled his eyes, and started to lead the way back through the passage before the council meeting ended.

Chapter Eight

When Erin opened her eyes, she'd been transported once again. It was daytime, she could feel the sun's energy, but the sky was dark. Thick gray clouds filled the sky, and the air smelled like rain and electricity. There seemed to be shadows all around, but then Erin got a closer look at them, and her blood ran cold. Thin humanoid figures, with branches jutting out of their bodies, filled the field. They were the color of thick smoke, and Erin realized the branch-like extensions were wisps of dark energy that seemed to constantly change. They had long fingers that curled, and what looked like two giant horns growing from their heads. Suddenly a fox streaked by, biting at the legs of the erebi.

"De!" Erin recognized her father's voice, and turned quickly. He was holding a long dagger in his hand, and Erin saw the blade was black from erebi blood. He was running, his eyes panicked. The fox ran before him, biting away any erebi that got too close. Erin followed after him and saw her mother on the ground.

Her pale skin was covered in black streaks; it took Erin a moment to realize her veins were black.

"Heal yourself!" Derek's voice was ragged as he looked her over. Odette's fingers started to turn completely black.

"I tried...it's not working. I'm infected...get out of here, Derek! Go and get our daughter!"

She started to cry, and Erin saw she had been stabbed on her side. Blood was spilling from her at an alarming rate.

"Mom..." Erin whispered. Why had Ana told her to do this? It was bad enough never knowing about her parents, but now she had to stand here, helpless and unseen, and watch her mother die.

Suddenly, the fox turned into a naked Sinopa. "Go, Derek, before we get completely overrun. There is nothing we can do. Go to your daughter. I'll make sure she's not alone."

"Odette, I love you so much." He kissed her hard and brushed back her hair. "We didn't have enough time."

"I know...I love you too. Please, go to Erin."

"I will...I will tell her all about you." Derek's voice broke, his whole body was shaking. He was trying to hold it together long enough to tell his wife goodbye, but he was starting to fail. Now Odette's arms were completely black.

"Take my ring, give it to her for me." She tried to hold out her arm, but couldn't. Derek picked it up and tried to pull away the ring. He was openly crying now, and it seemed the ring was stuck. Then Sinopa jumped to her feet as an erebus

started their way. She grabbed Derek's dagger and ran forward, sending the weapon
straight into the erebus' gut. She turned back around and screamed.

Erin and Derek had both been focused on Odette, and didn't notice when an
erebus came from behind. Now it hovered at Derek's back. Odette yelled out his
name, but he was weaponless and reacted too late. The erebus plunged its long
dagger-like fingers into Derek's chest.

"No!" Both Erin and her mother screamed as Derek's face registered shock.
When the erebus pulled free, he fell to the ground beside Odette, and didn't move.

"Derek!" Her mother sobbed and tried to turn on her side so she could look
at him. Erin was on her knees beside him, trying to see if he was still alive, but
already knew the answer. Then the world twisted around her, and she was falling.

Erin woke from her deep sleep with a jerk. She sat up in her bed and screamed until her voice was gone. "No!" Her heart shattered as everything she saw came crashing down on her in reality. In the dream, her feelings had been muted and her mind in a fog. Now, however, everything was hitting her with a weight she could not handle.

She wasn't sure how long she lay curled in her bed, but her body was out of tears and her voice was gone before she finally moved. She'd gone her whole life not knowing if she was wanted; feeling different, and being passed from one family to another as if something were wrong with her. Now, she finally knew the truth. She knew she had been loved and protected. She *was* different, but she had something wonderful in her that her mother passed down to her. Now that she knew she was part fae, she would do everything she could to embrace and grow that part of her.

The ringing doorbell drew Erin from her thoughts. and she looked around. She was still in the clothes from her weekend away. Looking at her phone, she saw she missed six calls from work, and two from Gabe. When she noticed the date, she cursed and realized she missed two full days of work with no notice…*and* she missed her own birthday. The candle had burned down to the wick and wax was melted all over her chest and onto her rug.

Ana hadn't warned her she could sleep for days. It felt like that should be a disclaimer printed on the back of the candle or something. Her doorbell rang again and Erin rushed to answer it, wondering what else she might have missed out on. Then she saw Gabe, his brow creased with worry, his hand already reaching out to ring the doorbell again.

"Gabe!" His eyes raked over her, lingering on her face and her clothes, and she shifted. Judging by the scrutiny in his stare, he knew she'd been crying, and recognized that she was in a very creased version of what he last saw her in.

"What happened to you?" His words came out gravelly as his gaze darted behind her.

Erin stepped away from the door so he could come in, eyes self-consciously fixed on the ground. "How did you know where I lived?"

She asked for curiosity's sake, but also to give herself the chance to come up with a story.

"I'm sorry...I tried calling you for your birthday, and I never heard back. So then I went to the bar, hoping you might be working. I just wanted to give you something I found for you, and maybe take you out for dessert. But then your boss," Gabe waved a hand as he tried to place the name, "Greg, said you hadn't shown up for your shifts. He'd been trying to call you but you never answered. Then I got worried. After you left the way you did on Sunday...and then just fell off the face of the earth..." He ran his hands through his hair as though he were trying to erase all of the stress she had caused. "He wouldn't tell me anything yesterday, but I went back today and he said he tried calling again but you still hadn't answered. I told him I wasn't going to leave until he told me where you lived so I could check on you. Finally he gave me your address, and I came right over. You should probably call him now too, let him know you're alive and that I didn't show up and kill you or something."

Guilt over the worry she caused nagged at her, and she sighed. "I'm...I'm sorry. It's hard to explain."

"I'm serious, you should call him before he calls the police on me. I may have been a little tough on him." Gabe's voice was laced with irritation, which — oddly — made her heart warm. "What are you smiling about?" he demanded, even though the corner of his mouth softened in fondness.

"Nothing...sorry..." She couldn't stop herself from grinning at him one more time, only because she could almost see him fighting against steam coming out of his ears, or joining her in grinning too. "I'll be right back. My phone is in my room. Make yourself at home."

Erin took a shaky breath when she got off the phone with Greg. She'd worked as both a waitress and bartender at his pub for the last three years. It was her main source of income, it was within walking distance of her apartment, and it was a job she no longer had. Not that Erin could blame him, he'd sounded really sorry to let her go, but she'd disappeared, missing shifts that he'd covered himself. She could hear Gabe moving around the apartment, but had to give herself a few minutes to pull all of her broken pieces back together.

She was part fae. Her parents loved her, but died fighting to protect the world. She was going to have to pay rent while down two jobs, *and* the man in the other room was someone she'd cared for all her life, and she couldn't tell him anything that she'd learned.

When Erin finally emerged, she found Gabe standing in front of her sofa looking up at her small collection of classic cameras. His gaze was locked in wonder on the very same one he'd given her. Something warm swelled in her chest at the memory. He'd been working odd jobs all summer because he was desperate for a bike. She had no idea how he planned on keeping said bike while in the group home, but he was determined. She'd met him when he got done being a stock boy at a local grocery store and they wandered around a thrift shop to pass the time. That was the day she'd fallen in love. She'd seen that vintage 1940's Kodak Retina II with the folding rangefinder, tucked into a worn leather case, and something in her blossomed to life. Gabe had laughed and grinned playfully when she'd held it in reverent hands and pretended to take his picture.

That week she spent hours pouring over a library book she picked up about cameras. She spewed random facts at anyone that looked at her too long. Then, Gabe snuck up to her room in one of the rare moments she had it to herself, and handed over a small bundle wrapped in newspaper. He'd used his hard-earned cash to get her that camera and a pocketful of film.

"It's still the best gift I've ever been given." His green eyes flashed to her, and there was something in that gaze that made her cheeks warm. She moved to stand beside him and stared up at the small display she'd spent a productive afternoon on.

"It looks like you have a decent collection going now." She had nine colorful frames hanging on the wall in straight lines of three. The top and bottom frames had small shelves in them where she had a camera displayed. The middle had favorite pictures of hers on either side, but right in the center was the camera Gabe had given her.

"It's still my favorite though." She whispered more to herself before looking back at him. She wished she could have pulled off taking a shower before coming back out, but she didn't want to leave him sitting in her living room waiting for her. Actually, after a quick glance around, she realized she probably left him out here too long as it was. She had piles of stuff scattered around her apartment as usual. Travel books and her "idea notebook" for shoots was taking up half of her breakfast bar, a basket of laundry sat on her table, shoes were kicked off by the door—

"I feel like I spent an entire summer looking at that camera instead of your face. Once you got your hands on that thing, there was no stopping you." His voice was warm, and she could feel his smile down to her toes. Then he seemed to take her in again and worry etched itself on his features. "What did Greg say?"

"Oh." All the work she'd done to build herself up before coming out of her room came crashing back down. She dropped onto the sofa with a deep sigh. "Well, he's glad that I'm okay, and that you didn't murder me, but I'm also fired."

"I'm sorry." Gabe sat down beside her, leaving the middle cushion as a buffer between them. He didn't sound surprised, but it *did* seem like he was truly sorry about it. "Are you going to tell me what happened?" he finally pressed.

Erin chewed her lip for a moment, trying her best to work out what to say. The last thing she should do was lie to him, but she couldn't exactly tell him the truth, either. Instead, she just shook her head. "I love seeing you again. I love being around you. It feels...like coming home after all these years."

"But?" he asked cautiously when she didn't continue.

"*But*, some things have come up the last few days. Some information came to light, and I'm not quite sure how to deal with it all just yet." Erin let out a deep sigh. "I have a lot going on all of a sudden, and I can't really share it with you, even though I'd like to."

"Listen, I didn't mean to be *that* guy, that kisses a girl, and goes all stalker on her. I just thought we could spend your birthday together if you didn't have plans, that's all. I got worried, though, when it seemed like you just disappeared. If you need space, I can give you space." Gabe took her hand and held it between his, his gaze forcing her to look up at him.

"I want you here, I want you with me." Erin finally looked up and met his gaze once more. "If you want that too, I just need you to be aware there will be some things I can't talk about, okay?"

Erin waited for him to pull away and turn down her offer. It was a terrible way to start off their relationship. It didn't exactly inspire trust to tell someone you have important stuff going on, but you can't tell them about it.

He stared at her for a while, and she could tell he was really thinking it all over. He wasn't stepping into this lightly, but he was also still holding her hand. After a lifetime, he gave a quick nod. "I accept that. Is there *anything* you can tell me though?" Erin's stomach grumbled loudly as interruption and Gabe chuckled. "Would you like to go and get some food first? I feel like I'm always trying to feed you."

"I really need to work on the pictures from the weekend. I can't afford to lose *that* job too."

"If the TV won't bother you, I can run for some take-out and come back? Keep you company while you work?"

She grinned widely. "I love that idea." It would also give her time to take a quick shower and figure out if there was anything from this story she *could* actually tell him.

℘ ℘ ℘

Doyle stood at the door and watched the two fae sisters interact. He didn't want to feel anything for them, especially not guilt over their situation, but he couldn't deny there was something there. It was his fault, after all, that the two found themselves here. It had been a few days since he last saw them and with just a glance, it was clear the younger fae was not doing well in his realm. She'd grown frail, and they hadn't been held captive for more than a month. From what he could tell, she hadn't been able to hold down any of her food in nearly a week. From the look of her glazed eyes, and the thin sheen of sweat across her brow, he suspected she now had a fever.

Briar looked up and he saw the worry in her gaze. Her slender fingers rested on Fern's forehead, stopping their gentle movements through her hair. "I need to see Lyra. If she expects me to spend any time forcing my mind to see the future for her, I need to know that my sister is going to be okay. She promised she would think about it. I need to know her answer." The fae held her chin up, her eyes blazing with determination. He wouldn't lie, he liked her energy, but he worried it was going to get her killed. "Doyle, *please*. I'm willing to help, I just don't want my sister to die. I'll do whatever I have to do, just take Fern home."

"I'm sorry she's not doing well. Is there something I can get to help?" He took a step closer so he could see Fern better, but Briar's wings shot out and wrapped around her protectively. He froze in place, and actually had to remind himself to breathe at the sight of what was supposed to be a harmless fae, looking more like an avenging angel.

"Yeah, a ride back through the portal!" she snapped. "Her energy comes from the magic in our realm. The longer she is away, the weaker she gets!" She released her sister and stormed over, stopping just short of running full into him. He had about a foot on her in height, but she didn't seem to realize it. She met his gaze and didn't flinch away, even as he saw his own red eyes reflected in her deep purple. "The only reason she was taken too was because I was trying to get her to safety through the portal. I just want to let her go home to her family. I was supposed to keep her safe."

Her eyes started to shine as they filled with tears, and Doyle stiffened at the sight. He brought his hands behind his back before they betrayed him and reached out to comfort her. She was their prisoner, and she was the answer to bringing down the queen. He'd do well to remember that. "I'll see what I can do." He glanced behind her to Fern, lying on the ground. Their kind, along with the humans and elves, killed and pushed away his kind since the beginning of time, and now a fae was asking him for help. The sad thing was, he actually *wanted* to give them his help. From what he could tell, Briar and Fern were good people. Stubborn and a little strong-willed for being captives, perhaps, but he couldn't see either of them killing simply because someone was an erebus.

"Lyra has something that belongs to the queen. She was requesting I bring you to her so she could pass it along. I'll take you, and do my best to back your request. My suggestion is you try very hard to make those powers of yours see something to give her in return."

She froze at that, and seemed to deflate. "Briar?" Fern called her sister back to her side as she doubled over. He watched in silence as Briar brushed back limp hair and wiped away drops of sweat.

"I just need a little longer, Fern, and I'll get you home." She rolled up their blanket, and made Fern lie down on it before kissing her temple and coming back to him. He wished they had just left the younger fae behind. Even with Kali's army roaming around her realm, she would have been safer there.

Briar would be safer, too. It wasn't exactly in her best interest to go around trying to negotiate. "Do you have a family?" Briar's voice was quiet as they started down the passage. Her wings were once again pulled tight against her body like a shield.

"Don't we all have families? We have to come from somewhere. Despite popular belief, erebi don't just spring up out of the ground with the sole purpose-"

"I didn't mean it that way!" Briar stopped and let out an exasperated sigh. It almost made him smile to hear it, and see the irritation on her face. "I mean do you have people that are invested in this fight? Whose lives depend on you? I've never had this weight before." Her shoulders seemed to sag under an invisible pressure. "My mother and I were extremely close because of our shared ability. Observers are very rare, and when one exists, everyone wants to use us for their own gain." She motioned absently toward him. "We are pressured to mate with another Observer, or to mate with as many different fae as we can to try and find the right combination to create another one. That's what they did to my mother. She and my father were never in love, but she was paired with him as no other male Observers were around. And when my abilities began to show, she was pressured to mate with him again...but they had both already moved on and refused, which really pissed off the queen."

Doyle wanted to keep moving and get the conversation with Lyra over with, but Briar leaned against the stone as though she were planning on a long story. *Great.* "We were bonded by that. She knew the pain of the gift and how hard it is to control. The toll it takes...but none of that compares to knowing Fern is locked in that room because of me. That just being in this realm is slowly killing her, and there is nothing I can do about it other than beg for help. If she dies, it's my fault, but I promise you, I'll drag all of you down with me." Her eyes met his in the darkened passage. Her mouth was pressed in a grim line, and he saw that strength in her he'd recognized before.

"I'm asking if you have someone because I want to know if you understand. If she dies, you need to know that it doesn't matter what you and Lyra do to me, I won't give you an inch of help. So you should really back me up in there and get her to help me, or find a way to sneak Fern out of here."

"Well, if you are trying to practice your argument for Lyra, I wouldn't suggest leading with that. She doesn't take kindly to threats."

"I couldn't care less what she does and doesn't like. I want to bring down the queen too, if only because she killed the only person who understands me and what my life is. So do you? Have someone?" she repeated, her persistence starting to grate his nerves.

"Your kind has already taken away anyone I had, so believe me..." He moved quickly in the darkness and pinned her to the wall. He wanted her to feel the strength of his anger, of his pain. Everything she spoke of he understood, because he had already gone through all the loss she was worried about dealing with. "You come from a pretty world, *Fae*. You see the sun and the moon. Your biggest worry is producing more powerful babies." He leaned closer until he could feel the warmth of her breath across his mouth. He saw the specks of purples and blues in her eyes.

"I live in darkness. Everything I had to love was ripped from me simply because of what we were. Never hurt a hair on anyone's head, but as erebus we must be evil, right? We must *deserve* to die." He scoffed bitterly. "Don't come to me like you understand *pain* and *vengeance* because your mother's dead and your sister's sick. If you want to come close to understanding my loss, we'll go right back in that room and I'll tear Fern to pieces right before your eyes." Her pupils dilated in fear, and he was close enough to her he could feel her heart pounding in her chest. He stepped back, pulling himself together before he did or said more he would regret. "You are afraid, I get it. I already said I would do what I could to help your sister. I don't want either of you hurt, I just want to see the queen fall so this madness of conquering other realms can finally be put aside. All I want is a chance at a life where I could be treated with the same respect as someone of your kind. Do you think you can try to help me do that?"

She was still standing against the wall, her eyes wide and watching him. Finally, she nodded. When he turned and started walking toward Lyra, he heard her follow. At least he could have a bit of silence before she brought on whatever chaos she was about to leach from Lyra.

.℮ .℮ .℮

Erin sent in her final photographs to the vineyard manager for approval. Then she readied herself to go and meet with Ana. There was so much she needed to talk about, needed to find out, that she wasn't sure where she would start. During the drive over, she thought about her night with Gabe. It was so easy being around him, even when her mind was trying to deal with finding out she is only half human. They'd settled side-by-side on the sofa and ate Chinese while he searched for something on TV. He also gave her a small birthday gift: a mug with a picture of an old camera and writing that said "I shoot people". It made her laugh, and she had to wash it right away so she could use it for some tea after dinner.

After her stomach stopped grumbling, she revealed that she'd found out information about her parents. That got his full attention, but she skirted around the details. She told him their names and that they had been killed, but she wasn't sure what else she could say without having a lot of explaining to do. Her relief was immense when he didn't push.

Then she worked on the pictures, and he simply kept her company and helped her stay awake to get her work done. After sleeping for two days, she had no idea how she could be tired again, but the drowsiness hit her hard nonetheless. Once she finished, he reviewed the pictures with her to make sure she wasn't missing something drastic in her sleepiness. Other than demanding she delete the ones of him, he told her everything was amazing, and then he kissed her. Slow and tender, his hands holding her face. His thumbs made small circles on her cheeks as he claimed her lips as his.

Erin parked in front of *Mystifying* and laid a hand on her lips at the memory. Just thinking about it had her heart racing. So much was changing in her life, now she just needed to start to take control.

Chapter Nine

Ana came down the stairs from her apartment to find Melody hunched over one of her school books. "I found another one last night." She wasn't sure how the young witch managed it; being a freshman in college was hard enough, only to add in all of Melody's...extracurricular activities.

"Oh Ana, I'm so sorry I wasn't here." Melody spent the night with a friend so they could study and work on a project together. "Are you okay?" Ana felt the witch search her for injury. The elf waved her off.

"I'm fine, but something needs to be done. If Kali is sending erebi through portals here, they are likely getting through all the seams. We may have a war on our hands." Ana went to make herself some tea before getting started on her work for the day. After fighting off the erebus the night before, she'd been too wired to get much sleep; it didn't help that she also kept worrying Melody would come home, and another enemy would get through.

"I don't understand, shouldn't the queen of Skia be controlling this? I mean, I understand the erebi are pretty much left to their own devices, but wouldn't the queen want to stop an all-out war?"

Ana shrugged. "Honestly, I doubt she cares. The way I see it, if Kali is successful in drawing the realms into war, the queen is only going to gain more power. *And* Kali's mother is an ancient erebus; she's very strong and powerful. The queen can't really control the ancient ones, only try to hold them back from full destruction."

"We need more hands if we are going to start hunting them down," Melody said softly. Ana became keenly aware that Melody was doing her best to avoid speaking of Aria. She felt the loss keenly, but could see the pain etched on Melody's young face. Her eyes were red, her normally rich skin had lost its luster, giving her a pale, withdrawn look. It worried Ana to see her so, especially when there was little she could do to help her. The door chimed before Ana could respond. She turned and found Erin standing at the doorway, almost as though Melody had summoned her with her words.

"So, next time you want to give me some hokey magic spell, you might want to warn me when it is going to put me to sleep for two days."

Ana's brow rose elegantly at her entrance, but Melody responded first. "You must have had a strong connection to your parents to relive so much. That spell usually only gives small snippets, and people are only out for an hour or so, right Ana?"

"Yes...it was your mother you connected to?" Ana responded thoughtfully.

"Yes," Erin replied, her initial flash of anger fading into confusion.

"Ah, fae mothers pass on some of their magic in the womb. The sharing of magical energy only increases the bond between a mother and her child. If you were asleep for so long...she must have loved you very much."

Erin didn't speak for a moment, and it looked like she was dealing with churning emotions. Her next words dripped with sarcasm, however: "Well it certainly helped me lose two jobs at once. Bosses tend not to appreciate you missing work with no call for two days."

"So, you made a connection with your mother. You were able to see and understand your predicament better?" Ana watched Erin nod, and shared a look with Melody. She didn't want to push, but they were going to need Erin if they had a chance of fighting off the upcoming storm. "And have you made a decision about what you want to do next?"

"You said you could help me hone my powers. I want-" she shook her head, "I *need* to embrace that part of me."

"Okay, why don't you sit down and you can tell us what you saw? At least what you want to share," Ana added when she saw the dance of emotion cross Erin's face. Erin sat next to Melody and recounted everything. The elf refrained from asking questions, and stayed quiet when Erin seemed to struggle. It was hard enough to listen to it when she had no real connection to anyone; she could only imagine how hard it had been for the halfling to watch it first hand. When Erin finished, she sipped the tea Ana sat in front of her.

"So what's next? What powers do I have? How do I learn to control this?"

"Slow down," Melody answered. "There isn't some magic button you can push to switch over, it's going to take some time."

"You may want to rephrase that." Erin spoke under raised eyebrows, though a smile played at her lips. "I'm sorry...I just..." she sighed. "A lot has happened and changed, and I just need to get this under control."

"I understand," Ana cut in. "Unfortunately, fae powers are not the same from one being to the next. Your mother's friend had a connection to animals and could change, some can heal, some can read minds or see into the future or past, others have a deep connection to nature and can make things grow at will. From what you have shown so far, I believe you have that connection to nature, but we will have to see what other abilities you show, if any. Now, I believe you mentioned you were fired?"

"Yeah...I missed a few phone calls while I was *napping*."

"Well, we recently..." Ana and Melody made eye contact again. Without speaking, they decided against telling Erin about Aria for the time being. "We recently had an opening come up. If you would like, you could start to work here. Then we can work on training you too, during down times. It would give Melody more time to focus on school; I'm afraid I've been running her a bit ragged the last few days."

"Are you sure?" Erin looked astonished at the offer, giving her the impression that the halfling wasn't used to having good things handed to her.

"I can show her the ropes," Melody volunteered.

"You will do no such thing," Ana replied primly. "You are going to go to a park or library to focus on your work. I can show Erin around just fine."

Melody seemed ready to argue further, but it wasn't often Ana pulled out the mothering tone, and she seemed to realize there was no use in drawing out the inevitable. She grabbed a bag from under the counter and gave Ana a hug before saying goodbye, and heading out the door.

"So, if you are free for the day, I can go ahead and show you around the store and get some paperwork done? Then we can start training tomorrow?" When Ana turned her attention back to Erin, she saw the halfling had watched the interaction and was giving her an odd look. Belatedly, she realized her relationship with Melody must look strange to an outsider; she only looked a few years older than the witch, and with their past, they could go from acting like best friends one moment to acting like mother and daughter in the next.

"That sounds great actually. Thank you...really, Ana...it was hard seeing those memories, but now I have a piece of my parents, and know that I carry a part of my mother. That wouldn't have happened if I hadn't met you."

Ana gave a sad smile. "I'm truly sorry for your losses. I lost both of my parents and my only brother, but I had time with them. I'm sorry you had to miss out on that." She rubbed Erin's shoulder, but could tell the other woman was uncomfortable with the affection, so she quickly withdrew her hand. "Okay, let me give you a tour."

.ℓ .ℓ .ℓ

It was clear Fern knew something was up. When Briar returned from her meeting with Lyra, she knew one way or another she'd just sealed their fate, and she couldn't bring herself to talk about it yet. Fern lay curled up in a tight ball, but she was watching her silently. Her eyes were glassy, and when Briar played with her hair, she pulled away chunks that were starting to fall out. Lyra might not have liked that she walked into that room with demands, but if Fern wasn't sent home she was going to die.

The erebus had gotten something of her sister's, but Briar refused to take it until Fern was sent away. Lyra didn't even raise a hand against her, just stared at her in surprised silence. Doyle bruised her arm squeezing her to his side as hard as he was. She wasn't sure if some part of him was trying to keep her from harm, or if he was too surprised to realize he was holding her so tightly.

"Are you ever going to tell me what happened?" Fern finally spoke. Her voice was weak, and it broke Briar's heart to hear her once ray-of-sunshine sister sounding so hollow.

"I'm not sure yet." For all she knew, Lyra would leave them locked up in this room until Fern died, and then make her demands. She had hoped Doyle would stand with her, help her with her argument to take Fern home, but all he did was stand as a mute, bruising her arm as they waited for Lyra to respond. It would have been nice to have someone on her side.

Suddenly the door swung open with a loud creak that sent chills down her back. Her wings jerked tight against her back in response, and the sudden contraction hurt. What she would give to be back in her realm where she could stretch them out to their full capacity and take flight once more. But the second she saw Doyle's expression, she knew that would not be her fate. No matter what she did to help now, she would never see home again. But hopefully Fern would. She stood just as Lyra, and two other erebi she didn't recognize, filled the small room she had been locked away in. Fern started to struggle to sit up too. Briar shot out a hand to still her sister, and kept her post standing protectively over her.

"You know, despite what you might think, I like you, Observer." Lyra smiled and looked her over. "You have guts. You're not quite like the other fae I've come across. A bunch of weak nature-lovers, but you have a spine. I mean," a hand flicked up in the air as if she were trying to pull an answer out of thin air, "how else could you explain a fae walking into a room of erebi and refusing to do what is asked of her? All for a little half sister. Maybe it's just because I want to kill *my* half sister, but I just don't get it."

Fern whimpered when Lyra's cat-like eyes darted to her. It took everything in her not to shove the erebus away when she leaned closer to inspect the younger fae. Her heart pounded in her chest but Lyra pulled back with a sigh. "She certainly doesn't look well, now does she? So I'm willing to help you, Observer. But you've put me in an awful fix. You stood in defiance when I had a room full of people. I can't let them think I'm playing under the thumb of some fae, especially not when I wish to bring down their queen."

"Of course I'll help you bring down your sister. I want the army out of my realm more than you do, and your sister's orders got my mother killed."

"Yes, well now I'm going to want more from you than that. I mean, the whole reason you are here is to help me. So for me to send one of my men back to your realm and ensure your sister gets home safely? I'm going to need some kind of payment to show me you are truly loyal to me and my quest."

Her eyes flicked to Doyle. Whatever Lyra was about to ask for, that had to be the reason he entered the room looking like her world was about to end. He met her gaze, and the vision washed over her. Before she could stop herself from reacting, she doubled over on the floor. Her head exploded with the pain of the vision while her body screamed in a mirror of the torture to come.

"Ah, so she *is* able to see the future after all. Well, what will it be?"

"Briar," Fern's small hand rested on her back, brushing over her folded wings. "Briar, what is it?"

"When?" Was all she could manage. She couldn't answer her sister yet. She couldn't bring voice to what they had planned for her.

"My two friends here can take Fern home right now. They will take her right up to her doorstep and hand her over to her parents, safe and sound." Which meant this could very well be her last moment as a whole fae.

"Doyle."

"Excuse me?"

"She knows Doyle, can he take her home?" She looked into his scarred face and found all the color had drained away. In the few talks they shared, she at least knew he did not mean Fern harm, and he would do his best to protect her. He was the only one she could pretend to trust when her sister's life hung in the balance.

"Fine." With a quick swipe of her fingers the two erebi came forward and grabbed her. Doyle stood frozen for another moment before he scooped Fern into his arms. She looked so small and fragile but when she started to scream her voice was suddenly stronger than Briar had ever heard.

"No! What's happening? Briar, what are they going to do to you? Don't hurt my sister!"

"Hush, Fern." Tears were threatening to choke her but she had to put on a brave face. "Doyle is going to take you home. Nothing is going to happen to me, my little flower. I'm just going to help them as I said I would. Go home and get well again. Everything will be fine."

"Briar!" She tried to kick out, but Doyle held her tight against him, trapping her arms and legs. Tears were streaming down her dirty little face and Briar drank in the vision. She was saving her life. That was all that mattered.

"Fern, I love you." And then she lied: "I'll see you soon." Doyle walked past Lyra and out of the room even as Fern continued to struggle against him. She would calm, and as soon as she stepped foot back in their realm, she would start to gain her strength back. Her sister would be okay. Now she needed to worry about herself. Wing removal was more than excruciating, it was known to make fae lose their minds, and even their abilities. She would have to be strong, or she would lose more than her wings tonight.

"Well, let's get it over with then."

Lyra gave her a sad smile before turning back to the doorway and ushering in a brute of an erebus that nearly filled the room with his own bulk. Lyra stepped forward and brushed back a strand of her hair as the two other erebi held her arms back. The second the copper skin touched her she felt a vision of those same hands holding her wings and giving them as an offering. Another woman stood before her with long curly black hair.

Briar's head shot up to look at Lyra, "keep the wings, you are going to need them to gain your sister's favor. We are going to need something from her before this is over." Lyra looked taken-back for a moment, but then she nodded and withdrew, leaving her to the room of erebus planning to rip her apart.

.℘ .℘ .℘

By the time Erin left for the evening, all necessary paperwork for her new employment had been finished, and she was set to begin her training the next day. Ana was relieved that the woman had come to some sense of peace about her parents, and that she'd opened herself up to the reality of magic.

Even so, the elf knew that they had a long road ahead in training her. As she moved through the routine of shutting down the shop and making her way up to the apartment, Ana took a mental inventory of everything that she knew about fae magic; even as a protector...even as a former elven princess...woefully little of her knowledge would help Erin.

Not even bothering to kick off her shoes as she would've any other night, Ana sagged onto the edge of her mattress, the weight of this oncoming tempest suddenly feeling like more than she could bear. *'Aria would have been able to do so much more for Erin,'* she lamented to herself. Picturing the two fae interacting left a crack in the elf's carefully-crafted wall against her grief. Before she could bolster her defenses, it came crashing down around her. Waves of pain, until then so carefully held at bay, left her breathless.

Elves were not built to withstand significant loss...and yet she had lost nearly everyone she'd ever cared for. Faces flashed across her mind as she remembered her beautiful realm, lost forever: her family, her people...a love that never had the chance to be anything more than a daydream. Already she'd borne the toll of so much death for seventeen years; how foolish she'd been to believe that she might have some reprieve.

Ana buried her face in her hands and released the sobs she'd been smothering for Melody's sake. She wasn't sure how long the tears fell before a soft voice startled her.

"Ana?" Equally soft steps approached while the elf struggled to regain her composure. The bed dipped under Melody's weight as she sat down, and the witch settled an arm around Ana's shoulders. It took her a moment to blink back her tears, to call on her regal training and compartmentalize. When she finally met Melody's gaze, it was clear the struggle was futile. "Stop that right now! I see you pulling away... just tell me what's going on."

Ana sighed, a ghost of a wry smile tugging at her lips. "I just... I wish Aria were here. She would be able to help Erin...and with all of the issues that will arise with Kali's return."

Melody made a face, and the elf's smile was a little more solid. "How *was* your day with Erin?" Melody's tone helped distract her from her dark thoughts.

"Why do you say it like *that*?"

Biting her cheek, Melody shrugged. "I'm just not sure I like her," she admitted. "She's so sarcastic, and it's like she goes in fists first rather than waiting to hear the whole story."

"Yes...she may be a bit rough around the edges, but I feel good about her. She hasn't had an easy life...and you remember what it was like to find out you had powers. I think we should give her a little leeway," Ana chastised gently. "But the day went well, she certainly seems ready and open to learn." Melody nodded, and the elf surged to her feet, pushing away the last of her emotion. "Okay, are you ready for some dinner? I'm sure you've had nothing but junk food *all day*."

.℮ .℮ .℮

The next day Erin arrived at the store, nervous about her first day of training. Ana told her they could do a spell to see what powers were evident so they knew what to focus on. Even still, she wasn't sure how she felt about magic and powers, not to mention whether or not she was ready to dive into all of it. She kept having a flashback of Queen Gossamer's eyes turning red, her hands burning her mother's skin before pulling away her wings. For all the good magic could be used for, there was probably twice as much darkness. Then there was also her mother's haunting words, that she would be safe until she started using her magic, then she could be tracked by the same erebus that killed her family.

"Good morning!" Ana called cheerfully.

"Where's Melody?"

"She'll be back from class soon, and then we can do the spell. I have a few things to get from the back. Are you okay getting the store open?"

Erin nodded. Ana had shown her what to do the day before and it wasn't her first time working retail.

Ana disappeared into the back room, which gave her a chance to take in her new place of employment, touching up spots as she moved around the store. Gabe had offered to stop by with lunch later, and now she almost wished she had taken him up on it. It would be nice to see his face, but she was nowhere near ready to talk to him about what she was learning. Just the *thought* of it set her nerves on edge.

She'd just finished wiping down the display case when the door chimed to announce Melody's arrival. The young woman looked a little better today than she had the day before. Her natural hair was twisted into two buns on top of her head, her dark skin looked clearer and her eyes more vibrant today, where yesterday they'd been dulled and red like she'd been crying.

"Morning. Where's Ana?" The witch was a little short with her, and the small smile didn't quite reach her eyes. Erin got the distinct feeling Melody was not a huge fan of her...not that she could really blame her after the way she'd acted. Melody nodded at her response, and announced she was going to run up and change. She was alone for only a moment before Ana returned carrying her supplies. Erin watched as the elf carefully set up in the clear space at the back of the store. Her chest tightened as she watched, nerves quickly setting in at what she was about to do.

Melody came bounding back down the steps, her eyes alight with the prospect of performing a spell, and grabbed a few crystals to add to the center of the circle Ana created. Erin could feel a heaviness between the two women across from her, but couldn't put her finger on what it was; before long it seemed as though the task before them was enough of a distraction from whatever was bothering them.

"Okay, are you ready?" Melody questioned, rubbing her hands together and sitting down with her legs crossed between two candles. Ana followed suit, so Erin did as well.

"Do I need to do anything?" Erin asked, wondering what one was supposed to do with their hands during a spell.

"Nope, you just sit there." Melody smiled at her, but it almost felt taunting.

"I'm not going to fall asleep again, am I?"

No one answered her this time, leaving her to watch as Melody focused her powers on lighting each candle around the circle. Finally Ana's voice spoke out, "Erin, just focus on the crystals at the center of the circle."

Erin did as she was told; she tried to look for all the cracks inside and pinpoint the exact colors that waved through. Melody's voice washed over her as she chanted softly in the background. She started to feel warm as the chanting grew faster. Erin wanted to look at Ana and Melody, but her eyes were locked on the crystals and her mind started to grow fuzzy. Then her arms reached out before her, her fingers stretched...and flowers started to bloom under them. The flowers turned to blood, pooled on the hardwood, but as quickly as it appeared, it was gone. Erin felt a great surge from within, and words started to appear, carved into the floor.

In one swift breath, the words disappeared and the candles went out. Everyone was quiet for a moment, and Erin dragged in a breath, feeling weak. She didn't know what any of it meant. The second her eyes tore away from the crystals, all of her energy was sucked away. The room seemed to swim for a moment, so she steadied herself as they allowed her a moment to settle.

"So, what do you think?" Melody asked quietly.

"Powers over nature, healing, and she probably has the power of telepathy, at least with other mystical creatures."

"What...what does all of that mean?" Erin asked quietly. When she looked to Ana however, she saw the elf was looking into the distance, seemingly focused on something.

"Ana?" Melody rose to her feet at the same time that the door to the back room flew open. Four dark figures entered and started to spread out before any of the women could make a move.

Erin instantly recognized them from the erebus that killed her parents. She wanted to scream but shock left her frozen, her lips stuck together as though they were glued. Ana, however, was on her feet and rushing to the counter where she pulled a dagger free from under it. One erebus, glowing eyes fixed on the elf, started toward her. All Erin could do was watch the wisps of black lick at the air as it moved in to attack. She could almost see her mother and father on the ground, surrounded by the dark beings. Melody held out her hands and a burst of glowing, white energy shot from her and hit the erebus square in the chest, sending it flying away from Erin.

Ana came bounding back and stabbed the erebus closest to her, but the one Melody knocked back was on its feet again and hissing angrily toward them. The three remaining erebi spread out, forcing the women to divide their attention. "Erin, get in the middle," Ana commanded sharply. The authority in her voice had Erin scrambling to get behind her. Melody covered her other side automatically while the erebi started to circle.

Ana moved quickly. As soon as an erebus got close to her, she moved in a fluid arc to stab it in the chest. It screeched in pain before falling, but it's cry seemed to provoke the other two. They moved in unison to attack and managed to knock into Melody, sending her falling to the floor. On the way down, Melody hit her head and stopped moving. Erin had no idea how to fight back, but she rushed to cover Melody with her own body. The erebus that knocked Melody down swiped an arm and hit Erin, sending her flying. Ana quickly took down the third erebus so she could go to protect the others.

Shakily, Erin rose to her feet and saw Ana was not going to get to Melody in time. So she ran, full speed toward the erebus, plowing into its middle and taking it to the floor. For just a moment she was fascinated at how solid it was when it looked like smoke, until it reached out to swipe at her with its dagger-like fingers. Vines sprung from the floor and wrapped around its arms suddenly, and Erin watched in astonishment as the erebus struggled on the floor, its dark, swirling energy becoming erratic.

"Erin!" Ana called her attention. She saw Ana was holding out her dagger for her. "Stab it in the chest."

Erin hesitated for a moment, but felt the vines weakening, so she grabbed the dagger, and plunged it into the erebus's chest.

Ana was gone from her side and hovering over Melody before the dark spirit disappeared. The witch was sitting up and holding her head, but was clearly okay.

"Erin, are you alright?" Ana asked, helping Melody to her feet.

Erin stood and looked around, the dagger still clenched tightly in her fist. Two of the erebi were gone, and as she watched, the third disintegrated into smoke and faded into the floor. "They are dead, their dark energy is getting pulled back into their realm," Ana explained softly.

"I'm going to need a drink." Erin held out the dagger to return it. Ana accepted it with a tired, wry, half-smile.

Chapter Ten

Erin moved slowly behind the other two women. Adrenaline was fading from her body, leaving her hands a little shaky, and she started to notice a throbbing in her cheekbone. Other pains made themselves known by the time they entered the apartment above the store, and Melody went for a sofa to plop down with a groan. She caught sight of herself in a mirror hanging against one cream colored wall and froze. Already her face was swollen, and a large bruise was blossoming on her cheek and jaw from being thrown. Her hip hurt from landing, and she saw a few small bruises up her arms. Damn.

"Erin." Ana's ever soothing voice broke the trance she was in. Her photographer's eye saw all the shades of bruising and immediately worried over how long it would take to heal. She healed quickly, but it wasn't likely to happen fast enough for the date she had planned for that evening. "Erin, why don't you come here and try to heal Melody."

"I'm fine! It was my own fault-" Melody started to argue before Ana cut her off.

"I know you'll be fine, but this is the perfect time for her to try to flex her healing abilities. It will be easier to heal yourself after you've had some practice." Ana turned back to Erin. "Your body will naturally work with you, but for now, we need you to recognize the power you possess so that you can control it. Being able to see an injury can make that easier."

"So I get to be the guinea pig?" The witch sent the sharp jab toward Erin as she reached up a hand to rub at her temples.

"I...I don't know what to do. I've always thought my body healed quickly, but..." she trailed off, staring wide-eyed at Melody. It already seemed like the other woman didn't like her very much. If she somehow made it worse, she would probably leave the apartment with a curse or something attached to her.

"You won't hurt her. You'll either help her or leave her in the same condition she is already in. You said you want to train, this is a good place to start." Ana took her arm and moved her toward the sofa. "Go ahead and lay down, Mel." Ana waited while Melody rolled her eyes and sunk lower on the sofa, gathering a pillow under her head for support. "Okay Erin, place your hand on her and hover your other hand over the wound. That will help concentrate your energy." Erin did so, making a fist before stretching out her fingers and laying them on Melody's arm, hovering the other over her head. "You can close your eyes to focus on the wound, but you want to visualize Melody being healed. Think of her pain and your desire to end it."

Ana's directions came out as soothing instructions, and Erin closed her eyes to do as she was told. She thought of the way Melody looked when she had been knocked out on the floor. She thought of how the girl winced when she scooted lower on the sofa, jostling her head. "Concentrate on your breathing, your heartbeat, and you should get a…little ball of warmth at the pit of your stomach. Focus on it growing, working up your arms and out of your hands into Mel."

Erin tried. For a moment she thought she felt a little glow inside of her, but then she lost it. A full minute passed in silence as she tried desperately to reach it again, but nothing else came to her. "I just can't do it!" Erin dropped her hands away and turned away from Melody's form. She was frustrated, her body was sore, and she kept seeing the glowing eyes of the creatures that'd tried to kill all of them.

"The spell we did and your burst of power during the fight may have drained you. Using powers and magic is like exercising. The more you work at it, the stronger you become, and the more you can do without rest." Ana helped Melody sit back up on the sofa before turning her bright eyes back to her. "It's okay. You'll get the hang of it; we just pushed you a little too far today. That was a great show of power down there during that fight, pure instinct. Have a seat; I'll make everyone some tea." Ana took off her sweater and draped it over a chair before disappearing into the kitchen.

Erin sat and tried to relax despite her failure. Melody sat across from her with a stoney expression, but it softened when her eyes fell on Erin's cheek. "Are you okay?"

"Yeah..." She tried to think of the best way to phrase the turmoil going on in her. "Those...*erebi*, demon guys...I've seen them before."

"You have?" Melody sat up a little straighter.

"When I connected with my mother. They are the same creatures that killed both of my parents. There was a whole field of them. One stabbed my father from behind...one infected my mother and her veins turned black. How were they here?"

"There is a portal to other realms in the store. Ana is a...protector of sorts to the portal. She helps the mystical creatures that pass through, and protects Sula from creatures that want to cause problems. Lately, there have been more trouble makers than innocents." The young witch shook her head wryly. "Ana likes to tell a story about a time when all the realms were together as one. A powerful witch ended up ripping the world into pieces because of a broken heart. The portals are tears in those walls. Some portals are small tears; they only lead to one spot in one realm. There are a few larger portals though, and these are the ones that need to be watched and protected. The portal beneath us is one of the larger portals. The magic of the larger portals can send you to a few choice spots in each of the realms." Melody readjusted on the sofa, leaning forward with her elbows resting on her knees. It seemed like she was getting into her tale, and Erin couldn't blame her. Though it felt like she was listening to a fairy tale, now she knew better. This was part of her life now. This had been part of her *parents'* lives.

"Portal travel is not easy, though. Those that have purely magical blood are able to go through with the most ease. The elves and full-blooded fae, they are better able to control the portals and travel easily. You and I would be considered mixed blood; we have magic, but we are also human...well, I'm a little *more* human, but you get the idea. We can travel through them, but will reach the other side a little worse for wear than Ana would. We also have less control, only really able to go where another large portal lies, versus being able to land at any of the portals available to that realm. Pure-blood humans would not be able to travel through easily, it turns out. A human stumbles upon a portal, and ends up...*falling in,* you could say. But they could get lost, hurt, or even ejected because they lack magic. The erebi shouldn't be able to travel through the portals at all; many of them have magical abilities, but they drain energy. They counterbalance the fae, who create energy. It seemed they were unable to travel through the portals for a long time, because the portals would protect themselves and eject the erebi. When Ana was a girl however - when your parents were alive - they found a way to get the portals to accept them."

"And let me guess, they didn't waste time using this new found ability?" Erin offered.

"You could say that. They tried to invade the other realms. Your parents were part of the front line that kept them from invading Sula, though it wasn't their main focus at the time. They wanted Eloas. They went for Ana's kingdom, brought down Ana's parents, and took over the realm. So many erebi there would eventually cause the realm to collapse...it's likely they simply drained the realm of its magic to make them stronger. Now we believe they are trying to rise again, and this time they are going for Loinnir."

"When I was connected with my mother, she told my father I would be safe until I started to use my magic. The erebi are attracted to magic? They can track those with powers?"

"Not all of them are feeders. There are many different kinds. But yes, there are those that drain magic, and they are greedy. They are attracted to those with power because taking it will make them stronger."

"So the stronger I become, the easier it would be for them to find me?" Erin did her best to keep her voice even, but fear gripped her heart. She had the sudden image of her sleeping in her bed while one of those creatures came stalking down the road, sensing her power.

"Now that you have come of age, they would be able to notice you either way. But yes, the more powerful you become, the more that power will radiate."

Erin thought about that, and Melody seemed in no hurry. It was odd to spend so much time talking with her one-on-one, when she got the occasional feeling that the witch didn't want her there. There wasn't a huge age gap between them, but enough of one that they were at different stages of life. She knew Melody was finishing her first year at college, and she knew the young woman had been with Ana for some time. She didn't know what happened to Melody's parents, and as an orphan, she knew better than to ask. It was an unspoken rule in foster care, you don't ask about the parental units. But she couldn't let her curiosity go completely unsatisfied. "Ana said you came into your power very early. That must mean you are quite strong."

"Yes, almost as early as I can remember. There had always been this *fire* inside me. When I was thirteen there was no denying what I was. Unexplainable things would just....*happen* around me, especially when I was upset about something. I started trying to work on it, control my powers on my own. Then one day my mom walked in on me doing a spell." Melody's face fell at the memory, and she looked in the direction of the kitchen. Erin could see Melody gathering herself.

"They said I worshiped the devil, that a demon had infested my soul. They kicked me out." She let out a small snort. "They weren't even religious people. So then I was a thirteen year old girl living on the street. I lasted about two months, too, before I went back to them. I thought they'd had time to come to terms. That they had just been scared, and probably regretted what they had done. I thought they missed me and just didn't know how to find me. So I went home." A bitter smile spread across her face and Melody turned back to look her directly in the eye. "They'd moved. Told the new buyer that their daughter died in an accident. So I was on my own, for good."

Melody took a deep breath before continuing. "I wandered the streets, sleeping where I could, getting food where I found it. I continued going to school, but everyone had stopped talking to me. I didn't tell anyone what happened, I just cleaned up as much as I could and went on my own every morning. I didn't want to end up in foster care or anything...I wanted to be able to practice my magic without worrying I would get kicked out. I wanted to stay in control, at least keep the little control I had. I turned fourteen, and I remember finding a bakery. They were giving away free samples so I went in and took one. It was a bite of a cake, but it made me feel *human* again." The young woman took on a wistful look as she delved deeper into the memory. "I wandered around afterwards, and ended up getting drawn to this store. It was late; the store was closed at that point, but for some reason I felt safe, so I slept in the back alley. Early the next morning Ana came downstairs and found me. She'd been on her own for two years. The couple that owned the store before her was gone. She had lost her family, her brother was lost coming through the portal. I think we needed each other...so she took me in. She got documents made up that said she was my guardian, and got me in a new school when the next semester started. I was able to start over and she was like a mother figure to me. She taught me to use my powers, helped me with homework, talked about boys." Melody shrugged but Erin could see the smile.

"It's wonderful that you two were able to find one another. What your family did was awful, but at least you and Ana were able to create a family of sorts." Erin thought of Gabe and their childhood together. They had always been each other's family, and she truly believed they made it through because they had each other.

Ana came back with a tray of steaming mugs. Erin watched her in a new light. Melody had been abandoned; she could have ended up in foster care, or a home. She'd suffered through the streets, but she could have been sent to some of the people Erin had been sent to. She could have been hurt. Instead, Ana had found her and taken her in, loved her like they were family.

Ana sat the tray down in front of them, drawing them from their reminiscing, and Erin watched while Ana added some honey to her own tea before returning it to the tray. Something caught her eye when Ana set the honey down: she remembered seeing that the elf had a tattoo before, but something about the lines held her attention this time. "What's that?" Erin lurched forward to point at the marking.

There was a sad twitch to Ana's mouth as she pulled back her sleeve. On her right wrist was a tattoo of a broken triangle with two dots inside, a symbol that Erin recognized. "It's a moon glyph. It is customary for notable elves to carry some sort of mark. As a royal member I had one to match my family; it represents the crown."

Erin studied the marking even though she already knew the lines. How could she not? She ran a hand through her hair, and the others must have noticed something was off, because Melody asked her what she was thinking.

"Sorry, it's just odd is all. My boyfriend, Gabe, has the same mark on his wrist." She noticed Ana jerk at that information, but the elf quickly recovered. "Humans know of moon glyphs too. It's quite possible he simply saw the design and liked it," she offered with a shrug. Or, at least what Erin would think was a shrug. Ana had more of a...*graceful rising* of the shoulder. *Elves.*

"I guess...he's had it since he was a kid. He doesn't remember how he got it, just showed up at the group home with it."

"What?" Ana really did startle at that. She set her mug back down and turned her full attention to Erin, who felt Melody's eyes dart between them. Now she felt uncomfortable. Sharing his story with two people he didn't know felt too much like she was betraying Gabe, but they were both watching her intently, and she *did* know them. So Erin took a steadying breath, and began recounting how Gabe came to the home without any memory of what had happened to him or where he had come from. Both women hung on every word, but there was something in Ana's eyes that made Erin look for an escape.

"We actually have a date tonight, I should get out of here or I'm going to be late." She stood and caught sight of herself in the mirror. With all the talking, she'd forgotten about her face. "I'm sure this will go over well." She muttered, touching the large bruise and cringing away.

"Sure, of course, I think we should both go and lay down for a bit." Ana stood too. "It's been quite the day."

"Yes, and it looks like I'll have some explaining to do," Erin groaned before escaping the apartment and the intense elven gaze.

.℮ .℮ .℮

Ana traced a finger slowly over the glyph long-ingrained into the skin of her wrist. Certainly not the only tattoo on the elf's body, this particular one had been her first, and was the one that identified her as a member of the royal family. Unlike tattoos in Sula, elven tattoos were drawn with magic; they were not painful and would never fade. Royal markers were given on a child's first birthday, while friends and family gathered to celebrate. Other markers might be given later in life, to show a high ranking guard for instance, and it was always a moment of celebration for her people. She could still remember being dressed up to attend her brother's ceremony. Toron had been a chubby little sprite with wild blond curls and a smile that lit up the whole room. He let out a brilliant giggle when they placed the mark on him and the magic caused his arm to glow, and then he'd reached for her to hold him.

From time to time, a customer would ask her for ideas about magic-related tattoos. Runes and glyphs were particularly interesting to most that asked, but few took much notice of the moon glyphs used among the royals and guards in Eloas. The possibility of a stranger sharing the same mark...

Was there a chance that Erin's boyfriend was in fact the brother she'd lost so long ago? The one separated from her when they fled their home realm? Could it really be *that simple* after all this time? Or was the similarity nothing more than coincidence? She had searched for Toron, unsure whether he even made it to Sula or not. But because of the spell put on him, he was disguised completely as human and she was unable to trace him. All of his elven traits were hidden and undetectable.

She was tempted to do the spell again, just to see if anything happened, but in the end, she knew it would be a waste of energy and resources unless Toron found a way to lift the spell from himself. She was getting ahead of herself, and she knew she needed to pull back before her hope rose from the dead. Ana couldn't deal with more heartache just now. Instead, she would see how everything played out, and wait until she had more information.

.ℓ .ℓ .ℓ

Gabe called Erin on her way home from the store. He let her know he was running late, which gave her a little longer to try to fix her face. She would have given anything to have control over her healing ability so she could just make the darkening bruise and swelling jaw disappear. She thought about just canceling. Tomorrow it would probably be gone and he would never need to know; but she missed him, and she just kept seeing those wispy creatures — the same ones that took her parents away from her. She *needed* him. It should scare her to need someone again, and it did, but it also brought her relief. Once upon a time they leaned on each other, and it made her extremely happy to know he was there again.

She pulled on her tightest jeans and tucked them into boots that would add an inch or two. Then she picked out her "going out" shirt that showed off more cleavage than her normal attire. Erin redid her hair since it fell flat during her fight earlier, and then she was careful to apply makeup. The coverup she used worked on the lighter bruises on her arm, but it only kind of covered up the one on her face. She knew it would get noticed by Gabe but hoped he wouldn't be too freaked out by it. When he called again, to let her know he was outside, she almost panicked and told him she couldn't come down.

"Erin, you okay?" Gabe asked in his warm tone.

"Yeah, yes. I'll be right down." She took a deep breath and vowed that no matter what, she wouldn't lie to him. It would be easy for her to make up a reason for her bruise, but she refused to do that to their relationship. She would tell him the truth when she could, and she would tell him that it was something she couldn't talk about when she couldn't say.

Erin made it halfway down the stairs when she realized she didn't lock her door, so she turned around to dash back up and turn the lock. She was regretting the boots when she finally reached the landing, but she'd rather fight another erebus than walk up the stairs again to change them.

"Why are you out of breath?" Gabe laughed at her when she climbed in his car.

"I thought it would be fun to take the stairs a few times before I came to see you, you know, really get the heart pumping." She grinned at him but froze when she turned and found him taking her in slowly. His gaze lingered at her hips before rising higher. She watched his Adam's apple bob when he took in the swell of her breasts, and heat washed over her. Suddenly the car felt so much smaller, too small for the two of them.

"You look-" He was staring at her face now, and she watched as his eyes darted back to her cheek a second time. Before she could turn away he reached up to turn on the overhead light so he could see her cheek better.

"Gabe-"

"Erin…" Her name was a soft question as he now assessed her more carefully. "What happened?"

"I am starving, how about you?" She tried to ignore the question, which was the wrong move, because now his soft, questioning gaze sharpened on her.

"Erin."

She leaned back in her seat and looked out the front window. She would not lie to him. "It's hard to explain. But I'm okay, I promise."

"You look like someone punched you in the jaw! If you still worked at the pub I'd be worried you got in the middle of a fight or something. Erin, what happened to you today?"

Flashes of Melody knocked out on the floor, the feel of a blade in her hand, the rise of the magic in her, all came flooding back. If she thought too hard on the events of the day she was going to totally lose her crap. She just wanted the comfort of Gabe's company. "I just had a really long day, but I still wanted to see you and I really am starving. Do you think we could just go and get some food?"

She dared a glance in his direction, and watched the fight of emotions until his mouth settled into a frown. He let out a long sigh before putting the car in drive and pulling out. She wanted to ask about his day, but his knuckles were white where they gripped the steering wheel and he wasn't looking at her. Her chest tightened. She wasn't used to Gabe being upset with her, and she couldn't deny that all signs pointed to just that.

It was only about a ten minute drive to the seafood restaurant he'd asked her to, but she sent herself into a tailspin during those ten minutes. If they stayed together, one day she would have to tell him the truth. What would happen then? Would he think she lost her mind and try to get her to get help? Would he just think she was lying and leave her? Would he actually give her the time to prove what she was saying, be able to wrap his head around it, *and* choose to stay with her? She couldn't tell him, though, not until she had more control over her powers. She needed to understand what all of this meant for her before she tried to include him, even if that wasn't exactly fair to him. She glanced at him again, and his gaze flashed to her, but cut away as he pulled into the parking lot.

"Gabe..." She needed to connect with him in some way but had no idea how to proceed. His name hung in the air between them before he let out a sigh and stretched out his fingers on the steering wheel.

"Is there someone else? Did he do that to you?" When he finally looked at her his gaze was open, ready to accept whatever she said, even if she broke his heart.

"Gabe, no, I told you I wasn't seeing anyone-"

"Yes, but then you run off right after we agree to be *more*. You disappear for days. Now you show up looking like someone punched you! You won't tell me what's going on, and normally I could understand that. I know you need to work through things before you put the information out there, but you are hurt. Someone *hurt* you and I can't just ignore that."

"Gabe, I told you there would be things I couldn't tell you. You agreed-"

"I agreed that you were dealing with stuff and you weren't able to talk about it yet. Yes, I did agree to start a relationship with someone I deeply care about and trust, knowing that you were not ready to be completely open with me. But I didn't agree to stand aside while you apparently join a fight club or something!"

Erin chewed her lip, doing her best not to cry. She was ruining this, and it was the last thing she wanted to mess up. "I swear, if it was something I could tell you, I would. I *will* tell you all of it one day, but I can't right now. I know that it's not fair to you, but I need you to trust me and wait a little longer. I promise that I am not in a relationship with anyone else, nor do I have some past boyfriend banging at my door. I..." She sighed and picked at the hem of her shirt. "I told you I found out some stuff about my parents, and I'm still exploring what all of that means. No one is hurting me, this was just an accident and I don't foresee it happening again. If you can't wait, I understand. I really do. I understand it's not fair what I'm asking, but I'm asking anyway, because I don't want to go back to my life without you."

Gabe's hand closed around her unharmed cheek and he turned her face towards his. "Are you safe?"

The deep green of his eyes almost erased the memory of the erebi attacking. She could almost block out the memory of her parents falling in that field, leaving her orphaned. This was all part of her world now. The stronger she got with her abilities, the more she would be like a beacon to creatures that would want to hurt her. She was afraid, but she also knew she had Ana and Melody. She would get stronger and be able to fight back as she had earlier. She didn't feel like she was lying when she told Gabe that yes, she was safe. His forehead rested against hers until her stomach growled, lightening the mood a bit as they both chuckled. "I guess I should probably feed you, huh?"

"Before midnight, or I might turn into a gremlin." His finger brushed her bottom lip and everything stilled inside her.

"We should get moving then, I'd be pretty upset if you became a gremlin." Neither of them made an attempt to move though. She could almost taste him on her lips. Then his gaze dropped back to the bruise on her jaw, and he leaned away from her. "We should get in there." Erin watched him climb from the car and knew this wasn't quite over yet. He was hurt that she wouldn't talk to him, and she was going to have to find some way to fix it until she knew more about herself and her abilities.

Chapter Eleven

Briar was dying. Heat washed over her in waves. One moment she was freezing, and the next she thought she was going to wither away from heat stroke. She couldn't open her eyes, it took far more energy than she had. Just the movement of breathing in and out was making her feel sick. Every nerve and muscle in her body either ached or screamed out in active pain. A shiver ran down her spine and, once again, she was lost to the darkness.

"Hurry, we have to move!"

"Why, Mama?" Briar spoke with a quiet, male voice. She looked into the worried expression of a woman with familiar red eyes.

"One of the protectors!" Briar was dragged forward faster than her smaller legs could handle and she stumbled a few times. Then she heard the movement behind her, and turned just in time to see a man and woman rushing after them.

While she knew of the protectors that guarded main entries into realms, she didn't understand why they were after a child and his mother.

A moment later, the man reached them and snatched Briar, pulling her back and shoving her to the ground. The side of her face exploded in pain. "Doyle!" The woman screeched in terror. and Briar looked up, trying to see her, but blood ran into her eye and her vision clouded. The man moved past her fallen body and went to Doyle's mother. Even as the erebus reached out to gather her son into her protective embrace, the man reached her and ran her through with his sword. Her red eyes widened, and Briar's mouth let out the most pitiful cry of despair.

"Elise, get the boy." The man turned and Briar heard the woman coming from behind. Briar stumbled to stand and run, but froze as a battle cry rang out. Lyra seemed to fall from the sky, though she must have leapt from one of the trees. Lyra grabbed Briar's arm, and used the human's surprise to her advantage. She shoved them out of her way and ran with Briar in tow. Out of breath, blood pouring down her face, Briar was finally given reprieve as they got a safe distance away.

"You okay, boy?"

"Mother...."

"Nasty humans. All the races like to say how terrible the erebi are, yet they kill us without question. Come, I don't know why your mother brought you to Sula but it's not safe here. That couple will be tracking us. You stick with me, I'll make sure you're safe." Lyra took the smaller hand into her own, but paused to grab a cloth from a pouch on her side and pressed it to the large gash on the side of Briar's *face. Then they took up a slower pace and made their way back toward a portal into the erebi realm.*

The breath was sucked out of Briar's lungs as she shot up. Pain coursed through her back, and it felt like someone was ripping her skin away.

"Shh, I'm sorry. I'm just changing your bandages. I guess if you were in your realm you would probably heal quicker." Doyle's face leaned over her, and she caught sight of the long scar over one side. She could still feel the pain from the vision and lifted her hand to her own cheek.

"Fern?" She tried to speak her sister's name, but wasn't sure if she even made any noise.

"Your sister is home safe. I didn't let your family see me but I watched her go to your father, and he took her inside. Now lay back. This will hurt a little." She wasn't sure her body could take any more pain. Sure enough, when he pressed his hand on the tender skin of her back, her mind carried her off to a safe place of darkness.

.℘ .℘ .℘

Erin stared out the car window as Gabe drove her home. Dinner had been a quiet affair. Neither of them seemed to know what to do to move past their stalemate. It didn't help that the waitress noticed her not-so-covered bruise and gave Gabe the cold shoulder all through their meal. They were almost back to her apartment when he reached across the center console and held his hand out for her. It was suddenly hard to swallow as his hand closed around hers, and he brought it up to his lips to place a soft kiss on her knuckles. "I want to do this with you, Erin. I want all of it. You've always been part of who I am. We've been to hell and back together. So I want you to know that I'm here with you. I'm all in. I know you need time, but in exchange for that time I need a promise from you."

"What is it?" Her heart was hammering in her chest.

"You have to tell me if you are in danger. I don't care if you think I can't help, or if you are worried that I might get hurt. I need you to promise, if you are not safe, you tell me. I don't know what all is happening, or what you've found out about your parents, but if you get pulled into trouble, I need to at least know something is going on. You have to trust me with that if you want a relationship with me."

"Okay, I promise." She squeezed his hand as he pulled into a parking spot outside of her apartment building.

When he turned to look at her, desire lit her up from inside. "I'm all in." He leaned forward and captured her lips with his own. He tasted like the chocolate mints they'd both grabbed handfuls of when they left the restaurant, but his familiar forest scent clung to his skin. His hand pressed to her back and scooted her closer to the console, but there was nowhere else for her to go after that. She wanted to be closer, to be wrapped up in him.

Not much time had passed since they reconnected, and even less since they decided to date, but it felt like their whole lives had been leading up to this. They'd always been meant to be, and if there was anything she learned from being an orphan, life was short and unpredictable. No one knew how much time they had, and she didn't want to waste a moment of it. "Gabe, come upstairs with me. Spend the night." She was breathless, and practically begging, but he'd seen her at her worst moments. Right now, she just wanted him like she'd never wanted anything or anyone else in all her life.

"Are you sure?" He whispered against her mouth in a husky tone.

"If you are." She smiled against his lips, pressing soft kisses to the corner of his lips.

"I've never been more sure of anything than I am about my feelings for you, Erin. You never have to worry about that, no matter what." He let her go so he could climb from the car and race around to open her door for her. This time, he pulled her flush against his body and claimed her mouth with the hunger of a man that had been waiting a lifetime for this, *for her*.

Erin was standing in an open field. Sinopa, the fae in fox form, was at her side. There was something different about the air, some energy that told her this was all wrong. She turned and found Gabe down on one knee, gazing at her like she held the world in her hands. Then he held something out for her, but when she leaned in she found it wasn't a ring, but a dagger. "Gabe?"

Sinopa let out a small yelp at her side, her teeth bared as she stared off in the distance. Shadows were creeping in —not shadows, Erin realized, but the infection erebi. "Gabe, we have to go!" She reached down and tried to tug him to his feet, but he refused to move.

"I'm all in, Erin. You have to promise to tell me if you are in danger."

"We have to go! I can't fight that many-" Sinopa took off running towards the approaching hoard, but she disappeared in the darkness and then the beasts were on them. Erin didn't even have time to scream before the pain started-

"Erin! Wake up!" Erin shot up, sucking in breath against the pain, only to realize she didn't *feel* any pain. She was wrapped up in warm blankets, Gabe's shoulder was her pillow, and his hand was caressing her cheek. "You were yelling. It's okay." He pressed a soft kiss to her forehead and she struggled to remember exactly what she'd been dreaming. "Do you want to talk about it?" His voice was rough with sleep but he pulled her closer against him, tucking her into a space that seemed to be made just for her.

Any lingering fear from her nightmare faded as she snuggled deeper into the safety of his arms. "I don't even remember now. Sorry I woke you." She pressed a soft kiss to his chest in apology. He opened his mouth to speak, but then shut it. "What is it?"

"I was about to say something, but I'm too tired to know if it's too lame or not, so I decided against it."

She chucked and kissed his neck this time. "I just woke up from a nightmare like a child, it's okay to be a little lame. This is a safe space."

"Hmmm." His fingers trailed down her spine and a small moan of contentment escaped her. "It was something along the lines of being perfectly okay being woken up by you, any time of the night, if it means I get to sleep with you in my arms. This is something I think I could get used to."

"All in?" She whispered as she started to drift back off.

"All in." He sealed the promise with a soft, tired kiss to her forehead.

.℃ .℃ .℃

"Briar! I thought I'd lost you!" A warm male voice engulfed her as familiar arms pulled her against a large chest. He kissed the top of her head, and then her eyes adjusted to the dark room and she looked up into Doyle's face. His red eyes were searching her for injuries, his face creased with worry, making his scar crinkle. She wanted to smooth it with a kiss.

"You'll never lose me." She was shaking; tears were falling silently down her face. He wiped them away before drawing her even closer and claiming her lips.

His mouth was desperate against hers, demanding that she respond and show *him that she meant it. The passion pulled the breath from her-*

"Lyra rescued me when I had no one else." The scene changed so suddenly that Briar's lips felt empty from the loss of his kiss. "I trusted you! I helped you get your sister to safety, I've helped you in all your plans along the way. I thought we wanted the same thing."

"Doyle, please! Hear me out-" His hand lashed out and grabbed her arm. His grip hurt, and gave her no room to try to pull away.

"No, I've heard enough. You have lied to all of us, now you'll have to pay the price." His gaze darkened dangerously. Any softness she had found in him was gone, and he was simply the little boy who lost the life he knew just because he was born an erebus. The boy who wanted revenge and didn't trust other beings. He held a dagger to her throat, and she saw no regret as he pressed it to her skin.

Briar struggled to pull in a breath, her body shaking uncontrollably with chills. A sweat-soaked blanket sat tangled at her feet, but she didn't have the strength to pull it up. Had she seen a vision of what the future could hold? As her future stood now, she and Doyle could either come to love each, other or he could turn against her and kill in order to protect Lyra. The idea that they could come to love one another seemed far-reaching. Even still, she knew, more could happen to bring about an altogether different outcome.

She managed to roll from her side to her stomach and rested her throbbing head against her arms. She thought of him changing her bandages earlier — *or had it been days ago?* She couldn't be sure, but she held on to his promise that Fern was safe. She just had to be strong and heal. If she survived this she, could worry about how to survive her questionable future in Skia.

"You have to drink something." Someone was tilting her head up, and a foul-smelling liquid was placed against her lips. She gagged and tried to turn away, but the hands on her were strong and steady. "You can do it Briar." Small amounts of the liquid slid past her lips and she sputtered, trying to spit it out even as her body craved it. It burned down her throat, but she could feel her body suck it in like dried soil getting a few drops of rain. She managed a few more gulps before she was able to open her eyes, and found Doyle there once more. The man that would either love her or kill her...the man she couldn't trust even if sometimes he seemed to be on her side.

"Good, that's good. How are you feeling?" His voice was soft, and he didn't bother to wait for a response before continuing. "You were out for a while this time, but your temperature seems to have settled." It was true, she didn't seem to be chilled or burning for the first time since a part of her was literally ripped and cut away from her body. Just the thought made her want to pull her wings tight against her as extra protection. Her muscles tightened and then screamed out as the pain shot through her. Suddenly alert, she doubled over and managed to get her palms against the hard rock floor...only to realize that she wasn't touching stone at all, but a mattress with bedding. For the first time, she looked around the room and realized she was no longer in the cell, but in an actual room with a door. She guessed that the door was locked from the outside, and the walls were still carved from stone, but she was on a *bed*. She had a *pillow*.

Doyle seemed to read her mind. "Ah, well. You did all this to gain Lyra's trust that you would help us and not run away right? Of course, if you died on the hard floor you wouldn't be much help. It's not much, but it's yours until your work with us is done."

"You did this?" Briar questioned. His hands had been on her to keep her from falling off the bed, but he let her go and moved back, his gaze hardening.

"I did what I had to to make sure you lived. It was stupid of Lyra to do this to you, especially before you saw anything useful," Doyle muttered. The weight of him left her bed, and Briar fought against the wave of nausea as she was jostled. "Here, see if you can get a little food in your stomach, then you need to rest more. You managed to avoid infection, but your wound is still raw." He set a tray down with a cup full of more foul liquid and some bread. "If you can keep that down we'll work on getting you something more interesting."

She lifted the bread to pick off a few pieces, and saw a ring sitting at the corner. Drawn to it, she reached out and felt ill as soon as her fingers touched the metal. Dark energy surrounded her. The visions came as they never had before. The small control she had over her powers was gone, and wave after wave ran her through. Some part of her realized she was screaming. She saw Doyle run back to her and could feel his hands grab onto her. She watched as more erebi poured into the room to see what was happening, but her mind's eye was elsewhere, *everywhere*.

"Briar? What's happening? Briar!" Her body jerked away and pain tore through her as her stitches came apart. Briar's throat grew raw as her screams continued to pour from her. Flashes of possible futures hammered into her mind until her head felt like it would explode. It was too much. When she was younger she would have trouble with too many visions hitting her at once, but her mother had been around then. She'd helped her and taught her how to navigate; right now she felt weak, and her powers were like a small leaf fluttering in the wind, just out of her grasp.

She'd known when they ripped her wings away that this could happen; other fae had lost their minds when such a large part of them and their magic was taken away. The wings of a fae were the purest part of their magic...and now hers are gone. Her only safeguard against the visions eating her alive probably sat in some cabinet in Lyra's room, waiting for the right moment to be used as a bargaining chip.

Desperate to keep hold of the present, she grabbed Doyle's collar and tried to meet his gaze. But it was too late...instead of his red eyes, she saw another face dance across her gaze as the visions pulled her under.

.℘ .℘ .℘

Ana looked up from the register with a smile. "You guys are all set! Please stop back and let me know if the tea helps!" The couple nodded and waved. As soon as they were gone, the elf turned to her friend. "Alright, what is going on with you today?"

"Huh?" Erin looked up from her phone, surprised, and a flush rose on her cheeks. "Sorry."

"You've been spacey all afternoon. Is everything okay?"

The fae sighed. "Yeah...it's just...I don't know. It feels like everything with Gabe has moved so *fast*."

"Fast? I thought you grew up together," Ana pointed out, trying not to think about her recent suspicions of who Gabe might be.

"We *did*, but then we spent ten years apart..." She shook her head and tossed her phone into her bag. "So much can change in ten years, what if he's not who I knew him to be? What if *I'm* not who *he* thinks I am anymore?" Erin scoffed at herself. "Who am I kidding, *I* don't even know who I am anymore. What if...what if he finds out the truth and freaks?"

What if he finds out he might actually be an elven prince and freaks?
"You have always trusted him, haven't you?"

Erin nodded. "He's my best friend."

The fae's words sparked a memory, an ache for one she'd once held as close as Erin held Gabe. One that had been left behind...lost with the rest of her loved ones and her home. Her smile faltered, and she had to fight back a wave of regret. "Erin...has he given you any reason to believe that he has changed...*truly* changed since you knew him?"

Her friend's brow furrowed in confusion at her serious tone. "No...but-"

Ana put her hand on the fae's shoulder with a small smile. "I know you are still trying to navigate everything, still trying to figure out who you are in light of all of this new information, but you're still *you*, just...you with a little bit more excitement in your life." Both women chuckled until Ana grew somber once more. "Trust your heart, Erin. Don't let your doubts stop you from letting him in, from giving him your whole heart. We never know when our time will come." She drew in a shaky breath and blinked tears from her eyes. "I let my fear stand in the way, once...I didn't tell him I loved him...and now, he is lost to me forever."

"He was an elf?" Erin questioned softly.

Ana nodded. "Don't make the same mistake that I did...don't push Gabe away."

181

Chapter Twelve

Two Months Later

"Ow!" Erin let out a string of curses as pain shot through her shin. "Shut up!" She turned on Gabe, who was still lying in bed, laughing at her. She sat on the edge of the bed and rubbed her leg.

"I'm sorry," Gabe cooed as he sat up and rubbed her shoulders. She couldn't help but smile when he started to kiss her neck and run his hands down her arms.

"I can't, I have to go to work!" She jumped from his arms before turning to face him. "*Please* finish unpacking. I can't keep living with all of these boxes lying around." Things between them moved quickly, but it all felt so natural that Erin decided to just go with it. After Gabe spent that first night at her apartment, it was hard to spend nights alone again. They both felt it, so Gabe stayed over more often than not. One evening Gabe had to go back to his apartment for fresh clothes; Erin ignored the fact she was still keeping secrets from him, and told him she thought he should pack up his stuff and make it official already. He'd picked her up and flung her over his shoulder, collapsing onto the sofa with her perched on his lap. He'd told her he'd been waiting since their first kiss for her to ask him to move in. He didn't go back to his apartment that night.

"You know, you could quit. This apartment is less than the one I shared with Jason. We could pull off paying for it between my paycheck and the money you make from your photographs." Gabe grabbed her hand and pulled her back toward him. "You can focus on photography, like you want to do." His hand held her cheek with tenderness before he kissed the tip of her nose. "You deserve that. You don't have to keep juggling everything."

Erin wanted to cry at the sentiment. His eyes were sincere, searching hers. But she couldn't accept his offer, and she couldn't tell him why.

In the two months that she'd spent with Ana, she was starting to gain control of her powers. It still took a lot out of her, but she was learning. The job at *Mystifying* was far more than a paycheck, and it was all part of a life she couldn't share with the man that she loved. Erin knew she had to tell him soon. She should have told him before he'd moved in, but she was terrified to lose him. He was starting to have more questions for her now though, since he was starting to see how much time she was spending at the store. She was more in control over her powers now, she was more secure in who she was…and she didn't have any reason to still be keeping it from him. Her promise to herself not to lie to him was starting to look tarnished from her secrets. She looked at him now, open and loving, doing his best to give her the world. "Gabe, I really appreciate that…but I couldn't do that to you. I really don't make enough with my photography, and it's never consistent work-"

"But it could be! You are wonderful at what you do. You get plenty of jobs, but you always have to fit them into your schedule. If you had all your time to devote to your business you could do so much more."

"We can talk more about it later, okay? But Gabe, Ana is willing to work around any scheduling issues I may have, she already did once. And we really need me to keep this job, okay? I like fancy living," she teased. Erin wrapped her arms around Gabe's neck and gave him a grin. "You know, dinners, wine…" She leaned in and kissed him until he backed away.

"You aren't playing fair, especially because you are about to leave me for the day." Gabe groaned. While he pushed her away, his grip on her was still hard, like he was going to put up a fight when she tried to leave.

"Just think of all those people that will be showing up for your class in two hours. Body Combat today right?"

"Ah, I like how you changed the subject." Gabe released her and started looking around for a shirt. "Yes, Body Combat class and then three personal training sessions. Then maybe dinner, wine, *fancy living*?"

"Sounds good!" Erin kissed him goodbye before escaping the apartment without further harm from stray boxes. Her stomach churned with guilt as she left him to get ready for his day. They were starting a life together, but he had no idea what kind of life she was really living. Erin took a deep breath and swore to herself she would talk to him soon. She wouldn't let time slip through her fingers. She couldn't hide from who she was, especially when such a large part of her wanted to share it with him. She was going to have to put on her big girl pants and trust that he'd hear her out and choose to stay with her.

She truly believed they were soul mates, put together when they both needed a friend, and brought back together now that they were ready to be more. She had to believe that he would somehow come around to her not being *quite* human. She would age slower than him, looking the same as she did now when they should be old and gray together. Any children they had could carry magic as she did. She would always have some form of danger following her, as certain erebi would be drawn to her power. *What could he possibly have against any of that?* She slammed her forehead on her steering wheel and let out a groan.

℘ ℘ ℘

Doyle hesitated at the doorway. The heavy door that locked the fae on the other side was carved from the dark wood of a viper tree. His realm was filled with all kinds of lethal mysteries, and a viper tree was just one of them. The sap was poisonous and seeped into the skin after just a moment of exposure. The wood could be used for building once it was dried and sealed, but it was dangerous work; it was almost guaranteed that multiple deaths had taken place just to put this door between him and the woman causing him so much stress. For *weeks* now she had been lost to them; she gave no response when talked to or touched, and Lyra was losing patience.

It was taking everything in him not to snap at the erebus. In all the years they'd been together he'd never been this angry with her choices. Pulling Briar's wings had been a stupid decision, but to then push her to have a vision before she was fully healed was even worse. Briar had been willing to help, and if not for this set back they could already have their answer.

Two guards passed by him, so he decided it was probably time to check in on the fae. She looked so much smaller than when she'd first come. Her wings, even tucked tight to her back, had given her an almost warrior-like look; now, though, she looked frail. The blue of her hair had faded, and her violet eyes were dull and unresponsive. He could only imagine what was going on inside her head. Whatever it was, was keeping her locked away for the time being.

"Briar, if you can hear me, you need to come back. Lyra has grown tired of waiting, and if she thinks you are truly gone, she'll bring Fern here, just to see if killing her in front of you will wake you. You *have* to snap out of this if you want your sister safe." He watched for some response, but she gave nothing. His stiff posture loosened and he sat on a side chair. At least he could get a few moments of quiet here. He'd been coming daily to check on her and force feed her so she didn't wilt away to nothing. They did this to her, so he would sit at her side and pay his silent penance for bringing her here.

"She can't do it alone." Jumping from his seat, Doyle found Briar blinking back at him, her eyes finally filled with life once more.

"What?" Instead of answering, she fell from the bed and, on her hands and knees, proceeded to throw up.

$$\wp\ \wp\ \wp$$

"What are you looking up?" Melody leaned over Ana's shoulder before the elf could close the book. "Spell removals? What for?"

Ana had spent the last two months searching for answers to where her mother's cloaking spell had gone wrong and stolen Toron's memories. She still didn't know for sure if Erin's boyfriend could be her lost brother, and she'd managed to keep those thoughts to herself. She asked Erin to bring him by, or get together for a meal, but Erin seemed adamant on keeping him away from all things mystical.

"Just research." Ana gave a reassuring smile and hoped Melody wouldn't probe. She felt the witch's eyes searching hers but the door chiming in the background drew away her attention.

"Welcome to *Mystifying*!" Melody called cheerily. Ana watched Melody go to show the customer around before she packed away the book. Once again, the information she sought seemed to elude her. The spell that was placed on Toron was complex, but it shouldn't have done anything to his memories of life before going through the portal. Without knowing what went wrong, there was also no way to know what further damage might be done by just releasing the cloaking magic. And so she remained in a conundrum: If Gabe *was* Toron he would be completely unaware…and she would also have no way to *prove it* unless she could lift the spell.

"Ana, do you mind ringing her up? I need to run."

"Of course, have a good day." Ana waved goodbye as Melody hurried off to her summer course. Menial small talk made the transaction quick and easy, and Erin ran through the door just as the customer was leaving.

"Sorry I'm late!" In the last months she'd let her hair grow out some and now had it styled in an asymmetrical bob. She'd dyed it black with blue highlights, and already seemed to be debating the next color combination. "Gabe was trying to tell me I should quit."

"What?" Ana looked up in surprise. Erin didn't talk about Gabe that often, almost like she was trying to keep even his name away from any association with her magic. No matter how Ana attempted to pry for more information, Erin remained guarded and tight-lipped about him.

"Well, I can't exactly tell him this is more than a *job*. He was trying to be a wonderful boyfriend and have me follow my passion of photography," Erin explained. She sat on a stool and held her head in her hands. "I feel like I can't even remember when my life was that simple. Now I'm juggling normal human girl life with fae learning her magical trade...how do you do it, Ana?"

Ana smiled sadly and shrugged. "I didn't have any other options. *You do.* You could tell him, include him in this new world."

"Yes, magical abilities, being a fae halfling, erebi attacks...*that's* the way to sweep a man off his feet."

"From everything I gather, you've known him most of your life. This is not a..." Ana searched for the appropriate word, "a *fling*. But if you are planning on being with him for more than a few years, you are going to have to tell him. I already told you that your aging will slow immensely now that you have reached full maturity. He *will* notice that you never seem to look older. It may take him a few years, but he's going to catch on. And what if you want to have children? They very well could have abilities-"

"Stop! Please...ugh, give me a task to do." Erin leapt from the stool, but not before Ana caught the look of intense fear that crossed her features.

The elf sighed and relented. Ana set her up with instructions for an herbal brew and watched her get started. "Are you able to stay after today? We could work on some fighting moves. You are getting more in control of your powers, but you need to start working with a weapon."

"I still haven't figured out telekinesis. You *are* sure I have that ability right?" Erin asked with trepidation.

"That is what the spell revealed. It's a very hard skill to master, and it may be a weaker power. But you have been able to heal and call upon nature to help you. Powers take energy from you; if there is a long battle going on, it is more efficient to fight with a weapon and have your powers to fall back on."

"You know, even with my increased use of powers, we haven't had another erebi attack. Nothing has come through that portal," Erin pointed out.

"Yes, so this is the perfect time to make sure you are trained to the fullest." Ana didn't want to say it to the others, but she worried they were just dealing with the calm before the storm. Erebi coming through the portal before could very well have been sent to get intel; if they were right, and Kali was behind the increase in portal activity, Ana was sure she would not be stopping until either the job was done or she was dead.

"The fae sighed. "Fine, but I have a date tonight. I've been here late every day this week, and Gabe just moved in two weeks ago. We still have to finish getting him unpacked, for the sake of my shins."

"You know, Melody and I could come and help. That *is* what friends are for, after all. No magic talk of course, but-"

"Really it's okay. Just, let's plan for another night okay?" Erin stood with the bottle of freshly combined herbs and added a label to it before sliding it onto the shelf.

"You know, it's about time I switch out some of the counter inventory." Ana tried not to flinch at losing another chance to see Gabe. "If you go in the back room you'll see a box marked 'counter'. Can you grab that? I like to switch up the display now and again, and I haven't done it since...your arrival." She felt a pang at the thought.

Aria used to switch out the cases. It had always bothered her when she had to look at the same things too often. Ana lost track of it, considering she'd never had to worry about it before. She may have been busy training Erin, researching spells, and worrying about her brother, but Aria was always there in her mind. She had sent her friend off to her death, and now, months had gone by and she was *still* not able to avenge it. Kali had a plan, and unfortunately Ana did not have any moves until Kali took her next one.

Ana turned quickly at the sound of Erin's gasp and found her staring into the box with her mouth unhinged.

"Is something the matter?"

"I..." Erin covered her mouth, and when she looked up she had tears shining in her eyes. Ana's heart started to race, wondering what could have upset her. She came to Erin's side and peeked inside the box, half expecting a dead animal. Instead she found the items that Aria had recycled the last time, sitting peacefully where the late fae had left them.

Erin reached in a trembling hand and pulled out a dagger that was laying inside. She turned it over and looked closely at the engravings.

"Erin, what is it?" Ana's voice was gentle as her eyes tracked the tear rolling down Erin's cheek.

"I've seen this before, in my dream. It was my father's. He had it with him during his last battle..."

"Let me see what I can find about that," Ana said, pulling her concerned gaze away from Erin after a long moment.

"Ah, here it is!" Ana found an old file that had never been scanned into the computer system. "Sometimes people bring us stuff that they believe has mystical properties. Sometimes those that travel through the portals bring items or trade items from their realms. Ever since I arrived here, I've kept track of what came through. The owners before me, the previous protectors of the portal, did the same, they just did so on paper."

It was about two hours after Erin found the dagger, and Ana noticed she still had it with her. Ana read through the paper quickly before handing it over. "It looks like a fae gave it to them before going through the portal. They wrote that it belonged to a great warrior, and close friend of the fae. They died in battle, and she couldn't bear to keep it with her." Ana found Erin's eyes shining.

"It must have been Sinopa. She was my mother's friend, and she was a fae. She could change into a fox." Erin paused to chew on her lip. "She was there at the last battle, but I didn't see what happened to her. After my father was killed the memory ended. So, this really was his then?" Erin asked, staring at the dagger like a precious jewel.

"It's from Loinnir, your mother must have given it to him. There are some notes here at the bottom, so they must have done some research on it." She turned the paper so Erin could see the tidy scrawl. "It is named *Willow*, and now it is yours."

"What?" Erin looked at her in surprise.

"Of course, it belongs to you. That dagger has been in this shop longer than I have, and it *never left*. It's been waiting for you all these years." Ana reached out and closed Erin's fingers around it with an encouraging smile. "It looks like we just found out what weapon you will be using."

.℘ .℘ .℘

"Lyra, just give her a minute!" Doyle stood over Briar's pale form as she managed a few bites of bread to try and settle her stomach. As soon as Briar woke from her trance, Lyra had been notified and showed up only minutes later. Doyle told her calmly what Briar said when she woke, and Lyra kept asking question after question, trying to figure out what Briar had seen and what she meant.

"We have been waiting for weeks for her to show any sign of life. Now she finally does something useful, but she won't say anything helpful! My sister must be stopped before she rips this world apart more than it already is! I don't have time to just sit around and wait for this fae to have a meal and work out what she is and is not going to tell us!" Lyra screeched though her pointed teeth, her long ponytail whipping as she jerked her head toward Briar.

"Do you know what my life has been like for the past few weeks?" Briar's voice broke through with some of her old strength. Her eyes regained some of their color, and she looked ready to rip Lyra's daggers from their sheaths and stab her with them. Lyra seemed to notice the look she was getting, which only made her eye the fae with surprised respect. "I have been mentally and physically living all the ways this *idea* of yours can go wrong. Over and over I've watched and *felt* all of us die. I've lived *thousands* of ways your sister beats us, tortures us, and kills us. You gave me that cursed ring to touch, and because you ripped my wings away, my powers - and my control over them - were weak. I had no way to navigate the bombardment of visions. So I'm *sorry* the agony I've been stuck in has been inconvenient for your timeline."

Doyle stood gazing at the beast of a woman that sat beside him. Her hands were shaking and her usually tawny skin was pale, but she held Lyra's stare and refused to turn away. "I don't have an answer for you. All I know is in all those visions, we failed. Any little changes we made did nothing to the end event. The queen *always* won." She shrugged tiredly. "So all I can tell you is you can't do this on your own, unless you just secretly have a death wish. I have no way of knowing who to go to for help, or if there even *is* anyone who *can* help us. When I am not in their presence and don't have something that belongs to them, it is very hard for me to grasp any kind of future they might have. So if you don't mind, I'm going to give my pounding head a break for five minutes, and eat this damn piece of bread before my body shuts down completely, and you don't have *any* hope of finding a way to bring down your sister."

With a glare a fae had no right possessing, Briar tore away a large piece of bread and shoved it in her mouth.

Chapter Thirteen

Erin was in her own world, lying on her stomach, her laptop propped up in front of her, and music blasting over her speakers. She was lost in concentration, trying to pick out her favorite photographs to update her website. Gabe chuckling drew her attention. She turned and found him grinning at her, his book still held open in his hands, his back propped up against the headboard. This was the first day since he moved in that they both had off work with nothing left to unpack, so they'd been enjoying most of it together in bed. He'd been quietly reading while she worked, but now his eyes glittered with amusement.

"Something funny in your book?"

"No, I'm finding my amusement elsewhere."

"Is that so?" She closed her laptop, shutting the music down mid-word.

"I kept being distracted from my book by your feet swinging in my face." He grinned at her. "While they are adorable feet, and they were swinging right in time to the music, they are a little hard to read through."

"Man, you've only just gotten unpacked and you are already clearly tired of living together. Well, it was fun while-" She never finished her teasing, because he'd sat his book aside and then reached over to grab her and pull her on top of him. Her lips danced with his, and she let out a contented sigh when his hands moved up her waist and back, coming to cradle her face so he could deepen the kiss.

"I think," he was a little breathless, "we both know that I do not have any regrets about moving in with you." He rolled so they were both laying on their sides, their noses almost touching. "How is the website going?"

"Almost done, I was just deciding between some photos for the reel at the bottom. It's so hard to pick between them."

"Do you want me to look at the ones you are stuck on? Let you know what I'm drawn to?"

"Yeah, that sounds good actually." She started to lean up to grab her laptop, but he pulled her back down next to him.

"I"m not ready for you to leave yet." He kissed the top of her head and warmth filled her from head to toe. She'd never felt so loved, and feeling so now made her heart ache. She felt so full that she was only just now realizing how empty she'd been before. Of course, the happiness set off the guilt that churned in her stomach. She still needed to tell him the truth. He was giving her all of himself, but she was still holding back so much.

"Do you think I could get signed up for your Body Combat class?" Her darker thoughts had pulled her away from the moment. Now she was thinking of all the practice she'd been doing with Ana and Melody; she was thinking of moves she'd failed to block and other bruises she'd gotten but had been able to heal.

"Sure, there's room. You've only taken a few yoga classes though, now you want to take up some combat courses?"

Since they'd started dating, she'd taken a few classes his gym had to offer and spent some time there working out, but she hadn't asked to take a class with him before. She thought it might be embarrassing to stumble through the class with Gabe as the teacher. She was more confident now in what her body could do, and thought the combat class could help her with her fighting.

This was a moment she could take to be honest with him. She could tell him everything she'd been dealing with, she could open up and see where it took them. She opened her mouth to say she had something she needed to talk to him about. She had every intention of doing so, but then he started tracing fingers up her spine. Such an easy motion, thoughtless in its intimacy, and the words grew thick in her throat.

"It doesn't hurt to know the right way to punch, does it? Plus, I get to see my man at work. I have to make sure none of the women in your class get any ideas." She thought he'd chuckle at her joke but instead she felt his body go tense near her. His hand stilled, and then he moved to tilt her face up to his.

"Erin, you are still safe aren't you?" His gaze was serious and concerned as his gaze darted between her eyes.

"I'm safe. I just thought..." She'd already pushed the truth, and couldn't think of another way to avoid why she actually wanted to take his class. He didn't seem to need the rest of her explanation, however; instead he pulled her flush against him, like he could use his body as a shield to anything that might try to hurt her.

"You haven't said anything else about your parents or what they were involved in. I thought you weren't really doing anything else with that. The idea of you having to punch someone to protect yourself just gave me a mini panic."

She cursed herself and her fear and snuggled in closer. He suddenly felt so far away from her. "Do you think you could read to me for a while?"

He let out a small sigh and she knew he was aware she was changing the subject. She was letting this void of her omission grow more and more between them. After a moment, he nodded and reached over to grab the book he'd been reading. She let his deep voice wash over her, letting the rumble in his chest sooth her. His fingers started up their thoughtless task of tracing her spine and brushing through her hair. She should be luxuriating under his tending. Instead she sat frozen, almost afraid to breathe, because she knew it was all going to come crashing down sooner rather than later.

.℘ .℘ .℘

Doyle was in the practice room, using his downtime to take out some frustrations on a dummy. He was just noting that his blade needed to be sharpened when the door slammed behind him. He nearly jumped out of his skin and turned on his heel, sword ready, when he spotted Lyra. Her arms were crossed, her brow raised, as she looked from him to the sword. "I need your help." He wasn't surprised to hear the words. The queen had noticed the heirloom missing from her belongings, and her wrath had been raining down on all of the realm while she tried to figure out the culprit. The only good Doyle saw from it was that Briar had been given some respite as Lyra worked to make sure she was at her sister's side, in union with her, before eyes could turn her way.

"With the fae?" After their little confrontation, Briar had been silent about what she had been living through in her visions, or what they could do to find a way around what were apparently their impending deaths.

"Not exactly," Lyra responded. "I need to be seen in complete alliance with my sister. You are my most trusted, and she is well aware of it. I am going to offer your help in Loinnir." Doyle looked up at that. Of anything she might ask, sending him back to Loinnir seemed so far off track from what they wanted to accomplish. "I've already spoken out against her decision in allowing Kali to go there. I want to be able to go to her and say that, while I don't trust Kali and her brother, I do want the best for our realm, and if taking over the others will bring us more power than I want it done as quickly as possible. You are a skilled fighter, and you are quite likable, though..." She swiveled a sly look in his direction, "I can only guess how you manage that."

"Well thank you so much for that vote of confidence."

"You know what I mean. With all that you've been through, you aren't exactly trusting or forthcoming, and with all those battle scars, you aren't even easy on the eyes. But still you manage. You draw others toward you, and that can be used to further our cause. Especially with the fae we have locked away. First I have to gain the trust of my sister, but then *you* are going to gain the trust of our little friend. You stood up for her once, she trusted you to take her sister home...she'll trust you where she'll question me. Tonight I'll tell Flereous you are going. I don't want you to stay long, just long enough to help Kali, be seen, and then return to me to deal with our *other* issue."

"I think you are overestimating my influence on Blue."

Lyra shot him a smile that made him uneasy before she shook her head. "No, I know women. She needs someone to trust right now, and you'll make it easy for her to trust *you*. Go and tell her goodbye." She shot to her feet and tapped a finger on her leg, just above her favored blade. "Take the lizard boy with you. He's been nosing around the girl. Make it clear we are trying to use her for information about Loinnir; it will double our efforts if he thinks we captured her in order to help Flereous along."

Doyle could do nothing but nod, when he really wanted to argue against getting Malux involved in any way. From what he could tell Malux was not a lovesick puppy, but an injured bird just waiting for his wings to heal so he could fly away. Malux might want the queen gone just as much as they did, but he'd also spent longer than Doyle had been alive being tortured into submission. That inner conflict could get them all killed.

"I'll see if I can find him." With a nod, Lyra left him. He turned his sword over in his hand, looked at the dull blade, and then sliced into the dummy with all his force. Then he left the room to follow the orders he would much rather ignore, leaving behind the dismembered dummy and the borrowed blade.

℘ ℘ ℘

"Ana, let me help you."

Ana looked up from her book and found Melody watching her from across the room. "I'm just doing some studies; you should be focused on that paper you have to write."

Melody rose from her chair and sat down her laptop. "Tell me what is going on with you. For *weeks* now you have scoured every magical text we have. You've been looking things up online, and I *know* you hate to do that. You are looking for something specific. Just tell me what it is. Maybe I can help."

"You are too intuitive." Ana sighed and pushed the book away from her. "I'm researching a reversal spell that my mother taught me. A spell made to hide all magical aspects of someone-"

"Your brother?" Melody whispered. "You are trying to find him again?"

"I'm trying to make sure the reversal spell would still be safe if something had gone wrong with it. It had worked when my mother cast it, but something must have gone wrong if he wasn't there when I came through the portal behind him."

"Do you think you could find him if you reversed the spell? It could be dangerous though, he'd be living like a human, and you don't know where he is. If all of a sudden he became 100% elvish...it could get him killed."

"I may..." She was afraid to talk. If she spoke the words aloud, and she was wrong, it would be like losing him all over again.

"Ana?"

"I may already know where he is. I haven't said anything but...I *think* Erin's Gabe is my Toron."

"What?" Melody blinked in shock and sat back in her chair.

"From everything she's said about him...we have matching tattoos on our wrists, he showed up at the group home and doesn't remember his childhood." Ana started pacing the floor. "If the spell had any weak points, it could have erased his memory of our elven home when he went through the portal. If he went through the portal and ended up in the wrong place, or even wandered from the store before I came through and had no memory of what happened because the spell had gone awry...he could have ended up in the home with Erin. It *could* be him. But clearly Erin doesn't want us around each other, because of the tension she already has with him from keeping secrets. If I can find the spell though...and meet him? If it *is* him, I can make him remember."

The sound of the doorbell below grabbed her attention. A quick glance at the clock showed it was time to open the store and Erin had probably shown up for her shift. "I have to go and get the store open, and let Erin in. You finish your paper before coming down. I know the second you set foot in the store you are going to be distracted." Ana gave a soft smile before setting off to go downstairs. She felt Melody's silence follow her, and did her best to cut off thoughts of their conversation while she headed to work.

.℮ .℮ .℮

What Briar wouldn't do to taste fresh air. What she wouldn't trade for a taste of fae water, fresh from the stream where she used to pick flowers with her mother. She wasn't sure which part of her soul she was missing the most today: her home, her wings, her mother...it was all gone, and now she was surrounded by stone walls with a dark realm's earth pressing down on her from all sides. The smallest thing drained her of energy, and she knew she was running out of time. She needed to figure out how to bring down the queen *and* try to find a way out of her situation. She wasn't stupid, if she proved useful she would be too valuable to let go. If she proved *useless*, well, then Lyra would take far more than her wings.

A short knock sounded at the door and it opened a moment later. Doyle and Malux entered, Doyle looking uncomfortable and Malux looking perfectly in place in Skia; ironic, considering he was the only one born human out of the three of them.

"I haven't seen anything new-"

"I know you have been working hard trying to help us bring a quick end to our wars, but I'm not here for that," Doyle interrupted. His eyes darted to Malux, and she quickly remembered the half dragon was a "pet" of the queen's. The queen they were trying to overthrow. She narrowed her eyes; while she understood his meaning

205

perfectly, she wanted to watch him squirm, thinking she might slip and mess up his plans. "If you aren't here trying to rip more visions from me, then why? Simply wanted to keep me company?" His gaze burned through her and she almost struggled to take in her next breath.

"Quite the opposite actually. I simply wanted you to know I am going back to Loinnir for a bit to help. I thought you might want to send your family a message." He stood with his back stiff, his face blank. She tried to read him for some hidden threat, but he seemed sincere. With a flick of his wrist he pulled a pen and sheet of paper from his pocket and handed it over. "If you wish to write a note to your sister you may. I'll find a way to pass it along." He leaned closer until he filled her space and they shared breath. "I will, of course, have to read it beforehand, so if you speak of me, use *kind* words."

"Then I suppose I won't speak of you." Briar snatched the paper like a child being given candy and sat down even though she wasn't sure what to say. In the background Malux's staunch face broke into a grin and she heard him chuckle. Doyle turned slowly to glare at the other man and Briar hid her face quickly by looking down at her blank sheet.

After a deep breath, she decided to just scrawl a simple note of how much she loved and missed everyone, and that she was doing well. It was hard to write down the words that she was okay when her back still screamed at the loss of her wings, and she could very well be trapped in a strange realm for the rest of her life, but she managed, and hoped they would take her words and find comfort.

Because she couldn't help herself, she scrawled a little comment at the bottom just to see if Doyle would actually read it. Then she did a quick fold until the paper was shaped like a flower and handed it over. Her fingers brushed Doyle's and she had a flash of the vision from before, the one of him holding her like she was all that was precious. She jerked her hand away before she could fall deeply into the vision.

"Well, I'll happily pass this along. I shouldn't be away for long." She felt his gaze resting on her and felt like he was trying to tell her something, but she didn't understand. "I brought up some food for you too, let me grab that." He returned a moment later with a tray of more bland food from Skia. She nearly exploded with jealousy that he was going to go into Loinnir, and would eat and drink the food her body was so desperately craving. If she were a weaker being, she would beg him to bring her back something; instead she chewed on the inside of her cheek and eyed the tray. "Thank you. I guess I shall see you soon."

His fingers brushed hers, and the gentle caress made her back stiffen. Without a backward glance he left the room, but Malux eyed her silently.

"You can't trust him," he finally said, his eyes hooded as he leaned casually against the wall.

"I'm sorry?" She looked into the broken face and tried not to choke against the first bite she took.

"I know Lyra and Doyle are planning something and using you to do so." Briar tried to force her expression into a mask before she confirmed his idea. "I"m not exactly an idiot. Lyra has been brooding around here wanting her sister dead longer than I have. The queen is no friend of mine, so you have no need to worry about me outing you. But you should know, Doyle has blind trust when it comes to Lyra. You should keep that in mind when you share any visions. If he has to choose, he'll always choose her. For all that's wrong with Lyra, she saved him and took him in. He won't forget that. *You* shouldn't either."

He watched her carefully to make sure she understood, then gave her a small nod before leaving her alone once more. She thought about the visions she'd had thus far, and felt the pain of a blade cutting into her as Doyle discovered she planned to betray Lyra. She had already been aware he could be a danger to her, but Malux's words only made her feel more alone.

Curious about the queen's pet, Briar rose and touched the door handle Malux had just released, and focused on the energy he'd left behind. A second later she had to pull away before the pain and darkness pulled her under. Malux didn't leave a clear memory or vision behind, but a swirl of chaotic pain. She could hear his screams and feel his body being shredded from the inside. She might not be able to trust

Doyle, but she believed Malux when he told her he was no friend of the queen.

.℮ .℮ .℮

A few hours later, Erin was finishing up a project while Ana worked on a protection charm for a customer. Up until this customer, Ana had walked her through all the steps of whatever custom request came in. Ana had been taking the time to show her how to mix herbs, combine crystals, and choose the correct candles to bring about the best results. It was all very confusing, and knowing what she now knew, Erin wasn't sure how simple things like crystals and herbs could really make a difference.

When this customer came in, however, Erin instantly recognized the way the woman skirted around the store, her eyes darting to every corner. She remembered seeing kids that had come from homes far worse than any she had ever seen. How they seemed to jump at the smallest things. Ana seemed to recognize something in the woman too, because she gave Erin a small project to occupy her time. She helped the woman in a corner of the store, away from the front door so the woman wouldn't startle if someone came in. When they were done Ana moved back around to the desk to get the woman her change, and Erin saw her pull out a card of a woman's shelter. Their eyes met and Ana gave her a small smile, her eyes sad, before she went back to the woman. They talked for a few more minutes and Erin sat at the counter, waiting for Melody to return from class.

Ana came to her side and they both watched the woman leave, gripping her small parcel to her chest. "Is she going to be okay?" Erin asked quietly.

"I think so. The charm I gave her is pretty strong, and I hope she calls the shelter if she needs it. Sometimes we don't just need protection from things coming in through the portals."

"Don't I know it." It slipped out before Erin thought about it. She froze and felt Ana's gaze fall on her, but Melody arrived, hands full, so Ana rushed forward to open the door. The younger woman juggled a pile of books and a laptop bag, and plopped it all down on the counter with a sigh of relief.

"How are your summer courses going?" Erin asked with a raised brow.

Melody shrugged. "I kind of wish I took the summer off. I miss sleep." Erin grinned. She'd only taken a few classes to help her with business and photography, but those classes were taken along with two jobs at the time, she could see where Melody was coming from. Melody got distracted by her cell phone and Ana sat next to her with a sigh.

"What do you say to practice since we are empty at the moment?"

"Sounds perfect." Erin noticed Melody's eyes flash toward them before darting back down to her phone. Ana apparently noticed too, because she paused and watched Melody for a moment before turning her attention back, a small crease between her eyes. "I think we should practice with weapons today. Work on your hand to hand."

"I still haven't been able to communicate telepathically. Shouldn't we work on that?"

"Well, in battle, powers can be hard to work. Telepathy is useful, and we should work on that more, but I want to make sure you can defend yourself if anything happens." Erin wanted to focus on expanding her powers more. It still took a lot out of her when she used them, and she knew she needed to keep working on them. When she looked back into the elf's eyes she found the woman watching her with a small smile.

"Okay, we'll try to work on that for a bit first." Ana motioned to the back of the store and they sat in the corner, the same area where they had done the spell to find out what powers she had. Ana crossed her legs and sat like she was about to meditate; Erin followed suit and worked on opening her mind and loosening her muscles. Ana concentrated on her and started to communicate with her mind.

"You want to focus on me and what you want to say. Then you push it from your mind. You have to keep your focus until you get the hang of it." She nodded, and tried to push away the worries of whether she would be strong enough, if she would master her powers, and what would

happen if *or when* Gabe found out about this secret life of hers. *"You have to open your mind, almost until it feels fuzzy."*

She felt the intrusion of Ana's voice and gave herself a mental shake. She *had* to do this. She stared into the eyes of the woman before her and tried to think of the words to the song that never ends. She sang the words over and over in her head and tried to push them out and away. She thought of getting the song stuck in Ana's head and nearly laughed, but thought the elf might look down on her if she broke into laughter when she was *supposed* to be concentrating. Then she felt an odd surge of energy. She thought something was finally happening so she tried harder to push the words away, but then Ana leapt to her feet and ordered Melody to lock the front door.

Erin gaped as both women flew into action; Melody rushed forward to lock the door while Ana grabbed her dagger from under the counter. The door to the back room jerked open, and the sight that greeted her stole her breath away. She'd expected to see the same infection erebi from before. Instead, a woman swayed at the mouth of the portal, her face nearly engulfed in the pitch black of the infection apparently taking over her body. They could do nothing but stare in horror as the victim clawed at the darkness. It pulled and stretched her features as she tried to fight it off. She had large golden wings that seemed to fill the space of the backroom. They were stretched out to their fullest, and shivered as they too tried to bat away the erebus. Her scream cut off abruptly, and she dragged in a shuddering breath before falling to her knees.

"What *is* that?" Erin moved to try and help, but Ana stopped her from entering the office with an outstretched arm. "We have to help her, she's dying!"

"We can't touch her...it might infect us too. It's too late. There's nothing we can do for her." Erin caught Melody's shoulder and used it for support, and the three women watched in horrified silence as the darkness spread through her wings. It was an awful sight to see, the beauty of her golden wings turn black, and then gray. Erin screamed when she realized the black energy was eating away at the wings. Soon they were gone completely, and the dark energy worked down the victim's body as she collapsed forward, utterly still.

Ana stumbled backwards, drawing the others away from the office. "Is she...dead?" Melody questioned softly.

Ana nodded. "The erebi are getting closer to this realm. We need to get rid of her body; we can't risk the infection escaping somehow and getting free. I've never seen a possession like this before; I've only seen in spread through blood."

"It's the middle of the day, we can't exactly go around carrying a body with us and not get strange looks." Erin spoke in hushed tones while she stared at the body on the floor at her feet. She kept seeing her mother's body as her veins had turned black and her body began to change. She wondered if the infection would have eaten away her wings, too, if she'd still had them. She thought she might throw up when Melody snapped at her.

"A fae just died and there was nothing we could do about it. This is not exactly the time for sarcastic comments."

Erin looked up in shock, her mind still dancing between the present and the past. Melody was looking at her with fury, and Erin realized belatedly how her words might have sounded harsh. She *did* tend to fall back on sarcasm when she was upset about something. She opened her mouth to apologize, but Ana stepped in. "She *is* right though, Melody. We can't go anywhere with her until it gets dark. Even if I pull the car around the back of the store, it would still be too easy for us to be spotted."

"Won't..." Erin started to speak but quickly paused and glanced toward Melody. The witch refused to meet her eyes, but Ana looked at her patiently. "The erebus bodies just disappeared, won't that happen?"

"If a fae body is placed on the ground outside it can be taken in by nature when its magic is released, but because she was infected by such dark energy...I don't think nature will take her."

They walked to the center of the store and Ana tucked her weapon back under the counter. Melody went to switch off the shop lights so no one would try to come in.

"Life is never dull with you guys," Erin mumbled under her breath, unable to think of anything else to say.

Ana stepped between her and Melody, and Erin caught the witch rolling her eyes toward her. She certainly wasn't winning the woman over. "If the erebus didn't fully take over before she died, and she's no longer fae so nature won't take her, we need to figure out another way to take care of her body. Can't exactly have the police come and pick her up, can we?" The elf sighed tiredly. "Erin, why don't we get started looking into what to do with her?"

Erin nodded mutely while Melody slipped away upstairs. She came back down with a blanket, which caught Ana's attention. "I'm just going to cover her. I don't like the idea of her just laying on the floor like that..."

"Okay, but be careful not to touch her, just to be safe."

Melody opened the door, but was quickly thrown back onto the ground. Ana was on her feet in an instant as a dark shadow darted across the room. "Erin, go to Melody!" Ana ran to get her weapon again, while Melody struggled to her feet. Her heart drummed in her chest and adrenaline pulsed through her. Erin came beside Melody but didn't offer her a hand; Melody was already on her feet, and looked like she might hit her before she accepted her help. Erin turned, and when she finally got a good look at the monster she realized it was the fae, her veins as black as her eyes. Her hands were turning into claws and the skin on her arms were completely black.

"Mel, are you okay?" Ana yelled.

"I'm fine...the erebus actually *turned* her?"

Before Ana could answer, the erebus flung itself at her and knocked her to the ground. Ana stabbed at it, but it rolled away and landed between them and Ana. Erin saw the elf's face pale as the erebus drew closer to where she and Melody stood.

"The wait is almost over, Kali is ready for her revenge." The erebus's voice was oddly high, and sent goosebumps racing down her arms. It moved to pounce again, but Melody thrust out her hands, and the erebus froze in her spot. Ana didn't hesitate, instead lunged forward and buried her dagger into its chest. With a high wail, the erebus made one last attempt to get to her, but Erin's feet finally seemed to break free from imaginary cement and she leapt. She grabbed the erebus from behind and pulled it onto the ground, rolling away as soon as it hit the ground next to her with a thud. With one last hiss, the erebus was dead.

They all watched in silence, hoping the infection would leave the body, but it never changed back to the fae. The erebus had destroyed her, body and soul. Finally, the body dissolved into smoke and dissipated. Everyone stood frozen, staring at the space her body had just occupied, until Melody's cell phone began to chime a happy tune, startling all of them.

Chapter Fourteen

Ana stared silently as Melody raced up the steps to answer her phone, leaving her and Erin alone in the store. Erin was still visibly shaking from the encounter, her eyes lingering on the place the energy had disappeared into. The store had become too quiet; the light music that played in the background was almost ear-piercing against the hollow of the room. She looked around. A shelf had been knocked off of the wall, items scattered over the wooden floor. The door to the office was thrown open, and Ana could still feel remnant energy pulsing from the portal.

Giving herself a shake, Ana moved forward and shut the door to the office. When she went back to Erin, the halfling had moved, starting to pick up some of the fallen items. The fae's hands shook, and after a moment she let out a deep breath and turned dark eyes up to her. Ana had noticed Erin's eyes tended to change their color based on her feelings. They were hazel, and usually hovered at a light muddled green; right then, they were dark brown. "Erin, just leave it for a minute. Are you okay?"

"It just took her over…" Erin stayed on the floor, crouched on her knees. Ana had a feeling her friend was seeing more than just the fae they'd lost. The elf knelt next to Erin and laid a hand on her back. Ana sighed and retreated when her friend jolted under the touch. She heard Melody coming down the steps before the side door opened, and when the witch re-entered the store Ana saw a new glow to her. Melody's brown eyes were bright when they met hers, and she flashed a wink. Clearly she was up to something, but with Melody, Ana could only guess. Erin finally stood at her side, letting out a shaky sigh and giving herself a small shake. It seemed like both women were about to say something, but someone tapped on the front door, which had everyone freezing. Melody was the closest so she walked over slowly. "I'm sorry, some shelving got knocked into, we are currently cleaning up."

"Oh, is Erin still here? I just wanted to see if she had eaten yet and if she wanted to run out for lunch." Erin stilled next to her, and Ana knew who it was that stood on the other side of the door. Melody turned away but didn't look at Erin; instead her gaze fell on the elf, eyes wide in question.

"Go ahead and let him in, Mel." Ana spoke softly, but her heart was pounding and it felt like her throat was closing up. This would be the moment of truth. Erin ran ahead and hugged him when he came through the door. Then Erin turned and gestured towards the other women.

"Uhm, this is Gabe, Gabe, this is Melody and Ana." Erin returned her attention to Gabe with a sheepish smile. Her eyes turned lighter as Gabe wrapped an arm around her shoulders, wiping away the grief that had been there moments before. "Sorry about the store being closed...we had a bit of an accident."

"It's nice to meet everyone. Do you need help? I'm great at hanging shelves." Gabe was looking right at Ana, but she didn't dare blink back in response. She was frozen in place, drinking in every detail about the man in front of her. She tried to compare it mentally to the young boy she lost so many years ago: the blond curly hair, the bright green eyes that instantly reminded her of their forest at home...those eyes...

"Ana?" Erin raised a brow. "Everything okay?"

"Sure, we'd love help!" Melody chimed in, skipping ahead of them. She picked up one of the shelves that had been knocked off the wall and handed it over to Gabe. Both Ana and Melody looked down to his wrist and saw his tattoo.

Melody shot her a look; even without words, Ana knew she was asking if it was him: *her brother.* Even if everything else could be written off as a coincidence, she could feel it in her bones. He was family, they shared blood, and they might be the last survivors of their realm.

She returned the look with the smallest of nods and Melody gave her a sly smile she couldn't read.

Once Gabe had the tools in hand it only took him a few minutes to hang the two shelves. Erin passed the product up to him, and then it was like nothing had even happened.

"What did you guys do to knock those off the wall?" He asked as he put weight on one to make sure it was good to go. It didn't even budge under his strong arm.

"Uhm, I knocked a ladder into it. We were putting out new products."

"Oh well, Ana, any chance you can let Erin go a little early today?" He turned his eyes to Erin with an affectionate smile. "It's beautiful outside, I was thinking we could take the drive to Bodega Bay, get some dinner and you could shoot some pictures. I know you've been wanting to go there."

"Actually," Ana cut in before Erin could say anything, "I do need her for just a bit longer. If you can excuse us, I just need her upstairs for a moment. I promise it won't take long."

Erin looked confused, but followed her up to the apartment, leaving Melody and Gabe in the store. "Is something up, Ana?"

Ana didn't hesitate. She needed to get the words out quickly before she lost her nerve. "You remember how I have the same tattoo as Gabe? I told you it was a mark of my people, part of our tradition?"

"Sure..."

"I've mentioned that I had a brother to you, but I never told you the whole story..." Ana started to explain how she and her brother had tried to escape the war in their realm but were separated, and she was never able to find him. Then she told the half-fae about the spell, and how something must have gone wrong and erased his memory. Erin listened to the whole thing, but the more Ana got into, the deeper the crease between Erin's brows furrowed.

"You think *Gabe* is your long lost brother?"

Ana shook her head, "I *know* it. I thought it before, when you first mentioned the tattoo, but seeing him now..." A broad smile spread across her face. "I *know* it is him, but I still have to find a way to lift the spell that's cloaking him."

Erin stared at her with something akin to concern in her eyes. "Ana...I know it must have been really hard to lose your brother. But do you honestly expect me to believe that of all the people in all the world, I am dating *your* brother? Don't you think that is just a little too convenient?"

"No more than you walking into this store right as your powers started to ripen." Ana felt herself become defensive, but she kept her voice even. "Those with power are drawn to places and people with power. I don't think it was any coincidence you wandered in here, and I don't think it's any coincidence that you two were childhood friends and met again, *right outside this store.*"

"So the only reason I love him is because he is really an elf and has powers?" Erin's voice grew harsh. "What, the only people that would want me must be some kind of screwed up, right?"

"Erin-" The elf shook her head, desperation seeping slowly onto her face.

"I'll see you later Ana." Erin didn't give her a chance to explain further. She was out the door and down the stairs before Ana could say any more.

.℘ .℘ .℘

Doyle stepped through the portal with as much ease as he could muster with skin that felt aflame. The sensation would pass quickly enough, but portal travel for those with erebus blood was never a pleasant experience. To take his mind off the pain, he tried to imagine how life would be different if that ancient witch hadn't ripped the world into separate dimensions. Clearly she had been mistaken to believe separating the races would stop wars and the constant passage into death. The fae were the only ones to have managed to live peacefully all these years, and now even *that* peace had come to an end. Instead, the erebi kept in constant battle for the better realms, the humans fought amongst themselves, and the elves did their best to protect the portals.

The feeling of solid ground under his feet drew Doyle from his thoughts, and he blinked against the bright sky and vivid colors. Always a shock to the system. Two guards stood nearby and watched him acclimate. One with cat eyes and lizard skin gave him a small nod of understanding. As guards, they probably passed through almost daily to pass along news and messages. "I'm supposed to answer to Kali, where is she?"

"Who sent you?" The voice was thick and sounded like it was being dragged across gravel. The cat eyes watched him with suspicion. Doyle was well aware he was smaller, but he looked vicious. Using that to his advantage, he squared his shoulders and met suspicion with a glare of annoyance. "Lyra, sister to Queen Flereous."

The second guard spoke in a brutish language, so quickly he didn't make out what was said, but Gravel Voice gave a quick nod before pointing him on his way. With a mocking flick of his finger against his brow, Doyle saluted and then went on his way. It was a short distance, but there still should have been a fae in passing. Instead, there were only erebi as far as he could see, and the once-deep-purple moss under his feet was changing into a brown with blackened edges as he neared the center.

It was supposed to be a win for his kind; he knew that even as a cold hand reached into his chest and squeezed at his heart. It would still be some time before the erebi fully started to drain the realm of its magical energy, but he already felt the loss for the crisp air, bright, bold colors, and the continuous song of nature ringing out. Maybe the other races were not wrong in their assumption of his kind. Without the balance of the races, the erebi would just continue to drain their realm into dust. Now, Kali was making the effort to do the same for Eloas and Loinnir, and with no real magic remaining to protect it, Sula would then crumble under the erebi. They had no idea that the wars they wage among themselves are nothing in comparison to the wars and dangers happening just outside a thin film of separation.

"Stop! Please!"

Doyle's hand rested against the hilt of his blade as he quickly searched the area for the source of the cry. Fellow erebi continued to move with no concern, so it took him a moment to catch the flash of thick black curls of a woman running past him. Gold wings glinted against the sun, and then she was swallowed by the crowd.

Wanting to see if he could help, Doyle pushed past the moving bodies just as the fae fell to her knees. Her almond colored skin paled as she let out a banshee scream. It was then that Doyle saw the small boy clasped in the arms of an infection erebus. He had only a few seconds to act in order to save the boy, but stopped short and moved his hand away from his weapon. If nothing else, he needed to remember he was here to gain Kali's trust; saving a fae from an infection erebus was no way to do that. He wanted to tear his eyes away, but if he was going to allow it to happen then he had no right to hide from the consequence of his inaction.

Despite his burning desire to just end the boy's suffering quickly, Doyle knew that any movement to stop the erebus would bring question to his loyalty, so he watched in silence as the wisp of dark energy took hold of the young fae. Guilt cut into him as the boy released blood-curdling screams of agony. By the time the cries cut off, the boy's mother was in a sobbing heap on the ground. Once-soft skin hardened into a shell that reminded Doyle of volcanic rock, and the wisp moved on, leaving the boy to collapse lifelessly. Doyle knew when the boy rose once more, he would be nothing more than a shell for the infection's energy.

With a shaky breath he hadn't known he was holding in, he glanced once more to the mother fae, skin white as a sheet. If not for the heaving of her chest as she mourned, she could've been confused for dead. Erebi moved around her like she was nothing more than abandoned trash that they didn't care to pick up. There was nothing he could do, nothing that wouldn't bring questions of his loyalty, no matter how much his skin crawled to do *something*.

He moved on, knowing - even though the sight was gone - he would never lose the memory. Kali was behind this. Queen Flereous was allowing it. He needed to stay focused so he could get the queen away from her throne. He reached the stone castle Kali was using: an ancient structure used by the early fae while they were still used to needing walls to protect them from the other races. Since then, they'd abandoned true structures for smaller buildings closer to nature, and many of them simply empowered trees to grow their branches into a hut structure, or influenced grass and vines to grow tall and tangle into walls and a roof. They should have kept to the stone walls, but even still, he knew it wouldn't have saved them. The fae were peaceful creatures who would give up their own freedom in order to preserve nature.

The stone castle was held up more out of defiance of the years than from any actual structure, with vines climbing up the sides even as they began to turn black from erebus energy. Doyle wandered in, and it didn't take him long to find Kali. She gave him a wide grin when he arrived, and Doyle couldn't help feeling that those that thought he had a fearsome face had never looked into the face of true evil.

Kali, the daughter of an ancient, had stark white skin that made her visible even in pitch black. She had long onyx horns jutting from her head and solid black eyes to match. Her teeth came to points, and her grin read as a warning.

"Lyra's most trusted servant. You would be useful if *Lyra* was trusted." She tilted her head, and he wished she had pupils so he could tell exactly what she was looking at. "Lyra means to prove her loyalty by sending you. The easiest way to test her loyalty would be to kill you, and send you back to her piece by piece." She paused, and he knew she was waiting for a reaction. He stood stoic even as his pulse quickened, making his skin warm. "Better yet," she purred, "I shall test *your* loyalty. I've had a collector put out feelers for the most powerful fae. I mean to use them to bring an end to the elvin resistance, and I also hope to draw out an old enemy that should have died long ago. The collector will give you the names, and you will retrieve them."

"Of course."

"Bringing down Ainadelothien and the rest of the royal family will end my vengeance, and give our queen power over all the realms. Is that what you are here to help me with, or has Lyra sent you under false pretense?"

Doyle gave a brief bow. "I am here to serve my queen." He didn't need to elaborate that *Lyra* was *his* queen.

"Then Bogor shall lead you to the collector, and you may start your retrieval."

Bogor turned out to be a pock-faced erebus with a snout, and tusks bulging from his bottom jaw. He was clearly no more than a brute; the small conversation Doyle started was answered with a snort and snarl. He got his names and locations for the collector, and was then shown a room to rest in before beginning his work the following day. He wished to go outside and watch the night sky come alive, but knew eyes were watching. Instead, he remained in his broom closet of a room and tried to remember why Ainadelothien sounded familiar to him. He focused on that rather than the list of names whose lives were now entrusted to him. Lives that would be *ruined* because of him…lives like Briar's. If she were still in this realm, he was very sure that her name would be on this list. He didn't sleep; closing his eyes only brought up the image of the fae mother and son. More lives against his name...two more checks against his kind.

So who was Ainadelothien, and why did Kali hold such a grudge against her?

.℘ .℘ .℘

"Are you okay?" Gabe asked. They'd driven their separate cars back to the apartment to grab Erin's camera, and then take one car to the bay.

"Yeah, I think I'm just getting hungry." Erin gave a warm smile and took Gabe's hand. They were almost to Bodega Bay, but it wasn't a short drive from the city and there had been a tense undertone to their ride.

"When we get there I can run ahead and put in our name if you want to walk a bit and get some shots in. I'm sure there will be a bit of a wait."

"Sure, that sounds good." Erin absently turned their entwined hands so she could look at Gabe's wrist. She let go so she could trace the design with her finger. "Don't you think it's odd that this never stretched or faded? You got it as a kid...it should have stretched out..."

228

She didn't want to believe it. How could it be possible for Gabe and Ana's brother to be the same person? How could he possibly be an *elf*?

"I guess so, I try not to think about it much." Gabe shrugged. "I mean, who tattoos a kid? My guess is, I was abused or something, and that's why I don't remember. Every time I look at this thing or catch a glimpse in a mirror of the one on my back..." He shook his head in disgust. "It makes me sick. Even if I don't remember, I still feel this emptiness in my chest. I have much more pleasant things to think about, like the woman sitting beside me." Gabe took her hand back and laced his fingers through hers.

Erin watched him silently, processing his words. "You never told me how much they bothered you before. You never really talk about how hard it was to grow up as an orphan."

"It wasn't that bad, I had *you* with me. You were always my best friend, and you were there for me just like I was there for you." He shrugged. "And I got lucky with my foster homes, you had a harder time with that than I did." Gabe squeezed her fingers and finally pulled into the parking lot for The Tides. They got out to a salty breeze and the sound of seagulls calling to one another. "Go ahead, I'll put our names in. I'll text you when the table is ready, okay?"

Erin smiled and took her camera. She had no idea how she managed to find someone who *got* her. At first she'd been worried she might lose him because of what she found out about herself, but now she was worried she might lose him because of who *he* might be.

If Ana was right, then he was going to find out his whole life had been a lie. While it might be good for him to find out he has a sister, his parents and whole world are gone. Everything he thought about himself would be gone. She certainly wasn't going to tell him anything until Ana could absolutely prove it. Right now, they had a few coincidences that seemed to add up, but if Gabe was told everything and Ana ended up being wrong —or wasn't able to find a way to lift the spell placed on him — it might just break him.

.℘ .℘ .℘

"Well, she seemed to leave in a hurry," Melody commented lightly when Ana made her way back downstairs. To the elf's relief, the shop was basically back to normal, no indication of the danger that had weaseled its way in. The thought made her shake her head; so often Ana, Melody, and Aria had been the only ones to know about all of the supernatural beings that tried to come into Sula. So often, the rest of the human world was completely oblivious to the fact that there was only one little shop standing between them and potential chaos and disaster. *Hopefully they would be able to keep it that way...*

"Yeah, well...she was skeptical when she first walked in here, and that was just about her own power. The thought that the love of her life, her best friend, is the long lost brother of the woman who, not long ago, turned her life upside down? Having to face the reality that everything is connected? That's a lot to ask of anyone. I can't say that I blame her for being upset." She ran a slender hand down her face with a weary sigh. "So...what was that look about earlier, anyway?"

Melody gave her a perfect imitation of her earlier smirk. "I might actually have a way to lift the spell. Asher, Marisa's father, sent me the recipe for a potion. Which by the way," Melody grinned, "is only proof you should have told me about this sooner. He said you dip a lapis lazuli crystal in this potion and touch his skin with it," Melody explained. She hesitated, and her face took on a look of concern.

"I get the feeling there's a catch here?" She knew Asher and Marisa well; Asher was a warlock that came into *Mystifying* often, and his daughter was in Melody's Wicca group. She knew Asher's family was very involved in their magic, so she could trust his recipe.

"There's a special ingredient needed," the young witch murmured, her eyes landing on the pendant around Ana's neck. "It requires something organic from the home realm in order to work for whatever species is targeted." Ana reached up to touch the glass encasing the last piece of her home. The small teal flower had been given to her at her coming of age celebration, just months before the attack. She unclasped it with trembling fingers and dropped it into Melody's hand, feeling like she was handing over a piece of herself. "I'm sorry, Ana. If there was another way-"

"I know. We have to. Just let me know when it's done? I'm going to re-open the store before customers start to ask questions about us closing up in the middle of the day."

Ana didn't turn back, but heard Melody begin to gather ingredients before escaping to the quiet of the back room. She felt naked without the necklace, and did her best to push away the image of her father standing before her, how he smiled at her and held out a hand to pull her into a dance. She could still feel the light material of her elven gown swishing around her, the hall alight with glittering candles. When the image of her mother, brother, and father's guard came to her mind, she pushed it away with a violent shake of her head. There was a chance she could bring her brother back, but not the rest of them. Her home was *gone*, and she would do well to remember that unless she wanted her heart to break into pieces all over again.

Chapter Fifteen

Two days later, Ana felt the loss of her necklace as a heavy weight that could not be lifted. She assured herself that soon she would have her brother back, and the flower, the last thing from her home, would be forgotten in her joy. Melody joined Ana downstairs, holding a small black box and drawing her from her thoughts.

"It's finished, the rest is up to you." Melody smiled and handed over the box. Ana opened the top to peek inside and found the smooth blue crystal with gold flecks resting inside. The crystal for enlightenment. From what she'd (finally) found, it would serve to protect his existing awareness, as well as unlock the memories lost to him until now, as it restored his true form.

"Thank you, Mel. I don't know what I would do without you." Ana gave the witch a hug.

"Don't I know it." Both women turned as Erin came into the store. The day before had been her day off, and Ana hoped Erin would be open to talking now. Holding the cure for her brother had her wanting to run to him immediately. But she had to try and do things the right way. Erin had a lot she kept from him, and she deserved the time to tell him her side before his world came crashing down.

"'Morning," Erin said quietly, not quite making eye contact when she came in.

"How was your date?"

Erin's eyes met hers, and Ana could feel the fae trying to work out what to say. It looked like their conversation had not been forgotten, and it was time to test the waters.

"Melody has completed Gabe's cure. You should speak to him tonight and let him know what is happening."

Erin turned vicious in one breath. "You *really* believe he is your brother?"

"I know it's hard to believe, but yes. Once I touch him with this stone he will take his true elven form and be able to access the powers that go along with it. He will be his true self. You *must* want that for him." Ana tried to be gentle.

"Of course I do! I only want him to be happy. But what about his memories? Will *that* bring them back?"

"It should. I'm not sure how damaged they are. They could be suppressed because of the spell, or they could have been destroyed. I believe they will come back...but I'm not positive." Melody touched her shoulder and Ana knew she had to head out. She gave a nod in farewell and saw Erin didn't even seem to notice. Her eyes were far off as she thought through what was said.

"Why does it have to be so soon though? I could tell him about me and give him a little time to comprehend that first. I *know* how hard it is to find out you aren't who you thought you were. It might be nice to let him come to terms with that first."

"Erin, he and I have waited years. He's my brother, and he deserves to know that. Just as you deserved to know about who your parents were."

"Ana-"

"Erin," her voice became a little harsher, "he *is* my brother. I thought he was dead all these years, and now he is standing before me. If you found out your parents were alive, would you want to wait a little longer before being reunited? You have tonight to tell him, otherwise I'll do it." Ana stepped into the back office, trying to get some space. She wanted to have patience, but her mind was buzzing with anticipation. All she wanted was to have Toron back. She needed to know she hadn't *completely* failed her parents.

.℘ .℘ .℘

Doyle rose before the sun, desperate to escape the suffocation of his room. He hoped Bogor was busy today, and that he would be given more freedom to roam after bringing in the named fae the last two days. He wanted to deliver Briar's note, and maybe see if there was any information he could pick up by walking around with his ear to the ground.

Luck seemed to be on his side when he escaped the building without seeing Bogor. He'd just reached the outskirts of Kali's camp when he froze at the sight of a fox, not wanting to startle it. He knew what it was, but had never seen one before. His eyes took in the thick red fur and dark eyes that watched him warily. Touched with amazement, he crouched low on the ground and held out his hand, rubbing his fingers together in an attempt to draw the animal closer. It lifted one front leg like it might approach, but then turned and took off into the forest.

"Probably smart." He turned and continued the journey to Fern's home. What would they think if they saw Briar today? Some of her color had returned, but her hair and eyes were still dull in his realm. The glow of her skin was gone. And her wings...

There was nothing worse than the memory of her wings. For weeks he'd believed the had destroyed her. He spent hours looking at them in the glass case in Lyra's room...such a magical force contained in a box, waiting to be gifted to gain favor per Briar's vision. It nearly made him sick to his stomach to think of the queen holding something so precious. He caught sight of Fern's hut, set away just a bit from the rest of the fae town. Doyle paused, tucking himself behind a tree, and waited. There was movement inside, but he couldn't tell just yet if it was the young one he wanted or another family member, which he was determined to avoid.

Then he remembered his promise to read the note. After dealing with rounding up powerful fae the last few days, he had been too tired to think about it. Now he had time while he watched the hut to find out what Blue had tried to pass along. He grabbed it from the hidden pocket in his weapon's belt, rested back against the nearest tree, and unfolded it, knowing there was no way he'd be able to recreate the delicate flower she'd folded.

My lovely sister,

I know with your kind heart you have the horrible tendency to worry yourself sick. Please, for my sake, do not do so. I am overjoyed that you are home safe, and that gives me the strength to be in this strange realm and do what I am here to do. It is my truest heart's desire to be home with you again, but I want to know our realm is safe before I do so again. Until then, I shall spend every free moment dreaming of the taste of our water, the smell of our flowers, and the comfort of home.

All my love,

Briar.

PS. I believe I am developing an unhealthy attraction to Malux.
Next thing you know, the always-angry Doyle will begin to grow on me.

Doyle let out a snort and re-folded the note. Even locked in a dungeon, the fae still expelled energy to poke fun at him. A shadow passed by him, and he nearly jumped out of his skin when the small-statured Fern popped up next to him.

"I thought I saw you. Where is my sister?" Wondering how the mite got a jump on him, he quickly searched the nearby forest, but didn't see anyone else.

Looking at Fern was like looking at a completely different creature than the one he'd carried home not long ago. There was color in her cheeks now, her eyes were bright, but he could still trace sadness there. Probably on account of Briar, and having her realm overrun with his kind.

"She is still in Skia, completing her work." He held out the note. She reached out, but didn't take it from him right away. "It's okay, she wrote it before I left. I told her I was coming and she wanted to assure you she was well." Even though she was broken, had nearly died, and even now seemed to be a shell of the fae he'd first brought through the portal.

238

"Of course she would tell me she is fine, but is she really?"

Had she read his mind somehow? "She is fine. Of course, she *is* a fae in the erebi realm, so she is not as healthy as she could be, but she is doing her best to help us so she can return home." Fern snatched the paper from him but didn't open it. He didn't remember her being brave enough to question him, but maybe after being held hostage, and passing through the portal with him, she wasn't as shy as before. "You look well. I'm truly glad to see it. Is there a message you would like me to take back?"

The small fae looked away from him before shaking her shimmering gold curls. "No, the family is as well as can be, but you probably already know that the erebi are eating away at our realm, and our people." Her voice shook, "but our family is...as whole as can be."

"I'll let her know. I hope to return her to you soon." Big, clear eyes looked up at him, and he got the impression she didn't believe him. Then she scampered back to her home without another glance in his direction. He thought of the note, of the family he helped rip apart, and the other families he was ripping apart by helping Kali. If it helped bring down Flereous, if it brought peace to their realms, he had to believe it was worth it. With a look around the forest, he thought maybe, *maybe* he could help make things just the tiniest bit better for Briar for when she returned.

.℃ .℃ .℃

239

Erin started her drive home, her mind still buzzing from her argument with Ana. It hadn't taken the elf long to find a way to lift the spell, and now her time was almost up. What would happen when she told Gabe about being half-fae? What would he do when she told him he is likely an elf, and has a sister?

She groaned aloud and banged her head on the steering wheel after parking in front of her apartment. Once again she was getting home late, but instead of wanting to run up into Gabe's arms, she was dreading going inside. She finally willed herself to go up and found Gabe sitting with his feet propped up on the table watching TV.

"How was your day?" he called the second she closed the door.

"It was...fine, yours?"

She could hardly hear his answer over the sound of her heart pounding in her chest. "Exhausting. I did too many classes today. I actually want to head to bed but I wanted to wait for you to get home." He shut off the TV, stretched his arms over his head, and then came over to her. He pulled her into a hug, and his familiar scent enveloped her. Becoming desperate, she turned in his arms and found his lips.

For all she knew, after she told him, he would leave her. She found it hard enough to accept what she was, it would be asking far too much of him when she told him the truth. This could be her last time with him, so rather than asking, Erin deepened the kiss, and felt him react to her. His hands found her hair, and her skin prickled with goosebumps.

"What is this all about?" Gabe asked with a familiar light in his eyes, his voice deeper than before.

"Just kiss me," she demanded and pulled him to her again.

As they lay side by side some time later, Gabe wrapped his arms around her and pulled her against him. Usually Erin would love to be in the comfort of his warmth, but tonight the half-fae stared at the wall across from her and tried not to cry. She had to tell him before she completely lost her nerve. She took a shaky breath and whispered his name.

"I have something I need to tell you." She only got a grunt in response, so she turned in his arms to face him. "Gabe?" He was completely out, and she couldn't bring herself to shake him awake. Instead, she snuggled her head onto his chest, soaking up the sound of his heartbeat, and accepted the extra time.

.℮ .℮ .℮

His return was not celebrated. In fact, Doyle didn't think anyone even noticed as he strode into the caverns and made his way toward Lyra's room - not that he was complaining. His visit to Loinnir had been trying, the return to the darkened caves grueling, but after this meeting, he could return to his own room and collapse into sleep for a day before returning to the task at hand.

"Doyle! Back so soon?" Lyra stood and flashed a grin in his direction. Chaotic energy flowed off of her.

"Has something happened?"

"Yes, not only have I gotten my sister off my back after sending you to help that little wanna-be Kali, but our little pet has *finally* made herself useful."

"Briar had a vision?" As exhausted as he was, he became more alert at that information. He needed *something* to move them forward. He needed some end in sight to know he was doing the right thing. Lyra wasn't perfect, but she would be a far better queen than Flereous. As powerful as Lyra's sister thought she was, her entire reign was spent trying to appease the ancient ones rather than trying to move their people forward. The ancients, in their deep pit, only craved power; if allowed they would devour everything: souls, worlds, even fellow erebi.

"She did, though it took some convincing to get it out of her." Lyra folded herself into a chair, perfectly at ease, while his spine tightened.

"*Convincing?*" Dread filled him. He had worried about Lyra taking advantage of his absence, and now he wanted to race to Briar's room to see what state he would find her in.

Her eyes darted toward him, piercing even as she tilted her head and grinned. "Had to go a little easier on her this time. Pulling her wings only put her out of commission." She waved a hand as though shooing a fly. "She said we couldn't do it alone. She still doesn't know *who* it is we need, but she saw an amulet. A very powerful one, conveniently owned by my sister, a gift from her mother. Apparently I will need it in order to get the help we will need."

"Do you know where it is?"

"I've seen it before, but very rarely. I believe she keeps it in the vault with her *special* collections."

His stomach muscles tightened. "There is no way to get into that vault without her." He knew where she spoke of. Malux would also know it very well, as he once spent three months locked up in there while she tried to *tame* him. Only Flereous' touch could open the door thanks to an ancient magic. A ward was placed on the room, so only someone that entered with Flereous would be able to enter again and Flereous didn't exactly throw parties in there.

"Yes, the testy, untrusting little wench. However, when I pulled Briar's wings she told me to save them because I would need them. I think now is the moment. Not only are they fae wings, but wings from a seer. Many dark magics would prosper if feathers were used in the spells. My hope is she will take them to the vault to ensure they are protected. And I will carry them for her, get a look around, and see if I can't find the amulet. Even if I can't get it then, if I can find the location we might be able to get in again somehow. Maybe we could even force Malux to act out so he gets locked up again." She giggled to herself, and Doyle had the feeling she would love to see Malux locked away again. He wasn't sure what spurred the hatred between the two, especially since they had a common enemy, but it had existed since the beginning.

"When do you plan on gifting the wings to her?"

"I shall wait a day or so. You only just returned; if I'm too nice to her, she will suspect something."

"Sounds like you have it all planned out," Doyle mused. "If you are okay, then I believe I will find some rest. I had a busy visit to Loinnir. Kali had quite the to-do list for me."

"Of course. I appreciate your service. You helped put us in a decent position to make our next move. We shall talk more tomorrow." He bid her good evening and left her alone. It was nice to have their next step, but it could wait for the morning. While he was completely exhausted, the word *convincing* kept repeating in the back of his mind, and he felt the need to check on the fae. So Doyle made a left through the tunnels and headed toward Blue's room instead of the bed that was calling to him.

.℗ .℗ .℗

The next morning, Erin woke to an empty bed. A quick search of the apartment revealed a note on the fridge telling her Gabe had a personal training session and then would be home. She checked the time and realized that she'd slept in, and he would be back within the hour. To kill time, she pulled up some photos to edit and tried to ignore the nagging pull of the conversation to come. She'd bought herself one more night, but could not put it off any longer. It wasn't fair to him. After all, her news might bring him happiness, and that was something she had no desire to keep from him.

Seeing he would be home any minute, Erin got up to make some lunch. She'd just started frying bacon for BLT sandwiches when Gabe walked in.

"Cruel woman! Making bacon for a man that just pushed her to the brink of cardiac arrest with cardio." Gabe gave her a wide boyish grin and reached around to grab one of the finished bacon strips.

"I believe it would have been more cruel if I fed it to you *before* you left and sent you to work *smelling* like bacon. Then you might've been attacked." She grinned when he snorted with laughter, but her mind was racing over how to tell him the truth. *Gabe, you have a sister, and you are an elf, and Ana may be able to bring your memories back. I just have to take you over to the store so she can lift a spell placed by your mother.* Really, was there any good way to say such things? She thought of her own rocky emotions about being a half-fae. The only reason she'd come to terms with it was because she was able to see into her parents' lives. But according to Ana, the cure still might not give him his memories. There was a chance the spell had damaged them for good. If that was the case, she would be taking away everything he'd ever known as truth, and not giving much back.

She waited until he scarfed down a serving before taking a deep breath. "Gabe, there is something we need to talk about."

"I *knew* something was on your mind." He sat down the second serving he was picking up and gave her his full attention. "I wish you would stop waiting until things are eating away at you before you tell me." He reached across the counter to hold her hand. She wondered if he could feel her pulse hammering away.

"I know...I'm sorry, I just don't want you to think I'm crazy. You know I love you-" The doorbell rang and cut her off. Erin paused midsentence and stared at the door, wishing she had the power to see through wood.

"Hold that thought." Gabe rose to answer it, even as Erin told him to ignore it, but it was too late. He opened the door and found Ana standing on the other side. *Not yet, you stupid elf!* Erin violently tried to push the thought into Ana's mind, but either the elf did not hear or chose to ignore her. Gabe invited the elf in, and as they stood side by side Erin wondered how she hadn't seen the resemblance before. It was clear they took after different parents, but it was there.

"Ana, maybe now is not the best time," Erin cut in as Gabe and Ana made small talk about the weather outside. Ana's eyes flashed toward her and Erin knew the elf understood she hadn't told Gabe.

"I told you to tell him, Erin! He's my brother, and after years of thinking he was dead, it would be nice to have him back. I refuse to keep waiting while you drag your feet. You had your chance."

"I was trying to tell him! Go away!" Erin saw once again her thoughts were not passed on so she thought an ugly stream of curses. Of all the powers, of course *that* was the one she couldn't get a handle on!

"We have some sandwiches leftover if you want one? Erin just made them."

"Oh, thank you, but really I came to talk to you."

"Me?" Gabe's eyes looked between the two women in confusion.

Ana glided around the room, taking in everything about the apartment. "Erin pointed out we share the same tattoos, and I have some answers for you."

Erin watched Gabe's expression turn from confusion to surprise as his eyes glanced to his wrist. He looked at Ana. She drew back her sleeve to show hers

"I have one-"

"On the base of your neck, right? They are called moon glyphs. The one on the wrist means 'crown', the one on your back is 'balance'. I have one on my back too, but it means 'hope.'"

"I...I don't think I understand."

Erin stood helpless as Gabe looked at her. She was frozen in place and speechless. She wanted to say something, say *anything*, or walk over and hold his hand, but she stood frozen.

"It is the tradition of our people."

"Our-"

"This may be best if you just wait until I get it all out," Ana murmured, face sympathetic. "You see, there is a lot Erin has not told you. There is a reason she came to work in my shop and stays late most nights: she has been training since she found out the truth about *her* parents."

That got Gabe's attention. She knew he had so many questions about her parents, but he knew the topic was not allowed. Erin saw the quick flash of betrayal in his eyes and knew it was only going to get worse. She crossed her arms across her front as if it could provide some security. The intensity of Gabe's gaze became too much, and suddenly the wooden floors beneath her feet were incredibly interesting. She was used to being alone. She was used to people turning away from her. But she couldn't bear to look into *his* eyes and watch the love fade from them. Losing him would hurt far worse than any other loss she'd dealt with.

"Gabe, does the name Toron mean anything to you?" Ana asked hopefully.

He continued to glance between the women in confusion. "No...listen, what is going on here?"

"Your real name is Toron, you just don't remember," Ana rushed before she lost him. "Your markings are not human tattoos. That's why they never stretch or fade; they were applied with magic-" Ana held up a hand before Gabe could interrupt her. "It is an elven marking. The crown is to identify you as part of the royal family. We both share this because we are siblings. There was a war in our realm, and we escaped."

Gabe chuckled. "Is this a joke? Is Erin playing a prank?"

"Hear her out," Erin whispered, her voice cracking. She saw the color in his face drain when he heard the sincerity in her voice.

"Our mother placed a spell on you to hide your elven features. You were young and unable to perform the right magic to do it yourself. However, there must have been a hole in the spell, and when you passed through the portal, it erased your memory. I've been searching for you ever since. It wasn't until Erin came to my shop that I ever thought I had hope."

"What about Erin's parents?" Gabe seemed to be pushing aside everything Ana told him, though Erin saw the angry red working its way up his neck and ears.

Ana glanced her way and saw Erin wasn't going to say anything at this point. "Her mother was a fae and fell in love with a human. They died fighting to protect our people. Erin has been training with me to control her magic."

Erin felt his heated gaze on her and finally moved. She went to the counter where she had a small potted flower. She gently touched the petals and willed the plant to grow. Before their eyes, the flower quickly overtook the size of the pot; its leaves spilled to the counter and Gabe's eyes nearly popped from his head. While Gabe was distracted by her performance, Erin saw Ana reach out and touch his arm. His reaction was instant, his whole body going stiff.

"What did you do?" Erin yelled in alarm.

"It will only take a moment," Ana answered calmly, though her blue eyes were shining brighter than usual.

Gabe's ears sloped to their true form and his very presence seemed to become lighter. Erin could swear even his hair lightened. He blinked hard as the stiffness left him. He held out his hands and looked taken back. "What did you just do to me?" His voice was soft with wonder.

"You feel it, right? All of nature. I can train you to control your powers better. Until then I have a cuff you can wear, it will hide your elven features again." Ana pointed to her ears, and Gabe reached up to touch his own.

"*What did you do to me?*" This time his anger was catching up, and Ana actually looked stunned.

"I lifted the spell placed on you. Now that you are in your true form, do you remember anything?"

"No, I remember ten minutes ago my life was normal, and then you come barging in and tell me you are my sister and I'm fresh out of Dungeons and Dragons! Did you drug me or something?"

"Gabe-" Erin tried to interject, completely understanding the war of emotions playing across his features. She came around the counter to stand before him, but he stepped back.

"You knew, all this time? You just thought, what, that I shouldn't know the truth about myself? You always need to have the control, right? You decide what I know and when I know it. You decide to learn about *your* magic, but ignore *mine?*" His voice continued to rise with each sentence.

"Gabe..." Erin couldn't say more. She started crying openly, hating the anger she felt radiating from him.

"Gabe, put this on." Ana held out the bracelet once more. "It will help lessen the changes you are feeling right now. Until you learn to control it-"

Gabe snatched it from her and put it on, but his eyes didn't leave Erin. "I can't believe you would lie to me about all of this. All the times I asked about coming to visit at the store and you kept me away. You didn't want me to meet Ana? You didn't want me to meet my *sister?*"

"Gabe, I only just found out about you and Ana. I've known about my parents and my magic, but I thought you'd think I was crazy! I *swear*, I just found out about you, and I was going to tell you."

"Yeah, when *you* felt like it. As usual." He threw his response out like a slap, and Erin felt it to her core.

Tears were streaming down her face now as she felt completely broken. "Please, Gabe-"

"I'm going for a walk!"

"Gabe," Ana tried to interject, her blue eyes flashing worriedly to Erin.

"No, I'm done listening." The door slammed behind Gabe as he left the apartment. Both women sighed heavily as silence fell like a shroud over the room.

"Erin, I'm sorry. I didn't think it would be like that." Ana placed a hand gently on Erin's shoulder, but the fae shrugged her off abruptly.

"I was going to tell him! I tried last night but he fell asleep! He *just* got home and I was starting to talk to him, and you rang the damn bell! I just needed a *little more time,* but you *had* to tell him this *second.* Well, you win! You've got your brother back, and he's all yours, because now he'll want nothing to do with me!" Erin lashed out, hating herself for lying to him all this time, hating herself for not telling him about his true self right away, hating herself for screwing up the only thing good in her life, and hating Ana for bringing all her screw ups to light. "Get out, Ana."

"Erin, once he cools down it will be okay. He's just upset."

"I said get out!" Erin turned on her heel and disappeared into her bedroom, slamming her door shut behind her.

Chapter Sixteen

Ana came home to a dark store and an empty apartment. She remembered Melody was meeting with her Wicca group that evening, and almost felt relieved. The elf was completely drained; she'd truly believed Gabe's memory would come back and he would be happy to see her. Instead, his memories remained in the dark, and she'd overridden his mind with far too much information at once. It *would* have been easier if Erin had told him about herself, then it wouldn't have been quite so shocking to find out the truth about himself. Even so, Erin hadn't deserved to have his full reaction thrown on her.

The craving for tea was so strong she could nearly taste it on her tongue as Ana sank heavily onto her sofa, but any energy necessary to make it was gone. She wanted her brother back; she wanted to tell him all about their home, and see the wonder on his face when he finally took a moment to connect with nature the way their kind was born to do. All these years he had been missing out on who and *what* he truly was; she wanted to show him all the good that would come from them finally finding one another.

Movement behind her had the elf's body tensing even before it registered in her mind.

"And the moment everyone is separated, she will strike her revenge." The voice was bone-deep familiar, and Ana turned to find Kali, in all her dark wonder, standing in her living room. Black horns against pale skin, eyes from the darkest pits, and a wicked grin that spread from one ear to the next, baring small daggers of teeth. She was made for nightmares.

Ana's heart was drumming wildly in her chest. "It's been a long time-"

"I'm afraid our business is not complete. I may not have brought *total* destruction," Kali moved fluidly around the room, circling like the predator she was, "but I have something of yours now, and I'm betting you'll give up any chance you have of saving them in order to get back what I took."

Confusion furrowed Ana's brow. "What are you talking about? What do you have?"

"It's already too late." Another too-wide grin before Kali pretended to pout. "I hope it wasn't your favorite." With a wink, Kali turned to smoke and was gone. Ana stood, out of breath, the heaviness of Kali's dark energy threatening to overpower her. *What was that about total destruction? And what in the world could she have taken?*

"Mel!" Ana rushed to her phone and dialed her young charge's number. It rang four times, and Ana was sure all of her hair must have fallen out before the witch finally answered.

"Ana? How did it go? Did the spell work on Gabe?"

"Are you okay?" she demanded, her voice hitching as she gasped in a breath.

"Ana?" Mel's voice changed quickly to a tone of worry.

"*Mel*! Are you in a safe place?"

"Y-yes. What's happening?"

"Stay there for now, *do not* leave the Wiccan circle until I call you back!" Ana didn't wait for an answer before hanging up. She drew a slower breath to quell the tremors as adrenaline fled her body. Then she dialed Erin's phone, praying the fae would pick up despite her anger.

.℘ .℘ .℘

Erin sat on the edge of her bed wondering what to do. She could try to run after Gabe…he had to be so lost in his emotions. He had every right to be angry with her, so she couldn't begrudge that; and if she lost his love, well, she knew she deserved that too, even if it wouldn't stop her from loving *him*. She would try to do what she could to help him, she just wasn't sure what the right move was at the moment. It might be better if she gave him a bit of space and let him come to terms with everything that happened, she realized. Then they could rationally talk it out.

She started to pace, and wondered if he would even come back. He could go to Jason's and crash there, or he could come back while she was gone, take all of his stuff, and never see her again. She might never have a chance to even say goodbye.

The thought was too depressing, so she shook her head and searched for her shoes. She would go after him, and at least tell him she was there for him when he was ready to talk. She could tell him she loved him and just wanted him happy-

The sound of the front door closing jarred the fae from her thoughts, and she was darting from the bedroom in an instant. She expected to find a disgruntled Gabe standing in the kitchen, but found an unfamiliar erebus instead. The world seemed to slow as she thought through her options; her father's dagger was hidden under her bed, but she wasn't sure she would be able to make it back to the weapon in time to defend herself. The erebus before her was unlike the others she had seen; he had two gray horns protruding from the reddish skin of his forehead. He had a nose like a pig, yellow eyes like a cat, and teeth like sharpened daggers. Large pointed ears stuck out from the sides of his head, and he seemed to be twice the size of Gabe.

"What do you want?" Erin made fists at her side in an attempt to make herself look more intimidating.

A dark grin spread across his face. When he spoke, his voice was deep and ragged, and it cut her to her very soul. "You." His head tilted to one side. Then he lunged toward her.

.℮ .℮ .℮

Ana raced to Erin's apartment. If Erin hadn't kicked her out...Ana pushed the thought aside. There was no going back now. She just had to get there, and hope she did so in time. A sick feeling turned in her stomach as Ana thought of all Kali might do to Gabe if she figured out who he was. Luckily, that fear was put to rest quickly when Ana pulled up to the apartment building and found Gabe walking up the entrance. She was out of her car and running to him before he noticed she was there.

"Ana? What are you doing here?" He asked when he turned at the sound of her keys jingling at her side. He ran a hand through his hair and looked her up and down, his gaze lingering on their matching features. "Listen, I'm sorry for earlier, but I really need to speak to Erin. Could we talk tomorrow-"

"Where is Erin?" Ana was so relieved at seeing him that it wasn't until he brought up her friend that the rest of her fear reared its head.

Gabe's mouth dropped open at her tone, then his eyes darted towards the building. "I'm just getting back, she was still in the apartment with you when I left."

"Come on." She grabbed his wrist, just above the cuff she'd given him, and started pulling him along towards the building. He tried to ask her again what was going on, but she ignored him. Ana was doing her best to feel out their surroundings, hoping she wasn't dragging them into a trap of some kind. When they got to the apartment door, she reached out and tried the handle. It gave easily. "It's unlocked."

"I've been talking to her about that, but she's awful about locking her door. She probably wasn't sure if I had my keys with me or not either. Ana, what is-"

"Shh." Ana moved in front of him, blocking his body with her own. He tensed behind her, but she still didn't explain. Instead, she stepped in carefully, but she didn't make it far before she froze. "Take off your cuff," she whispered. If something was about to go down, she needed him to have all of his senses available to him. She could tell he wanted to ask more questions, but he did as she asked.

She slipped off the ring she wore to mask her own elven features. Even before she did, she'd felt the static of dark energy. Once the ring was removed, she needed a moment to breathe as the force of it slammed into her, no longer muted by the cloaking magic.

"What is that?" Gabe was clearly trying to place the dark feeling in his apartment, breathing sharp and hitched as he also processed the change in his senses.

"Erin?" She called out instead of answering him. She made her way to closed doors on the right side of the apartment. That room proved empty. Ana turned to find Gabe holding Erin's camera with a frown on his face.

"Where is she?" His voice was heavy with demand. "It's very likely she left here without locking up, even without her phone, but she would have taken her camera. Tell me what is going on."

"We need to leave, now." Ana grabbed him by the elbow and dragged him from the apartment, ignoring his protest and the fact that he was still holding the camera. It wasn't until she pulled the door shut behind them, that he jerked from her grasp.

"Ana, tell me what is going on! Where is Erin?"

"We can't talk here. I'll explain, but you have to come with me." He stared her down, a spark of panic in his gaze. Then, with a quick nod, he agreed to go with her.

.℮ .℮ .℮

Briar sat huddled under a pile of blankets that Malux had been kind enough to sneak in for her. She was tired of being surrounded by stone, tired of fighting back a chill, and more than anything, afraid she would never see home again. How much had she taken for granted before? The lush greens, the deep purples, the bright blues. That crisp water on her tongue, a fragrant flower tucked behind her ear, her beautiful wings stretched out and free behind her.

At least all of her distraction-free time was giving her a chance to work out some kind of plan. She wanted their queen knocked off her throne as much as the others, but she'd be dead before she let *Lyra* sit up there in her stead. The question remained, however: who was best for the job, and how did she get them there? She needed something to strike a vision, give her a future she could accept. At the moment, she only had the vision she'd given to Lyra. The black amulet. Lyra needed it in order to get someone's help, or at least she *hoped* that was what her vision meant.

Briar groaned and rolled her head slowly. She couldn't remember the last time she opened her eyes to a clear head; there was a constant pain at the base of her neck, spreading over her skull like cruel fingers. Visions had always been painful, but after her wings were taken, she didn't seem to have any power to control it anymore. Instead, she heard and felt *everything* in each vision. Lyra might think she had her game-of-pain down to an art form, but anything she brought on was nothing compared to the multiple deaths she lived through in her own mind.

A quiet knock had Briar struggling to sit up while clinging to her blankets, and she had to fight to ignore the ache throughout her entire body with the movement. She called for the visitor to enter, expecting Malux. They hadn't spoken again, but an understanding existed between them; he had been tortured by Queen Flereous, she by Lyra, and they both wanted the sisters out of the picture. She had felt his pain, felt what his life had been reduced to from his curse, and that knowledge created a bond with him that couldn't be broken. Even if they ended up on opposite sides before this was all done and over with.

Instead, she found herself gazing at the scarred face of the man who would either love her, or kill her. "Doyle, you've returned." His eyes flicked over every bruise, every cut, every broken piece of her, and she wanted to burrow even further under her blanket to hide from the piercing look. She cracked a smile, her only form of self-protection. "These caves sure missed that sour look of yours-" The joke died on her tongue when he made it to her side in three long strides and sat beside her on the bed.

"How much more damage is hidden under those blankets?" Doyle's voice was quiet, dangerously so.

"Enough to spur a vision that can actually help us." She wanted to just shrug it off, uncomfortable with the way he was looking at her. There was murder in his eyes. That, combined with his normal scowl, was enough to leave her cringing.

"Yes, I heard about that," he murmured. "Thank you for your help once again. I saw Fern."

"Really?" She sat straighter, eager for news.

"She passes on that your family is well, and I can personally say that she looked quite well herself. You getting her home saved her life." Tears welled in Briar's eyes, and he sat in silence while she struggled to pull herself together. Just as she'd found herself pining for home, Doyle returned, smelling like the fae forest, speaking of her family...it was enough to rip her apart. "On that note..." He reached into a parcel hanging from his hip. "I thought since I could not take you home, I could at least bring a little something from home to you. And it seems you might need it more than I thought, seeing what Lyra did to you." He passed the whole thing over to her, eyes skimming over her visible injuries once more. The trembling of her fingers made it impossible to undo the knot herself, so he reached over and pulled it free. His skin barely brushed hers as he pulled back, but she was startled by his warmth.

"Doyle..." she gasped as she pulled the wrapping back and saw an array of small gifts.

The man shrugged with a ghost of a smile. "Was nothing. You earned it. Now I'll leave you to eat and get some rest." He reached out as though to pat her knee, but pulled back at the last second like he'd thought better of it. He was out the door before she could utter her thanks. Alone on the bed she laid everything out, taking in the small bits of home he'd brought back for her. Sometimes the smallest gesture...

Briar looked over the large vial of fae water, reveling at the warmth of it in her hand. To someone without fae blood, fae water would always be cold, whether drinking it or touching it. To a true fae, however, the water was always cool and crisp on the tongue, but warm on the body; they never had to worry about a cold bath or a warm glass of water. She kept it tucked against her to keep her warm as she brushed careful fingers over the biscuits, cookies, and dried fruit. The familiar scent left her mouth watering, the taste practically dancing on her tongue already. It was the smallest item though, bundled like an afterthought, that tugged on her heart the most: a string wrapped hastily around a fistful of colorful flowers from her home. Out of their realm the plants lost some of their luster, but when she buried her nose in them she was overwhelmed by scents from home, and for just a moment, she was standing there with her feet in the lush grass, her veins alive with the world around her.

She stuck one of the flowers behind her ear, and grabbed a biscuit with a practically giddy grin.

The next morning, Doyle brought her a tray of food and looked her over. "You ate the treats from home."

"Yes, thank you." Her newest meal was far from appetizing in comparison.

"It helped heal you," he observed with an air of approval. "Probably one minute in your own realm and you'd be completely restored."

"It was kind of you to bring what you did." He sat the tray down next to her, and Briar stood. His gaze caught on the flower behind her ear, and the smallest flash of a smile tilted his lips.

"I'm just glad it helped. Lyra shouldn't have done what she did. I've tried to argue that just because we are erebi, it doesn't mean we are *evil* or that we only want to bring harm. But then she goes and does something like this...again."

"She saved you once. If she was *strictly* evil she wouldn't have done so. And you took care of my sister, took care of me...even brought me food from my home. I'm well aware erebi aren't inherently evil, you've shown me on many occasions since we've met. May I ask...do you wish to put Lyra on the throne because you believe she is the best for the job, or because she saved you?"

Doyle took his time answering. "I believe our current queen does not look out for the best interest of our kind. She sides with the wrong ideology. The queen craves power and rare items, and having everyone under her feet. I believe Lyra would do better. She doesn't want to start wars with the other realms. I don't think she's perfect, but she is *better*. She also listens to me, so I hope that if she gains the crown she will take my thoughts into consideration, and I might be able to do some good." He spoke carefully, and gave her the impression this was not the first time he'd thought of this.

"Why don't you just leave? You are an adult now, you could go into another realm and start a life for yourself," Briar pointed out.

"Which realm would that be? Eloas has been under attack for years, your realm is *currently* under attack, and Sula is next. I can't run from this problem, I have to try and stop it."

She was pulled toward him at his words. There was quiet desperation in him to do something good, to make a real change, and it brought a glimmer of hope. She reached out and touched his hand only to fall over herself into a vision.

The black was spreading. Dark veins creeping through the plants, spreading and killing. Fae on the ground, calling for help, children running and hiding from passing infection erebi. The fear filled her, the weakening spirit of her realm surrounded her. She saw him there. She watched Doyle and Lyra move through the realm, hiding from fellow erebi, ignoring the fae. They went to the top of a hill and looked down at a battlefield. Erebi, more than she had ever seen in one place, filled the land below. An erebus of white with pitch black horns and eyes stood on a platform. Footsteps came from the side and Doyle and Lyra moved behind brush nearby. Lyra pulled the amulet from a hidden pocket and held it in her hand, waiting for the footsteps to come closer.

Briar tumbled away, trying to pull herself back to the surface. She felt Doyle holding her, calling out to her, but she couldn't reach him. Instead, her stomach turned and she was dragged away again.

"Blue?" His hands were on her, his voice a whisper in her ear. The pain in her body was gone and she fell into his touch. Doyle's scarred face tilted down toward her, traces of anger and hardness absent, replaced with an actual smile, just for her. She rose up on her toes while he gathered her close to his body, brushing her hair back with a gentle touch. Then his lips fell to hers-

"Blue! Dammit, you stupid fae." She was being carried. Awareness returned sluggishly, her head pounding. The erebus rested her on the bed, and the fae almost reached out to pull him close, a reflex, before she remembered. The touches they shared were from a future that might never be. As much as her mind hurt, it only took the span of a heartbeat to decide; she needed to know. She reached up and touched his cheek, willing herself to fall in again. Doyle tried to draw back, but she followed.

"What are you doing?"

"Shh..." and reality shifted once more.

"You were planning to bring her down? I trusted you. I stood up for you!"

"Doyle! You said you wanted what was best for your realm, for your people! Do you really think she's it? She ripped away my wings in exchange for my sister's

life! But forget about that, I am only one. She has been grabbing for power from the beginning. That won't stop once she gets her crown. I had to do something-"

"You betrayed me." He gripped her arm, his eyes flashing with regret.

"Doyle please, if you look outside of yourself you will see the option I'm giving is for the best-" His grip turned hard and she saw the flash of movement as he reached behind him. "Doyle, don't-"

She jerked herself free from the vision and found him staring at her, eyes void of the betrayal she'd just witnessed. The future of her death by his hand still loomed. There might not be a way to change that until the moment arrived. She might never know the love he could hold. "Hey there, Blue. You okay?" He sighed in relief when her eyes finally focused on him.

"Yes, my head isn't too happy with me, but I'm fine."

"Do you have any of the fae food left?" He reached over and rubbed the base of her neck then moved his palm down her spine. Shocked at the familiar touch, Briar couldn't help but jerk away. "I'm sorry, did I hurt you?"

"No, my mother..." Her throat tightened. "She would do the same after I had a vision. I'm okay, I have some food and water left. You should go, give me some time to rest."

"Sure..." He got to the door before turning back to her. She didn't need a vision to know what he would ask. She saved him the breath.

"I saw you and Lyra in Loinnir. She had the amulet. There was an erebi army below you. You guys were waiting for someone."

"It must have been Kali's erebi. Did you see who we were waiting for?"

"No, but they were approaching."

"Okay, thank you for telling me. I'm not going to tell Lyra yet. We'll wait until she has the amulet, and let her know we need to go to Loinnir after. I don't want her pushing you to see more. I might not be able to stop her later, but I can at least give you time to recover now." That regret seemed to return, but this time it was accompanied by concern rather than anger. She wanted to do something, *say* something to turn him from Lyra, but no words came, and she found herself alone once more.

Chapter Seventeen

"What do you mean she's been taken?" Gabe demanded, concern clearly overriding any lingering anger he'd felt towards Erin. Ana shot him a stern look before glancing around to make sure no one on the street seemed to overhear them.

"We really don't want the cops snooping around right now, trust me. Keep your voice down until we get inside and we can talk in private," she hissed. Gabe stalked past her into the store, and Ana made quick work of securing the locks behind them.

"So are you going to tell me what's actually going on now?" Melody called as she left the office. "Oh...hi, Gabe..."

"You really couldn't tell me that my *girlfriend* has been *kidnapped* while we were at my apartment?" Her brother hardly spared a nod to

Melody before turning on Ana once again. "You guys are just full of secrets around here, aren't you?"

Ana sighed, holding up a placating hand. "Let me explain, okay? I don't know what Kali may or may not have done to your apartment when she sent someone to take Erin. We couldn't talk about it until I knew we were safe."

"Who the hell is Kali?"

"She's...she's the erebus, the *demon*," Ana added at the bewildered look her brother gave her, "responsible for destroying our realm. She came to me to tell me that she'd taken something of mine. When I was sure Mel was safe, I called Erin. When she didn't answer, I rushed over. Mel, can you get the supplies for a tracking spell? We need to find her as soon as possible; who knows what Kali is planning." Melody nodded and hurried off to get what they needed. "Gabe-" She paused when all the color drained from his features.

"She promised she would tell me if she wasn't safe." He practically fell into the stool by the register. "I know she needs time to process stuff, she always has. She's never had anyone but me that she could count on, so she's used to dealing with things on her own. I knew that, so I tried to give her space. But she promised she would tell me if she was in danger." He ran fingers through his hair, let out a bone-weary sigh, and then looked up at her. "Let's just find Erin, okay?"

Ana nodded solemnly, her heart aching with the desire to comfort her little brother. She could only imagine how overwhelming all of this was for him; *she* was in shock, and she had all of her memories intact with a lifetime of understanding the dangers of the supernatural world. As Gabe began to pace nervously, Ana watched him, and wondered how different their lives would have been had they never been separated. Would Erin have found them? Would they have been better prepared for Kali's return? Would she have even stayed to take over the store and role of protector over the portal?

Melody returned with all of the necessary items and began to work. "Okay, I've got everything. Are you ready?" Ana glanced over to Gabe and nodded. The three of them sat down around the map that Melody had set up on the countertop. The siblings watched in silence as Melody worked through the spell. Hope swelled in Ana's chest, but eventually that hope dimmed as Melody's brows began to draw together and her lips thinned in frustration.

"What's wrong?" Gabe questioned, his voice timid. Melody glanced up at him, and her frustration shifted to remorse.

"It...it's not working," she murmured.

"Does that mean she's dead?" Gabe's voice was hushed in disbelief.

"No, Kali wouldn't kill her. She needs Erin to draw in Ana. They probably have a spell in place to hide her from being tracked. Give me a little more time, I can keep working on it and try to fix it." Ana nodded and turned her attention to Gabe.

Her brother met her gaze and shook his head. "I...I need to go. If this...*spell*," he seemed to stumble over the word, "is going to take time to figure out, I need some time to process everything." He pushed himself to his feet and backed towards the door.

"You are welcome to rest upstairs while we work. We don't know what Kali is planning next. If she knows who you are-"

"If she knew who I was, I'd imagine she might have come after me first, considering I'm your brother. Seems like she's trying to cause *you* pain, would only make sense to go after the only family you have left." The hollow, nonchalant tone of his voice felt like a sucker punch, but she couldn't disagree with him.

"Be that as it may, I would still feel more comfortable with you here. If we find something, it will be much easier if we are all under the same roof." That's when his face crumpled under her gaze.

"Ana, my whole world just got turned upside down. Half of my soul was just taken from me...I need to be home; I need to be in *our* home."

Her heart broke for him, but she couldn't agree to let him go back. Not when someone took Erin and they didn't know where she was yet. Moves were being made, and the last thing Ana was about to do was let any of them be alone. "I understand Gabe, I really do, but you also need to be safe right now. Besides, as soon as we find out where Erin is, we will move quickly so we can get her back. It's best if you are already here. Come on." She stood and motioned for him to do the same. "I'll show you around upstairs and then I'll come back to help Melody."

He looked like he might argue but then he picked up Erin's camera and stood too. He gave one tight nod in agreement, his eyes flashing towards Melody before falling back to her. "Okay, if anything comes up you'll get me right away?"

"Of course." Ana led him up the narrow stairwell to the apartment. "It's only two bedrooms, you can take my-"

"The sofa is fine." His voice was gruff, and she could almost see his energy seep from him. Too much had happened to him for one day. She didn't think he'd be whole again until Erin was in his arms once more. It was clear the two of them loved one another deeply. Once upon a time, she'd believed there was such a thing as soul mates, and if there was, it was clear the two of them were it. Fated for one another, their paths never should have crossed once, and yet they'd found each other twice now. She believed they'd come together once more.

She couldn't see Kali killing Erin until she thought she could get to Ana. They had some time, she was more worried about what might be happening to Erin before they could get to her.

Ana set up the sofa with some extra pillows and blankets, but Gabe could only nod silently in thanks as he clung to Erin's camera. She had a feeling he wouldn't be getting sleep anytime soon, but she could at least give him some space.

"Help yourself to anything in the kitchen, and obviously we are just downstairs if you need something. Try to rest." She gave him a small smile, and then left him to return to the store.

Melody was chewing on her bottom lip as she stared down at the map when Ana returned. She knew better than to ask; it was clear enough that Melody hadn't found anything new. She stayed nearby just in case her help was needed, but knew better than to insert herself in the process.

"Did it work?" Melody asked quietly, looking up from her spell. "Did he get his memories back?"

"I lifted the spell but his memories haven't returned. Now Erin's been taken." She gave a sad smile. "We have to find her and get her back. We lost Aria already, we can't lose her too. She didn't even know about this being a danger, and now...I can only guess what Kali is having done to her. We have to find her quickly."

Melody nodded, "I'm going to call Asher and Marisa. Maybe with some extra help we can get through this." Melody gave her arm a squeeze before walking past her to the cell she'd left on the counter. It was going to be a long night.

$$\mathcal{C} \, \mathcal{C} \, \mathcal{C}$$

Doyle tried to shake the feeling Briar left with him. It was clear that the visions were taking their toll on her, but they needed to keep pushing her to have them until they knew exactly what they needed. He wanted it to be over, but it took time to form an uprising. Skia hadn't had a queen or king overthrown before. One would imagine, out of all the realms, his would be the one to most often overthrow their leaders, but the reality was quite the opposite. Flereous had been sitting on the throne for over two hundred years. She was deeply rooted with the ancient ones - they loved her in fact. She let them feed on as many human souls as they could get, she let them send as many of their minions as they wished into other realms to do their bidding. The ancient ones were a plague, and their full-blooded children like Flereous and Kali were hardly better. They fed on destruction, while most others of his kind simply wanted to live, to *survive*. The erebi with ancient blood started the wars, leaving the rest of them to fight and die for a cause they didn't believe in.

Was *he* actually any better? In order to get what he wanted, Doyle had been more than willing to sacrifice others. How many fae had he just thrown to Kali for no other reason than she had provided their names, and he needed her trust? Briar was a perfect example. He was simply standing by as Lyra tortured the fae, to spur visions that were *clearly* ripping her apart. He didn't sneak her back to her own realm, didn't give her the freedom she deserved. He brought her trinkets from home and accepted her thanks, as if she didn't deserve *so much more* from him.

At what point would his darker acts outweigh his good? What else would he sacrifice to get done what he felt was right for his people? He didn't like the thought. It was too easy to envision Briar's body laid out before him, her eyes dead, all the bright colors dull and faded, his name the last on her lips. If a time came when Briar needed to be killed for the cause, would he move to stop it? He didn't have an answer, and that didn't make him feel worthy of her gratitude, or the trust she was placing in him.

He entered Lyra's sitting area, and found her lounging on a deep plum chaise as though her life had no worries. Her leather-clad body moved to attention when he came in. "We have a window today." As always, her voice was deep and sensual, but today there was a nervous anticipation lightening her tone.

"A window?" He stood with his feet wide and arms tucked behind his back, a normal stance for him when in her presence.

"My sister is meeting with one of Kali's representatives to discuss how her brother is doing in Eloas. She is to be free afterwards, so I was able to get a small meeting with her. I will need you to go with me, and bring Briar's wings. I can only hope she will lead us to the vault and allow you to carry them for her. Once we are in, I can attempt to find the amulet if we are able to distract her. If not, at least then we will know the location and see how she got in exactly, so maybe we can retrace her steps. I want to use our little blue friend first though. Maybe she can see something new, now that a plan is in place."

Lyra nodded toward the door, and Briar was brought in behind him. Doyle's gut twisted at the sight of her, pale with dark bags under her eyes. He knew the vision earlier had drained her, but only now could see just how deeply. The erebus hated himself for being party to this; Briar had asked him to leave so she could attempt to recover, and now she was brought here so another vision could be forced on her.

"How is my favorite seer?" Lyra cooed.

"Enjoying your hospitality, though my view leaves a lot to be desired."

Lyra chuckled at the response, even as his spine shot into a straight line. Briar's words were laced with a bitterness he hadn't detected in her at any other point of her capture. Her sister had been near death, her wings ripped from her body, and still nothing like the tone she had now. He looked her over, and despite the fact that he could practically see the pain radiating in her head and through her body, she stood with a stiff back, her eyes not looking anywhere but at Lyra. Her gaze held steady, defiant. There was a true hate in her for Lyra, and that made him uncomfortable. He knew Lyra had gone above and beyond in mistreating her, but he had only ever witnessed Briar's kindness. He hadn't even been aware fae could hold those kinds of feelings. How bad had Lyra been to do that to her?

"Well, we can't all live in luxury," Lyra crooned. "Now, my dear, you know the deal. You can work with me the easy way, or we can force your cooperation."

"As I said before, that isn't exactly how my visions work. But you haven't listened yet, so I'm not sure why I bother."

"You know, I like you more and more every day. You were so *timid* before. Now look at you, talking back to mama. A little worse for wear, maybe; I can't see any men jumping up to sweep you off your feet, but you are certainly becoming far more interesting in *my* eyes."

"You aren't exactly my type," Briar deadpanned as Lyra stepped forward until she was practically nose-to-nose with the fae. He wanted to spring to action, dive between them and keep words or fists from flying.

"As much as I enjoy dry banter, I do believe we have limited time today," Doyle interrupted, doing his best to keep his voice neutral.

"True enough." Lyra straightened, her long hair swaying back and forth with her quick movement. "We have a plan for getting the amulet, and I want to see if you are able to give us any information. I thought you might be able to tell us if what we have in mind will work, or if we'll have some trouble. Anything that might prove your *usefulness*."

Briar chose to ignore the last dig, and her deep eyes turned to Doyle for the first time since entering the room. "Are you aware of the plan, and are you going with Lyra?"

"Yes." Her gaze bore into him, making him shift his stance to dispel the sudden discomfort. Briar shook from the grip of her guard and came to him.

"May I have your hand?"

"Why him instead of me?" Lyra nearly whined.

"Because he doesn't wish me harm. You *enjoy* forcing the visions from me, and that partially blocks my ability to naturally draw your futures to me." Her gaze broke from his and he could nearly feel her exhaustion. "Doyle stated you have limited time, so I don't think you really have any to waste on your enjoyment. He, however, only wants me to have a vision to help his cause. He wants it to be as easy on me as it can be, so his mind is far more open to my probing."

He had no idea that the desire of the other person could change how easily she was able to see a vision. He thought of earlier, how a simple touch of his hand seemed to throw her right into a vision. He hoped it would be just as easy for her now, so she could get back to her room for rest. Over the years he'd spent a lot of time meditating; he found it relaxing to turn off his mind and open himself to his surroundings. It seemed like good practice for him to look outside of himself while gaining a center. He used his training now to open himself up to her, hoping it would give her the ease to see what she needed.

Briar held out her small hand for him, and their eyes met again. Hers were tired, but also warm, like maybe she was thinking of some hidden joke; and then he was distracted by the touch of her soft skin against his calloused palm.

Nothing happened at first. She just stared up at him, and he started to worry nothing would come to her. It wasn't long, though, before Doyle picked up on the changes as she fell into another vision: her body stiffened, her eyes took on a clouded, far-away gaze as they began to watch something entirely different. Her body started to shake, so he gripped her harder, giving her his body to lean on, but keeping his palm against hers in case his movement would break their bond. Breaths passed by in silence before her knees gave out and she fell completely into him.

"*Shit.*" He caught her easily, and released her hand in order to sweep the fae up into his arms. She felt so light. She was wasting away to nothing in this realm, and there was nothing he could do to help her.

That wasn't entirely true. There was just nothing he seemed willing to do in order to *save* her. To save her would be to give up their one advantage in this fight.

Awareness seemed to be gradually returning to Briar just as he eased her down on the chaise, and then all at once as she jerked awake. Her skin seemed void of color and her lips tinged blue; he had the sudden absurd thought of pressing his lips against hers in order to restore their natural rosy hue. Almost like she'd read his mind, her eyes flicked to his mouth before traveling back to meet his gaze.

"You will get into the vault, but I didn't see the amulet. I don't think you can get it today, but you will be given a clear picture of the room, and how the queen enters it. Pay attention to the details, it might help you re-enter."

"That's all you have for us?" Lyra's voice held a tinge of disbelief.

"Your sister will be in an annoyed mood when you go to her. The news she will get won't make her happy. She will want to take it out on you when you first come to her, but then you present her with my...with my wings, and she is grateful." Briar stumbled over the words, her tone laced with pain. Doyle wished that he could comfort her somehow, but knew nothing would. Briar continued, eyes focusing on the female erebus. "She will allow Doyle to carry them into the vault, you hang back at the doorway so you don't draw attention, and it seemed like you get a very full view of everything. Doyle goes deeper into the room...I couldn't see his face but I believe he gets a pretty nice look around also. Then she gazes at the wings for a moment before leading you both back through the path." Briar reached up like she was going to rub her head but caught herself, and her spine stiffened once more. "Might I make one request of you?"

"I certainly can't stop you from asking," Lyra snarked.

"I would like to see my wings one last time before they are handed over." There was no hiding the pain in her voice, her plea was like an open wound.

"Dear." Lyra stepped forward and took her chin into her hand. Sitting beside Briar, Doyle could feel her try to pull back, but Lyra did not relent. "It is time to move on from the past. They are no longer *your* wings, you gave them to me in exchange for your sister." She jerked her hand back. "Take her back to her room. Doyle, are you ready for our task?"

"Yes of course." He took his normal stance once more, but his eyes didn't stay on Lyra. Instead he followed Briar's dejected form as she was led back out. Something twisted inside of him, and anger nearly flared out before he was able to gain control. Some part of him wanted to see Lyra in pain, just for a moment, to know that she could even *feel* it. He wasn't so sure there was any ounce of feeling left in her.

"Good, go fetch the wings then. We should be ready as soon as my sister returns from her meeting."

$$\varphi \ \varphi \ \varphi$$

"Gabe?" Erin's head was throbbing, and she wasn't quite able to open her eyes. She remembered her argument with Gabe and Ana, and then...she wasn't sure. She forced her eyes open when she realized she was sitting on a cold floor and her arms were numb. It was dark. The floor was made of stone, and the only light was seeping through a heavy looking iron door. Her arms were chained above her head but her feet were free. The air felt different. It was more than being locked in a dungeon, it felt oddly familiar...

The fae realm, Loinnir. It felt the same as it had in her dream when she saw her mother. The faint smell of flowers, the buzzing in her veins, the crispness of the air. But how did she *get* there? Erin remembered the large, horned, brute attacking her in her apartment, and prayed Gabe didn't come back any time soon.

Slowly, she started to pull her legs in to stand. Her arms had fallen asleep along with her legs so it was a bit of a struggle; with every move, her whole body filled with the nasty prickling feeling of blood flow returning. She finally stood and just leaned against the stone wall for a few minutes, trying to be as still as possible until the feeling finally went away. Then she tried to take in more of her surroundings. It was too dark beyond the iron door for her to see, and she could only move to the middle of the room with her chains.

Ana, it would be great if you could hear me right now. Erin did her best to force the words from her mind, but felt like nothing happened. No response came. "Freaking useless...genetics could have at least let me talk to animals or something instead." Erin walked back to her wall and started to twist the chains taut. She planted both feet on the wall and tried to push back, hoping to break the chains.

"You could at least groan a little or something," she mumbled when nothing happened. Her mind started racing, lamenting her lack of options, when she heard footsteps approaching from outside her door. Alert, she waited, her eyes trained on the opening door. The erebus from her apartment approached first, his eyes glowing like a cat's in the dark. Then a woman with chalky white skin, and vicious horns that matched solid black eyes sidled up beside him.

"So you are one of the *mighty* friends of Ainadelothien, elven princess. Tsk Tsk." She shook her head with a pout. "So easy to catch. Now what should we do with our new toy, Bogor?"

The erebus that attacked her just grunted in response, but a split tongue darted out to lick at his lips. Chills ran down her spine. She'd had her fair share of bad situations, but this moment had to top them. Unhealthy coping mechanisms almost had her asking who did their cosplay masks, but self-preservation managed to win out.

"Who are you?"

"Oh, she never told you about me? How disappointing. I am Kali. She escaped me with her brother many years ago, and I'm planning on finishing the job. Seems her brother didn't survive the portal, but there is still the princess."

"What does that have to do with me?" Erin thought frantically. The erebus before her was the reason both her and Ana's parents were dead. At least she didn't know Gabe was Ana's brother.

"You are her friend, she'll come for you." Kali gave a small shrug. "After all the gifts I sent her from Loinnir, she'll figure out she needs to come here for you."

"You took her kingdom, killed her family, why can't you just let her be?" Her voice was bitter, but Erin was thankful she was able to keep it steady. Bogor kept making half circles around her, inching closer.

"My job is incomplete, and I just *hate* for things to be incomplete. I must say, elflings are certainly stubborn beings...but once I take away their princess, my brother will finish his work. Your kind however, much easier to press under my thumb. Been here only a few months, and already most of them are bowing down to me. The war is still being fought with the elves though, and I can't have their princess returning with hope. She *will* come for you." Kali smirked knowingly. "After we killed her friend Aria, I'm sure she learned her lesson about leaving her toys laying around."

Erin tried not to look surprised, but she wondered who Aria was, and why she'd never heard of her. Apparently, Ana hadn't shared *all* the dangers that awaited her in learning her powers.

"But until then, Bogor has been in desperate need of a plaything. He plucked a few fae of their wings, but that grows tiresome after some time."

Internally, Erin was shaking. The image of her mother having her wings ripped from her body nearly made her sick, but she refused to show it. No matter what was going to happen next, she would not give them the pleasure of knowing her fear or pain.

Chapter Eighteen

Ana was starting to doze, sitting on the floor with her back against the wall, where she'd been trying to keep Melody company. She wasn't sure what time it was anymore, early morning she'd guess, though the sky was still dark outside the windows. As she dozed, she thought of her brother as she remembered him: chubby cheeks, curly wisps of blond hair, bright, curious eyes. A memory she'd avoided for years pushed to the front of her thoughts.

She saw Ethelron, her loyal guard, a man she'd considered a friend, and had once hoped would be more. He had found an injured wolf pup. He'd cared for the fluffy thing and started training her. She'd walked into a room to find him standing at the doorway in his usual guard pose: legs spread, shoulders squared, body tense and alert. Then she'd heard her brother squealing with joy, and came to stand beside Ethelron to find Toron rolling on the floor with the wolf. The two of them wrestled on the ground before Toron popped to his feet and took off running, the pup chasing at his heels. When she'd dared a small glance at Ethelron's face, she'd found his usually stern set of lips tilted into a smile that was nothing short of the glow of the sun.

Ana found herself living in the memory, studying the face set in a rare moment of contentment, when a crash in the apartment above jolted her from the drowsy memory and to her feet. "Stay here," she spoke quietly to Melody, whose face was drawn in exhaustion. She'd been working non-stop, even after Asher and Marisa had tried to help. After several hours, they left with the promise to return the next day if needed.

Ana moved quickly up the stairs before Melody found the words to argue, but stopped short when she found Gabe sitting on the floor next to the sofa, as though he'd fallen off. She froze, unsure what was happening. He turned his head towards her, his eyes wide.

"Aina?" His voice was hushed with awe, and her heart raced. "I..." He swallowed and ran a shaky hand through his hair, "I remember."

She wanted to run to him, but her feet wouldn't obey. *He remembered.* Melody's spell had worked, it had just...taken some time. Relief flooded her, until he closed a fist over his chest as though in pain. "I remember everything-" Then he looked up at her and tears started racing down his cheeks.

She raced to him then, gathering him up in her arms and stroking his hair as she'd done when they were children. She knew there were happy memories in there, memories that he would be able to take comfort in, but right now he was probably too busy feeling the ache of loss for their home and their family.

"We have each other now, and we *will* get Erin back, not all is lost." *Not all is lost*, she repeated to herself, taking comfort in her own words as well.

.℘ .℘ .℘

Doyle followed Lyra down the winding halls carved from stone. She moved in silence before him, and he let his mind wander as they made their way deeper into the caves. He had the sudden craving for fresh air and open skies, and wondered how Briar was able to stand it. If he felt this suffocated, *she* must feel buried.

Lyra, on the other hand, seemed unaffected. In fact, the deeper they went, the longer and more sure her strides became. She wanted to rule this realm; she felt she was born to do so. He had never argued or even thought to wonder if she was really the right person for it. She'd saved him when he was alone and afraid; she'd taken him in and given him purpose. She wouldn't bend over backwards to keep the ancients happy, and she wanted the wars in the other realms to end. But for the first time, walking quietly behind her down the dark caves, he saw something else. She felt she *deserved* the crown, and she was willing to do all it took to get it. She'd beaten an innocent fae that was doing her best to help, and she'd bring others into their fight with no knowledge about them other than the fact that they would help her win. So, for the first time, he wondered what she would do after, to ensure she kept the crown, if they were able to place it on her head.

They met Malux in the hall, and the half-dragon met Doyle's gaze and held it longer than was usual. He and Malux had never been friends; Lyra went out of her way to taunt Malux, because of his association with her sister, which left them at odds. But this was one area where Lyra had royally messed up: Malux had no love for their queen, and he probably wanted her brought down just as much as they did, he was simply unable to make a move against her. After centuries of torture and pain, the half-breed was a puppy in the queen's lap. Lyra could have shown him kindness, could have given him someone to turn to. Instead, she taunted and poked and kicked the puppy when he was already down. She could have had a teammate on the inside.

Malux's gaze flicked down to the large glass case he'd been carrying. Briar's wings sat inside, spread only enough to glimpse the strength present. It was nowhere near their full potential; he'd seen them in action right before they captured her, when she and her sister had been trying to flee. He now knew that she had just witnessed her mother's death, or saw it in a vision, and was trying to get her sister to safety. At the time though, he'd had the collector yelling at him that she was powerful and they needed her. He'd had orders to keep anyone from going into the portal, to capture something useful.

Even still, it didn't stop him from being struck by her beauty. Her face had been tense, desperate, her eyes wide and searching, her wings stretched out behind her in all their power and strength. They moved the air as she'd pushed Fern to the portal, trying to also get the fae the other erebus had injured. She had only been captured because they had tried to save the other fae. Now, he held her wings in a glass case, ready to pawn them off to the queen they wished to overthrow.

He could feel the sharp judgement in Malux's gaze before Lyra barked at him: "Is my sister back from her meeting yet? Maybe you could be useful, and run ahead to let her know we wish to see her."

"She is not back yet. I can lead you to her seating area and send her in as soon as she is back," Malux responded dully, hardly flicking a glance in her direction.

"I don't exactly need someone to show me the way. Make sure she attends to us the second she returns."

"I shall notify her that she has guests, but I don't exactly have control of the queen's movements. I'm sure she'll get to you when she deems her time available to you." Malux strode off, leaving Lyra to huff and stomp on toward the sitting area. Doyle jostled the large display and continued after her now noisy footsteps.

They waited two hours. Smoke was practically coming out of Lyra's ears by the time Queen Flereous finally graced them with her presence. They had covered the display with a large sheet, but she didn't even bother to look toward it. She was miffed. Both sisters stared one another down for a few breaths while his back stiffened and his hands tightened on one another behind his back. Flereous always had the ability to strike a man dumb. Dark hair curled down over her breasts, her cleavage displayed just enough to make one's mouth water. Her skin was pale, her eyes dark. Sexual energy exuded from her; even the smallest flick of her wrist could leave someone on their knees before her, begging for a moment of attention.

Doyle was able to see that, see her power over others, while being completely unaffected. He had eyes, he could appreciate what she brought to the table...but he knew the power that flowed through those veins. He knew what went on in her mind and heart, and that somehow saved him from becoming one of her little lap dogs. Malux seemed unaffected by her powers also; where others would fall over themselves for some of her attention, he shied away from it. Malux had seen far too much of her attention over the years, of *all* sorts, and had never benefited from it.

"I've had a long day already. I hope you are here on important business, as I don't really have time for a social call from my *sister*." The word was spat out as the queen looked Lyra over from head to toe. She hardly changed day to day. Where the queen loved to don gowns of rich fabrics and designs, changing multiple times a day on occasion, Lyra usually wore some form of her favorite armor. The leather wrapped around her, leaving skin exposed as a dare to attack, while twin daggers were strapped to her thighs and a spare was hidden at her ankle. Her hair was always pulled back into the same tight ponytail atop her head, leaving it to hang down her back. The queen's hair, on the other hand, was used as an additional accessory, changing as often as a woman might change the necklace she wore.

"I am sorry your meeting did not go well." Lyra's eyes flicked to Doyle. They *had* been warned that the queen would not be in the best mood when they first got to her. A clear sign everything would work out in their favor. "We actually came bearing a gift for you." Lyra nodded to him. He gave the sheet a pull, wondering if he should have done so with more flourish, and stepped back so the queen could get a good view of their gift.

Flereous gave a small gasp and stepped forward, resting fingers against the glass as she leaned in. "*Magnificent.* Dare I ask what grand mistake you have made that you wish to butter me up?"

"Hm, now I regret bringing them to you. I should have saved it for a time I needed a favor. No, dear sister, I simply came across these and knew I could not let them slip through my fingers. I thought they would make a great addition to your collection."

Doyle watched the expression change on the queen's face, and knew she didn't quite buy the story, but she also wasn't about to let such a great prize slip away from her. "Well, I offer you my warmest thanks. Since your pet has carried them this far, could he carry them the rest of the way? My own seems to have run off after letting me know you were here."

"Of course." Lyra gave a small bow of her head and Doyle bent to pull the case back up to him, smothering a glare of frustration. When this was over he wanted a strong drink and his bed. The wings had weight to them, power that kept calling to be reunited with their owner. It was like the force in them grew stronger and heavier the farther away from Briar they got. Once his hands were on the case, *no he didn't need help, thank you very much*, he followed the queen down an even more winding path. Lyra fell in behind him, and the erebus wondered if she was making observations about the way he walked as he had done to her hours earlier. At one point on the path, he had to stop and turn the case to fit through the walls.

Finally, the queen slowed and made a few more sharp turns, moving through splits in the cave with ease. He hoped Lyra was memorizing all the twists because his focus was on keeping the case in hand. They stopped before a wall. When he looked carefully, he could see places where the rocks did not line up exactly. Flereous moved a rough spot in the stone, exposing a keypad. His grip tightened as he focused on her movements. He couldn't make out the keypad, but he tried to memorize the way her hands danced over the keys, six buttons, none seemed to have a double sequence. The rock separated into a small doorway, which they all stepped through.

"Hm, I think over here would be good." Flereous touched the bare skin of his forearm — to allow him through the ward, he realized — and pointed to a spot deep in the room to the right. He nodded at her and followed her direction while his eyes scanned shelves and bookcases. Paintings hung on the wall, cases of mysterious substances were littered everywhere. There was a clear organization, it just wasn't clear to *him* because he didn't know what anything was. No sign of a dark amulet, or jewelry, or anything else that would tip him off that the amulet might be near a certain area. When he turned though he caught Lyra's eyes and knew she'd seen something. The confident set of her lips told him she was happy.

"They look wonderful there! A great addition to such a strong collection," Flereous crooned as she practically floated towards her macabre collection of fae wings.

"Yes, they do look lovely. Makes me wonder after the fae that used to bear them. Do you know the previous owners?"

The queen shook her head, tracing her fingers along the edges of the case lovingly as she responded. "Not much, I'm afraid. One that was attempting to flee her realm, the wings were ripped away as punishment I believe. A collector brought them back as bragging rights and decided to sell. Then *I* came upon them." She gestured towards another set close to her newest acquisition. "I suppose I actually owe you my thanks. The fae must have been powerful, I can feel the energy here." Flereous placed her hand on the glass again and Doyle had to turn away before he protested.

Hot rage shook him to the core, and he only wanted to get away. Finally both women moved toward the door, which let him move away from the case. The reminder of his own crimes. He did better paying attention to the turns as they moved their way back out of the caves, but even as the walkways grew larger he still felt suffocated. He needed to get away.

The second the sisters stepped back on the main platform outside of the queen's sitting room Doyle excused himself, gave a quick bow to both, and then made his escape. He knew Lyra would want to go over what they had learned, but for right now he needed a moment to himself. A moment to get air, to have the sky above his head, even if it was the heavy clouded sky of the dark realm.

Maybe one day, *one day* he could stand under clear skies of another realm and be able to call it home. But he doubted it; he would never be able to escape. He would end up buried under the stones that surrounded him now.

.℃ .℃ .℃

Ana sat with Gabe while Melody finally went to get some rest. Now that Gabe had his memories back, though, there was no sleep for the two of them. She just sat in awe as he came to terms with what happened, and told her about some of his time after going through the portal. It was hard to miss that Erin was in all of his stories, and the more he talked, the more an urgent tugging began in her chest to get her back. She did not want to lose someone who had become a close friend. Even more than that, though, she was terrified of her baby brother losing the one person that had been there for him all this time.

Together they discovered that with his memories, some control over his powers had returned. He was able to speak with her telepathically, and his strength increased now that he had magic flowing freely in his veins. The higher the sun rose, the more at ease he became with the heightened elven abilities. Even with his memories returned, there was still a barrier between them that she could feel. They'd spent more time separated than they had as siblings; it would take time for them to figure each other out and begin to grow a relationship again.

When Melody came downstairs again some of the red had faded from the whites of her eyes, but they were still puffy. She brightened when she caught sight of her and Gabe sitting together, and flashed a smile. Ana knew the only reason she'd convinced her to go and rest in the first place was because she'd been trying to give the two of them space once she realized Gabe's memories had returned.

"Asher is coming by again to try and help out some more. There has to be something blocking the tracking spell, but we will find a way through it." Melody gave a confident smile as she started to gather supplies. "Why don't you guys get something to eat and then train? Give a girl some space?"

"I'm sure we have a fight coming up, so training would be good." Ana glanced at her brother, and he gave a small nod of agreement. His mouth fell to a grim line as he watched Melody. "Come on." She tucked her hand into his elbow to pull him away. If they stayed, he'd just sit and obsess over where Erin was, not that she could blame him.

"You'll tell us right away if you find out anything?" He asked, his hand coming up to rub at his chest.

"I promise." Melody gave a reassuring nod just as Asher came to rap his knuckles at the front door. This time, when Ana tugged at his arm again, he followed.

.℮ .℮ .℮

A day passed, but it felt like a year. Erin hadn't had anything to eat or drink since she'd been pulled into Loinnir. She managed to deal with Bogor without showing her weakness, but worried about what he would have in store today. Her body had healed the damage done, but it left her feeling drained in a way she'd never known before.

Her hands were tied by her sides this time, but she was still finding rest impossible. Every small sound had her heart racing, worried that they were coming back. She wanted to be strong, and if it took all of her energy, she was going to keep it together when they were around.

Ana, if you can hear me, now would be a good time to come and get me.

"Erin, dear! Hope you got some rest!" Kali appeared, her skin almost glowing in the darkness. "Oh goodie, I love it when healing powers are involved. Just keeps the fun *coming* right?" She placed a large leaf on the floor, and Erin saw an assortment of flowers and fruit covering it. Beside the food, Kali deposited a small bowl of tightly bound leaves with crystal clear water. The water seemed to have an internal glow about it that made Erin's stomach feel warm just looking at it. "Oh yes, fae food...not exactly my taste. Eat up. Bogor is leading a fight against some rebel fae, and then he'll be looking for you."

Kali moved closer, pulling out a knife from her tight clothing, black against pale skin. She moved the blade delicately over Erin's skin, but the halfling held herself still and forced herself to look into Kali's solid black eyes. "Maybe I'm bored though, we could have fun testing those healing powers of yours. You know, if they are used too much in a short space of time, they will stop working. It has to be rested. It takes a lot for that to happen though."

"I'm trying to be polite...but you forget, you are in *my* realm. My mother's blood runs through my veins, and it is calling out to me. I *will* not be broken, not by you or your ugly brute. *You* will lose." She felt the slice of the knife across her shoulder and tried to rein in the quick pain. Instead she spit out the little moisture left in her body and watched it land on the erebus' cheek. Kali reared back with a hiss and slapped Erin across the face, making her whole face numb. "Hmm, I thought you'd melt like the wicked witch. Oh well, one can only hope," Erin gritted out. Even though it bought her extra pain, she liked that she was able to get a rise out of her captor.

"Enjoy your meal, *halfling.* We will see if it is your last."

Erin watched her leave before turning suspicious eyes towards the food. She was starved, but for all she knew everything was poisoned. With determination - and not a little bit of effort - she looked away and tried to go back to sleep. Her body felt warm as her powers naturally started to heal the bruise already swelling on her cheek and the cut on her shoulder. She thought she healed quickly before all of this happened, but once she'd started to hone her skills with Ana, she could now heal almost instantly.

A pitter-patter on the floor caught her attention; it was light, not one of the erebi. It almost sounded like a dog. Erin peered through the door until she saw a red fox start to sniff at the metal. It was just barely able to squeeze through, and then sat in front of the door. The fox watched her silently, and Erin wondered if her eyes deceived her. She *knew* that fox.

"Sinopa?"

The fox cocked its head in surprise, and then transformed. The woman now crouched in the cell looked the same as the day of Erin's memory. Sinopa's orange-red hair and naked skin seemed to emit a light of its own. "You know me?" Her voice was quiet, with a musical lilt.

It broke her. Erin felt the tears roll down her cheeks; seeing her mother's friend standing before her in such a dark place was almost like seeing her mother return from the dead. This fae was the last person to see her parents alive, had fought side-by-side with them, and, Erin had assumed, died side-by-side with them too.

"I saw you, with my parents, when they died."

"Oh, you lived Odette's memories?" Sinopa came to sit beside her, keeping her voice quiet to stay undetected. Her eyes were sad as she spoke of Odette. "I was surprised when Kali brought you to our realm. I knew you instantly. You look just like your mother." Sinopa's mouth curved into a melancholic smile. "I saw you once as a baby, when I came to warn Odette about the erebi growing in strength. It was my fault your parents left you. I'm sorry for that."

Erin shook her head, but couldn't form words.

Sinopa gestured towards Kali's offerings with a wry smile. "The food is safe to eat. I watched them prepare it. They want you to have your strength."

Erin's mouth watered instantly at the mention of food. She knew she could trust Sinopa, so she grabbed for the water first.

Somehow it was ice cold, and seemed to spread moisture back to every limb after just a sip. There was a hint of honeysuckle, and after a large gulp her veins seemed to tingle with magical energy again. She wondered if full-blooded mystical creatures felt like this all the time. Now that Gabe's spell had been lifted, did he feel the constant pull of energy within him? She reached for one of the pieces of fruit while she listened to Sinopa.

"I'm sorry I couldn't come sooner. I watched them bring you here, but Bogor stayed with you, and then a guard was put in place. Right now they are preoccupied with a small uprising though, so this was my chance."

"Can you get me out?" For once, Erin felt hope of escape. It faded quickly, however, when Sinopa shook her head.

"Not yet, not by myself. The fae still want to fight, but the erebi are pulling us down. I can't get you out alone, and I'm not sure when I can gather others to help me get you out. But you will be safe. Kali does not want you dead."

Kalie doesn't want me dead yet, was all Erin could think. And while she might not kill her, she would certainly make sure her time in Loinnir was not a luxury vacation. "Can you travel through a portal? One comes out in Sula, in a shop...my friend, Ana, can help. She's probably looking for me right now. But with your help, she could sneak in and not have to search once she's in the realm. You could lead her to me."

"I know the portal well. It is some distance from here, but I can get there by morning." Sinopa placed a hand on Erin's cheek. "I'm sorry."

Before Erin could ask what exactly she meant, Sinopa was a fox again, trotting toward the door. She turned her eyes to Erin one last time, then slipped through the door and disappeared into freedom. Once again, Erin was left to face Bogor for another round of playing practice dummy.

Chapter Nineteen

Erin sat on her bed at the group home. The housemother made her roommate leave the room to give her space, but Erin knew it would come all too soon. The questions, the sneers, the sideways glances from people that pretended they knew what happened. Erin looked down at her bruised knuckles from where she punched Joey, her last foster parent's seventeen-year-old son. She remembered how the punch reverberated up her arm, and the satisfying crunch of his nose. The bruises on her knuckles were worth it; it was the bruises on her arms and face she wished would disappear. They were the ones that called out that she was a victim, that he'd gotten the upper hand.

The ones on her knuckles spoke otherwise. They showed she was a fighter. Even though he ripped her shirt and threw her down, tried to get on top of her...she looked at her knuckles and remembered. She fought back. She *won. Her bruises* would fade, but Joey would deal with a crooked nose for the rest of his life, as a reminder of what an ass he actually was.

Erin looked up when she heard her door open. It wasn't her roommate returning, it was Gabe. She felt his eyes on every bruise, just like earlier. He'd seen her at school and demanded answers. He'd been the one to make sure she never had to go back to that house. Hell, he was back at the group home too, because he'd demanded it, to make sure he would be there for her.

"Heard you broke his nose, you left that part out." His voice was dry, leaving her thankful it wasn't full of pity. She couldn't bear it if he looked at her like a victim.

"You heard right." She smiled shyly, and was met with one of his wide grins.

"That's my girl," he praised as he sat next to her on the bed and put his arm around her. Erin sank into the hollow of his shoulder, and fit perfectly. She felt safe. He kissed her temple and rested his head against hers. "I missed being in the same house as you. No one to nag me about homework when you aren't around." He brushed back her hair, and she went stiff.

Joey yanked it, holding her down. She couldn't move, he had her pinned.

Gabe quickly let go and moved away, feeling her change. "I'm sorry..." His voice was quiet.

"It's fine. I just want to cut it all off."

Gabe shrugged and got up. He didn't say anything, just left her alone in the room. She felt empty in the pit of her stomach. He could have at least said *something. Before she could think too much about it, though, he was sneaking back in her room, a pair of scissors held in his hand. "So do it." His eyes held a dare, and she smiled despite herself.*

"You always have to have the control right? You decide what I know and when I know it."

Erin jerked awake at the anger in Gabe's voice. She might never see him again, and the last thing he knew was that she'd lied to him. She deserved every bit of his anger; she just hoped if she died, he would remember their good times. The times when they were tender with one another, *happy*. She hoped he wouldn't just remember when she was selfish and scared, a liar to the one person she loved in the world.

Erin tried to move, but her body hadn't quite healed itself from her last visit with Bogor. The erebus never said a word to her. He only came in with a leery grin and eyes that danced with the idea of bringing pain. She managed to keep silent, but the inside of her mouth was constantly being torn up from biting back her cries. Just as she hadn't let Joey break her, she wouldn't let her new friend. The light coming in down the hall was reaching her door, so it was morning. Sinopa should be reaching the portal, reaching Ana. Bringing her help. She just had to hold on. Just as she thought it, Bogor's hulking form blocked out the light into her cell.

"Ah, my silent charmer. What, no flowers?" She raised a brow and forced a smirk. His eyes shone yellow and reflected like a cat's. "Where's your dominatrix? You look lonely." With a grunt he lifted her to her feet, and pain raced down her spine.

She thought of Gabe, coming to her room when she felt so lost and broken. He hadn't looked down on her, he hadn't looked at her with pity. He'd been happy to see her, had pride that she'd fought back. She closed her eyes and remembered that look as he'd leaned against her doorway, looking far too casual for someone that had to sneak up to her room to avoid trouble with the housemother.

The erebus unchained her and moved her to the middle of the room. She struggled against him, but it was like fighting with a brick wall. Then she was hanging from ceiling chains and watching him pull out a long whip. *Oh shit.* There was a low rumble coming from his chest, and she wondered if he was laughing. The first hit struck her across the back, but also whipped around to her side and sent her feet flying out from under her. She cried out. She hadn't meant to, but the pain was so sudden, and sent every one of her nerves on high alert. The rumble in his chest increased. His tongue darted out, and he came to stand before her. He wanted to rub in the fact that he got a reaction.

Erin struggled for breath and tried to keep tears at bay. She almost felt defeated when one slid down her cheek. Bogor tilted his head to watch it. Erin gathered her strength and grabbed the chains above her head. Using all the force she had, ignoring the pain across her back, she pulled herself up and swung her body, her feet kicking out to find the center of his chest. He stumbled back a few steps and snorted in anger.

"This would be much more interesting if you unchained me and let me fight back, you know." Her voice was strong, but her strength spent, so she fell limp on the chains. He moved to her back again and she heard the crack of the whip before she felt it slice across her skin. Without pause he brought it back and sent a third one, this time hitting her shoulder. She nearly threw up.

"Having fun? Unfortunately, I need to pull you away for a time." Kali stood on the other side of the cell, ignoring Erin's presence completely. Bogor huffed in disappointment but followed her out, letting the whip fall to the floor with a dull thud. They left Erin hanging from her wrists, her legs no longer able to support her weight. She was going numb with pain. Erin knew it would take Ana and Sinopa another day to get to her. She just had to hold on another day. *Hurry it up you stupid elf!*

.℘ .℘ .℘

Briar woke to a pounding head, and groaned in the most un-ladylike fashion. She felt like someone had shaken her until her brain rattled and then abandoned her to her bruised mind. She could feel her heartbeat; with every pulse her head felt like it would explode. She really outdid herself this time; she'd indulged herself with her visions of Doyle, and quickly lived to regret it when she was called in to have another vision. At least Doyle had been there. For all the questions she still had about him, she at least knew he didn't wish her harm. His openness to her visions took some of the stress off of her, so she could slip easily into what she needed to see.

Briar rolled over and curled under the extra layers of blankets Malux had brought her. The mattress beneath her was stiff and unforgiving, but at least it was something. Certainly better than the stone floor, though probably not by much. A knock at the door echoed in her head, bringing tears to her eyes. She just wanted to drift back into peaceful sleep, where she wasn't unbearably nauseous. She just wanted to be left *alone*.

The knock sounded again. She couldn't manage actual words so she just groaned and rolled so she was facing the door. There wasn't any more strength for her to draw from, let alone power. Maybe with her wings she would have been stronger, better able to bear what they kept placing on her, she'd been better able to maneuver through her visions before, control how much they affected her, but now she felt weak and had about as much control as a leaf caught up in a tornado.

Doyle must have read her groan as an invitation, because he stepped in, clad in dark fabrics that seemed to wrap around him. His scar somehow seemed darker, standing out in sharp contrast against the rest of his face.

"Were you successful?" Briar mumbled. The effort to sit up proved too much, and her head landed back on her bundle of blankets.

"Your visions were too much for you." He didn't ask, only stated the obvious in a way that made her want to punch him. "Come on..." He was at her side in two long strides, but instinct had her shying away from him. If he were to set off another vision her skull might *actually* fracture in two. He paused and seemed to assess the situation. She did her best to ignore him and closed her eyes. The light was hurting them. "If I don't touch your skin, do you think you'll be okay?"

Why was he insisting on touching her at all? Why wouldn't he just let her *be* so she could try to sleep? The fae's exhaustion was the only thing that kept tears of frustration at bay. Strong hands abruptly slipped under her arms. He pulled her off her feet and tucked one hand under her knees, while the other supported her back. She knew she had lost weight. She had been small to start with, but now she could count each of her ribs when she lifted her shirt. They'd been bringing her food, but never quite enough, and what she did eat was hard to stomach. Add that to the multiple sessions of nausea the visions kept bringing on, and she was melting away into nothing.

Doyle held her close to his chest and his warmth seeped into her. A familiar scent clung to him, almost like walking through a forest after a storm; earthy, charged energy. She didn't ask where he was taking her; if he was taking her to Lyra, he was probably taking her to her death. At least her head and body would stop aching. If he was taking her elsewhere…well, she didn't really have the power to try and guess. Instead, she closed her eyes and rested her heavy head on his shoulder. He walked for a while, and Briar started to realize she didn't feel the earth pressing down on her as heavily. They must be walking closer to the surface of the caves. Doyle shoved open a heavy door with his shoulder, and she gulped in fresh air.

Well, as fresh as it would get in this realm. She choked and sputtered for a moment, but then took another deeper breath. A strong smell of sulfur came from the west wind, and when she blinked up at the sky she could only see dark clouds over dark clouds. Not even a *hint* of actual sky. But at least it wasn't stone. At least it wasn't earth crushing her from all directions.

"Are you okay?" Doyle searched her face as he sat her down gently. He remained crouched before her, brows creased with worry. She nodded, but the cloth he drew gently across her cheeks alerted her to the fact that she'd started crying.

"Why did you bring me up here?" She managed to push the words out, but her tongue felt thick and clumsy in her mouth.

"Yesterday we went to the vault and I had this sudden feeling of claustrophobia. I had to step out of the mountains and go for a short walk before going back to Lyra to discuss what we saw. I just had this sudden urgency to get out…and I thought of you. I've seen your realm. All the beauty, the colors and tastes. Everything is fresh, and new, and open. So far, you have done everything in your power to help

310

us. You haven't complained, you haven't fought us, and we've treated you in the worst way. We've hurt you, taken important things away from you, and to top it off, we took away the sky. You haven't had a breath of fresh air once since you've been here. You've been under stone every minute of every day, and I don't know how you stand it. It's amazing to me you haven't gone insane. Instead, you have continued to amaze me." His words stirred something strong, awoke a bright light inside her. He could kill her, *but* she had seen the alternative. She had seen the tenderness within him. She *craved* it.

"Thank you."

"I am glad to have your help, but sometimes I wish I had just let you through that portal. I don't know where you were going, but you'd have been *so* much better off," he murmured.

"I am no one. Just a pawn in this game of chess between two sisters. Easily discarded." She didn't say it with bitterness. It was a fact Briar had come to live with.

"Maybe to Lyra." Doyle didn't say anything else, didn't say what she was to *him*, but she didn't argue and simply enjoyed being outside. They sat in comfortable silence for some time. The shading and sky never changed, so she had no way of knowing just how much time was passing, but Doyle didn't seem in a hurry to take her back to her room.

"Lyra should have let you see your wings again."

"As she said, they aren't mine anymore." It was a physical effort to speak those words...Briar didn't want to think of her wings locked away under the earth of this foreign realm.

"But they are, and they still possess immense magic. When I was taking them to the vault, it was like they were getting heavier the farther we got from you." The erebus shook his head in mild disbelief. "At first, I thought it was just my arms getting tired or something, but there was far more to it."

"There is a deep connection, yes," Briar whispered. "They were a part of me, the magic that flows through my veins flows through those wings. For the rest of my life I will feel their loss, I will feel them calling to me." The air was helping her head, but she felt tired from so much talking. She wasn't sure she was explaining it right, but couldn't bring herself to speak further.

"My people have been persecuted for simply being what they are. The ancient ones are far too powerful to be destroyed, but *they* are the ones who crave and push for the chaos. Most of us are just trying to live our lives. You see our realm." He moved a hand across the expanse before them, and Briar's gaze followed. A tangle of woods sprawled out to the east, she could make out a molten pit to the west— source of the sulphur stench. The sun hadn't moved so much as an inch in the time they'd been sitting, so she could only assume it never would. Maybe one side of their planet was always dark, while the other was forever left in this harsh light. "It's not so wrong to want something better. Not to destroy, but to enjoy. I used to think it was worth whatever it took to get some freedom to my people; freedom to enter other realms without being killed, freedom to try and make this realm better without the ancient ones demanding some form of payment for any small change. But now, I wonder if maybe we don't deserve what we *have*. We were given this lot because of our past sins against the other races. Once, any race could have any life, but all they chose was war and destruction. I'm starting to wonder if there *is* any good in us."

"Of course there is," Briar insisted, drawing his gaze back to her. "There is good and bad in each of us. The wars of the past were on everyone. Everyone fighting for power, for land, for *more*. It wasn't just the erebi. There was no reason for Malux to sneak me extra servings of things I've been able to eat, or bring me extra blankets. There was no reason for you to bring me up here, or bring me items from my home."

"I'm afraid my bad far outweighs my good, but there is little I can do about the past. Come, I should take you back down. You do look a little better, at least." He swept her off her feet again, but this time she protested.

"I believe I have enough strength to get back down on my own two feet."

"No. You need to preserve what energy you have. Just because there is the slightest tinge of pink in your lips again does not mean you should push yourself needlessly." He carried her back down to her room, but didn't leave right away. "Is there anything else I can get you to help?"

"I think not. You didn't tell me how everything went yesterday."

"Just as you said. Lyra saw where she believes it might be. We will just have to find a way to go back down there and try to get past the code she had."

She nodded, but instantly regretted the jostling. Doyle watched her sympathetically, before he disappeared back through the door. She idly wondered what he did when he wasn't with her. Briar turned to go back to her bed and her pile of blankets, but stopped in her tracks.

There, on top of her pillow, was a very familiar feather. With a shaky hand she reached out and touched it, and felt whole for just a moment. Somehow he had gotten a feather from her wing and brought it to her. The smallest thing, and yet she could feel the power radiating through it, calling to her. The fae felt revived just holding it.

For all of his worry over his bad outweighing his good, he was certainly making an effort to rack up points for the good column. She clutched the feather to her chest and didn't bother stopping the tears from racing down her cheeks.

.℘ .℘ .℘

Feeling more like her former elven self than she had in years, Ana woke with the sun the following morning. The blond glanced at her nightstand, her ring resting atop her favorite book. She considered it for a long moment, thinking of the habits that formed in her time running the shop. For years now she had been leaving her enchanted jewelry on at all times; she'd long since developed the ability to work beyond the cloaking spell when she needed to, and she'd never had the need to utilize her full abilities before now. She hadn't considered how much the cloaking might have impacted her sleep, her overall well being. Spending the night without it, though, left her feeling recharged.

"Goodness knows we're going to need that," she muttered to herself as she planted her feet on the floor. The rest of the apartment was quiet, and she quickly found that it was empty. The only sign that Gabe and Melody had even been there was a plate of waffles and an orange waiting on the table. With a tiny smile, she grabbed the plate and the syrup, and padded downstairs to the back room of the shop.

"Good morning," she murmured to Melody, who was sitting cross-legged on the floor surrounded by books. "Mel...you exhausted yourself looking for an answer yesterday. I don't want your school to suffer when we can help it. Let Gabe and I do some hunting."

"Already ahead of you," Gabe corrected. He strode into the office with his nose already in a book on realms. Ana gestured to him as if to say 'see?' Melody raised an unamused brow at her. A thought struck her, and she prayed her young friend didn't see through her idea. "You need to go to class. Your professors aren't going to understand if you tell them an erebus showed up and took your friend, and you've been spending all of your time trying to figure out how to find her."

"Oh no, no way. I'm not going to hide away in school while Erin needs us! My professors love me, they will get over me missing a few days. Nice try, Ana. I'm going to go grab a few more books." Ana could easily read the frustration on her friend's face. With a heavy sigh, she dropped into the chair behind her desk and took a bite of her waffles.

"I'm gathering that she fits in very well here, even as a human. Definitely just as stubborn," Gabe teased. Tension radiated from her brother, but she was grateful for his attempt at some levity. All of them were standing on the edge of a knife; desperate to find their missing teammate, a breath away from exploding at one another. Part of her wished that she could spare him from this pain, could return him to the blissful ignorance that had been his existence for so long. The significantly larger part of her, though, was eternally grateful that he was by her side once again.

"She's always been irreplaceable here. Some days, I'm convinced she could run this place better than I do. I don't want her to get hurt in a fight that should have never come to this realm to begin with."

"Maybe not," Gabe agreed, "but I've also gathered that she is fiercely loyal to her family. She's not about to let you stop her from fighting to keep that family whole." With an affectionate flick, her

brother shifted the focus to Ana's ear. "Natural looks good on you."
Ana gasped in surprise and brushed her fingers across where he'd just
touched her.

"Oops...good thing we're not open yet. Let me go-"

The elf was silenced by an abrupt shift in the air of the room,
and suddenly she and Gabe were not alone in the office. A beautiful
redheaded woman stood before the portal. Ana was awestruck by her
ears, large and fox like, sticking out of her hair. She glanced at her
brother, and nearly laughed out loud at the startled, bashful look on his
face as he quickly looked away. "Fae often don't have the same
perspective on nudity as humans," she explained, her eyes returning to
the stranger. "Many of them are also shapeshifters, taking on the form
of a specific animal. Fox?"

The woman nodded solemnly. "We don't have time for
explanations," she insisted firmly.

Ana nodded, and glanced again at her brother. "Mel! Hey, can
you run upstairs and grab my robe? We have a visitor, don't be
surprised when you come back here!" She heard her friend call back
an acknowledgement. "How can we help you?"

"My name is Sinopa. Your friend Erin is in need of your help."

Suddenly, all of the discomfort in the room was gone, replaced
by tension and anticipation. "You know where she is?" Gabe
whispered. Sinopa nodded.

"Then what are we waiting for? Let's bring her home." Melody was unfazed by Sinopa's nudity, and the fae took the robe without comment.

The elder elf shook her head. "First of all, I'm going alone. There is no way I am allowing Kali to get anywhere near either of you. Second of all, Sinopa looks like she needs something to eat and a moment to breathe." Ana turned to the fae. "Come on, let's go upstairs and you can relax for a bit." As they made their way towards the stairs, Ana felt a hand wrap around her arm.

"You are *insane* if you think we are letting you go without us," Melody hissed. Ana shot her a stern look, opting to gather some fruit for Sinopa instead of responding. The fae smiled gratefully at her and dug right in.

"More people means more opportunities to get caught. It means slower movement through very dangerous passages. We would be safer going alone," the fae added between bites.

"I'm sorry," Gabe interjected, "but how do we know that this isn't a trap? I have already potentially lost my girlfriend. I *will not* lose my sister as well. We are going with you; we'll have to be careful, but if that's what it takes to get Erin and bring her home safely, *that* is what we are going to do. I appreciate you coming and giving us this chance to save Erin, but I don't know you, and I can't trust you with two people I love."

"I am paying a debt, I am not a stranger to Erin." That got everyone's attention, and the fae found herself at the center of attention. "Erin's mother, Odette, was one of my *best friends*. I was there when her wings were *ripped* from her body because she was in love. I was the only one at their wedding. I saw Erin once as a baby, when I came to warn Odette about the war beginning in Eloas." Sinopa's eyes darted between Ana and Gabe. "I was on that field, fighting off erebi and trying to keep them from getting to Eloas. I watched my friends *die*. I *watched* Erin become an orphan. I was outnumbered and there was *nothing* I could do. So please know, what I do is for my people, to protect them, and to save my best friend's daughter from her parent's fate." Sinopa spoke strongly, her eyes daring anyone to come against her. "I loved Odette. Even though she did not care for me in the same way, she was still my best friend, and I will be loyal to her, even in memory. Even if the only thing I can do is help her daughter."

"I'm sorry, I really am," Gabe spoke up. "But these are *my* people. I lost my home, my friends, my family. I'll not stand idle while you and Aina run into danger."

As exasperated as Ana was at the thought of putting her brother and friend at risk, she couldn't deny that she felt some relief knowing she'd have people she trusted watching her back, as well as someone that would be able to get Erin home if something happened to her.

Erin was still hanging from her wrists as the light faded from the hall. It had to be getting dark, and yet no one came back for her. She wondered what happened to keep them away, but counted herself grateful for the respite. Despite the agony of hanging from her wrists and having her arms asleep for most of the day, some energy had returned and her body had started to heal again.

For the hundredth time since arriving, she tried to focus on the nature around her. She pulled vines up from the ground and had them wrap around the chains above her head. She had done so before, but hadn't been able to get enough strength behind them to break the metal. She felt nature flow through her and her ears seemed to buzz with the use of power. Finally, the vines reached the chains and started to weave in and out of the links. Erin noticed one of the circles give just a little, but then the metal refused to budge anymore. The chains were too strong and thick, there was no way she could get down.

With a groan of disappointment, Erin gave up. To keep trying would be a waste of energy; her power would better serve her by healing her body to be ready for a fight when Ana arrived.

Chapter Twenty

Doyle sat with Lyra before sketches sprawled across a table; one of the queen's vault, and one that detailed every item on the shelf where Lyra believed the amulet was hidden. At the center of that sketch was a silver box, outlined in red, with ancient writing in dark contrast to the silver"This is a dark spell scrawled on here, very dark magic, very old. This right here," she pointed to one section, "speaks of an amulet. It must be in there."

"So the code to get in-"

"Sorry to interrupt, b-but the fae is demanding an audience," an erebus stuttered from the doorway.

Doyle frowned toward Lyra, but she simply arched a brow. "Then why has she not been brought in?" The man scurried away and Lyra stood. He followed suit, taking his normal stance a few steps behind her. Had it only been a day since he saw her last? Briar stepped through the doors, her head held high. Her face had color, still dull, but it was at least there. Yesterday he had been worried she would fall over and shatter to pieces. Lyra had yelled at him for being gone so long, because he kept Briar on the roof for as long as he could, hoping it would help her.

"I thought I might be of service." Without waiting for an invitation, Briar stepped forward and looked over the sketches. "Seems you are missing the most important one. The pencil?" Doyle watched as the two women seemed to have a standoff. As forgiving as Briar had been of him, that forgiveness had not transferred to Lyra, and she made no effort to hide it.

Lyra held out the utensil, but not toward Briar. Instead she held it behind her so he could reach out and grab it. He and Briar met each other's gaze, and he couldn't stop himself from rolling his eyes before grabbing the tool and stepping forward to hand it over. Now that he was closer, he could still see the bags under the fae's eyes, the lingering pain at the corners of her lips, the bones that stuck out far too much on her small frame. But it was an almost-cocky grin she gave him when she took the pencil and leaned down. Her hair fell to one shoulder, and then he saw the feather. She had it hidden by her hair, knotted in so it was touching her skin, but tucked away from clear view.

When she stood again, there was a sketch of a keypad with symbols rather than letters or numbers. "Which of you had the better view of Flereous when she entered the code?"

"I did." Doyle took an automatic step towards her, entering her personal space. "I couldn't see the pad at all, only her back. I don't think there were repetitive choices but I can't really say more than that."

Briar held out her hand but he hesitated to take it. She needed more time to heal. "Doyle, it's okay. Open your mind and try to focus on the memory of what you saw." Her hand waited patiently for him. Somehow she smelled like flowers.

"Doyle, let's get this over with," Lyra interrupted, her arms crossed and voice impatient.

Forcing himself into focus, he thought of Flereous, how her body moved before the keypad. Briar reached out and grabbed his hand, then leaned over her rendition of the keypad. Lyra dove forward to grab the pencil as Briar fell into her trance. Briar's fingers reached out and tapped the different symbols, Lyra wrote them down as she watched. Briar's other hand kept a steady grip on his even as she stopped tapping. She didn't rise from the trance immediately, and when she eventually did, she looked stronger than she had the other times he'd watched her have a vision.

"The amulet won't be in there...but there *is* a spell you will need. The amulet," Briar searched the sketch, "is right here." She pointed to a shelf above the box, then grabbed the pencil and did a quick but thorough sketch of a simple necklace with a black amulet at the center. "Get this, get the spell. I believe that is all I can help you with right now. Our next move is close, but hinges on this. I don't foresee issues getting into the vault but I cannot guarantee anything. Any choice either you or Flereous makes could change things. Be quick. Be careful."

Only then did Briar release his hand, taking her warmth with her when she did. She turned and left them before Lyra could think of anything else to try and pry from her.

Doyle and Lyra talked over their plan, and waited for the perfect moment to sneak down to the vaults. The queen was caught up with an *amorous affair,* so Lyra believed she would be otherwise entertained for the rest of the night, giving them time to get there and back out undetected. Lyra led the way, having a better memory of which turns to take. They ran into a few people on the way to the queen's sitting area, but no one paid them any attention. Once they entered the narrow walkway, they didn't see anyone else.

"Okay, the true test of the observer fae's powers." Lyra held out the paper where she'd written the code Briar showed them. She pulled back the rough stone that would reveal the keypad, and entered each symbol carefully. They both held their breath, until the wall moved. Doyle was the only one the ward would allow through, so Lyra waited outside of the barrier while he grabbed the amulet and spell. It almost seemed too easy. They closed up, and with racing hearts, they started back up the path. They were just at the landing for the sitting area when one of the queen's lackeys came around the corner. She caught sight of both of them standing at the entrance to the path and stopped in her tracks.

"What are you doing down here?"

"Excuse me? I am the queen's sister. You dare to question me?" Lyra stepped forward, all irritation and haughtiness.

"You aren't supposed to be here. No one is." The woman stood her ground. Doyle noticed Lyra's back straighten, ready for a fight.

"*They* are. They are with me, I had orders from her majesty. It doesn't really concern you, but they recently brought the queen a collector's item, and the case it was in had a crack. I took them down to replace it. We disposed of the old one, and we're on our way. You are now interrupting us." Malux approached from behind them and waved a hand, dismissing the woman with an air of nonchalance as she slinked away. Doyle wondered if Lyra was gaping at Malux in the same way he felt he was. Malux's dragon eye seemed to see through him when Malux turned his attention to Doyle.

"Briar saw trouble and sent me to you. You should make sure you take care of that girl. If she didn't want to help you, she could have ignored the vision she saw." His eyes darted to Lyra and Doyle tried to ignore the twinge of jealousy over hearing someone else stand up for Briar. Malux gave a small bow to each of them, and then continued on his way, as if he hadn't just stopped them from getting beheaded, or worse. He and Lyra shared a look before fleeing the scene.

$$\mathcal{C} \; \mathcal{C} \; \mathcal{C}$$

Ana drew a steadying breath as the nervous energy in the small office of *Mystifying* threatened to smother her. Sinopa, shifted into her fox form, was practically prancing to cross through to Loinnir. Melody seemed to be giving herself an internal pep talk, and Gabe - *Toron* - kept glancing between her and the portal.

"Are you sure?" Ana whispered beside him, reading the fear in the lines of his forehead. She wondered what was going through his mind, and wished that they'd had more time, and better circumstances, to reconnect before throwing themselves headlong into danger to save Erin.

"We don't have any more time to waste. Who knows what they are doing to Erin. Let's go."

Sinopa laid in the center of the portal. Everyone reached down to touch her fur, so she could lead them to the correct location on the other side. Ana steeled herself for the unpleasant experience of this particular mode of travel, and felt for her brother who hadn't experienced it in so long. The sudden lurch nearly toppled him and

Melody, but they both seemed to regain their footing easily enough. Ana had to breathe through a wave of nausea, and gave an apologetic smile to her companions when they both paled for a moment as well.

"Everyone okay?" Melody spoke up, her voice shaky. Everyone nodded, and Sinopa whined at their feet, trying to urge them on. The small group started to follow.

No matter how many times Ana traveled to Loinnir, she was always awestruck by the explosion of colors and nature that put even her home realm to shame. Loinnir was full of deep blues, bright purples, hues of pinks and yellows seemed to hang from every branch and cover every flowered field. The air was crisp and fresh, filled with the songs of birds.

As they walked close to one field of flowers, a hoard of what looked like butterflies rose from the grass. Gabe stopped in his tracks to watch them take to the air, but Sinopa stood in front of him protectively and tried to lead him away. Ana watched realization dawn on him that they were not butterflies after all, but pixies.

"Great," she groaned. They both remembered pixies that lived in Eloas and quickly tried to move on. It was too late, though. The small beings had already taken an interest in them, and went straight for Melody, who had never come across the creatures before.

"What-" Flashes of small green bodies with bright yellow eyes were visible as the hoard surrounded the witch, nipping at Melody's dark skin with sharp little teeth. "Ow!" Melody tried to swat them away, and Ana and Gabe quickly joined in, batting the small creatures back toward the flowered field.

Sinopa took charge with a few short little yips. She jumped and caught one of the pixies in her jaws and shook it. The rest of them seemed to watch in horror as the pixie got dizzy and flew from Sinopa's mouth with a high-pitched scream, and flew off before the fox set her gleaming eyes on them.

"Are you okay?" Ana asked, looking over Melody carefully.

"Sure, not exactly a fan though." She rubbed at a small circle of bites, and their group started to hurry from the field before the pixies grew brave once more.

They didn't make it much farther before thoughts that weren't her own invaded Ana's mind: *She knows about Gabe! Keep Gabe safe! Forget me!* The elf froze at Erin's voice, and grabbed her brother's arm.

"It's Erin, I hear her!"

"What?" Melody looked around them in confusion, searching for their friend.

"No, she used telepathy!"

.℘ .℘ .℘

Something was happening. Erin could feel a change in the air, like an electric buzz. She'd spent the night hanging from the ceiling, but was grateful no one returned to continue the torture. She had been close to losing it, and with the time to heal and rest a bit, she was feeling strong again. Early in the morning, a group of brutes looking like Bogor showed up to take her down. They chained her back to the wall, and left without a word.

She was desperate for a change of clothes and a shower. Her current outfit was mostly ripped away from the multiple cuts, lashes, and hits she'd taken. Dried blood, sweat, and her own fluids caked her skin. Almost like an answer to a prayer, a group of fae showed up to her door not long after she had been moved.

"What is going on?" Erin pleaded when they came in. They were fae, they *had* to be on her side, right? One turned, and she saw familiar gashes on the woman's back. Someone had taken her wings from her. That explained her chalky coloring and downcast eyes. These fae had been broken. Her mother was strong, she'd accepted the removal of her wings for love. These fae had probably been tortured into submission, and then had Bogor set loose on them for his own amusement.

"Please! *Talk* to me! Tell me what is going on!"

Nothing. They silently brought in a bucket of water and sponges. They left her chained, but ripped her clothes away and washed her. The water was warm on her skin, but it took multiple scrubbings for the grime to finally chip away.

"Am I about to be part of some sacrifice to the Kali god? Because I think I'll pass." Erin had no idea what was going on. The fae moved in silent grace. Their movements almost seemed choreographed. The skin on her back was still tender and she felt the welts from the whip that were still healing. It was better than open gashes across her back, but even the warm water made the skin goosebump and sharp pain hit her. She held as still as possible as the dried blood was scraped away.

Finally they were done, leaving her raw and aching. One fae, with hair that reminded her of Ana, produced an outfit. They released one hand at a time so they could drape her arms through the dress.

"What is happening?" Erin yelled, feeling panicked now.

"Oh nothing my dear. You are our guest, we thought you should be treated as such." Kali spoke from behind the fae and clapped her hands together. Quickly, the small group of women gathered up their items and fled. Erin forced her fear back down, refusing to allow Kali to see any more of it.

"Where's my friend? You rushed off with him last night, and he hasn't been back to see me." Erin feigned a pout. "I certainly hope he didn't die in a battle."

"You really do have a smart mouth don't you? Is that smiled upon in Sula? As I see it, it seems like a good way to run off any suitors."

"I make out just fine, thanks," Erin sneered.

"Yes," a flash of sharp teeth, "with the prince of elves from what I've heard." Her smirk grew at the shock in Erin's eyes. "You *do* realize I have eyes on your people? I could have struck them down a thousand times without lifting a finger, but that just doesn't make for good entertainment."

Erin's heart stopped. She knew about Gabe, she knew he was Ana's brother. Now they would be after him. If Ana left him behind to come and rescue her, the erebi could get to him. His memories hadn't come back, he hadn't had time to train, he would be a sitting duck.

"I wonder how our dear princess feels about her brother screwing a halfling. You know, the elves are very high-browed. They look down on other beings; the erebi, the humans, the fae, it doesn't matter. None of us can stand up to their *beauty*. They are so in love with themselves, I find it hard to believe they get anything done."

"And yet you said you have still not won against them. Guess that makes you pretty weak," Erin spat.

"There's that mouth again." Kali swung her hand across Erin's mouth with a force that snapped her head to the side. "I really would love to cut out your tongue. You know, your healing powers won't fix *that* my dear. And you would be so much more tolerable without it."

She knows about Gabe! Keep Gabe safe! Forget me! Erin tried again, and again. She kept running the words like a mantra through her mind, pretending she was putting them in a box and throwing them at Ana's head. Anything to get the stupid words from her skull and into Ana's.

Kali's fingers pinched Erin's mouth, drawing her attention and making her lips pucker. "I really don't see why she keeps the friends that she does. A weak human, a halfling…"

Erin jerked her head free. "Well, I've seen the friends you keep. I don't think you should be one to judge. It's clear you enjoy the sound of your own voice, though. I wonder if that's why Bogor has so much aggression. He just has to listen to you all day-" This time a knife cut across her cheek. She wasn't even sure when Kali *got* a knife, but she felt the fresh slice in her skin and her vision went dark. "You know, I thought you said I was company. If you really want to show me a good time, you guys will unchain me and let me fight *back*. But I guess erebi aren't about a fair fight."

"Erin?"

Erin froze. She felt the small push of a mental invasion. Ana's familiar voice echoed in her mind.

"In due time my dear. Until then, I hope you won't mind if I forget your lunch." Kali stalked from the room, but Erin was no longer paying her any mind; she was concentrating on Ana's voice.

"Erin? We are here. We are coming. Just hold on. We are coming."

"Ana, for once, hear me*! They know about Gabe! Forget about me, keep Gabe safe!"* She felt a tingle at the base of her skull, like the fuzziness someone would get after hitting their head.

"Erin! I hear you! We are coming! Gabe is with me, he's safe."

Gabe was with her? She thought it was a good idea to bring him to the middle of an erebi war when he only just found out about his powers? Her abilities had pretty much been rendered useless while she was here, and she had a lot more time to deal with having powers than he had.

"*Erin?*" An all too familiar voice pushed into her mind. Erin was thankful she was alone because she gasped as the deep voice of Gabe washed over her. "*Erin, I'm sorry. I'm coming. I love you.*"

I love you, I love you, I love you. She wasn't sure if the words left her mind this time. She wasn't sure if he heard her. But she heard *him*, and her soul was revived.

"It's time." A harsh, rattling voice broke into her happiness. She found Bogor standing before her.

"It speaks?" Erin asked in genuine surprise.

"Get up." Bogor ignored her and yanked her to her feet. One quick movement, and he had her out of the chains and was dragging her behind him. *Time for what?*

Chapter Twenty-One

Briar waited for someone to come for her, and when no one did, she started yelling through the door. She could sense some darkness in the wooden barrier, and avoided touching it. She continued shouting until her voice was hoarse, and finally heard footsteps pounding down the hall. The door flung open, and Doyle stood in her doorway, dagger in hand.

"Are you okay?" He demanded after searching her room with quick, darting eyes.

"Just sitting here wondering if I sent Malux in time. It's been hours and no one thought to come and tell me if it worked or not." She was angry. She shouldn't care if they were all killed - she would be able to escape and go home if they had been killed. But she *did* care, at least for Doyle. He only wanted the best for his people, and she had come to care for him. She wanted the future she could see with him, but Briar insisted to herself that she *shouldn't* care. The very different alternative was still there, and she couldn't trust which way he would turn. With the luck she'd had in the last year, it seemed far more likely he'd stick her with that dagger.

"I apologize." Doyle lowered said blade and swiped his forehead with the palm of his hand. "Yes, Malux got to us just in time. Thank you. I was only trying to give you time to recover from your last vision. Lyra has been making herself visible to the queen, so that if the amulet is discovered missing, they won't think of her. She's been all around the realm this morning."

Briar looked into the red of Doyle's eyes. All he had been through, all he had lost. Would he lose more before it was over? "It's time to make your next move. I need to speak with Lyra."

"You saw more?" His brows rose at that. She started pacing, loving that she finally had enough energy to move. She had meditated over her feather, trying to search for more clues. Flashes came to her: their need for Malux's help when leaving the caves, Loinnir, the flash of battle, the erebus with white skin and black horns. She saw Doyle and Lyra waiting for the person they needed to give the amulet to. She could *smell* the forest. The presence of so many erebi was slowly killing the area, but it hadn't stopped her from gulping in the smell of home. She gained energy just from being there in her mind.

"Still not a face..." She did regret not having that detail, but nothing she'd done had been able to bring it into focus. "But I got a clearer picture of the woods, the area in which you'll need to wait. I should be able to give you enough information for you to find the spot, and then all you will have to do is wait for the person to show up."

"Come with me." Doyle took her by the elbow and started her toward Lyra's sitting area. It was empty when they walked in. Deep in thought, Doyle summoned one of the lackeys and told them to fetch her. Feeling daring and self-indulgent, Briar went for the chaise and lounged. *Actually* lounged. Her bones and muscles sighed in relief. Doyle turned back to her and froze. Something flashed in his eyes, though she couldn't be sure what it was; it was gone before she could try to place it.

"Oh dear," Briar feigned a gasp. "Will she kill me if she finds me sitting here?"

"You have proven too valuable. Let her stew a little." He actually cocked a grin. Her heart stumbled in her chest. She wanted to respond, throw back a little joke, but Lyra entered the room. Her cat-like eyes were immediately drawn to the fae on the chaise. Briar couldn't help it, she had something the woman wanted, and she was going to make her beg. Briar leaned back again, caught Doyle's small chuckle, and waited for Lyra to speak first.

"So I've been busy all day trying to keep our names clear, and I'm summoned away to watch the fae sit around? Is that what I am to understand?"

"Certainly not." Briar didn't sit up, but gave an innocent smile. "It's time for you to go to Loinnir. You don't need the spell, not yet. But the person who needs the amulet is there, or will be soon. You need to get there, get to a hill above a battle, and wait in the woods for them."

"And how am I supposed to know this mysterious person?"

"She is going to come with us." Doyle spoke for the first time since Lyra entered. Lyra shot a look at him and Briar sat up, her pretense of ease long gone.

"Excuse me?" Lyra sneered.

Doyle seemed unaffected by the nasty look on the woman's face, and stated again: "She is going to come with us." He broke his usual stance and gestured toward her. Briar almost flinched, afraid that if he drew more attention to her, Lyra would pounce. "After all that she's helped us with, I don't think she will run. You can have a rune placed on her if you need. Place the other on me, and I'll be fully responsible for her. We haven't come this far only to go into another realm with a map, and a time and place to wait in the woods."

He actually let out a small huff and paced toward her. "We bring her and she can help make sure this goes smoothly. We would have failed leaving the caves yesterday if she hadn't been able to send

Malux to help us. She won't be able to send anyone across a portal if she sees something."

"Did she put you up to this? Bat her lashes and ask you to get her away?" Lyra stepped forward and placed a hand against his cheek. "She *is* beautiful. I certainly won't stop you if there is something you wish to take, but she is too valuable to just let her go running off to her realm."

"Don't treat me like a *child*. Please tell me one moment since you've known me when I have let desire or my own *well-being* dictate how I conduct myself within our cause? Briar could have let us get captured last night, and Malux would have freed her if we were out of the picture. No one else really knows about her, at least not that she is our prisoner. She had freedom in her grasp...and yet she sent help. She will help us until this is over, because she gave us her word that she would. If you want to put the mission at risk because you don't want her to go into her own realm, even though she is far too valuable to leave behind, then I wish to stay behind also. Maybe if she sees something, *I* could get to you in time. So why don't you tell me, which you would prefer?"

Briar gaped at him. The color of Lyra's face had turned to ash, and Briar had a feeling he had never talked to her that way before. Lyra was clearly stunned, but there were deeper workings within. She was actually debating how she would react.

"Of course you would never put our goal at risk." Lyra smiled, the indulgent smile a mother would give her child. "We will need to take precautions. Take her back to her room. I will send Jared to place the runes on you both." Lyra turned a hard eye on her. "When do we need to leave?"

"Tonight, if possible. You saw Kali first, and then it was a bit of a hike to where we needed to be. The morning at the latest, but I'm not sure how long it will take for us to walk."

"Tonight it is. While you are getting your runes I will tell my sister we are going to Loinnir because a contact of Doyle asked for our assistance. A battle is about to take place according to you, so Flereous should know of it already. She will hopefully assume that is why we are needed."

"We will see you soon then." Doyle took Briar by the elbow again, his grip urgent like he wanted to drag her from the room before Lyra decided to throw a dagger at her back. He didn't speak as they returned to her room, but the second the door closed behind them she turned wide eyes toward him.

"Thank you! I had no idea you would do that. I certainly was not expecting to see…to go to my realm with you." She'd almost said she wasn't expecting to see home again. Ever. She hadn't been. She had come to terms with the fact she would likely die in Skia, the mountains crushing her from above.

"It was the best thing for the mission. You don't have a clear face yet, and we all know that the smallest decision could change our course. Having you there will help us to know if something has been, or needs to be, changed." He said the words in his normal stoic way, but his eyes were soft as they watched her. "The runes that will be placed on us are no joke. They are temporary, but will tie us together. For forty-eight hours we will not be able to be far from one another; believe me, you'll feel it if you stray. If you try to escape, or make a run for it, you will end up regretting it very quickly. And if anything drastic is to happen to one of us, the other will also feel it. So please, Blue...don't try to run and get yourself killed. I won't die, but it won't feel pleasant either."

He had put himself at risk by standing up for her. Yes, she could help them in Loinnir, but she was also a risk. He believed in her, and he was willing to stake his own well-being on that. It wasn't something she would soon forget. "I won't run," she vowed.

.℮ .℮ .℮

The sunlight was fading in the distance, and Sinopa was starting to act anxious. Melody gathered a few sticks for everyone and created fire for torches so they could see better, but they all knew it would be time to stop for the night soon.

"How much farther is it?" Ana asked, catching a sideways glance from Gabe. Her brother watched in fascination as Sinopa seamlessly changed from a fox mid-step, barely glancing at them as she continued moving.

"I'd say another two hours at least. But I have a feeling it will take a bit longer than that."

"The erebi are getting closer." Ana could feel the dark energy growing, and knew the others could too.

"We should camp for the night. Gather our strength and hopefully avoid any fights as long as possible," Melody suggested.

"Melody, every second we rest, Erin could be getting closer to death," Gabe cut in.

Sinopa shook her head, her long tendrils falling forward to cover most of her body. "I told you, they want to keep Erin alive. She's bait for the princess."

"And I'm sure they are treating her like a beloved house cat, right?"

Ana rested a hand on Gabe's forearm and came to a stop. "Melody is right. We aren't going to get to Erin tonight. Even if we did, it would be after fighting our way there, and it's not like they are just going to hand Erin over to us. We need to be prepared. We can't get her out alive if we get ourselves killed." Ana turned to Sinopa. "Do you know of a safe place for us to camp for the night?"

The fae nodded, and started to lead the way off from the path they had been following. Gabe slowed to trail at the back of the group and kept a wary eye.

Everyone settled solemnly under the lip of a cave. Melody got a fire started as darkness blanketed the sky. Sinopa, the only one familiar with the realm, was the only one that did not turn her gaze upwards. Stars they had never seen before started to come alive; they were in constant movement with random specks of blue and red dotting the sky. Ana wondered if those orbs were other planets in the realm.

"We should have a plan for tomorrow." Sinopa's voice drew their attention back to the reality of their situation.

"Where exactly are they keeping her?" Gabe asked.

Sinopa told them about the dungeon and the guards.

"I should go on my own-" Ana held up slender fingers before anyone could start to argue. "I can cause a distraction. Sinopa can lead you guys to Erin and break her free, then come back for me. Hopefully Kali won't be expecting all of us."

"I should go with you. Melody and Sinopa can get Erin. You shouldn't be alone facing Kali. We should both be there," Gabe insisted.

"No, Erin said Kali knows about you now. If she has both of us together..." Ana shook her head fiercely.

"Then I'll come with you, Gabe can get Erin," Melody offered. "She'll want him anyway. I may be able to do a protection spell to keep Kali at bay until they join us again."

Ana relented with a nod. Sinopa turned back into her fox form and wandered into the woods a little bit away from them. Ana stopped paying attention to the conversation around her as she watched the fox carefully; Sinopa stopped at the foot of a tree and sat down. It seemed as though she was on watch duty, but Ana noticed she was not alone. There was a black crow, almost completely hidden by the darkness of the forest. A few breaths later the crow took off, and Ana wondered if Gabe had been right to question Sinopa's loyalty. The fox settled down with her tail curled around her snout. Though she was uncertain, Ana knew they would do Erin no good if they didn't sleep, so she nodded to her brother and friend, and the three settled in for what little rest they might find.

.℮ .℮ .℮

Briar was *home*. The cool fae air was crisp in her lungs, and her blood pumped renewed energy through her body. The loss of her wings, though, struck her so hard she nearly fell over. Her first thought had been to spread them and leap into the air. Instead, she remained at Doyle's side and tried to stay calm. They were just outside a large encampment of erebi. Ruins, long ago abandoned by her kind, had now been taken over by his. The ground beneath her was sick; the air grew stale the closer they got to the ruins...but it was still home.

Lyra walked ahead, but kept darting glances back at her, probably waiting for an excuse to kill. The portal they had shot through left her a little off kilter, but Doyle was at her side, and she was sure if she *did* fall over, he would catch her. He didn't want to have to deal with the after effects of her scraping a knee and their joined runes making him feel it too, after all. The rune placement had been simple, a spell over each of them, a small burning sensation, and then she was left feeling about the same as she had before. Only now she had a small marking on her wrist that matched Doyle. He told her it would fade once the spell was over, and reminded her it was not something to mess with. She couldn't go too far from him or she would *feel it*, whatever that meant. It didn't sound good, and she wasn't about to push boundaries.

"Stay close," he whispered in her ear as pitch black erebi swarmed near them. The energy she had been given by entering her home realm started slowly seeping away when they got close. She recoiled, not wanting to know what might happen if she accidentally touched one of them. Darkness hung overhead. Candles and large bonfires started popping up as they entered the ruins and made their way through a small maze of erebi and stone.

Doyle took her hand. Ever since she'd told him it was easier for her to enter a vision with him, he'd avoided skin-to-skin contact. She wasn't sure if he was doing it to keep from throwing her into an unwanted vision, or if he simply didn't want her to see something she shouldn't. Either way, he had been careful to only touch her elbow, where her arm was covered by a sleeve, or the small of her back, but no longer. Instead he gripped her hand and pulled her tight to his side. The action made her heart leap to her throat. The feather, as small as it was, *did* help her gain a little control over her visions. After Doyle gave it to her, she had been able to meditate and see things more clearly. She wasn't jostled so violently from one scene to another.

Lyra had hurt her own mission in taking her wings away. If she still had them, was still able to draw strength from them, she might have already solved the riddle before them. They moved through the castle, teeming with the infection erebi, and others of all shapes and sizes. She also saw her own kind; fae were scattered throughout, clearly being used as servants. Briar wanted to search each of their faces as she went by, see if she recognized anyone, see if they were being well cared for or abused. Something held her back from doing so...*fear*. It gripped at her throat, making it hard to draw breath. The only thing she could really do for them would be to get the erebi out of their realm as quickly as possible.

She tightened her hold on Doyle when they turned the corner, and she came face to face with the erebus that killed her mother.

"Doyle!" A grin spread on the she-erebus' face and sharp teeth glinted at the fae. "How nice to see you again so soon. The work you did for me before helped a great deal." Black eyes flicked to her and their joined hands before shifting to Lyra. "Lyra." The smile was quickly replaced by a thin line. At least she wasn't the only one who wasn't Lyra's biggest fan.

"Kali. It's been a while. What with you trying to fight a war on two fronts and all."

"This is hardly what I would call a war. These fae types are so easily...*bendable*. Have you caught yourselves a little pet?" Kali's eyes went back to her. It was disconcerting to stare straight into darkness. She expected Doyle to drop her hand, but other than a quick flinch of his fingers, he held her steady. "This is Briar. She has been helping us with a small project." Doyle held out his wrist and showed his rune. That seemed to be enough explanation for their closeness and why she was walking 'freely'.

"Ah." She lost interest as a pig-snouted erebus headed in their direction. Briar believed he was grinning, but she couldn't be sure as he had tusks sticking from his mouth, setting it at an odd angle. Before anyone could react he stalked right up to Briar, grabbing her upper arm and dragging her close. "You won't let me play with the other one. How about this one." He grabbed her jaw and turned her face to him. She heard Doyle's voice, terse, getting closer even as Pig Snout moved her away from him, but something else came over her; a vision came on, hot and strong. It wasn't the kind that pulled her under, bringing her to the depths, but it was *violent*. An assault on her mind as flash after flash passed through. She was still on her feet, she could still feel the rough hands on her, hear voices around her, but she was frozen, her mind elsewhere.

She saw a halfling, chained to the ceiling, her body beaten. She saw a group searching for the prisoner. They were getting close, traveling through Loinnir from the other portal. They were coming to try and rescue her. She saw Pig Snout pounding on the halfling for amusement. Kali stood in the background, clearly enjoying the show. Briar felt the pain in the woman's body, weak from healing herself over and over. She felt each wound and each ache inside her, and longed to run to her aid. Then, suddenly, Briar was standing in the forest, above the battle. Lyra stepped out to hand over the amulet and a face, one from the group, finally came into view.

Pig Snout's hands were off of her now. She felt like a rag doll being passed around, but her mind searched for what happened next in the vision. Why did they need to give the amulet to the group? Would it help them save the halfling? Why would the amulet give them leverage to get them to help bring down Queen Flereous?

But then Doyle was in her ear, his hands on her, bringing her back to reality. Her head pounded, her body ached with the halfling's pains. "Stay with me, Blue." His voice was strained and quiet in her ear. She was walking...she was going through the motions, and the clouds in her eyes finally started to lift. As soon as they were closed off in a room she expected questions, expected yelling or demands.

Instead, Doyle brought her down beside him on a sofa and dropped his head into his hands.

"What the hell was that?" Doyle managed.

Briar massaged her temple and shook her head, leaning back against the cushion. "I'm sorry. He grabbed me and I just went under-"

"No, is that what it's *always* like for you? Do you actually feel the things you are seeing? My head feels split open."

That made her look at him closer. He had the same stance she normally did after a vision. Belatedly, she remembered the runes they shared. He'd told her if something happened to one of them, the other might have some affects. Clearly, that had backfired for him. With a tired sigh, she let her eyes close and simply breathed.

"Well, what did you see?"

"I…" She glanced back to Doyle, who was still holding his head next to her. She wondered if he had seen the same things she had or if he just felt the after effects. "I saw the face of the person you need to give the amulet to. Pig Snout was connected to them somehow…a *mutual friend*. Once I had that connection, my mind just filled in the blanks we had been missing. Doyle, are you okay?"

"Fine. It's starting to fade. How are you even standing right now? I thought I was going to fall over right there in front of Kali and Bogor." He snorted then. "Though, I like your little nickname for him."

"Here..." She stood and walked around the back of the sofa so she could rub his spine as she liked after a vision. Her head was pounding, her body still hurt, but after being away from her home realm for so long, it seemed her body was adjusting quicker now that she could draw energy from the land around her.

"What a cute couple you two make," Lyra said dryly. "So. we need to start our way up the mountain then? We can't stay around here for too long, or Kali will give us stuff to do. Then my sister will hear about it if we disappear on her."

"Yes. They will reach us early tomorrow. It would probably be best to camp there and wait. Then, I think we will need to go to the second portal, the one where you caught me," she added for Doyle. "Once they are given the amulet, they will be walking into battle. We will use our leverage over them another time, but for now, we just need to give them the amulet and then get out. We can't come back to this portal, there won't be time." She felt his muscles loosen under her hands, so she pulled back and heard him sigh in relief as he stood and stretched.

"Thank you for that." His eyes were dark when he turned back to look at her. She only gave a small nod, and found Lyra's gaze shifting quickly between the two of them.

"Then we should get a move on. I'm going to see if I can grab some provisions. Stay here, finish recovering, and as soon as I return we will leave." Lyra didn't wait for a response or argument. She simply went right back out the door.

"Briar..." Doyle looked at her now, some new profound understanding on his face. With how quickly he recovered she doubted he'd been jolted as hard as he could have, though the taste he got was enough to tell him what it was like for her to have a vision. "My whole body hurts. I could feel what you were feeling, the head splitting, the pain through my body, but I couldn't *see*. Does something happen to us in the woods?"

"No. That was the pain of the mutual friend. Pig Face and Kali are beating a halfling in their dungeon. They are using her as bait. The group we need to find is coming for her. This whole thing is for them. I could feel it in Kali's gaze. This *whole* thing isn't about gaining Loinnir, not really. It's about that group...she's trying to draw them here."

"What does the amulet do?"

"I don't know yet. I saw who we give it to, and I know we will need to prepare the spell Lyra took. Somehow that gives us leverage to get their help. Like I said, we'll need it, just not yet."

"The halfling...do you know her? Is she...okay?"

"She's hurt and weak...I'm not sure yet if they will save her. I couldn't see that far. Too many decisions still have to be made on their part. I don't know her. Are you okay now?" She asked again, searching his face for signs of weariness.

"Am I? How are *you* holding up?"

A light smile tugged at her lips. "I'm home for the moment, so it's giving me strength. I can feel the magic moving in me."

Doyle took her in for a moment. "You have color again. For as short a time as you've been here, your color is back, you look-" He cut himself off and just gave a warm smile. Another smile, just for her. She wasn't sure what to do with that, so she simply smiled back. Lyra returned, and after a nod to each of them she led the way out of the room. They had a rendezvous point to get to.

.ℰ .ℰ .ℰ

"Am I getting through to anyone?"

Ana sat up with a jolt and felt Gabe do the same. *"They moved me. I'm outside and tied to a tree or something. I'm blindfolded, I can't tell you where I am exactly. They didn't move me far, though. Go back, they are setting some kind of trap and I can't help you. They had some fae put a spell on my bindings. I can't use my powers to get loose. Please, can* anyone *hear me? I have no idea if this stupid power is working!"*

"Erin, calm down, we are coming for you. We will be fine."

A quick look around the camp showed Sinopa was still asleep under the tree, and Melody was resting at the edge of the cave. "I don't think Sinopa can be trusted," Ana whispered, turning her body so that her back was to the fae. "I think she sent a message through another fae last night. There was a crow sitting with her when she left the fire."

"What do we do?" Gabe's eyes landed on the fox.

"We don't say anything. We don't tell them we heard from Erin, or that she was moved. We see what moves Sinopa makes first. Let's wake them now, we should get moving." She gently woke Melody, and called out to Sinopa. "It's time to get moving. The longer we wait, the greater risk to Erin."

The fox stared at her for a long moment, before turning and trotting away. With a pointed look at her brother, Ana followed and felt Melody and Gabe close behind her. They traveled in silence for a while, each keeping careful watch of their surroundings.

Ana was yanked from her thoughts by the sound of a twig snapping nearby. She glanced around at the others, and similar looks let her know that it hadn't been any of them. "Mel, come between Gabe and me," she whispered, listening intently for more noise. The young witch started to argue, but Gabe grabbed her by the shoulders and moved her. He faced away from Ana, and searched the woods around them.

"We've got company," Gabe hissed. Sinopa suddenly shifted back to her fae form and stepped back towards the group as well. From the shadows, black infection erebi surrounded them. "How do we want to handle this?"

"The only thing we *can* do is fight," Sinopa answered. "Do not let them cut or scratch you. This is how the infection spreads to a new host." Gabe and Ana drew their daggers, and Ana glanced over her shoulder at Melody. As prepared as any of them might have been, the terror was clear on Melody's face, and the elf vowed to do whatever it took to make sure she got home safely.

The erebi slithered forward out of the shadows, and the fight began. Sinopa growled and lunged for the nearest enemy, dodging a slash and burying a dagger into its chest. Ana took a deep, steadying breath, and tightened her grip on her own blade.

"Mel-"

"Shut up, Ana. I have a knife, I know how to use it. Don't get yourself killed worrying about me," Melody snapped. The witch quickly started muttering a spell under her breath. Ana knew it well, they practiced it often in case of a fight. The protection spell would make it harder for the erebi to cut their skin, but it would not save them completely. Pride swelled in the elf, but she stamped it down quickly. There would be time later to gush over the young girl she'd taken in years ago. First, they all needed to not get killed.

Easy enough, right?

She took out the first erebus easily enough, but when she turned to check on her friends Ana came face to face with a *much* larger erebus than the other one. "Oh...hello..." She ducked under the shadow's sweeping arm, and instinctively kicked at what should've been a knee. The resulting *crunch* and roar confirmed that hope, and Ana placed a solid kick to its chest. As it crashed to the ground, Ana followed and stabbed it in the heart like Sinopa had.

"Little help!"

Ana spun at her brother's voice, and saw him double-teamed. Without a sound, she yanked her dagger free and crept up behind one of his attackers. Before it even reacted, her knife had pierced its heart from behind. From there, Gabe easily dispatched the last remaining creature. The siblings stared at one another as they caught their breath.

"Well *that* was not fun," Melody muttered, kicking at the dark mass at her feet.

"Kali must have sent them out. If we don't keep moving, there *will* be more." Sinopa turned, a fire in her eyes Ana could not quite read. The elf followed her gaze, and saw a body sprawled further down. Sinopa started in that direction and the small group followed silently. "No," Sinopa gasped when they came around the collection of brush on the ground.

Ana looked in horror at the small group of fae bodies. They must have been a few minutes too late to save them from the attack. A woman and three children, their veins slowly turning black as the erebus blood took over the bodies that remained.

"What's happening to them?" Gabe asked quietly as their hands and feet slowly became completely black and the skin hardened.

"That's what happens when you are infected. Eventually they will become an infection also." Ana had to stop speaking for a moment and take a breath. Seeing the innocent face of the youngest child slowly turn black with infection squeezed at her chest.

She saw the fae before her, but she also saw her elven people that she left behind to save her own life. Who knows how many of her friends went through a similar change? "The infection spreads through the veins quickly, then it turns the skin black and hard to make it harder to kill them while they go through the change. Eventually they will take on more of the wispy, shadow look."

"No!" Sinopa said stronger this time. She stomped ahead, her hair flying wild in the wind. She held out her dagger and stabbed the woman in the heart with a devastating screech.

"What are you doing?" Melody yelled out.

Ana put out a hand to grab Melody's arm and hold her back. "She's stopping them from turning, she's saving them."

The elf could only watch as the fae stopped the others from changing. When she finished, Sinopa turned into the bushes and threw up. When her stomach was empty, she fell to her knees and openly wept. Ana wrapped her arms around the fae's shoulders and held her.

After Sinopa had her moment of grief, they moved forward with a new fire under their feet. Sinopa led the way with a quick pace, seemingly on a mission for revenge. Ana wondered again about the crow from the night before, and what the connection could be. They came to a clearing and Sinopa pointed ahead.

"They are keeping her right down there."

Ana and Gabe exchanged a look, wondering if they should voice that Erin had been moved. Sinopa could have turned on them during the fight, to let the erebi get to them, and she didn't; she could have let the fae turn...but she didn't. So *why* had she been talking to another fae in secret?

"She's not there anymore," Gabe spoke up, making the decision for both of them. "She communicated to us earlier that they moved her nearby, she's outside somewhere."

"No..." Sinopa's eyes started to search below them. Without a word she took off as a fox, sprinting down the hill. Everyone exchanged looks before running after her. They went through another collection of trees and almost lost sight of the fox, before she came to a sudden stop and changed back. She turned on them then. "Everything I did was to save her and my people. You should have told me earlier! It's too late for Erin now."

"What? It's not too late until she is *dead*!" Gabe barked.

"Isn't she though? The second Kali gets her eyes on Ana, Erin is dead. We *can't* get to her." Sinopa nodded toward the break in the trees. Gabe pushed past and saw what Sinopa saw. Ana slowly approached when Gabe's shoulders fell.

Erin was tied to a post in the center of a field. The field was almost black from the amount of infection erebi around her. They circled her slowly, ready to attack as soon as they heard the word.

Another erebus, with a large build and horns jutting from his head, hovered near her.

"She broke her promise, I should have known I couldn't trust Kali," Sinopa sighed.

Ana couldn't stop it. Sinopa's words barely registered before Gabe spun, grabbing Sinopa by the neck and pushing her against a tree. "What did you do?" He growled.

Chapter Twenty-Two

"Gabe, let her go." Ana touched his shoulder, but he didn't even look her way. Fury was radiating from him in waves, and she was reminded of how far he had come from the little boy he'd been before they were separated. How different he was from who she'd known.

"Tell me what you did and how we can fix it. You said you were *protecting* Erin."

Sinopa grabbed at his hand but his grip only tightened, making her lips turn blue.

"Gabe, she can't talk if you kill her! Put her down!" Ana sighed with relief when Gabe finally loosened his grip and Sinopa gasped for air. The fae held her neck as she coughed.

"I was trying to! I've fought these erebi before. I've watched what they can do. With everything we did to try and stop them from getting to Eloas, we still only held them back a few years!" Sinopa wheezed in another breath of air. "The fae cannot defeat them. I just wanted to keep my people from dying...so I spied for Kali and talked groups of fae into giving in without a fight. I thought it would be better to be *ruled* by her then have my people *annihilated* by her. I just wanted to help keep my people alive."

"By *enslaving* them?" Gabe growled.

"We can't win against them! Fighting just brings death. You think I want to walk through my home and see fae with their wings ripped from their body, because some erebus was bored and thought it would be fun? You think I *want* to stumble upon more dead children? Queen Gossamer was the most protected, and they took her early on. Stood her in front of everyone and stripped her down. They turned her, and let everyone watch as her wings died and fell away. Her skin and eyes turned black...and then she was one of *them*. I didn't know they could do that! I thought the infection just killed them...so yes, I helped Kali, and I *saved lives*. Then she brought Erin here. I knew she was Odette's child immediately, so I agreed to go to Sula and bring Ana into a trap. Kali told me if I brought Ana, she would let Erin go. I'm sorry." Sinopa started to cry, but Gabe blocked Ana from comforting her.

"So, what now?" he demanded.

Ana watched Sinopa shake her head. She felt the betrayal, but also understood the driving force behind what Sinopa had done. She didn't know Ana; war took sacrifice, and Sinopa was willing to sacrifice someone she didn't know to save the child of the woman she loved.

"Sinopa, what was Kali's plan?" Ana murmured.

"Erin was supposed to still be in the dungeon. I sent word we were on our way, she must have moved Erin then. Any move we make will set the erebi loose on Erin. The dungeon was supposed to be a trap. I lead you in and they attack you. But now, the whole place is a trap. You have to run. Both of you."

"We aren't leaving without Erin," Melody spoke up. "She is one of us. We aren't *cowards*, we won't leave her behind. We won't let her be enslaved or changed. We will keep fighting." Melody's words hit their mark, and Sinopa made an animal whine from her throat. "So now *you* have to decide if you are going to keep your word and try and save Erin, or if you are going to run away with your tail tucked between your legs."

ℰ ℰ ℰ

"As soon as your friend makes an appearance, I'm going to rip you apart. I was gentle before, boss's orders. But once she has the princess..." Erin cringed away from the feel of Bogor's claws against her skin. She hated that she was blindfolded. Being tied up was one thing, but not being able to see what was happening around her was making her mind go wild. She kept waiting to hear Ana or Gabe yell in pain in front of her. She tried reaching them again, but she wasn't sure if the spell placed around her had taken hold and was keeping her from being able to communicate. Hell, it could just be that she wasn't very good at her power yet. Even though she couldn't see, Erin certainly *felt* the dark energy all around her. It was like a storm cloud circling, and she could only imagine the swarm of erebi that had to be near.

"Maybe I'll keep your boyfriend alive. *If* he even bothered to come to save you. He can watch all the things I do to you."

"Bogor, stop it. Leave her be. They are near, I can *feel* them." Kali's voice joined them, and Erin wondered if she had been there the whole time. "Once they are in view you can have all the fun you want with her...you can split her in two for all I care. But you won't lay a finger on her before then."

"Oh, I wish you guys would stop teasing me with all this fun and not even let me watch," Erin mumbled.

"So eager to watch your friends die." The stroke of a clawed finger down her cheek made Erin flinch, and the she-erebus spoke so close that her breath tickled her ear. "You'll make a fine puppet once we let you become infected. I hear the change is very painful. The infection kills all of your cells during the process, burning you from the inside as it takes over. I wonder if that will be the worst of it, or what Bogor does to you while you are still a human mutt."

Then the sounds of explosions filled the air.

Ana watched as Melody tried to release Erin's binding with magic from where they stood. Her head dropped in failure after the third attempt.

"Erin said there was a fae spell placed on her bindings so she couldn't use her magic. One of us is going to have to physically cut it away from her. Before then, I don't think a protection spell or anything else will help her."

"I'll do it," Sinopa volunteered. "I can get through the erebi easier as a fox. I can get to her and gnaw her free. Then Melody can put the protection spell on her, and we can fight our way back to you. Even if Kali sees me, she might think I am running to warn her of your arrival. But some form of distraction in the meantime would be beneficial."

Melody grinned. "I think I might have a little show up my sleeves."

"We need to spread out. Sinopa runs in to get Erin. Melody should stay here so she can keep a protection spell around us and keep an eye on anyone in trouble. Gabe and I can run in when Sinopa is almost to Erin, and start thinning out the erebi." Ana paused, watching how Gabe kept his eyes on Erin from across the field, like he was willing her to feel his presence. When he finally nodded that he'd heard her, she spoke again. "Okay, spread out. The fireworks will be the cue."

Gabe went to the right while she went farther to the left. She gripped her sword at the ready, waiting for the right moment to run forward. She was tense, ready to bring this to an end. Kali escaped her once, but this time Ana was going to bring her to her knees. She'd taken her family, her realm, her friend, but no more.

"See you in the middle, Aina. Be careful."

"You too."

Just as the explosions started in the sky, Sinopa's fox body sprinted toward the erebi and began to dart through their feet. Ana watched carefully as she felt Melody's warm protection magic wrap around her like a warm blanket. That was her sign to go, so she leapt into action. Running towards the infection erebi, the elf was determined to take out as many as she could to make it easier for Erin to escape. As her blade sliced through the wispy bodies she thought of them coming to her realm, killing people she'd loved. She held back nothing as she fought her way towards the center, a single-minded focus of getting to Kali, and ending this war.

$$\mathcal{C} \; \mathcal{C} \; \mathcal{C}$$

As the shared ache of a brief (albeit very informative) vision wore off, Briar watched the group prepare to fight their way through the impossible in order to save their friend. She gave a silent nod towards the male to tell Lyra that was who they needed. The moment he separated himself from the group, Lyra rose and stepped toward him. He turned, a blade at the ready, and Lyra held up a hand to forestall an attack.

"I am a friend. There is no time to explain, but you must wear this. It is for protection." She held out her other hand with the long silver chain coiled in her palm. In the center rested the simple black stone. Silver wound its way around the stone and came to a sharp point. Briar watched as his green gaze took in Lyra once more, before his gaze darted back to the halfling at the center of the battle.

"There is no time, just trust me." Lyra quickly unwound the metal, grabbed his hand and pricked his finger with the sharp tip just as Briar had seen happen in the vision. "Now it is bound to you. It will save your life." She slipped it over his head before pointing back over his shoulder. "That's your cue, hero."

"How was that?" Lyra asked after the man disappeared into melee. Briar watched the start of battle before Doyle grabbed her hand and started pulling her away. They all started at a brisk walk in the opposite direction, not wanting to get caught up in the fray.

"Perfect...at least according to my vision."

Lyra gave a satisfied grin. "Well that is accomplished. Now you said we have to look into the spell we got with the amulet?"

"Yes, hopefully once the spell is ready, I will know what to do with it." As they made it farther from the battle raging behind them, the world became a little brighter, quieter, more like the home she knew before all of this happened. She stopped...she didn't care if Lyra came up and jabbed her in the side. Briar just needed to stop for five seconds and breathe, take it in, before she was taken back through that portal.

She closed her eyes, turned her face to the sky, and basked in the warmth of the sun. The breeze against her skin grounded her. She wasn't as attuned to nature as others of her kind, but she could still feel it. The life at her feet, the pulses of energy all around her. Skia was dead; there was no scent of flowers in the air, no sound of bugs moving over blades of grass, not even the movement of stars at night. The erebi certainly had to pay the price for their past greed.

"Lyra, can I speak with you for a moment?" Doyle requested quietly, reminding her of their presence. She refused to open her eyes though, not ready to come back just yet. She was given longer than she thought she would have been, before Doyle returned to her side. She felt his warmth, heard his gruff tone as he called her Blue.

"I'm sorry. It..." Tears blurred her vision, and when she patted her cheeks, Briar found more there. "It just feels good to be home, you know? I'm sorry. I know I can't stay, our work isn't done. I just didn't think I would ever be here again." The fae gave a feeble, faltering smile. "And here I am, standing in a meadow while my people fight for their lives behind me." Her stomach twisted in guilt.

"I think we should make a pit stop before we leave." Doyle's eyes were serious. With a jolt, she realized they were alone.

"Where's Lyra?"

"She started ahead. She is going to go through the portal herself. We will follow shortly. Our work isn't done yet, and we have your word you won't run. Add to that the fact that we have these," he touched the inside of her wrist where the intricate design of the rune lay, "and there is still time before they fade...so I asked for a little reprieve."

Hope blossomed in the fae's chest. "You got her to let us stay here a little longer?"

"I thought it would be good for you to gain as much strength as possible before going back to my realm. You need to be strong so you can see what we are to do next. The amulet was no small feat, and I can only hope it will pay off in our favor. But I don't think we will find out how that will be until you see something more." The erebus paused, a hint of affection seeping into his gaze as he watched her. "I also thought it might be good for you to see Fern again, before we leave."

"What?" Her heart nearly leapt out of her chest at the thought of seeing her sister.

"Come on, we don't have much time." Doyle started walking off without her, toward the village. Part of her wondered if Lyra actually left them to their own devices, or if she was lurking somewhere to listen in. She thought Doyle would know if they were being watched, but the feeling was hard to shake all the same.

"How did you do this? Why?"

"I simply told Lyra you should have more time in your realm, and that we had time left with the runes. Then I told her I had it handled, and I'd see her back on the other side of the portal. You helped us accomplish so much, you deserve a little something."

His body was tense, she could feel the difference in him as they walked. He was alert to danger as they walked, but the area was devoid of anyone. The erebi had probably all been called to the battle, and the fae were either involved as well, or hiding. Finally, she saw the outskirts of her father's home. The last time she had been here seemed like years ago. She'd just had the vision of her mother dying, she'd been desperate to get her family and escape. She had been broken then, knowing her mother was dead, but still hopeful. She'd still had her wings, and was going to get her family, and then get help. She had believed everything would work out then. Now, she stopped and just stared at the house, afraid to move closer. Fern couldn't see her like this.

Briar shook her head and stumbled backwards. Doyle turned to look at her, questions glinting in his gaze, but she was rooted in place.

She couldn't let Fern, or anyone else, see her like this. Her wings were gone, dark circles were still under her eyes. Being home had given her strength, had given her color back, but she wasn't whole...not anymore. She couldn't let anyone see just how broken she was, because then she would have to explain why she had to go back with Doyle, why she would have to give *more* before all of this was over. "Blue?"

She shook her head again, a quick jolt, and turned away. "I can't. Fern...she can't see me like this." His gaze was heavy on her back. Her muscles still tightened to draw the wings in close for protection, but there wasn't anything there. Not anymore. "I'll come back when all of this is over. It will be okay then. But not now, not when I will just have to leave again."

"Blue," Doyle implored softly, his voice drawing her back around to face him. "She misses you. It will hurt to see you like this...hell, it hurts for *me* to know what you gave up, but it will do her good to see you, to hug you, *and* it will give you something to take back while we finish this." Briar closed her eyes as though it could block out the truth of his words, too afraid to take the next few steps. "Look, I don't have family. I can't tell you what to do here. But I know you love your sister dearly, you protected her above all else. You should see her before we go back." He held out his hand, and finally, with a shaky breath, the fae took it and followed him up to the door.

Instead of knocking or opening it, she moved to the window and peeked in. She saw Fern inside with one of her other sisters and their mother. They sat on the rug, tying something, clearly involved in whatever task they were doing. Briar watched them for a few breaths. Fern was safe. That would have to be enough to take with her for now. "Okay, let's go. We have a long walk, and our time will run out soon. I really don't want to get on Lyra's bad side after this small achievement."

"Are you sure you won't see her?" Doyle asked.

"I saw her." She forced herself to look into his face. "That's enough for now." He nodded after a long pause, but they didn't head directly toward the portal. Instead, he stopped and filled multiple flasks with fae water from the stream. He tucked them away before going to a food shed, and filled two linen satchels with the various fae food hidden within. While he worked, Briar dipped her toes in the stream and lost herself in the feeling of its warmth.

Tossing away all thoughts, she sank into the water and let it wash over her. She had bathed delicately in Skia, but that water had been dirty to start with. To actually feel the warm fae water pull away grime from her hair and skin made her come alive. She wanted to undress and float on the water until she grew old and died. She didn't have the time for that, though, and when she looked up, Doyle was standing at the bank waiting for her. She dipped her head back under the water one more time before standing and made her way to the grass. "Sorry, I couldn't help myself."

He only shook his head at her, that hint of affection in his eyes once more, and the ghost of a smile tugging at his lips. He gestured toward the bounty he'd gathered. "Hopefully this will last you for a while. One fae snack a day, a little something to keep you going back in Skia. We can't let you get weak like you were before. You don't belong there. And I promise, one day I'll get you back here again." He brushed a finger across her cheek, and she suddenly found it hard to swallow. She didn't want to think of her visions anymore, she didn't want to wonder if *he* would be the one to kill her one day. She just wanted to close her eyes and pretend for a moment, *just a moment*, that he was hers, and she was his.

"Come on then, let's get hiking."

Going through the portal again was always a jolt to the senses. The weight of the mountain instantly landed on her shoulders, but she clung to the image of home and Fern in her mind, and tried to focus on every small detail she could. Doyle took her back to her room, and left her stores of food hidden under the bed so she could take what she needed as her strength waned. The erebus watched as she circled the room, feeling once more like a caged animal, and silence passed between them. The runes on their wrists were fading. She wanted to reach out to him, to fall into a vision of them together and let him *feel* that while they still had this spell over them, but Briar wasn't daring enough, and Lyra entered the room, shattering the moment.

"Oh lovely, you guys are back. I brought the spell. What do we do next?" Lyra passed over the paper, and Briar took it.

"I'm not sure. Why don't we try and find out?" The fae sat on the floor and placed the paper before her. She thought of the people she'd seen in the vision, the small group that now had the amulet. She visualized the halfling, and thought of Doyle and his desire to help his people. She thought of her single feather tied to the back of her hair so it always touched her skin. Gathering all of that, Briar closed her eyes, reached out, and touched the paper. The room disappeared as she fell into a line of futures with far too many twists and turns.

$$.\wp .\wp .\wp$$

Too much was happening, and Erin couldn't see any of it. She could hear explosions, but she couldn't understand what they were, or where they were coming from. Ana shouted in what the fae could only assume to be elvish, then Bogor growled beside her and stomped away. She wasn't sure if Kali was still with her, but lighter feet suddenly landed beside her. Erin jumped, unsure who the newcomer was, and only relaxed when fur brushed her hands and what felt like sharp teeth tore her bindings free.

Erin was just pulling away her blindfold as Bogor came running back toward her. Only then did she see the familiar fox at her feet. The erebus swept his arm out, catching Sinopa and swatting her away from them.

"Sinopa!" Erin watched in horror as the fox flew to the center of a horde of horned erebi that looked like Bogor. Sinopa whimpered as the erebi converged on her, the sound morphing into pained cries before dying away.

Rage blinded Erin. Thoughts of all of the things Bogor had done to her since she'd arrived — the pain and torture, and now taking her last connection to her parents — propelled her towards the erebus and gave her the ability to catch him off-guard. Bogor fell to his back, but his claws found her arms. Even as she felt the nails pierce her skin, she realized that she'd regained control of her powers. With an angry cry, the earth around them shifted. The hot ball of power in the pit of her stomach added to her strength as she brought down her fist into his face. Vines pinned him to the ground and grew back as quickly as he broke through them. A rock rose from the earth. Erin grabbed hold of it, seeing red, and she pounded it into his skull with a cry of vengeance. *The slashes on her back. The feeling of helplessness. Sinopa...*she didn't care if an infection erebus took advantage of her unguarded back. She didn't care if she got away alive...she just needed Bogor to feel pain.

He withered under her as he failed to break completely free from the vines so he could fight back.

"I thought you enjoyed a little bondage!" Erin hit him again, and blood gushed from his mouth. One of his hands finally broke free and he hit her across the face, but this time a vine of thorns caught hold of him. She dropped the rock, and started pounding on him with her fists. Ana's voice drifted through the haze in her mind. Distracted by the sound, Erin turned and saw the elf running into the small clearing.

"*Erin!*" Gabe's voice entered her mind. She searched for him and saw him burst through the horde of infection erebi on the opposite side of the clearing. His face lit up when he saw her, and the man she'd come to love so dearly started coming toward her. With Ana approaching from one side and Gabe from the other, Erin knew she only had a moment to finish the job. Bogor was still struggling under her. She had no idea if Sinopa was still alive. She had no idea where Kali was. She wanted to rest in Gabe's arms, but not with her torturer still alive. The thorny vines that rose from the darkness of her mind wrapped tightly around his neck. His struggles slowed, and she continued to punch until her knuckles split.

"Erin!" Gabe's voice called out beside her and brought her back to reality. Bogor was bloodied...*dead* by her hands. The vines she called from the earth were embedded in his skin and covered in blood. The magnitude of what she had just done hit her, and had her doubling over sick.

Gabe reached out and steadied her, drawing her away from Bogor's body. "We have to go!" The erebi were closing in.

"Too late," Kali hissed. Erin spun just in time to see the erebus appear between them and Ana, whose back was turned as she tried to keep the fight away from Erin and Gabe. Erin tried to move, but her body was frozen, still in shock over what she had done.

"*Ana!*" All Erin could do was scream her name in warning.

$$\wp \; \wp \; \wp$$

Ana watched in horror as Erin was lost to the world. Gabe broke free from the erebi and called Erin's name, but it only drew away the fae's attention for a moment. Then she was hitting the beast under her, over and over. The erebi started to close in, so Ana turned to fight them back, trying to keep a circle open behind her so Gabe could pull Erin away; she didn't know where Sinopa went, and she knew Melody's spell had faded. More explosions rocked the ground as Melody tried to draw attention away from their small group and get them another opening for escape.

Kali's voice hit her like an electric shock. She hadn't seen the erebus that caused all of this...but her voice was close by. Ana fought back a horned erebus coming too close, and was distracted when Erin screamed her name in panic. The elf turned just in time to see her friend's face, devoid of color, eyes wide like saucers. That sight was soon blocked by Kali, heading toward her with her claws outstretched, ready to rip Ana's heart from her chest. Ignoring the voice in the back of her mind telling her that it was too late, the blond settled into a fighting stance, dagger secure in her grip. Her weapon would come up a beat too slow, she knew, and Kali's claws would already be cutting her open.

The blow never came. Gabe dove in front of her at the last instant, taking it instead. His body fell back into hers, knocking Ana to the ground. Kali landed on top of them with a high screech.

"Gabe!" Erin's voice called out in desperation, but Ana couldn't move, couldn't *see* what was happening. She shoved at the weight pinning her down, until Kali threw Gabe aside with a growl. Free from obstacles, Kali pounced on Ana, but the elf was able to kick her back and scramble to her feet. When the erebus lunged for her again, Ana used her momentum to throw her to the ground.

The air suddenly awoke with electricity as magic flowed around them. Animal fae joined the fight from all directions, tearing at the infection beings. Ana noticed the fear in Kali's eyes as smoke began to rise around them, horned and infection erebi alike falling to their deaths and turning to dark energy to return to their realm.

"It's over, Kali, this is your one and only chance to surrender." Kali's lips curled in a wicked snarl, and Ana remembered the view of her realm on fire, Kali standing between her and those she loved, an open portal at her back. Ana pounced, knowing the erebus could disappear in an instant.

"Too bad your brother isn't here to see you finally take me down!" Kali spat in Ana's face as Ana's dagger came down into her chest. The elf felt the kill reverberate up her arm as the blade cut through bone. Despite the victory, her enemy's parting words cut just as deep. She forced herself to look away before the light fully left Kali's eyes. The fae were doing their part in keeping the erebi away from the group. Melody had finally gotten through, and stood over Erin and Gabe, her face horror-stricken.

Ana ran to their side, her heart pounding in her throat. *No, no, no...*

"Toron!" Her brother's elven name fell from her lips when Ana saw his chest torn open from Kali's attack. Erin held his head in her lap, her hands over the gaping wounds as she desperately tried to heal him. Ana realized she was sobbing his name over and over, and though her hands glowed with power, nothing happened. The world fell away as Ana realized her brother had just died saving her life.

Chapter Twenty-Three

"It's not working!" Everything was happening way too fast. One minute, Erin was watching, helpless, as Kali charged at Ana, and then Gabe's touch disappeared. Erin had barely registered him leaving her side before she was watching Kali claw through his chest. Horror only froze her long enough to watch the erebus toss him to the side like a rag doll, before she scrambled to her knees at his head.

"Erin..." She barely made out her own name as blood spilled from his lips and garbled his voice.

"It's okay, it's okay." Erin pulled his head onto her lap and held out her hands to heal him. A quick glance behind her showed Ana holding her own against Kali, so Erin concentrated on Gabe. She felt her power fill her with warmth and directed it towards his chest, waiting for the wounds to heal...but his chest was no longer moving with breath. His face was frozen, eyes open, mouth slack.

"Gabe! Gabe, heal!" He was too blurry to see now.

"Erin!" The voice reached her through a fog, sounding far away despite the fact that she looked up to see Melody hovering anxiously over them "Oh no...Gabe..."

"Gabe...please, Gabe, please," Erin sobbed, willing something to happen. *Why wasn't it working? Why was it taking so long for his body to heal?*

"Erin." Ana's broken, hollow voice drew her attention. "He's already gone, you can't bring back the dead."

"No! Gabe! Please!" Ana tried to touch her shoulder, but Erin jerked away and covered Gabe's body with hers. "Get away! He'll be fine! I'll heal him!"

"Erin…" Ana's voice was filled with pain, but it hardly registered with Erin. The war around them came to an end. As Kali drew her last breath, the infection erebi froze, no longer under Kali's control. The fae watched as they vanished in a swirl of smoke to their realm before they were killed. Cheers and celebrations broke out around them as the fae gained back their realm. For their little cluster, though, there was little to celebrate. Erin clung tight to Gabe's body, refusing to loosen her grip; her hands still glowed with power as she tried to bring him back. Ana fell to her knees beside them and looked at her brother before slowly tugging on Erin's shoulder.

"Erin, you have to stop now, he's gone. You are making yourself weak."

"Where is Sinopa? I lost track of her after she cut Erin free." Melody asked, her voice gentle. No answer came her way. "*Erin*, where is Sinopa?"

"Bogor hit her, threw her into a crowd of erebi. I don't think..." Ana and Melody met eyes as the response faded away.

Melody gently touched Ana's shoulder and gave a squeeze. "I'll go look for her."

"Erin, we need to move him." All around them the fae were gathering their injured and the plants were starting to claim the dead as their magic released back into the earth.

Suddenly, they were not alone. "You, you saved us! Sinopa sent word to us to be ready." A tall male fae with jet black hair stood over them.

"What?" Erin felt Ana pull away, and whatever connection she had to reality dissipated as she stared into Gabe's empty features.

.℮ .℮ .℮

"Sinopa told me to keep an eye on Kali. She wanted to get Erin away, but then she thought we might have to fight. We've been trying to keep the loss of fae at a minimum, but Sinopa thought we should stay ready just in case. It's because of you that everyone gathered to fight back. It's because of *you* that we are free once more."

"Thank you," Ana muttered. She tried not to think about how they could have helped by fighting back sooner; then maybe Erin wouldn't have been taken in the first place. "We need a place to rest, and take my, my brother." The elf tightened her fists at her side. She *had* to hold it together. Erin was lost to reality in her grief, so Ana had to hold it together for the both of them. Once she was alone, she could let her mind comprehend what happened.

"Oh, I'm sorry. I'll carry him. I live nearby. You can rest there. Where is Sinopa?"

"Mel, my friend went to look for her." The man gave a quick nod and changed into a crow. He circled above and then darted down a little farther. Ana watched him dive to the ground and quickly change back. He knelt beside someone, and Ana *knew*. The woman had kept her word and saved Erin, even in sacrifice of herself. She watched as the male fae gently stroked her hair and the earth slowly took her, blooming orange-red flowers in her wake.

He came back to them, his head held low, Melody following after him. He knelt down next to Erin and Gabe, and reached for Gabe's body.

Erin curled over him again with a snarl. "No! You can't touch him!"

"Erin, we have to move him." Ana's voice was suddenly stern, working to hide her emotion. She grabbed Erin's shoulders and pulled her away. She noticed Erin's knuckles were broken and bloodied, and she had a large gash on the side of her face...she hadn't bothered to heal herself. She probably didn't even notice her own physical pain.

Ana watched as the man gently lifted Gabe's body, and carried him through the cheering crowds of fae celebrating their freedom. No one noticed the sacrifices that had been made for them.

.ℰ .ℰ .ℰ

Two days later, Erin stood in front of her apartment door. The black haired fae, Kyrell, had helped them back to the portal. The small group carried Gabe's body back to Sula so that he could be buried at home. The elves had their burial traditions, but Erin didn't think she could watch. Instead, she had kissed his forehead and said her own private goodbye.

The fae wasn't sure how long she stood in the hallway...all she knew was that the second she opened her door, it would be real. The last time she'd stood in their apartment, he'd been angry with her. He'd told her she was selfish and didn't care about him. He'd stormed out, unable to look at her. Absently, Erin touched the amulet she now wore around her neck. Gabe had been wearing it. Ana said she didn't know when he'd gotten it, and she hadn't seen him wearing it before the battle. But he'd had it with him in his last moments, and now Erin gripped it like her life depended on it.

She finally crossed the threshold of her apartment with a shaky breath. The smell of him still lingered...the smell of the forest. Erin touched the counter and saw him sitting there, eating the lunch she had made. Before everything changed. Before she lost him. Before Ana stormed into their lives and crashed through her happy bubble.

The shrill ring of her phone startled her, and Erin saw Ana's name flash on the screen. Rage took over, and Erin chucked the phone at the wall before she could even think about it, and watched the pieces shatter to the floor. She went to her room and froze in place at the sight of her reflection in the mirror. Erin still refused to heal herself; her knuckles were still split and hurt every time she moved her fingers. She still had a gash across her cheek from Bogor hitting her face. It would scar. *She didn't care.*

Erin laid in her bed, resting her head on Gabe's pillow. She pulled the covers around her and shut her eyes hard. She was empty. No more tears. No feelings. No anger, no pain, no love. She was alive, but she was dead. She had nothing left. The blackness of sleep finally drew her in, and Erin didn't bother to put up a fight, only praying that she didn't dream.

℮ .℮ .℮

Ana sighed heavily as Erin's voicemail message played through her phone. She didn't bother speaking, ending the call instead, and dropped her phone back to the table. Hollow pain had long since settled into her chest, and the elf had to resist the urge to scream. They'd returned to Sula just days before, and Erin would not say a word to her. Ana understood, of *course* she understood. Her friend was grieving, *they all were*, and she was doing it in her own way.

Where Erin seemed to prefer solitude, Ana wanted to talk. To hear about what her brother had been like in his childhood here in this realm, to share stories of what he'd been like in Eloas. *Anything* to keep her mind off of the hole left behind by having her brother ripped away so soon after finding him again. Melody did her best to support her friend, but she'd barely known Gabe. It left Ana alone with her thoughts more often than not, and she'd shed so many tears it didn't seem like she had any left.

"Ana?" Blue eyes turned towards the door, and Melody sighed. "Still no response from Erin?" Ana shook her head. "I'm sorry. Maybe she just needs some more time. In the meantime, you need to *eat*, and maybe opening the shop might help keep you busy?"

The young witch received a humorless laugh in return. "I can't even *look* at food right now, Mel. I...I just...I can't." Ana stared down at her hands. "I spent seventeen years grieving the loss of my brother, but there was still this *hope* that he'd survived. That he'd been able to make a life for himself somewhere, away from the war that had destroyed our home. It was the only way that I was able to sleep at night. But then...then, Erin came into our lives, and G-Gabe. I found out that he was my brother, and for *five seconds* everything was right with my world. But then," she paused, her voice catching and eyes welling with tears. "Then everything went wrong, and my baby brother died to save *me*."

Melody rushed across the kitchen, and Ana found herself wrapped in a tight embrace. "None of this is your fault, do you hear me? *Kali* did this...Kali destroyed your kingdom, Kali chased you out of your realm...*Kali* took Erin to draw you out. She is the one who killed Gabe."

"I just...I can't help but think that he would have been better off if I'd never removed that spell. If he'd just...remained oblivious to the fact that he wasn't human. The worst thing he'd ever have worried about would have been why he couldn't remember the first eight years of his life."

Ana watched tears fill Melody's eyes before the witch pulled away. She rested her chin on the top of her head so she could no longer see her face. "Oh, Ana."

The elf leaned heavily into Melody's embrace, allowing herself a moment of weakness before straightening her shoulders and sitting back. "I'm not quite ready to open the shop and deal with strangers, but you're right that working will help keep me distracted. I think I'm going to head down and...do some organizing or something. Thank you, Mel."

Melody nodded sadly, and followed the elf with her gaze as she disappeared down the stairs. Ana dragged her fingers numbly along the wall as she crossed the threshold into the store. *Mystifying* had been *home* since she'd arrived in Sula, but at that moment, it felt hollow...empty. Her eyes dragged across the room but saw *nothing*. The last of her family was actually gone. She'd felt indescribable joy when she realized that her brother had finally returned to her.

Would she have been better off spending the rest of her life thinking that Toron had disappeared forever through the portal? *He* certainly would have been better off never knowing his past; he never would have traveled to another realm. Kali never would have known that he was still alive. Kali never would have had a chance to end his life just as he was beginning it...with Erin.

Erin. Erin would never forgive her for putting Gabe at risk...for letting him follow her to Loinnir, for putting him in the position to sacrifice himself for her. Hell, *Ana* would never forgive *herself*. She'd failed everyone: her parents, her kingdom, Aria, her brother, Erin...and at the rate she was going, Melody too, before long.

Ana let out a deep sigh and turned away from the storefront after making sure the door was locked. She was about to head upstairs, but froze when a shadow caught her eye. The vague shape of a dog, a very familiar *wolf*, lurked in the doorway to the office. Everything in her went still as she stared back. She was mostly hidden in the shadows of the store, and Ana needed to get closer, to see if it was really

Ethelron's wolf, or just a figment of her overtired mind. She was aching for home, aching for family. She wouldn't put it past herself to summon ghosts of her past. She moved to step closer, to get a better look, but in a breath, the wolf was gone, and everything in her fell.

Her grief was playing tricks on her mind. She was clinging to any sliver of hope she could find. Her parents were gone, her brother was gone. Her kingdom and everyone she'd cared about were destroyed by the erebus she'd finally managed to kill, *too late*. All that she had left was to pick up the pieces, and fight to make sure she didn't let down the one person she had left.

A sudden thought struck her, halting her in her steps across the floor.

"*This will not save your realm.*" In her rage and grief, she hadn't paid attention to the last words that Kali had said to her...that killing her would not save Eloas. *The elven realm.* Could that possibly mean that it had somehow managed to survive the siege seventeen years ago? It was possible she'd imagined the wolf, but maybe her mind was *trying* to tell her there was still something to hope for. Maybe this wasn't the end.

Acknowledgements

This series has been a part of our friendship from the very beginning. To see it in print is such a huge accomplishment for us and brings us so much joy to know we have come this far. While we had each other in this process, so many others have helped us along the way. From our parents letting us be little weirdos, acting out story ideas in the pool all summer, to all those that read the many versions of this book over the years.

So first and foremost we need to thank our families, for nurturing our creativity, and conveniently living only a few streets away from each other. You guys gave us the freedom to be ourselves and accepted each of us into the family, always treating us as one of your own.

We want to thank some of those that read this story, even in its infant stage, and giving us encouragement and feedback to help us grow : Quigley, Mike, Mackenzie, Nicole, Jackie, Steve, and Megan to name a few. You guys rock! You were so supportive, and your excitement over our story made us even more excited.

We also want to give a huge shout out to Megan Moore (@GraphiteGeek on Insta) for working with us on a perfect cover design and bringing our idea to life. We kept you busy with our back and forth, but we absolutely love how it turned out, and look forward to working with you on the rest of the series.

Of course we also have to thank our husbands Paul and Jamie. Thank you for understanding our friendship and, most of all, your love and support. And to our children, we love our little guys and hope you all grow up to be the best of friends.

We also want to thank all of you for picking up this book and giving us a chance to tell you a story that is so close to our hearts. Thank you so much! If you can, please take a moment to connect with us on our socials and post a review. We would love to hear from you!

Instagram: dorianmoore.books
Facebook: Facebook.com/dorianmoorebooks

Author Bio

The Dorian half of Dorian Moore works as a preschool teacher by day, but in her free time, she is a hoarding book dragon with a frozen coffee in one hand and a pen in the other. In school, it was believed she was an avid note-taker, but she was really writing stories in her composition notebooks and avoiding math like the plague. No character is safe, the death of characters was even mentioned in a toast at her wedding, but when she's not killing off characters, she's helping them find love. She lives in Delaware with her loving husband, two boys, and houseful of pets.

The Moore half of Dorian Moore is a therapist by day, writer by night. When she's not working with clients or writing, she's hanging out with her husband and young son in her hometown in Delaware (probably outside). She also enjoys recreational archery and finding new toys for her pretty purple Jeep (aptly named Hawkeye). Moore writes in the fantasy genre when writing with Dorian, and leans towards contemporary new adult romance (dabbling in the Christian fiction genre as well) in her own stories.